DEATH STALKS THE RETIREMENT PARTY

BY

RANDALL J. FUNK

<u>ALSO BY RANDALL J. FUNK</u>

Death is a Clingy Ex

Death Lives Across the Hall

Death Wears a Big Hat

Death is Sleeping with My Wife

Death Stole My Ride

Death and the Fanboy

Death is a Real Killer

Death, You Jabroni

Death Will Be Brief: Joe Davis Mystery Tales, Volume One

Published in the United States by Ghost Light Press, LLC

www.randalljfunk.com

ISBN:

Cover design by Ann McMan

First edition

Special Thanks to:

Michelle Hughes, for her help in preparing the manuscript.

Ann McMan, for her usual awesome work on the cover.

Beatrix Funk, who helped me create the landscape of the Porter's Bay area.

Everyone who has bought the previous Joe Davis books and helped me along on this adventure.

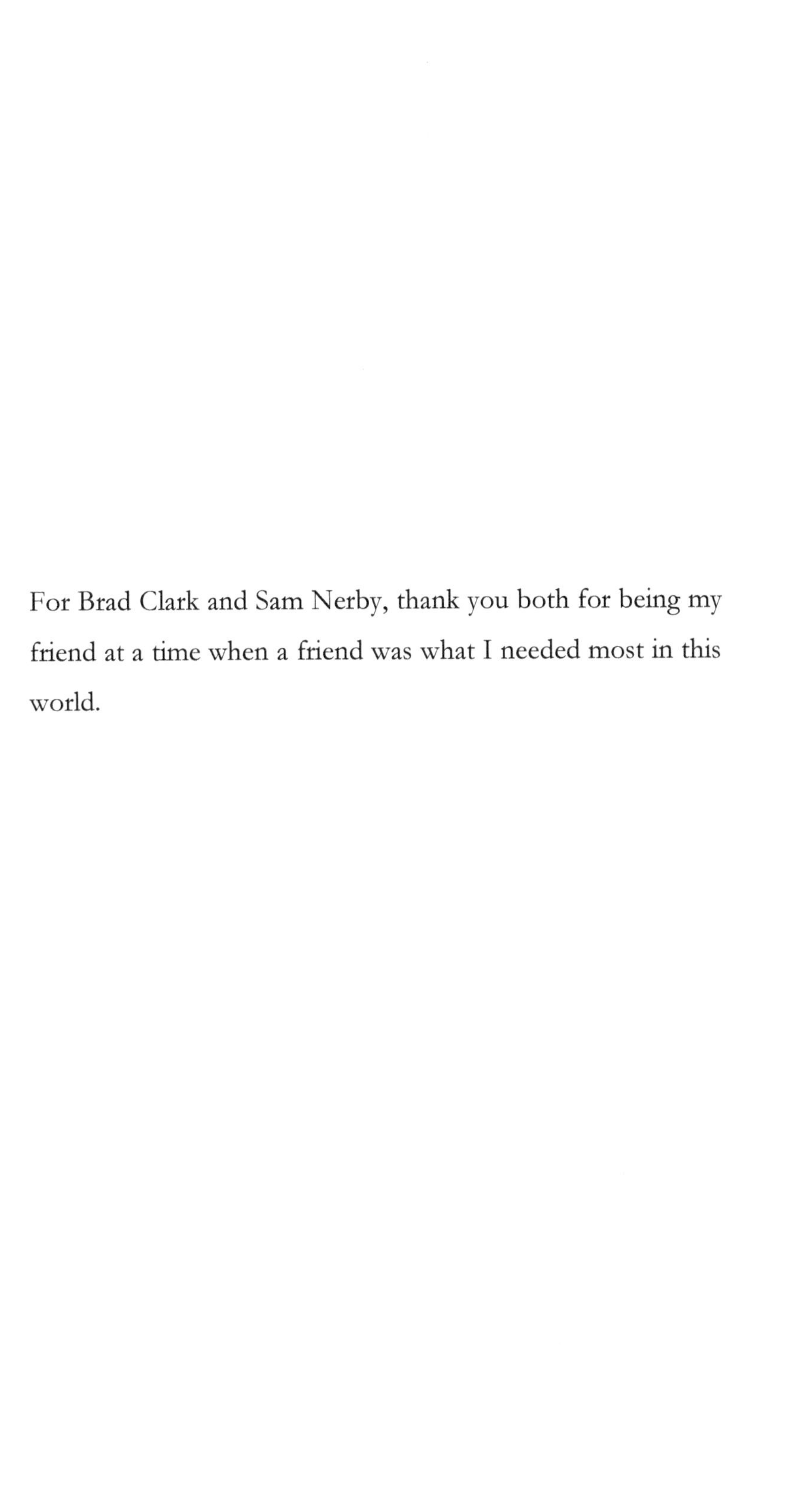

For Brad Clark and Sam Nerby, thank you both for being my friend at a time when a friend was what I needed most in this world.

CHAPTER ONE

The biggest myth about our parents is that they were ever real people. You can never make a kid of any age believe such a thing.

Now, I'm not seriously suggesting our parents are some kind of alien breed set loose upon this planet. (Although, let's not rule anything out.) When I use the word myth, *I'm referring to a story confined to the past with little reliable evidence to confirm it ever existed in the first place, like the Homerian epics or stories from the Bible or the Reagan administration. And that, like it or not, is how we treat our parents.*

Sure, we see pictures of them as younger people. We hear tales of the old days, either from them or from other relatives. We might even have video evidence of such things. But we never truly believe, deep down, they were ever people like we *are. They never had doubts and fears like us. They never had their hearts broken the way we have. They didn't get into trouble just for the sheer unalloyed risk of it. God knows they never tried to get laid in the same way we did. (Even though we are a walking contradiction of that notion.) Parents generally distributed food, money, clothing, advice (solicited or unsolicited) and—if you came from a home that was into this sort of thing—approval. Parents are an ATM, a*

Goodwill, a cafeteria and an internet search engine. But people? Perish the thought.

My name is Joe Davis. I get paid to write stuff like that.

And yes, I'm even writing when I'm on what passes for a vacation. Dealing with my parents, though, doesn't feel like much of a vacation.

"Let's get in there," my father says, tapping his fingers on the steering wheel, "The sooner we get it started, the sooner it ends."

That's the spirit. I'm in the backseat of my father's GMC Envoy, staring at the entrance to the Buffalo Lodge across the street. People are filing in, but Dad, despite his pronouncement, is in no hurry to join them. My mom, perhaps conscious that everyone in my hometown of Porter's Bay will recognize Dad's car, lays a hand on his forearm.

"Henry, why don't we get going?" she says, "People are waiting."

Dad greets this with a small noise in his throat, somewhere between a grunt and a scoff. Forty years of dealing with the idea that the customer is always right and even now, on the verge of his retirement, he can't escape it. He takes his hands off the wheel.

"Then let's go," he says, his voice barely above a whisper.

We tumble out of the Envoy and jaywalk across the street. Howard Street, one of the main arteries in Porter's Bay, looms to our left, a half-block away. All the shops and businesses are brown brick and mortar. Most of them were built in the Nineteen Twenties and while they've stayed clean over the decades, the architecture hasn't changed. Porter's Bay deals heavily in quaint. The sun is bending low in the sky. The air is warm but not humid and there's a breeze drifting in from Lake Superior. June in northern Minnesota. I fall in behind my parents, keeping some distance, like I did in junior high. My dad, dark-haired and stocky, drops his hands into the pockets of his tan slacks. His stride is, as always, unhurried and fluid. His black short-sleeved dress shirt billows out behind him as he walks. My mom, taller and blonde, slips her arm into his. She fusses with the white sweater covering her tan sundress. A few people hail them as they approach. There's some sweat on Dad's brow, which is uncharacteristic. Mom looks back at me.

"Your friends are coming?" she asks.

"They should be here by now," I say, "They left the hotel about twenty minutes ago."

Mom is talking about my friends from the Twin Cities. I grew up in Porter's Bay, but I haven't lived here in more than a decade. These days, I make my home in St. Paul and my living as a thrice weekly columnist for *The Daily Bugle*, an independent newspaper that became an independent website when they realized they could successfully ditch the cost of print a few years back. My column, *Cup o' Joe*, covers a variety of topics: pop culture, news, entertainment, sports, social situations, etc. All with the same depth and insight one normally finds in a Daffy Duck cartoon. It's the stuff with which I bored many a friend at the school lunch table, but now (barely) affords me a living and a weenie bit of celebrity.

"It's nice that they came," Mom says, facing forward again.

My closest friends—Mike, Carol, and Lars—all decided to make the trip with me, though they've barely met my parents and—in the cases of Carol and Lars—have never been to Porter's Bay. For Carol, it was a chance to honor someone she's heard a lot about. For Lars, it was a chance to get in a quick summer vacation. (Though I have no earthly idea what he needs a break from, given the general sloth of his existence.) For Mike, it was a chance to get out of the Cities and let the heat die down after his latest breakup. (Don't ask.) We decided to go in on a rental vehicle (a reasonably priced RAV4) and carpool it up here. It was almost worth it. (Almost.)

Dad stops outside the door to the Buffalo Lodge. "Joe, you stay behind me. If I make any attempt to escape, let me."

This isn't the easiest week for my father. It's filled with things he didn't want. Yes, retirement was his idea, but it was more about giving into age (and constant nagging from my mother) than something he truly wanted. He certainly didn't want the fuss that's accompanying said retirement. For forty years, my father has owned Davis Hardware. He's been a pillar of the community: serving on the Chamber of Commerce, having a seat on the board of the Porter's Bay Historical Society, being a member of the church council at Our Savior's Lutheran, helping to organize various charity drives, and doing his best to keep Porter's Bay clean and safe for the tourists who are the lifeblood of the town's economy. When he announced he was stepping down from Davis Hardware and handing the reins over to my young brother Owen, the community decided to honor him. To my father's everlasting regret.

"I shouldn't have said anything," Dad grumbled at dinner earlier, "I should have just kept my mouth shut and stopped showing up at the store. Nobody would have known the difference."

That right there should have told him why it's a good idea to retire. While no one could question Dad's worth ethic for the majority of his tenure, during the last few years he's ceded more and more of the day-to-day running of the store to Owen. Dad has become more a figurehead, chatting with customers and reading the newspaper for much of the day. If he *had* stopped showing up, people might have noticed, but the store would not have been impacted at all.

Dad opens the door for my mom and follows her into the marble-tiled foyer. We ascend the stairs to the main hall. Dad has been a lodge member for as long as I can remember. He played Santa Claus at the Christmas parties when I was a kid (replacing Bill Knox, who was "retired" from the position after getting liquored up and falling through the door of the men's room, prompting the kids to start crying and screaming, "Santa's dead!") A hue and cry go up the second Mom and Dad step into the lobby of the main hall.

"It's about time, Henry," one of the guys says, "We were starting to think you'd changed your mind and gone back to work."

Dad greets this with a weak smile. He and Mom are herded toward the main hall. I'm left in the wake and largely ignored, which is just fine by me. I keep wondering if someone will recognize me and if I even want that. This place brings back enough memories as it is. The Buffalo Lodge was built about a hundred years ago and still bears some old school marking: wooden paneling, dark oak crossbeams, marble stairs. Only the furniture and the carpeting—regularly replaced by the Buffalo—bear any modern feel. (And even there, the choice of green carpeting tells you the Buffalos' tastes have not been updated since the Seventies.) The lobby is filled with guests and the buzz of conversation from the main hall tells me there are many more people inside. The size of the crowd is overriding the building's air conditioning. I fidget with my blue collared shirt, check to make sure there are no wrinkles on my black slacks. After several moments, a friendly face appears from the crowd.

"I didn't realize your dad was this popular," Carol says, holding a Cosmo in a plastic cup, "You said everybody in town knew him, but I didn't think you meant *everybody* in town."

Judging by the stares she's getting from the locals, everybody in town may soon recognize Carol (or at least the guys will). Her dark hair flows past her shoulders and on to her sleeveless white blouse. Her blue eyes are clear and bright. Her smile reveals a row of perfectly white teeth. She wears a dusting of makeup and that's all she ever needs (if even that). Carol has brought a bit of big city glamor to my humble little hometown.

"Dad is most definitely public property," I say.

Carol takes everything in with a bit of amusement. "These are your people, huh?"

"These *were* my people," I say, "I haven't lived here in a long time."

"You've still got friends here, right?"

"A few," I say, "Andy, one of my best friends when I was growing up, has a meeting tonight. But he'll be at some of the other events. My other best friend from school, Sam, is going to be in town in a few days. He lives in Duluth."

"What about your brothers?" Carol says.

"My younger brother Owen is here, and my older brother Kevin will be coming in."

"Mike and Lars are here, of course. They're making the rounds. I hope they don't embarrass you."

"More than normal?"

Mike and Lars are friends I've picked up since leaving Porter's Bay. Mike has been my best friend since about five minutes after we got to college. Lars is my downstairs neighbor and the superintendent of my building. He's been in the picture for about seven years. If previous experience means anything, they're not doing much to burgeon my reputation in the old homestead. Carol sips her Cosmo.

"How many events are planned for your dad this week?" she asks.

I look up as I think. "It's the Buffalo tonight. The Historical Society is having a party. The Youth Sports League is having a softball game. The City Council is giving him the key to the city. And Our Savior's Lutheran Church is holding a big picnic on Sunday."

"Wow," Carol says. She peeks into the main hall. "It's nice to see your parents. I can't believe I've never met them."

"They don't come down to St. Paul much. They think it's a den of iniquity. Porter's Bay is a little more their speed."

Carol giggles. To a cosmopolitan type like her, a little town like this must seem hopelessly quaint. (Then again, *hopelessly quaint* is how Porter's Bay appeals to tourists. I think it was on a billboard once.) Carol nods toward the main hall.

"Are you going in?" she asks.

"I should," I say, "I wanted my dad to go in first. Enjoy his moment in the sun before the real star of the show arrives."

Carol snorts. She senses this whole thing makes me feel like I'm eight years old again. She slips her arm into mine and gently pulls me toward the main hall. "I totally forgot to ask: if Mike, Lars and I are here, who's taking care of your cats?"

Two cats, littermates, run my household back in St. Paul: Lenny, a butterscotch tabby who may be the reincarnation of John Belushi, and Squiggy, the nervous former runt of the litter whose black-and-white coloring and obsequious manner puts me in mind of a butler. Like all cats, they give off an air of self-sufficiency. And like all cats, their inability to work a can opener or change a litterbox undercuts that. I try to disguise my embarrassment.

"I, uh, I got Frank Pike to do it," I say.

Fortunately, Carol wasn't sipping her Cosmo, or she would have almost certainly done a spit-take. Sergeant Frank Pike of the St. Paul Police Department is not a fan of either my column or my general existence. We've bumped into each other several times over the past few years, usually involving a homicide he absolutely wants me to stay away from and that I assure him I will absolutely avoid, and we both know I am absolutely lying. To hear me say Pike is taking care of my cats is, for Carol, the equivalent of hearing the Vaders are going on vacation and Darth saying, "Don't worry, Luke will mind the Death Star until we get back."

"Sergeant Pike?" Carol says, "How in the hell did you pull that off?"

"I asked him," I say, "After the thing with the wrestling a few months back, he figured he owed me. And who the hell else could I ask? You guys are up here with me. I don't have a girlfriend right now. Pike was the only one I could think of."

"Will wonders never cease?" Carol says.

We step into the main hall, which is packed assholes to elbows. It's a reasonably large room with a high ceiling. The head table stretches along the far wall. Smaller round tables are scattered around the floor. A makeshift bar is set up in one corner. Portraits of former lodge leaders—my dad among them—line the walls. Everyone wears summer business casual. My parents greet various guests. Carol, her face glistening (she won't allow herself to sweat on formal occasions), waves her Cosmo toward the crowd.

"You know most of these folks?" she asks.

"I recognize a lot of them," I say, "Can't say I really *know* them."

Dad doesn't flinch from being the center of attention. He is in conversation with a short, wiry guy with slicked back gray hair and wire-rim frames. He also keeps an eye out for other people who might be trying to greet him. The other guy gives Dad his undivided attention. Carol leans toward me.

"That's your dad?" she says, "I thought he'd be taller."

"So did he," I say.

Carol smirks at that. "Who is he talking to?"

I jog the mental database. It takes a few seconds, but I come up with the name. "Eli Perry. He was one of my dad's partners. Back when he opened the hardware store."

"I didn't know your dad had partners."

"Three of them," I say, "The place was originally called Quality Hardware. Dad wound up buying out all of the partners after a few years. He was doing most of the work, so he figured he should get most of the profits. That's when he renamed the place Davis Hardware."

"And the partners were okay with this?" Carol asks.

I start to answer, then stop and give it some thought. "I guess so. Dad doesn't really talk about it. Come to think of it, he never had them over to the house or went to visit any of them. I've seen a few pictures, but that's about it."

It's one of those things you don't think about as deeply as you should. Sort of like accepting that your cat Mittens went to live on a kitty farm. It's only years later you realize *Wait a minute, who the hell ever heard of a kitty farm? And what kitty farm would gladly accept a fifteen-year-old incontinent cat? Come to that, the closest Mittens ever got to the outside was when he'd sleep in the sunbeam near the window. What use would he have for fresh air? Why did I accept that kitty farm horseshit?*

"It looks like they're getting along," Carol says, tugging at her blouse.

I can't say there's a lot of backslapping or hugging, but that doesn't seem to be Eli Perry's style. And hugging certainly isn't my dad's. We watch the conversation for another second before someone slaps *my* back.

"You have got to be one of Henry's kids," a big jovial voice says, "Am I right?"

The gentleman in question is a few inches shorter than me (placing him just below six feet). His face is round and red, and his wavy hair is going gray. The blue eyes practically twinkle. His chest and stomach push against his white short-sleeved dress shirt and his tie is askew. He holds a beer in a plastic cup and while he's not lurching or slurring, it probably isn't his first of the evening. He offers a hand that engulfs mine. I wait for recognition on my part, but none is forthcoming.

"Yeah, I am," I say, "My name's Joe."

"Pleased to know you, Joe," the gentleman says, "My name is Will. I'm an old friend of your dad's."

That throws a few sparks into the recognition boiler. "Will," I say, "You were one of my dad's partners in the store."

"That I was, that I was," Will says, "A long time ago. But I tried to keep up with you and your brothers." He mops his face with his blue handkerchief. "Now, let me see, you're the lawyer, right?"

"No," I say, "That's my brother Kevin."

"Oh," Will says, "Then you're the one who's taking the store from Henry?"

"No, that's Owen," I say, "I'm the…other one."

Will's face goes blank. He's trying to remember what *the other one* does for a living. Not coming up with anything, he slaps me on the back again.

"It's good to meet you, Joe," he says, "Hell of a nice thing they're doing for your dad."

"It is," I say. A fraught moment follows. Will and I have nothing in common except possessing names and knowing my father and we've already used up that bit of the conversation. If I don't do something, this could descend into the dreaded awkward silence. I turn to Carol, hoping I can buy some time by introducing her. But she's already slipped away into the crowd. (Damn sociable creatures, screwing it up for us introverts.) I turn back toward Will and say, "It was nice of you to come."

"Ah, I wouldn't have missed it," Will says, "I always liked Henry. We played football together in high school. Did you know that?"

"No, I didn't. Dad doesn't talk much about…" Then I realize the conversational pipe bomb I'm about to throw, so I end lamely with, "Football." Which is an utter lie, because from September to January, football is damn near *all* my father will talk about.

Will is satisfied with that answer, though. "We were all friends in high school. Me, your dad, Eli." His face darkens slightly. "Burt." He chuckles. "Survived Lou Barley, our coach. Meanest son of a bitch who ever lived. We all went to college, did some time in the service, then came back here and started the store."

I search for something to add and all I come up with is, "That must have been cool."

"It was," Will says, "It was hard damn work. Any new business is. We were lucky to have your dad. He had the drive to get things off the ground. Worked his ass off. Handled all the paperwork. Kept track of the inventory. Constantly worked with the customers." He drains a good deal of his beer. "After a while, it seemed like we were working for him. It made sense to buy the rest of us out. It was his store more than anybody else's."

"And you were okay with that?" I ask, treading lightly.

"Oh sure," Will says, "Hell, I knew I wasn't cut out for that sort of thing. Guess I was always meant to work for somebody else. Your dad was nice about it. Offered me a job at the store. But it would have been too strange. Better to just move on."

"Were the other partners okay with it too?"

"Guess you'd have to ask them." Will tosses that off with a light laugh. "Hey, I got nothing to complain about. I've got a beautiful daughter. I've had some good times. It's been a great life. I can't be anything but grateful." He downs the rest of his beer. "I could use a refill. It was nice meeting you, Joe. I'm sure I'll bump into you again."

He gives me another backslap and he's off. I desperately need a beer. I have a clear path to the cash bar, staffed by two overworked bartenders who are likely cursing whatever school of bartending ad first seduced them. There is exactly one piss-water domestic on tap. I'm tempted to order a glass of wine, but in my hometown, wine is for ladies only. The hard stuff might lead to a hard hangover, which I don't want while I'm staying with my parents. Serve me up the piss-water, barkeep.

Someone slides up to me just as my beer arrives. "An excellent choice, my friend. Not quality, but when in Rome…"

That someone is my friend Lars, who couldn't be farther from Rome. He has adorned his tall, skinny frame with a Nehru jacket, black slacks and white sneakers. A gold chain hangs around his neck. His quasi-pompadour is done up just so. One of his flipper-like hands cradles a gin-and-tonic. As always, he seems to be having a good time. I take a sip of my beer and promptly regret it.

"Everything going okay, Lars?" I ask.

"Ah but well, ah but well," Lars says, "Tis impossible I should speed amiss. But I have a bone to pick with you, mein Freund."

"Oh? And which bone is that?" (I'm not a fan of the verbiage in this conversation.)

"Why didn't you tell me that your uncle is the mayor of this lovely little town?"

Probably because I'm trying to forget it myself. About a year and a half ago, in what can only be described as an act of mass dipshittery, Porter's Bay elected my uncle Gordie as its mayor. The fact Gordie is in his late fifties, has never held a full-time job, currently pays the rent on his trailer home by working part-time as a pizza delivery man, and has never held elected office of any kind was apparently not a deal-breaker with the general populace. I haven't had to deal with Gordie's administration full-time (thank ye gods), but from the tidbits my parents have provided, Gordie has taken to the perks of the job, if not, y'know, the actual work involved. (And that is the most Gordie-like statement I can think of.)

I mumble into my beer. "Must have slipped my mind."

Lars's head snaps back. "I find that hard to believe. It must have been your family's proudest moment. I mean, this…" He gestures toward the gathering. "This is all well and good, as long as you overlook the celebration of your father's status as a herder of sheep to feed the capitalist beast. But your uncle Gordie? He's making a difference. Serving the people."

"You sure that's how you want to describe it?" I ask, "From what I gather, Gordie's main accomplishments are putting his buddies on the city payroll and staying awake through about half of the city council meetings. At least, the ones he bothers to attend."

Lars waves this off, using his usual expansive gestures. "There are always small, petty people who will find fault with those who dare greatly. The important thing is Gordie is a self-made man. Someone who pulled himself up by his own bootstraps. A man of humble beginnings—and middles, I believe—who has risen to great heights. He's the very embodiment of the American Dream."

"That's amazing," I say, scowling into my beer, "If you'll excuse me, I'm just going to go lay down in the street and die."

Lars clamps a hand on my shoulder. "Your uncle is making an impression. See? He's regaling Carol with his vision right now."

To my horror, Gordie has cornered Carol. Hizzoner is sporting his best white t-shirt, dirty sneakers, and faded jeans for the occasion. A battered Minnesota North Stars toque covers the bald spot on the crown of his head. He drinks cheap beer from a plastic cup and his walrus mustache droops over his crooked mouth. He's smiling, probably thinking he looks slick. Carol, on other hand, appears ready to chew her own leg off to get out of this metaphorical bear trap. Obviously, this situation cannot sustain itself.

"Y'know what?" I say, "You should probably get over there and join the conversation. If they're talking policy, you don't want to miss that."

Lars gives me a horse-toothed grin. "An excellent point, brother. All due respect but talking to you isn't getting me anywhere."

"The feeling is mutual."

"Later, good sir," Lars says, slipping through the crowd.

A few seconds later, Lars reaches the conversation. Gordie seems annoyed at Lars's presence, but it allows Carol to get the hell out of there. I've downed about half of my beer when someone stands up near the front. It's Bill Somrock, my former English teacher and former editor at the high school newspaper. A thoroughly decent guy and a good teacher. And as a good teacher will, he commands the attention of the room.

"Hello everybody, the program will start shortly," he says, "If you want to chat with our guest of honor or grab something at the bar, you should do it now."

That, of course, creates a gentle stampede toward the bar. I down the rest of my beer and join in. I'm close enough to a speaker to realize Dean Martin is playing. (Dad will be thrilled, if he can hear it.) I fall in line with someone who recognizes me. (Oh joy.) The dude looks vaguely familiar. He's got long dark hair, and a mouth that is pouty at all times. He's dressed for the occasion in a black t-shirt, jeans and sandals. He studies me for a second.

"Joe Davis, right?" he says, sticking a hand out. "Evan Erickson. I don't know if you remember me."

I *do* remember him, though we were never tight. Evan's sister, Elyse, was in my grade. She and I were buddies, bonding over a shared love of The Beatles. Evan was a few years younger and usually annoyed Elyse by doing kissy sounds whenever I was visiting. I shake Evan's hand.

"How's Elyse?" I ask.

"Good. Married. Got a couple kids. Lives in Portland now."

Evan weaves, ever so slightly. He's not holding a beer and I can't smell any alcohol on his breath. But the eyes are bloodshot, and he has a dopey expression. As I recall, Evan was a pretty big pothead back in the day. Looks like he hasn't outgrown the habit.

"Your dad's a great guy," Evan says, "I thought you should know that."

"Thank you," I say, "I *do* know that."

"I liked working for him at the store," Evan says, "Sucks that it didn't work out. But I don't blame *him* for that."

Oh yeah. I vaguely recall hearing something about Evan working in my dad's store. Elyse may have mentioned it on Facebook. I asked Dad about it on the phone a few weeks later and all he said was, "It didn't work out." Something in Dad's tone told me not to pursue it (and I wasn't all that curious to begin with).

"It's…it's good that you feel that way," I say, "About my dad, I mean."

"Your brother Owen, man, he's a prick."

I'm torn, obviously. Many is the time I've thought of Owen in just that way. But *I'm* allowed to think that. The privilege does not extend beyond the family circle. Evan stares at me like I'm supposed to make some sort of apology on behalf of the Clan Davis.

"I, I don't think I remember—" I say.

"Dude got me fired," Evan says, "Bunch of trumped up bullshit. Claimed I was never on time. Said I was impaired when I got there. Found twenty bucks missing from the till in my car and drew all sorts of conclusions. I know he's your brother and all, but he's a goddamn fascist."

I'm not going to disagree with Owen being a fascist. He's always had a bit of the control freak in him. (Unusual in a guy whose life is pretty much dictated by his wife and his father, but still…) However, he's also scrupulously honest (like my dad) and isn't about to make up a bunch of stuff as an excuse to fire someone. That doesn't mean I want to get in a pissing contest while waiting for booze.

"That sucks," I say, which commits me to nothing.

"But your dad is a good dude. I need you to know that."

"Thank you."

I dearly hope this is the end of this conversation. I'm not good at small talk and I'm *really* not good at listening to people make cracks about my family (even members of my family that *are* a bit tight-assed). But we're still stuck in this line.

"You need any?" Evan asks.

"Any what?"

"Herbage? You need some?"

Oh jeez. It's not that I'm opposed to herbage. I have a stash hidden away in my apartment. But there's no way I'm partaking in the Devil's Lettuce while staying under my parents' roof.

"I appreciate that," I say, "But I'm good."

Evan takes it in stride. "You got friends, don't you? You think they might be interested?"

My friends aren't staying at my parents' place, but I'm not going to facilitate a drug deal. Besides, I can't even locate them in the crowd. I *do* catch a glimpse of Mike in conversation with some woman. He'd kill me if I sent Evan over to interrupt.

"You'll have to ask them," I say, "I'm not sure where they are right now."

"Cool, cool. You let me know if you change your mind, 'kay?"

Evan slinks into the crowd. I get another cheap beer from the bar and walk to the head table. Mom and Dad are seated to the right of the podium. People still approach Dad for a handshake or a quick chat before the evening's program begins. Owen and his wife Mary sit near the end of the table. For once, Owen's expression doesn't look like somebody just cancelled Christmas. His stocky, muscular body is loose and relaxed. He runs a hand through his sandy blonde hair. Something approaching a smile spreads beneath his needle nose. He's trying to contain the euphoria he feels at taking full control of the store. Must be similar to what Teddy Roosevelt felt after becoming President due to McKinley's assassination. "Yes, yes, a horrible moment for our country, a great man has fallen, and also YIPPEE!!!!" A chair is open between Owen and Mom. I assume that's for me.

Owen turns to me as soon as I drop into my chair. "Glad you could make it."

I'm tempted to offer some snarky remark about how a four-hour drive isn't exactly crossing the Sinai. But Owen is being genuine, so I just say, "Wouldn't have missed it. When is Kevin getting in?"

"Flying into the Cities tonight," Owen says, "He and Jordan and the kids will be driving up tomorrow."

Swell. It will be good to see Kevin and the kids. Jordan is a different matter, but I don't want to dwell on it now. I scan the room. People are taking their seats.

"All of dad's old partners are here?" I ask.

"Yep," Owen says, "Eli is over there." He indicates Eli, at a side table nearer the front. "Will is there." Will is at a table almost directly in front of ours. "And that's Burt."

He says it in the same way one might point out the only eyesore on the block. Burt stands near the bar. He's on the short side and has a middle-aged spread he's carried into his senior years. He's in the advanced stages of male pattern baldness. What hair he has is gray and shaggy. He wears a tan suitcoat, a striped tie and dark blue jeans. He eventually joins Will's table. Will barely acknowledges him.

"Burt doesn't seem to be the most popular guy in the room," I say.

"I'm surprised he's even here," Owen says, "Dad says Burt was pretty bitter about him taking over the store."

Everyone takes their seats, allowing the evening's program to begin. Dad clasps his hands in front of him, gripping them so hard his knuckles are turning white. Mom lays a hand on his forearm, trying to calm him. (Her intentions are good, but it's a fool's errand.) Mr. Somrock steps to the podium and the room gives him a respectful hush.

"Welcome," Mr. Somrock says, "This is a very special occasion. We're here to honor a man who's been an institution in Porter's Bay for the last forty years. A man who has been a business leader and civic leader. A proud member of this lodge. A friend to the community. And I'm very pleased to say, a personal friend of mine."

Huh. Mr. Somrock and my dad are friends? That would have been a nightmare, once upon a time. To know he's friends with my dad makes me feel like I've missed something. Nonetheless, the praise of my dad continues for several minutes as his various accomplishments are extolled. Dad greets all this with a tight smile. He's never taken praise well on a personal level. Receiving it in a public forum must be absolute torture.

But he's forced to endure two more speeches from lodge members, talking about how much he's meant to both them and the community. This is followed by a video presentation, set to the tune of "A Very Good Year" by Frank Sinatra, showing Dad with various friends, civic leaders, and family. My mom dabs at her eyes. Owen cringes at a picture of him as a three-year-old sleeping on Dad's chest. (At his moment of ascendancy, he doesn't need images of him being dependent on Dad.) My friends get a kick out of the picture of Dad reading *Green Eggs and Ham* to me. After the video, the Buffalo present Dad with a gold pocket watch for his retirement. Then Mr. Somrock again steps to the podium.

"I think this would be a good time to hear from some of you," he says, "If anyone would like to share a story or give Henry some well wishes, please feel free to share."

Somewhere, Krusty the Clown is muttering *Oh God, this is always death*. Two people move around the room, ready to offer a mic to anyone who wants to say something. I've been at a few events where this has been done. Usually, at least one person delivers a speech that makes you wish they would have just cut one and saved themselves the embarrassment. I sit back in my chair, hoping my body language will confer that *I* will not be participating in this horseshit. Owen is stock still, betraying a muted tension similar to a junior high boy with a boner desperately hoping the teacher won't ask him to come up and show his work on the blackboard. The first few speakers offer bland—and brief—statements of congratulations and best wishes, giving us hope this thing may come off without a hitch.

Then Dad's former partner Burt raises his hand for the mic. He stands as someone dutifully delivers it. Burt totters slightly, his drink still in his hand. Dad tenses. Mom puts a hand on his shoulder. Burt breaks into a wide smile, revealing a set of yellowing, crooked teeth.

"Henry, I just want to say congratulations," Burt says, his voice a little higher-pitched than I would have expected, "I keep thinking about when we were young and trying to figure out what to do with our lives. You were the one who was always pushing us. 'We should get into business. Do something we love. If we do that, we'll never work a day in our lives.' I don't think we could have started the store without you."

That's greeted with a smattering of applause. Burt lowers the mic slightly, letting the applause have the floor. Dad rests his chin on his jowls and gives Burt an impassive face. Burt brings the mic back up to his lips.

"We were all in it together," Burt says, "We got it off the ground. The four of us. But you wanted it a little more than we did. At least, that's what you told yourself. Probably made it easier to shitcan the rest of us."

That huge crash must be the other shoe dropping. The room is filled with a tense, uncomfortable silence. Burt lets his words take full effect. Will reaches for Burt, trying to hold him back. Burt ignores him and addresses the whole room.

"He froze the rest of us out. That way he could justify everything he did. Go on and admit it, Henry."

Dad glares at Burt. Will reaches for the mic. Burt nimbly takes a step away, avoiding the grab and retaining the floor. There's a buzz in the room, as if someone should throw Burt out of here (a thing I wouldn't object to).

"I wonder if we should talk about Taylor?" Burt says, "You think everyone in here would be interested in hearing about Taylor?"

Dad stands up. So does Will. So does Eli. Some uncertainty comes into Burt's piggy eyes. Perhaps he's gone too far (though about what, I have no idea). Burt looks to each of his former partners.

"Maybe I should save that for another time," Burt says, "But it's something I think people ought to hear. If they want to know what you're really like, Henry."

Burt offers up the mic to one of the volunteers. Dad, Will and Eli slowly return to their seats. Burt saunters to the bar, the damage is done. The volunteers stand frozen, as does much of the room, uncertain about how to continue the evening's program.

If Dad didn't like these kinds of gatherings *before*...

CHAPTER TWO

When I was in high school, I once stopped by Cobb-Cook Elementary to perform a scene from the high school play. I hadn't been back at Cobb-Cook since the day I finished sixth grade, but I had (and still have) fond memories of it. As I walked around the school, I was overwhelmed by just how damn tiny *everything was: the classrooms, the lunchroom, the hallways. Hell, it seemed like the drinking fountains were no higher than knee level. How did this Lilliputian institution take on such epic proportions in my mind? I left there slightly depressed, realizing I had literally outgrown the place.*

Since then, I've come to the conclusion it's best to visit the past only in your mind. It can stay as epic as you need it to be (so long as you don't mythologize it to the point where you become one of those boors who says, "Back in my day…") John Ford may have been a miserable S.O.B., but he was on to something with that whole print the legend *thing.*

Nick's Corner Bar wasn't a place I visited in my childhood, but it holds a certain mythological value, nonetheless. Nick's was where my dad would stop off for a couple after work. It was where my mom and her friends would go after bowling. It was where my uncle Gordie would get into endless fistfights. (Gordie's record stands at 0-for-Life, with many by knockout.) Because I didn't set foot in the place until I was an adult, I had to imagine what it was like. My thoughts drifted to a *Cheers*-like pub, stocked with quirky characters and hilarious dialogue, where everybody knew your name and was perfectly willing to shout it when you walked in. The sort of place the Algonquin Round Table would have been perfectly at home. A place filled with cocktails and witty repartee and bonhomie.

Turns out, Nick's is your standard operational dive bar. And kind of a dump at that.

It's not as if we don't have options, bar-wise, in Porter's Bay. Many of those establishments will be cleaner, more relaxed, and more sociable than Nick's. But some subconscious desire to give my friends the entire Porter's Bay experience has driven me to choose Nick's as our post-debacle hangout.

"Interesting place," Carol says, cradling her vodka press, "When does the fighting start?"

"Right after the rednecks are done hitting on all the married women," I say, "We should probably leave before then."

Nick's sits at the corner of First Street and Howard Avenue. The place doesn't look like much. The tables and booths are imitation mahogany; all chipped and faded. The lighting is low. Even so, one can see the hardwood floors could use a sweeping. A picture window looks out on Howard Street. Various neon signs adorn the wall, advertising the likes of *udweiser* and *Coo s.* (Sadly, the Schmidt's sign remains fully functional.) The clientele is blue collar and ugly. Locals only. The mood will get ugly as well, sooner or later. After what happened at the event for my dad, though, it would feel like getting out of the fire and into the frying pan.

"Your dad ever slug anyone?" Mike asks, running a hand through the brush of brown hair atop his big bulldog head, "Because he sure as hell looked like he wanted to slug that one guy."

No argument there. After Burt's little speech, the rest of the evening was as awkward as you'd expect. There were a few other speakers, but their words were muted and the speakers clearly uncomfortable. Dad sat at the head table, glowering and probably not listening, which didn't help the situation. When the speeches were over, Mr. Somrock made a few uncomfortable remarks of his own (it was a unique experience to see Mr. Somrock at a loss for words), then the formal part of the event was over. And shortly after that, the event itself, as people were quick to flee the scene. My parents headed home while my friends and I walked over to Nick's.

"I have seen my dad throw a punch or two," I say, "but always in self-defense."

Carol huddles over her drink, perhaps wishing she had something to disguise her bare shoulders from the collection of troglodytes surrounding us. "Judging by the way that Burt guy was coming at him, he might have called it self-defense. And enjoyed it."

I sip my beer, still stewing about the whole incident. Said beer isn't helping. It's another cheap domestic. I wasn't going to order something snooty and give the rednecks a reason to come after me. When your company involves Lars, there's provocation enough.

"Not to get us on another subject, brother," Lars says, although that's exactly what he's going to do, "But I came up with a moneymaking idea regarding your little town here."

Oh, this should be rich. Back home, Lars fancies himself an entrepreneur. His enthusiasm is such that I don't point out he's an entrepreneur in the same way I'm a pro bowler. Just the act of doing a thing doesn't necessarily mean you're worth a great goddamn at it. Lars has tried and failed with many ventures, ranging from an urban alpaca farm (turns out alpaca do not like urban areas) to a self-guided brew pub crawl (some of those poor people have never been heard from since). They have all been, without exception, spectacular failures. He's like a Bizarro World Elon Musk (or, increasingly, a *this* world Elon Musk). His failure rate, though, has never deterred him (just as my gutter ball rate has never stopped me from bowling). Ergo, there's a very high cringe factor in Lars looking on my hometown as another money-making scheme.

I summon up the courage to ask, "What idea is this?"

"When I was at the event for your padre," Lars says, "I was talking to a woman from the Porter's Bay Historical Society. I guess, technically, I was hitting on her, but some genuine conversation came out of it. Who'd have thunk it, huh? Anyhoo, did you know Porter's Bay has a criminal history?"

I snap him a look. The only criminal history in Porter's Bay is a history of DWIs, drunk-and-disorderlys and urinatings in public, with maybe the occasional domestic conflict thrown in. To suggest more is to besmirch my hometown's heretofore smirch-free existence.

"What are you talking about?" I ask.

"There were gangsters here," Lars says, keeping his tone on the downlow.

Oh, *that* criminal history. "I heard something about that. Bank robbers and such used to hide out here, back in the Thirties. Is that what you mean?"

"Exact-a-mundo. This was a prime hangout for all your major crooks and baddies. A virtual den of iniquity here in the north woods!"

"That's overstating it," I say, "It was just a couple of people—Bonnie and Clyde a few times and maybe John Dillinger once—and they only spent the night on their way to St. Paul."

For those not in the know, St. Paul was considered a *safe city* by crooks of all kinds back in the Twenties and Thirties. As long as the crooks checked in with the St. Paul Police Department, made a small "donation" to the retirement fund and didn't commit any crimes within the city limits, they were allowed to come and go with impunity. The whole thing fell apart, of course, because crooks don't generally adhere to gentleman's agreements and the federal government began to get interested. Certain towns outside of St. Paul might have harbored crooks during this era because said crooks were passing through and under no circumstances was Roscoe the Local Sheriff going to trade bullets with the Barker Gang.

Lars, though, seems entranced by Porter's Bay's footnote in that chapter of history. "Do you realize you are sitting on a treasure trove of information?"

"Funny, I thought I was sitting on a rip in this Naugahyde bench," I say.

As per usual, Lars blasts past my snark. It's not that he misses jokes. He just runs several seconds ahead of them. "I'm talking a treasure trove of *history* here, my friend. Do you—

Naugahyde, that's a good one—do you realize what could be done with this?"

"You planning on making Porter's Bay safe for criminals?" I ask.

"No. Look, from what I gather, most of Porter's Bay's economy is based on tourism."

"It is," I say, "Especially this time of year."

"Exactly," Lars says, "There is money to be made— I'm talking big fat stacks of *dinero*—in exploring this part of your town's history."

"What are you going to do?" I say, "Offer tours of all the gangster sites in Porter's Ba—oh my God, that's exactly what you're going to do, isn't it?"

Lars slaps the table. "It's a surefire money-making enterprise." And he says this every time he comes up with an idea that eventually fails and leaves him in debt. But Lars always leaves the past (and several angry creditors) behind him. "People stay in and around Porter's Bay or pass through on their way to other locations. What better way to take advantage of this than to examine this town's sordid history?"

Oh boy. I didn't want Lars to *visit* my hometown, let alone get involved in the business community my father is about to abandon. Safe to say Porter's Bay would be trading down in that case.

"You sure you want to do that?" I ask, "People around here are pretty protective of the town's image. It's good for the tourist trade if people think we're a quaint little Norman Rockwell town. Saying a couple gangsters hunkered down here doesn't fit that."

"You worry too much," Lars says, giving me a flip of his hand, "People like honest-to-goodness history. They like a walk on the wild side. I'm ready to give them both."

No worries about *a walk on the wild side*. Lars can at least manage that. "Besides," I say, "I'm not sure there's all that much there. Just a couple gangsters, and a couple overnight stays. It's not like there were any crime sprees around here."

"That you know of," Lars says, giving me a smug look, "That's where research comes in, mon ami. I'll bet there's plenty to be discovered in the dark underbelly of this sleepy town. It's just a matter of kicking over rocks and finding the creepy crawlies on the underside."

"Who the hell are you?" I ask, "David Lynch?"

"No, no, brother. I'm merely a man with an idea. And an empty glass. I'll be right back."

Lars slides out of the booth and makes his way to the bar to collect another fruity cocktail. The Nehru jacket draws some looks from the locals. Lars is oblivious, tapping his hands on the bar and whistling a little tune (off-key). I turn to Mike and Carol.

"If he and that jacket survive the night, I'll be amazed," I say.

Mike straightens his black collared shirt. "Won't be the first time he's gotten his ass kicked."

"And it probably won't be the last," Carol says.

I sip my beer. "Can we be sure this whole enterprise isn't just an excuse to spend more time with the woman from the historical society?"

"I don't think so," Carol says, "When Lars comes up with an idea, he's pretty dedicated to it. Getting laid is just a bonus."

"Speaking of boners…" Mike says.

Carol swings her head his direction. "We weren't."

"Really?" Mike asks, "You didn't say *boners?*"

"No," Carol says, "I said bon*us*. You know what? That doesn't sound any better."

Mike stretches an arm along the back of the booth. "Anyway, I have to say I'm pretty surprised. I thought this town was going to be wall-to-wall uggos, but you got some babes."

In Mike's universe, that's a ringing endorsement. As Carol has stated many times, Mike is essentially a penis with an auxiliary human being attached. And she should know. She and Mike dated for about a year. It's been over for some time, but he frequently—and unintentionally—reminds her she spent a year of her life being defiled by Jughead Jones.

"I assume one of the *babes* was the woman you spent all night talking to?" Carol asks.

"Yes, she was," Mike says, not even attempting to conceal his shit-eating grin, "Her name is Julie. You familiar with her, Joe?"

"I'm afraid I am not."

"We had a great time," he says, "We're going on a picnic tomorrow."

"You're into picnics now?" Carol says, "Since when? I couldn't *drag* you on a picnic when we were dating."

"I've grown up a little since then," Mike says, "And Julie has a tremendous rack."

To be fair, Mike wasn't *always* this way. I first met him about five minutes after we got to college. He was a military brat; the scion of two helicopter parents who ruled him with an iron fist. Once he got to college and discovered he wasn't being supervised constantly, he not only embraced his freedom, he bent it over the arm of the couch and took it roughly from behind. He's not progressed much, if at all, since. Lars returns from the bar, oblivious to the disdainful looks he's getting from the redneck set. We're going to have to get out of here soon. All thoughts of that go out the window when I see Burt walking into the bar.

"Son of a bitch," I say, stiffening up.

Carol follows my look. "You got that right."

Burt looks around the place then spots our table. He walks our direction. This is going to be fun. Carol senses the trouble coming and spins toward me.

"What are you going to say to him?" she asks.

"I'm going to tell him what an asshole he is," I say.

"He's probably aware of that," Carol says, "Don't make the situation any worse."

That will be a hell of a lot easier said than done. The smug look on Burt's face does *nothing* to quell my distaste for him. He offers his hand when he arrives at the table.

"You're one of Henry's kids, right?" he asks.

"Joe," I say, ignoring the hand.

Burt lowers it. "Which are you? The lawyer?"

"No," I say. And I refuse to elaborate on my line of work.

"Too bad," Burt says, "If you *were* the lawyer, I was going to remind you there's a law against destroying people's property."

Okay, he's got me on this one. "Destroying whose property?" I ask.

For the first time in our very brief acquaintance, Burt looks unsure of himself. "You're telling me you didn't slash the tires on my car?"

Wow. People in my hometown are still doing that? It's like watching somebody lay rubber in the Dairy Queen parking lot. It's not like I'd do it myself, but it's nice to know the practice hasn't ended. Particularly when it's being practiced on somebody like Burt.

"That's what I'm going to tell you," I say, "One, I'm not into vandalism. Two, I have no idea what kind of car you drive."

I'm not sure which argument hits home with Burt. If I had to guess, my ignorance about his car probably holds more water than any testament to my moral fiber. He scrutinizes me for another moment.

"No big deal," he says, "This place is walking distance. Even for an old fart like me."

"Happy to hear it," I say, deadpan.

"No chance your brother might know something about it?"

"You'd have to ask him." I want to let it go at that, but I can't resist a further jab. "I doubt it, though. Owen is a good guy. Just like my dad."

Burt smirks in response. "Keep telling yourself that."

He waddles back to the bar. I start to get up. Carol puts a hand on my leg, stopping me. She guides me back into my chair.

"Don't give him the satisfaction, Joe," she says.

"Besides," Mike says, "You're not a fighter. What do you think you could do to him?"

"I could…" And common sense takes over. Mike is right. Fighting isn't close to being my strong suit. Flies have not only survived the thrashings I've attempted to deal out, they've taken pity on me and refused to press charges. Distasteful as it is, it's best to let this go.

That doesn't mean it's easy, looking at the guy who embarrassed my dad on a night when he should have been celebrated. I'm again considering getting up when someone approaches Burt and takes a seat next to him at the bar.

"Evan," I say, absently.

Mike cranes his neck. "The stoner at the bar? How do you know him?"

"Younger brother of a high school friend," I say, "I bumped into him at the party. I wonder how he knows Burt."

Carol shrugs. "It's a small town."

Lars throws a look that direction. "And who is the young lady?"

Evan and Burt are joined by a tall woman with curly hair and wire-rim glasses. She stands behind Evan, her arms folded across her chest, and lets him do the talking. I don't recognize her, meaning she wasn't in my grade at school.

"I have no idea," I say.

Evan glowers at Burt during the conversation. The woman places a calming hand on Evan's shoulder from time to time. Burt half-turns away from Evan and gives him a sort of dismissive gesture. Evan grabs Burt's arm and tries to turn him back. But he doesn't have the strength required. Instead, he gets up in Burt's face. Burt looks around, concerned somebody might notice this chat. The woman grabs Evan's arm. Burt gets up and looks for a table. Evan calls after him.

"You don't own me!" he says, "You hear that? You don't fucking own me."

The bartender approaches Evan and whispers something. I'm assuming it's a request (or more likely an order) not to make a scene. Evan slaps the bar and stalks out of the place. The woman follows. Burt joins some friends at a high-top in the corner. I turn back to the booth.

"I wonder what that was all about?" I say.

"Who knows," Carol says, looking around the bar, "You think maybe we should get going? The atmosphere in here is getting a little unfriendly."

She's right. A little pressure change occurred without me noticing it. The rednecks eyeball each other and, unfortunately, Lars. Just as we slide out of the booth, a burly redneck makes his way over and stands in front of Lars.

"What the hell are you supposed to be?" he asks, his voice gravelly.

"My name is Lars." He offers Mr. Burly his hand.

Mr. Burly looks like Lars just offered him a dirty diaper. "I don't give a fuck what your name is. What are you doing here?"

Lars says, in all honesty, "Drinking."

Mr. Burly tenses up like he's going to make a move. This is bad. Mike slips past me and leans close to Lars, whispering so that Mr. Burly can still hear him.

"Okay, here's your chance," Mike says, "You keep telling me you can get the Glock out from under that ridiculous jacket in less than three seconds. Why don't you show me?"

Lars, who is unflappable if nothing else (and may not be anything else), merely raises his eyebrows. A look of doubt creeps onto Mr. Burly's face. He leans back slightly. Mike gestures toward Lars's boot.

"Unless you think the knife is better for this," Mike says, "It sure as hell makes less noise, but I don't know if you want to clean this place up afterwards. Those serrated blades do a hell of a lot of damage."

"This is true," Lars says, rolling with it.

"Just don't tell your therapist I brought this up," Mike says, "He'll go blabbing to your parole officer and you'll wind up back in solitary. Like the time you bit that guy's nose off."

Lars inclines his head. "That *was* rather funky."

Mr. Burly backs off. His look is still hard. His eyes flick from Lars to Mike. He'd like to offer some crushing exit line; a warning to Lars or a reminder that he's damn lucky. But not wanting to risk Lars's ire, Mr. Burly just turns and walks back to his table. We head for the exit.

"That was fun," Mike says, "If I had known your hometown was like this, I would have hung out here *years* ago."

I'm sure he would have. Probably best I kept him away. For my hometown's sake, if nothing else.

***

Being back in my parents' house, even for a visit, always feels strange. This is, after all, the house I grew up in. My bedroom, the one I shared with Owen until I was twelve, looks largely the same; third door on the right on the second floor, tiny closet, ledge outside, still accessible from the maple tree in the side yard. The oak table in the dining room hasn't changed. My mom still has a plaque with the Serenity Prayer in the little kitchen. Dad still diligently makes sure branches and leaves don't accumulate on the top of the A-frame garage. The furniture in the living room gets swapped out every now and again but sits in the same arrangement: TV as centerpiece, couch facing the TV, Dad's armchair nearby. Mom still keeps M&Ms in the glass candy dish on the coffee table. Not a speck of dust can be found. She keeps the interior in fighting trim while Dad dutifully handles the yardwork. Just as it was when I was growing up.

But even with all this sameness, a feeling of alienation has crept into the place for me. It's home, but it's not *my* home, at least not anymore. Maybe that's why I feel comfortable but kind of anxious to leave at the same time.

In any event, it's where I'll be staying until the beginning of next week. Mike drops me off and I slink up the front steps, feeling oddly guilty, as if I'm sneaking in after curfew. It's not as if I don't go out drinking when I visit my home (it becomes particularly necessary during the family gatherings at Christmas and Thanksgiving), but I can never shake the guilt. Turns out, I didn't have to worry. My dad has been drinking in my absence.

In this area, my dad is a lot like me. He's not a drunkard, but he's hardly a teetotaler. He considers a martini or a whiskey sour after getting home from work to be a ritual. He enjoys a beer or two when watching a ball game. And he enjoys beaucoup champagne on special occasions. So, I'm not dismayed when I walk in and find him in his easy chair, nursing a whiskey on the rocks, clearly not his first.

"Have a good time at Nick's?" he asks.

"Good as it gets."

"Pull up a chair. Have a drink."

After an evening of cheap swill, I could use a decent beer. Fortunately, for this trip, I brought a six pack of Hefeweizen from Grand Brewing, my favorite brewery in St. Paul. (My parents' beer palates, sadly, aren't any more sophisticated than the general population.) I walk through the dining room and into the small kitchen to fetch a bottle from the fridge. Normally, I'd pour it into a glass, but my father would look askance at such a thing, I bring the bottle back to the living room and drop onto the couch.

"Where's Mom?" I ask.

"She went to bed. I didn't feel like sleeping just yet, so I came down here."

I set my beer bottle on the coffee table, making sure to put a coaster underneath. (If only my friends could be as attentive a houseguest as I am.) Dad has loosened the top button on his shirt. His feet are propped on the ottoman. Neither of us says anything for several seconds.

"You okay?" I ask.

"I'm fine," Dad says, a little too quickly, "I should have known Burt would pull something like this. That's how he's always been."

"How long has it been since you've seen him?"

"Years. We do our best to avoid each other."

I run a thumb along the mouth of my beer bottle. "He accused you of a lot of stuff."

"He did. I'm sure from Burt's point of view that's exactly how things happened."

"You think the other guys feel the same way?"

"I hope not." He lets out a sigh. "It was a long time ago, Joe. We were all gambling on the store succeeding. I knew that just showing up to work every day wasn't going to be enough. We had to work at it. When things needed to be done, if no one else was jumping in to do it, I did it myself. After a while, I realized I was doing three-quarters of the work and only getting one-quarter of the profits. What profits we had, anyway. I finally decided if I was going to take most of the risk, I should get most of the reward. So, I bought them out. And the rest, as they say, is history." He gazes at his nearly empty glass of whiskey, something vaguely sad in his eyes. "Or at least it should have been."

I try to make the next question sound casual. "Burt said something about *Taylor*. What was that all about?"

Dad snaps me a look. As usual, my attempts to sound casual have crashed and burned. (In my defense, there is only so much you can do with this material.)

"It was just a thing from when we were younger," Dad says, "It doesn't mean anything. I have no idea why Burt even brought it up."

Now it feels like the shoe is on the other foot. Dad tried to make *that* sound casual, but there's something there. Something he doesn't want to share. I sip my beer.

"Sorry about all this," I say.

"It's not your fault." He takes in a breath through his nose. "Maybe this is what I deserve."

"What do you mean?"

After a few seconds, Dad lifts his eyes. There's a slight movement in his cheek, as if he wants to say something to me. Then he looks away and finishes his drink.

"It's nothing," he says, "I just meant it's what I deserve for letting everyone do this. For my own vanity." He gets up from the chair and hands me his glass. "Would you mind putting that in the sink? I'm going to bed."

"No problem."

Dad shuffles toward the stairs. His shoulders are stooped, and he moves slowly. I've watched my dad age, but this is the first time I've seen him look…old. He stops at the foot of the stairs, his hand resting against one of the pillars, as if it's holding him up. "Even with all the crap tonight, it was still nice of you and your friends to come up here."

"Wouldn't miss it."

"Your friends seem like decent people. Although, Lars…are you sure he's all there?"

"I'm still trying to figure that out."

Dad bobs his head, as if to say, *I expected as much*. He goes up the stairs, each step a bit of an effort.

***

Anyone who has been acquainted with me for more than five minutes knows I'm a creature of habit. My job usually only requires a few hours of work every day, so I'm left with copious amounts of free time. To make sense of this landscape and not fall into the slough of despond, I've created a solid foundation of routine. Certain parts of my apartment are cleaned on the same day every week. I work out at the same time of day every day. I partake in the same activities at the same times of the year. It lends structure to an existence that could easily descend into chaos. One side effect, though, is that I don't travel well. I either have trouble falling asleep or I get completely disoriented when I wake up. Sometimes both.

This morning, for instance, I wake up and blindly reach to get my phone off the nightstand. I come up empty and realize the nightstand is on the other side of the bed. Confused thoughts abound. *Why did my nightstand move? Where am I? Wait, I'm in my old room. I'm at my parents' place. What year is this?* It takes a second to get it together.

I slip out of bed and pull on a robe. It's from my younger days and is pretty worn out, but my parents' house is not a place to walk around in a pair of boxer shorts and a t-shirt. I head downstairs. The aroma of bacon and eggs hits me.

It's the same breakfast Dad has almost every morning. (He's a creature of habit himself.) The local news plays on the little transistor radio in the kitchen. (The broadcaster is Mike Broker, a guy I went to school with. Complete jackass, as I recall.) I could use a cup of coffee, even if it is my mom's coffee. (For all her culinary talent, my mom makes the worst coffee known to man.) Mom buzzes around the kitchen, preparing breakfast. Dad stares out the little window to the backyard. I'm struck by the feeling something is wrong. Breakfast is on the table, but no one is eating. Dad has a cup of coffee in his hand, but he's not drinking. I stop in the entrance.

"Everything okay?" I ask.

Mom does the talking. "Burt Franklin is dead. He was murdered."

Suddenly, Mom's coffee is not the worst thing I can think of.

CHAPTER THREE

There are those who consider growing up in a small town to be idyllic. And in some ways, for me, it was. I had a lot of freedom to roam around. I could be out riding my bike and playing with my friends all day. As long as I was home in time for dinner or by my curfew, my parents weren't concerned. What was going to happen to me? Kidnapping, murder, assault, mugging…those were big city things. They didn't happen in our little town.

But I don't think that kind of existence is a good thing. First, it doesn't properly prepare you for the world outside of said little town. My parents still hate coming down to St. Paul because they think it's a den of iniquity. I try to tell them I live in a neighborhood that's more boring than theirs, but they refuse to listen. When I first moved to the Cities, I had the same feeling. I was constantly trying to make sure no one picked my pocket or tried to rob me. Now, there are still neighborhoods I avoid or places I won't go at certain times of the day, but eventually, I realized the Cities are not a post-apocalyptic nightmare. (More a pre-apocalyptic one.) That fear of the Other almost caused me to miss the Cities' rich life and diversity.

My parents might think avoiding the Twin Cities means they can avoid violence and murder. But sometimes those things will come to you.

For a few seconds, I don't know what to say. Dad doesn't move. Mom keeps cooking, apparently planning to feed bacon and eggs to the Seventh Fleet. (She likes to stay busy when stressed.) Finally, I say, "What happened?" Because that seems like a decent place to start.

"Burt was found in Bennett Park last night," Dad says, "An anonymous call to the police tipped them off. He was shot to death. They think there might have been an assault involved."

"Have they arrested anyone?" I ask.

"Not yet," Dad says, "They didn't even say if there were any suspects."

Wow. I wasn't thrilled with the guy, but I didn't want anything like this to happen to him. And in a place like Bennett Park. It's on the far side of town and used to be home to a kickass rocket ship slide. It's been a gathering place for little league games, picnics, performances in the park, what have you, for as long as I can remember. Not the sort of place you picture someone getting killed. I step over to the coffee pot and pour myself a cup. (Hopefully, the shock of the murder will take the edge off tasting my mom's coffee.) I turn down the volume on the radio.

"What was Burt doing in Bennett Park in the middle of the night?" I ask.

"That's a good question," Dad says, "For now, we have to assume only he and the murderer know for sure."

Odds are neither of *them* is saying anything. Mom invites me to sit at the table and she'll get me some breakfast. I tell her that she doesn't need to get me breakfast, but my denial is pro forma. Mom knows full well she's going to fix a plate for me, and I know full well I'm going to eat it. We go through this little ritual so I can maintain some air of independence.

"You okay?" I ask Dad.

Dad comes out of his reverie. "I'm fine. Just…surprised."

"Have you talked to your other friends?"

"Will called this morning," Dad says, "He heard it on the news, too. He said he was going to call Eli."

Mom glances at Dad as she puts the plate of bacon and eggs in front of me. "Do you know if Burt had any family?"

"I don't think so," Dad says, "He has a brother, but I heard they aren't speaking. I don't think Verna knows. I don't think they were speaking, either."

Mom's mouth tightens. "I suppose someone should tell her."

There is a story there. But the morning has been hard enough on them (not that last night was any bargain). I'm not going to push the issue. Mom wipes her hands on her apron and goes back to work on breakfast for fifty-seven. Dad pours his coffee in the sink and rinses out the cup.

"I should probably call around," he says, "See if people still want to go ahead with all this…retirement stuff."

"I'm sure they will," Mom says.

Dad makes no attempt to hide his disappointment. "I'll call anyway."

He steps out of the kitchen and heads for the phone in the living room. (Dad owns a cell phone, but he rarely uses it, regarding any invention more modern than the remote control to be the work of the devil.) There's a knock at the front door. Dad adjusts his route to answer it. Voices are audible from the living room.

"Good morning, Henry," a male voice says, "I'd like to talk to you."

"That's fine, officer," Dad says, "Come on in."

I go into the dining room where I can get a better view of our visitor. He's a uniformed Porter's Bay cop who looks vaguely familiar. His face is round, and his slash of a mouth seems to indicate he knows more than you. His brown hair is receding and his gut pushes up against the blue of his uniform shirt. His head is cocked back, possibly in an effort to look taller.

"Okay if we sit down?" the officer asks, trying to put some bass in his voice.

"I suppose," Dad says.

The officer looks my direction and says, "Hi, Joe."

Then I recognize the guy. Cliff Beardsley. Cliff and I were in the same grade in school and for a time anyway, I suppose you could have called us friends. I would go over to his house occasionally and we'd play with the same group of friends. That ended when we got to junior high, and Cliff figured his social status would suffer if he was seen with the likes of me. I'm not surprised Cliff wound up being a cop. (It feeds his need for social status and respect, and his defective intellect isn't considered a drawback.)

"Hi," is all I can muster.

Dad settles into his armchair while Beardsley sits on the sofa. "Can I ask what this is about?" Dad says.

"Burt Franklin is dead," Beardsley says, sounding like he's auditioning for some variation of *Law and Order*, "His body was found in Bennett Park last night."

"I heard that," Dad says.

"Where?" Beardsley asks.

Dad jerks a thumb toward the kitchen. "On the radio."

There's a pause. Beardsley is sweating slightly. "I understand you and Burt had an incident at the Buffalo Lodge last night."

Dad is quiet for a second, then says, "The incident was mostly Burt bringing up the past and me sitting there. If that's what you're talking about."

"It is." A beat. "Where did you go after the event at the lodge?"

"I came back here." Dad doesn't give Beardsley a chance to keep fumbling around. "Officer, can I ask—again— what this is all about?"

Beardsley ignores him. "Did you talk to Burt after the incident at the lodge?"

Judging by the edge in Dad's voice, he's losing patience. "There wasn't a lot to talk about."

"I understand you were given a pocket watch by the Buffalos. A retirement present?"

"Yes, I was."

"Do you have it now?"

"I suppose." Dad calls toward the kitchen. "Katherine, where did you put that watch I got from the Buffalos?"

Mom steps to the entrance of the kitchen. "I haven't seen it. You were the one who brought it home from the lodge."

"No, I wasn't," Dad says, "I remember handing the thing to you."

"No, you didn't," Mom says, trying to keep her own patience, "You set it down on the table, but you never handed it to me."

Dad throws up his hands and turns to Beardsley. "I'm not sure where it is. Is it important?"

"I'd say so," Beardsley says, "It was found on Burt Franklin's body."

By this time, I've worked my way to the edge of the dining room. A bubble of panic rises in my chest. Dad's face is completely blank, as if he's been told alien invaders would like to use the apartment over the garage.

"Burt had it?" Dad says.

"It was found next to his body," Beardsley says.

Dad steeples his fingers, holding them just under his chin. "Son of a bitch."

"What does that mean?"

"It means, how did the son of a bitch get my watch?"

"That's one of the reasons I'm here."

Dad debates how cooperative he wants to be. He's genuinely befuddled by the misplacement of the watch and genuinely alarmed it was found with Burt's body. Should he answer questions or is it time to call a lawyer? Dad drops the finger steeple.

"I don't know how Burt got my watch," he says, "I thought I handed it to my wife, but apparently, I'm mistaken. It was a busy night, and I was tired and, frankly, a little pissed off. I didn't keep track of the watch." He flips his hands open. "That's all I can tell you."

Beardsley's beady eyes are still suspicious. He's perhaps waiting for my father to break down and make a blubbering confession. Even if Dad *was* guilty, he's not the kind to do that, so Beardsley is SOL there.

"What time did you get home?" he asks.

"Eleven-thirty or so," Dad says.

"Anyone who can verify that?"

"My wife."

"Anyone *outside* the family?" Beardsley asks, unable (and not trying too terribly hard) to keep the snark out of his voice.

Dad doesn't take the bait. He folds his hands on his stomach. "I think the Seavers next door were in bed by the time we got home. I don't know about the other neighbors. You'd have to ask them."

"I will."

Dad twiddles his thumbs. He's reacting to the idea of a cop going door to door in the neighborhood and essentially asking, *Can you back up Henry Davis's alibi on a murder rap?* It's not the kind of image my father has wanted to project. Still, objecting to Beardsley talking to the neighbors would make him look guilty.

Beardsley leans forward and invades Dad's space, "And you were here all night?"

"Yes."

"Can anyone confirm that?"

Dad leans back in the chair and looks toward the ceiling. "No, I don't have any witnesses to me sleeping all night. I usually prefer it that way."

I stifle a laugh. Dad is still on top of the situation. Beardsley greets this in silence. He shows no sign of moving. Maybe Mom should offer him coffee. That would show him.

"When Burt was delivering his speech at the lodge," Beardsley says, "He mentioned something about *Taylor*. That's right, isn't it? Taylor?"

Dad noticeably stiffens. "I think *Taylor* is what he said."

"What was that all about?"

"I don't know," Dad says, "You would have to ask Burt. Except…"

Beardsley looks up from his little notebook. "Doesn't that seem strange? He'd be speaking in public and bring up something you didn't know anything about? Something he was apparently going to tell other people about?"

Dad remains as still as a Buddha. "Do you know how much Burt had to drink before he said that?"

"Not yet we don't."

"There you go," Dad says, "When he was younger, Burt would get drunk and go off about something, whether it made sense or not. I guess he was still like that."

I'm not buying it. I hate that I'm not, but I'm not. While he's subtle about it, Dad seems relieved to seize on a talking point to counter questions about Taylor. The problem is, Beardsley doesn't seem to buy it, either.

"You're saying Burt got drunk and threatened you with something that didn't mean anything to you and that you don't know anything about?" he says.

"That's all I know," Dad says.

Several seconds pass. Beardsley has no further questions, and Dad offers no further information. Finally, he offers Dad his card.

"Thanks for your time," he says, "I'm going to ask you not to leave town for the next few days, if that's all right."

Dad spreads his hands. "Where the hell would I go? Besides, they insist on making a big deal about my retirement. I *have* to stay."

Beardsley heads out the front door. Once he's gone, the room gets quiet. The radio filters in from the kitchen. *E-O-Eleven* by Sammy Davis Jr. Dad sets the card on the end table, next to the phone.

"I should have known Burt would get himself killed," he says.

"What makes you say that?" I ask.

This is the wrong time, psychologically, to ask my dad a question. He's just been interrogated by Officer Numnuts. He doesn't need me to join in. Dad gives the same look he'd give me when I was a kid, and he was about to unload on me. He corrals himself before the dressing down can begin.

"Because of the way he treated people," Dad says, "You may not have figured this out, but the man was an asshole."

In my defense, I *did* cotton on to that fact, both in public and private conversation. I make a half-move to fetch my coffee then remember what's waiting for me. The visit from the police has killed my appetite, so the bacon and eggs can wait.

"I don't suppose you slashed Burt's tires, did you?" I ask.

Dad rolls his eyes. It seems like *everyone* is accusing him of something. "Why in the hell would I do a thing like that?"

"It's the same question Burt asked me. And I gave him pretty much the same answer."

I tell Dad the story about Burt confronting me at Nick's. Dad takes a deep breath through his nose. This hasn't been a great morning.

"I didn't slash Burt's tires," he says, "I've never slashed anyone's tires. Not that I haven't fantasized about it a time or two." He fixes me with a look. "Let's keep that between us."

"Will do."

"At the risk of repeating myself, there was no shortage of people who wouldn't have minded slashing Burt's tires."

True dat. "I wonder what else the police have got?" I say.

"If Officer Beardsley is any indication," Dad says, "they've got my watch at the murder scene, and me with no alibi."

I suppress a shudder. "That's not always the worst thing. If you *had* done something to Burt, you would have made sure to have an alibi."

"I always thought if I was going to be a criminal, I should be the very best one I could."

Dad has a placid look on his face, but there's a little twinkle in his eye. All this, though, is too much for my mom. She starts back to the kitchen.

"I don't want to talk about any of this," Mom says, "Joe, come back and finish your breakfast. Henry, do you want more coffee?"

"I can get it myself," Dad says, working his way out of the easy chair, "I wonder if they have decent coffee in the big house?"

"Henry, that's not funny!"

Mom says it with more vehemence than Dad's smartassery deserves. The tension of the morning is getting to her, and I can't say she's alone. Dad's apparently glib attitude is a cover for real concern. (I know him that well, at least.) He holds up a hand by way of apology. We all retire to the kitchen. I resume eating my now-lukewarm breakfast. Dad gets himself another cup of gawdawful coffee. Mom rinses the dishes, her shoulders tense and her movements irritable.

Clearly, this is not what I came home for.

***

City Hall in Porter's Bay is a few blocks off Howard Street, right next to the library. It's a four-story building that takes up a whole city block. There's red brick on the outside and marble on the inside. Its most distinctive feature is a clock tower stretching up a few stories above it. A bronze miniature of the Statue of Liberty sits on the grounds out front. Like the high school, it's a monument to a time when Porter's Bay was a major shipping center and iron ore money flowed through the town.

The Porter's Bay Police Department is housed inside City Hall. Despite having grown up in Porter's Bay, I've been inside the building only once. When I was in high school, my dad asked me to accompany him to the police station to pick up my brother Owen, who had been detained (not arrested, mind you, Owen likes to make that very clear) for getting into a fight and beating the holy hell out of Monk Jones. (Owen, as you may have guessed, was a lot more fun in his younger and wilder days.) The fight was in the alley behind the junior high and drew a standing room only crowd. (I'm not sure why they thought a few hundred junior high kids standing in an alley *wouldn't* draw the attention of the police, but then again, they were in junior high.) I'm pretty sure Dad brought me along to make sure he didn't strangle Owen in the car on the way home. Dad handled the situation with aplomb. He joked with the cops, noted the lack of marks on Owen's visage as a sign of how the fight had gone, and assured the arresting (excuse me, *detaining*) officer that such a thing would never happen again. Owen was palpably relieved…until we got out of the police station and Dad grounded him for three months and read him the riot act the whole drive home.

I pull my mom's borrowed mini-Cooper to the curb in front of City Hall. I want to talk to the police about my father. Officer Beardsley's air of suspicion was easily detectable. I'd like to know if that opinion is shared by the rest of the department. The air is warm, and the sun is out. A slight breeze comes in from the lake, where most of the tourists are. A few straggle around City Hall, taking pictures. The Police Department is on the first floor, just down the hall from the main entrance. The sight of the marble floors, brass railings, wooden doors and little rectangular windows gives me a case of nerves. It reminds me I'm not a grown, relatively independent man in my thirties. I'm a scared kid housed in the body of a grown, relatively independent man in my thirties.

The cop at the front desk informs me Officer Beardsley is not, but I can give him a call if I have his card. I look past the expanse of desks to the offices near the back. The chief's office door is open, and the office appears occupied.

"Would it be okay if I talked to the chief?" I ask.

The cop frowns, further sagging the folds that make up his face. I'm not sure if he doesn't want to bother the chief or if he dreads the idea of waddling all the way back to the office to find out. He squints at me.

"What is it about?" he asks.

"The murder of Burt Franklin," I say.

I'm sure the phrasing is more dramatic than it needs to be, but I'm hoping to shock the cop into a sense of urgency. Judging by the look on his face, though, I've just shocked him into constipation. He rests a cushioned hand on the front desk.

"You have information?" he asks.

"No," I say, "I was actually hoping to *get* information."

"You a reporter?"

"Not really. I'm Henry Davis's son."

That shocks the cop into action. (I probably should have led with that.) He looks around, as if worried someone has overheard.

"Let me check with the chief," he says.

The cop makes his way back to the chief's office. I stand there, feeling conspicuous, trying to ignore any looks from the other cops. After what feels like a few hours (but is likely only a minute), the cop returns to the front desk.

"The chief's got time," he says, "You can follow me back there."

I'm not sure why the escort is necessary, given I can clearly see the path to the chief's office and the layout of the department is so wide open I couldn't even think about an act of mischief without getting caught. But I've never been a cop (which is best for both me and law enforcement in general), so I won't comment on procedure. The cop pulls up short of the office and lets me approach the open door.

The chief is a craggy faced guy in his late fifties. His physique is trim and a thick mustache droops over his lips. He moves with an easy grace and his blue eyes look untroubled. If there's a lot of stress involved in running the Porter's Bay Police Department, he doesn't show it. He steps over to me, casually offering a hand.

"Ben Davenport," he says, his voice a deep rumble, "You're Henry's kid. The writer?"

My eyebrows go up as I shake his hand. "I am. I'm surprised you know that."

"Henry talks about the three of you all the time. We've been friends since I had to detain your little brother for fighting outside the junior high."

Ah. He was there for the Great Family Shame. Glad he and Dad could use it as a bonding moment. Davenport waves me into a chair and moves back behind his oak desk, which is neat as a pin. He drops lightly into his seat and picks up a coffee cup that could use a wash. His brow furrows slightly.

"Lou said you want to talk about what happened to Burt Franklin," Davenport says, "How can I help you?"

"One of your officers talked to my dad this morning," I say, "I got the impression my dad is a suspect."

Davenport doesn't react. I get the feeling very little fazes him. "Cliff Beardsley is a decent officer. But he can come across as a little suspicious. Hell, he could stop you for a traffic violation and give you the idea he thinks you've got a trunk full of drugs. I wouldn't worry about it too much."

"I appreciate that," I say, "But it's a little hard not to worry when a guy insults your dad publicly, threatens him and then turns up dead the next morning. *And* you have a cop come to your house to question your dad about it."

"I understand. Just know this is an open investigation. All we're doing right now is gathering evidence. Officer

Beardsley might not have the nicest way of going about it, but he's just doing his job."

That I get. If my memories of Cliff are relevant, being a dick *is* how he goes about doing his job. Still, I can't get rid of my uneasy feeling. I shift in the hard wooden chair.

"Should I consider my dad a suspect or not?" I say.

Davenport doesn't answer right away. He gets up from the desk and closes the office door. His steps echo on the marble as he returns to his seat. He folds his hands on the desk.

"Like I said, we're just gathering evidence," he says, "But some of that evidence is…interesting."

Huh. *Interesting.* There's a word that covers a multitude of sins. (I've hung around Mike long enough to know that.) The uneasy feeling is turned up to eleven.

"You're talking about the gold watch?" I say.

"That," Davenport says, "and your dad's lack of an alibi. The fact that Burt threatened him. None of that looks good."

The boxes are ticking in my head. Motive? Yep, Dad had plenty of that. Opportunity? With no alibi, he had that in theory. Means? That one doesn't quite compute.

"Burt was shot to death," I say, "You have the murder weapon?"

"No, we don't," Davenport says, "We haven't found it yet. But we pulled the slug out. It was a .38."

Ah-ha. That definitely does not check the box for *Means*. "My dad doesn't own a .38. He has a few hunting rifles, but he's never owned a handgun."

"We're thinking the .38 in question was Burt's."

"What makes you say that?"

"Burt had a holster on him. Perfect to fit a .38. But the gun wasn't found. Burt also had a pretty good bruise upside his head. We're thinking he was knocked down, maybe out, before he was shot."

"The murderer whacks Burt over the head, takes his gun, and shoots him to death. That's the scenario?"

"It is."

Glurk. That doesn't fill me with relief. If the cops find the murder weapon and can't connect it to my dad, that's at least a point in his favor. It's all the points *not* in his favor that worry me.

"What about the watch?" I asked, "Were my dad's prints on it?"

Davenport shakes his head. "No prints on it at all."

I sit up a bit. "None? It was wiped clean?"

"That would be my guess," Davenport says, "Didn't even have Burt's prints on it."

"Doesn't that strike you as odd?" I ask, "Someone wipes the watch and leaves it at the scene of the crime?"

Davenport shrugs. "Somebody might have panicked. Might not have been thinking."

"Or they *were* thinking," I say, "And they were trying to frame my dad."

"That thought has occurred to me," Davenport says, "It's also possible the murderer accidentally left it at the scene. Which would implicate your dad. Like I said, it's an ongoing investigation. We can't take anything off the table yet."

And isn't that just as satisfying as hell? I can't tell if Davenport is on my side. I like him being friends with my dad, but not so much his refusal to run with the idea Dad is being framed.

"What time was the murder called in?" I ask.

"About quarter after one. Not sure how long Burt had been in the park."

I run that through my head. I must have left Nick's around ten-thirty or so. Burt was still there. He must have gotten to Bennett Park and gotten killed sometime between then and one-fifteen. I wonder what happened in between? I sit back in the chair.

"What happens next?" I ask.

"We're going to keep collecting evidence. We might call in the sheriff's department, depending on what we find. But it's too early to tell. As for your dad, just keep going with the week. People want to celebrate him. He deserves it."

I appreciate Davenport trying to be comforting, but he's so far short of the mark I can only get annoyed. "Might harsh the celebration's buzz," I say.

Davenport walks around the desk and sits on one of the corners. "I remember when that science teacher, Jacobson, got killed. You and your girlfriend figured that one out, didn't you?"

"We did."

"She's a reporter now. What was her name?"

"Lisa," I say, "Lisa Cleary."

"That's right," Davenport says, "You two figured out another one, too, didn't you? That woman from the pageant."

"Yeah, we did," I say, desperately wanting to know where Davenport is going with this.

But he puts the ball in my court. "You know what I'm going to say next, don't you?"

"That I had some good luck as an amateur, but I should probably stay away from this."

"That's right," Davenport says, "Leaving out the fact you have no training—which is a big thing, by the way—there's also the matter of you being personally involved. That's never a good thing."

"I suppose not."

"Besides, and this is just between you, me and the wall, Beardsley is not somebody you want to screw around with.

Cliff may not be as smart as he thinks he is, but he's not an idiot. He's ambitious. He hasn't said as much, but I know he's looking at this office when I hang it up in a few years. Far as he's concerned, nothing would look better on a resume than solving this thing before we call in the sheriff. You cross him and he can make your life miserable. And there's only so much I can do to sit on that."

"Oh?" I say, "Aren't you, y'know, his boss?"

A resigned look comes over Davenport's face. "He likes to bowl with your uncle."

"Please tell me you mean my uncle Mel down in Johnson County."

"No. Your uncle Gordie. The mayor."

Shazbot. My idiot uncle as Porter's Bay's highest elected official. The gift that keeps on giving. In theory, Gordie could use his power to quash any moves Officer Beardsley might make against my dad. But Gordie has always resented the respect my dad has garnered in the community and has subtly used the power of his office to needle my dad over the last year and a half. I doubt Gordie will call off the dogs. Davenport seems like a decent, level-headed cop, but as Bob Dylan wrote, you gotta serve somebody.

"I appreciate the warning," I say, getting up from the chair. I start toward the door while Davenport returns to his seat behind his desk. I hesitate at the door, then ask, "Do you think my dad is guilty?"

Davenport crosses his arms. "First off, I'm one of these funny types who think you shouldn't draw conclusions until you have all the evidence. On top of that, your dad is a good man. One of the best I know. But I've been in law enforcement long enough—hell, I've been on this planet long enough—to know nobody really knows anybody. I'd be as happy as anyone if it's proved he isn't guilty. But right now, I just don't know."

I suppose that's all I can ask of him. I just wish Davenport could offer a bit more. I thank him again and step out of his office.

Thoughts crowd in as I walk out of City Hall. Beardsley wants this thing solved and he doesn't strike me as the kind of guy to cross all the *t's* and dot all the *i's* before doing it. Davenport seems like that kind of guy, but he's got an incompetent and resentful mayor overseeing his work. Maybe I'm panicking, but what if they railroad my dad before the sheriff can get involved? I have nightmare images of my dad facing a murder trial. A lifetime of good works and good will wiped out even if he's found innocent. And if by some chance he's *not* found innocent…

By the time I get to the car, my mind is made up. *Somebody* has to be in my dad's corner. I might be the only one available. I slip on my shades and climb into the Cooper.

Here I go again...

CHAPTER FOUR

In the years after I graduated high school, I found out two of my friends and one of my teachers were gay. Now, that didn't bother me personally and given the significant redneck element in the town, I understand why they didn't say anything at the time. But in the case of one of the students, we had a pretty good friendship. I kept wondering why he didn't tell me. I've realized the reason since. Even in an era of the internet, social media and other forms of mass communication, the most frequently used in small towns is: gossip. In a smaller community where people are cloistered together, gossip spreads like a brushfire. That's why my friends and teacher never said anything about their sexuality. One word to the wrong person would have been akin to throwing a still-smoldering cigarette into a field of dry grass. Best not to trust anyone, even someone who seemed sympathetic.

And that's assuming the gossip is even accurate…

The Hub Diner is on Lake Drive, one of three main arteries in Porter's Bay and the one most visitors encounter when they first enter the town. The Hub is something of an institution, a gathering place for townies for decades now. The portions are large, and the menu leans heavily toward comfort food. When I was a kid, it was my parents' favorite place to take the family after church. Unfortunately, it was everyone else's favorite place to go after church. As a kid, I thought the pancakes were great, but not *Sit around for forty-five minutes before getting a booth* great. I've had other reasons for avoiding it since then. But I got a call from Carol, asking me to lunch. She has been out exploring the town this morning and wanted to check out The Hub. I decided I could use the distraction.

It was a good idea in theory.

The place isn't tremendously busy, just a couple of people at the counter and a few booths and tables occupied. The Hub looks like it always has: Formica tabletops, orange Naugahyde seats, tile floors. Everything clean and orderly. Servers in tan uniforms and white shoes. The buzz of conversation died off the second I walked through the door. Even now, everyone sneaks looks at me. As I've noted, my column affords me a weenie bit of celebrity. Right now, though, I'm a celebrity for an entirely different reason. Carol, looking resplendent in her white blouse and capris, seems amused by the locals, looking right back at them from our booth by the picture window.

"These people can't really think your dad killed Burt, can they?" Carol asks.

"Oh, they certainly can," I say, looking out over Lake Drive and the lake beyond, "My only concern is that the cop investigating seems to think Dad did it. And he's a buddy of my idiot uncle, the mayor."

Carol's face darkens. "That reminds me, I want to talk to you about Gordie. I have to say: he's an absolute pig."

"I saw the two of you chatting last night," I say, "It wasn't a pleasant experience?"

"He kept going on about how he was a very important man in this town, and he'd like to give me a personal tour and all this other horseshit. I tried to be polite, but I had trouble keeping that up. He did nearly all the talking. I'm standing there with my arms folded, half turned away. Did he not get the hint?"

"You were too subtle," I say, "You needed to throw your drink in his face and follow up by hitting him with a folding chair. Even then, he might have taken it as a kind of mating ritual."

That sends a little shiver through Carol. "At any rate, I was finally able to get away from him and do some other socializing. I talked to a guy named Rajveer. He owns an antique store on First Avenue. Maybe you've seen it."

"I'm sure I have," I say. Meaning I probably saw it and didn't note it because there are about seven-hundred-and-thirty-two antique stores in this town.

"Rajveer is a really nice guy," Carol says, "He just became a member of the Buffalo Lodge last year. We had a good chat. Just as we were wrapping up, I saw Gordie watching us. And he seemed really pissed."

"In Gordie's defense, he always looks a *little* pissed."

"Anyway, I visited Rajveer's store this morning. It's an incredibly cute little place."

"We specialize in incredibly cute little places here on the North Shore."

"So I've noticed," Carol says, "While I was there, Rajveer told me he got a notice from the city, first thing this morning. The fees have been upped for garbage collection. His private parking space in the alley has been commandeered by the city. And due to some ancient zoning law, his backroom might not even belong to him. The city, apparently, is looking into it."

"Oh, dear," I say.

"Gordie sees me talking to Rajveer and then the city comes down on Rajveer's store. Does that sound like your uncle is trying to drive him out of business?"

"Sounds like? No, I think that's *exactly* what's happening."

Carol blows out a frustrated breath. "We've got to do something."

"There's an election later this year."

"I can't wait that long. Gordie will have driven Rajveer out of business and ruined who knows how many other stores. Somebody's got to stop him."

I flick a look at Carol. "You seem awfully…interested in this guy."

She gives that a flip of her hand. "It's not like that. Sure, in another life, maybe. He's a nice guy and very attractive. But it's a no-go. Long distance relationships never work out."

I freeze in place. Those last words jar something from out of the past. Couple it with being here at The Hub and the server approaching and how those ugly-ass uniforms haven't changed in all these years, and I'm hit with a rush of emotion. It must show in my face because Carol taps the table.

"Joe?" she says, "Are you alright?"

I snap out of it. "I'm fine."

"You just…you kind of went away there for a second."

"Ancient history." The server arrives. "You know what you want?" I ask Carol.

Carol gets a Cobb Salad, vinaigrette dressing on the side, and I get a chicken salad sandwich on whole wheat toast. The server scoots away. Carol props her chin in her hand and studies me.

"You're going to look into this thing with your dad's partner, aren't you?" she asks.

"If the cops are going after my dad, he's going to need someone in his corner."

"Shouldn't a lawyer be doing that?"

"I'm just going to talk to a few people," I say, "See if there's something the police haven't considered. Which, given this police force, might cover a lot of territory."

Carol concedes that point. "Where are you going to start?"

"I know Burt was at Nick's Corner Bar at ten-thirty and he was dead by one-fifteen at the latest. I'll see what I can do to put that timeline together. And I should talk with Dad's other partners. Both of them knew Burt. Maybe there's something there."

"You think one of them might have done it?"

"I don't know. I'm like the cops. I'm just going to gather evidence. Unlike them, I'm not looking to gather evidence against my dad."

"Also, unlike the police, you're not trained to handle a thing like this."

I should have known I wasn't going to get out of this conversation without Carol saying something like that. I could get annoyed, but it's a conversation we've had so many times, I just take it in my stride.

"I would like to remind you that before last night, there have been two murders in Porter's Bay in the last eighteen years," I say, "And I was involved in solving both of them."

Carol's jaw drops. "You were? I've never heard that."

Again, the memories and the emotions swirl up. "Ancient history. Like I said." I try to forestall any further questioning. "There's an event for my dad at the historical society tonight. I'll see Eli and Will at that."

"Good luck," Carol says, "You're not going to be making any friends in this town."

I look around the restaurant. Some of the patrons look away. Some openly stare at me. I fight the irritation that rises in my chest.

"I think the ship has sailed on that," I say.

***

After lunch, I drop in at Davis Hardware. I usually make at least one pilgrimage back to the place when I'm home. After all, there's no lack of memories here: running up and down the aisles as a kid, playing in the stock room, hanging out with my dad behind the counter, stocking the shelves and helping customers when it was my summer job. The place has changed, subtly, over the years and will probably change more rapidly now that Owen has taken over.

He's never stated it outright, but I always felt my dad wanted one of his sons to take over the store. Owen was the obvious choice. My dad loves his children, but he's never blinded himself to who we are or tried to turn us into something we aren't. He probably knew early on that my older brother Kevin was too ambitious to stay chained to a hardware store (or Porter's Bay, for that matter). And I would be absolutely hopeless as a businessman. Owen wasn't a compromise choice, though. He always had more curiosity about the business than the rest of us. He actually wanted to work there rather than seeing it as an obligation to Dad. And once he graduated college and Dad took him on full-time, he worked diligently to learn everything about the business. He was clearly Dad's heir apparent.

The store sits halfway down Howard Street. A glass door is situated between two picture windows, one of which has _Davis Hardware_ stenciled on it. The front counter is to your left as you walk in. Several rows of merchandise extend away from the counter. The stockroom, loading dock and office are accessible through a small door at the back. As usual, the aisles are swept, and the merchandise is orderly. The popcorn machine near the front counter is relatively new. (Owen's idea, and last I checked, the bane of Dad's existence.) Owen stands at the front counter, talking to a customer. He is, as always, dressed professionally: white collared shirt, tan slacks, loafers. (No idea how he can spend a whole day on his feet while wearing loafers.) Owen is not an extrovert by nature, but over the years, he's picked up some of Dad's gift of gab. He'd probably do better if he didn't look like his balls are in a vice while talking. In this case, I'm less interested in Owen's conversational skills than in *who* he's talking to. It's Eli, one of Dad's old partners.

The conversation seems similar to the one my dad had with Eli last night. It's polite but not exactly warm. Eli wears a short-sleeve plaid shirt and gray slacks. His hair is combed back and there is a slight stoop to his shoulders. One hand rests on the counter. Owen seems relieved to see me. (There's a first.)

"Hey, Joe," Owen says, "This is Eli. You remember Eli, don't you?"

I offer my hand. "I don't think we've met. But I've heard about you."

Eli's handshake is dry and brief. "You're the lawyer?"

"No," I say, "I'm the writer."

He looks toward the ceiling, trying to place me. His voice is gentle and has a slight drawl. (I wonder where that comes from?) "The one with the internet thing?"

"That's, uh, a way to put it."

A flicker of amusement crosses Owen's face. "Eli and I were talking about the store. Back when it started."

Eli doesn't say anything. He just gazes at the lawn furniture on the far side. Owen looks to me to say something.

"I'm sorry to hear about Burt," I say.

Okay, it wasn't the most eloquent thing or even the most appropriate topic of conversation. But it *is* the elephant in the room. Owen looks under the counter, pretending he's trying to find something. Eli's face is cold but not unkind. I get the impression he's thinking of something appropriate to say as well.

He finally settles on, "Thank you."

"Why don't you guys take a look around the store?" Owen says, "Must bring back memories. For both of you."

It doesn't sound like the most inviting proposition. But I *do* want to talk to Eli. "Sounds good to me," I say, turning to Eli, "You want the grand tour?"

Eli doesn't move, blink, or betray any sort of human emotion. "All right."

We're not going to link arms and skip along, singing *We're off to see the Wizard*. But I'll take it. I let Eli take the lead. Owen beats feet to the backroom. Eli shuffles toward the far wall, where the screws and nails are kept. His movements are casual and contained. He puts his hands in the pockets of his slacks.

"We used to keep these on the other wall," he says, "Back when we first started the store. Prices were a hell of a lot cheaper."

"When I first started working here, they were along the back wall. They were cheaper then, too."

That brings a lightness to Eli's face. "Did all you kids work in the store?"

"At one time or another. My brother Kevin—he's the lawyer—he and I worked here during the summer, in high school and a couple years in college. Owen did too, but then, obviously, he stayed."

"Now he owns it."

"That's the case."

"It's nice that Henry brought you kids into the business."

It was. Maybe Kevin and I didn't appreciate it enough at the time. I don't know. Eli and I shuffle down one aisle and start up the next. He doesn't seem deeply interested. I get the feeling we're both doing this little tour out of obligation to Owen. At least I have the decency to have an ulterior motive.

"It doesn't sound like *everybody* was happy for my dad," I say.

Eli scoffs, lightly. "Burt could never let anything go. His ego. That was his downfall."

We round onto the next aisle. It's hammers of all varieties. Eli takes his hands out of his pockets, maybe as a way of increasing his pace. He'd probably power-walk if he had the ability.

"Hard to believe," I say, "Burt was still mad after all these years."

"That was Burt for you."

"Did you and Will feel the same way? About my dad?"

Eli eyeballs me. I'm not sure if he considers the question impertinent or if I've dredged up old memories. "Maybe at first. For me, anyway. Your dad and I were good friends. I felt like that changed when we opened the store. He was more devoted to this place than he was to his friends. Then he got rid of us." Eli puts a hand on my shoulder. "I need you to know that's how I *used* to feel. After a while, I realized your dad was just doing what he had to in order to make this business work. He did it better than the rest of us."

"You've gotten over it?"

"Absolutely," he says, "Your dad's a good man. He was probably right to get rid of us."

"What makes you say that?"

Eli turns slightly. "I tried starting another business, Not hardware. I wasn't going to compete with your dad. It was sporting goods. I had Burt involved. It didn't work. We closed down after a few years."

That makes it sound like Eli has no axe to grind against my dad. If he tried on his own and failed, why be bitter against Dad? We keep the grand tour going, rounding from one aisle and on to another. Eli and I are on different tracks. I look around and remember what was. He looks around and thinks what might have been.

"Did Will feel the same as you?" I say, "About the store?"

"Never heard him say a bad word about your dad," Eli says, "And Will's not the kind to carry a grudge. I think he got over it years ago."

"Did you and Burt talk last night?"

Eli gives me a sidelong glance. "We said hello. I wanted to talk to him afterwards, but he got out of there in a hurry. Probably for the best."

"Someone took the watch the Buffalos gave my dad. It was found next to Burt's body. Did you see anyone take it?"

Eli seems a little thrown off by that. It's a detail from the murder scene that hasn't been released to the general public. He's probably wondering how I know this but has the decency not to mention it. "I'm afraid I didn't. I didn't hang around afterwards. I just went home."

"Oh, you live around here?" I ask.

"I do. The Highland Park Apartments, just off Lake Drive."

Interesting. Everybody lives in town, but I don't remember meeting any of my dad's old partners while I was growing up. We round onto another aisle, having made it two-thirds of the way through the store.

"Burt said something about *Taylor*," I say, "Do you know anything about that?"

Eli's body stiffens. He breaks stride, just for a moment. "I don't know what Burt was talking about," Eli says, "That was Burt. If he hated you, he'd do anything to hurt you. It wouldn't surprise me if he made the whole damn thing up. Something he thought would rattle your dad. That's all I can think."

He can think it, but that doesn't mean it makes sense. If *Taylor* was fictional, what use would it be to threaten Dad with it? If there's no substance to it, why does everyone get both the heebies and the jeebies every time it's mentioned? It can't be coincidence that Burt brings it up and is found dead later that night, right? I'm ready to call Eli out on this particular bullshit when he suddenly turns to me.

"I should get going," he says, "I'm having coffee with somebody. I don't want to be late. Thank Owen for me. And thank you for the tour. I appreciate it."

Eli heads for the front door, a little more pep than I would have thought possible in his step. I offer a *Have a good one* to his back.

I start toward the backroom to tell Owen the coast is clear, and his cowardly ass can come out of the office. (That's going to be more or less a direct quote.) I can't help but think about this Taylor thing and wonder what the hell is going on.

If I'm not supposed to be suspicious, they're doing a lousy job preventing that…

CHAPTER FIVE

It was Napoleon who said, "History is a set of lies that people have agreed upon." (Well, he said it in French and my smattering of college French has left me woefully unable to translate it, so that's just a best guess.) There are times when I feel the same way. When you're talking about places from your childhood, you realize how small is the circle of people who have agreed upon this *lie. All you need to confirm that is to show a friend or a significant other the place you grew up.*

See, you can show these people the sights from your childhood. "Here's my old elementary school. Here's the old playground. Here's the hockey rink where we played football in the summer and fall. Here's the corner where Beans Madden pantsed Jeff Hoff as he was trying to ask out Tammy Fink." But those places don't have the same meaning to the person you're showing them to (which is a shame because the pantsing was particularly funny). They see a collection of buildings tied to events they can't quite picture. If they make a comment about something every now and again, it's due to whatever strikes them about it and not the nostalgia you've attached to it. It's disheartening because you realize, in a sense, your past—the thing that helped form you—is meaningless to someone else.

You still have your parents and your siblings and the friends you grew up with. But that circle gets smaller as time goes along.

My best friend Mike does and doesn't have familiarity with my hometown. He lived with his grandmother in Aurora, up on the Iron Range, for his final year of high school. During our first year of college, we took a road trip to Aurora, both for a vacation and to explore his comic book collection, which occupied about half of his grandmother's basement. Since Aurora is only about an hour from Porter's Bay, we took a side trip so he could see the old homestead and meet my parents. Time was tight and we only had the weekend, so it wound up being a very quick stop. He Eddie Haskelled his way through meeting my parents, saw a few markers from my childhood, and we were off. He barely got a glimpse of the place where I grew up.

I now think of it as *the good old days.*

"I should have remembered what small towns are like," he says, leaning back on the bench and tapping one foot about a thousand times a minute, "The dating pool is limited, so you get a lot of sexual repression. When you find something you like—genuinely like—the shit can get nuts. I may never walk normally again."

"On the bright side, you haven't walked normally up to now, so…"

Mike gives me the stink eye. We're sitting in the middle of Frank Porter Park, a big circular patch of grass and trees who's most distinguishing feature is a bronze statue of Frank Porter, the town's founder. It depicts him wearing boots and a wide-brimmed hat, staring presumably in the direction of Lake Superior (though he's more likely searching for ways to pillage the countryside to make a buck). I'm not sure if this was by design or if the town just evolved this way, but the park is located about two blocks off Howard Street, tucked in the middle of a neighborhood of no particular note. It's not exactly a great mark of the city's esteem for its founder. I used to eat lunch here from time to time when I was in high school. And it's a perfect gathering place for me and Mike, a man frequently held in low esteem.

I swirl my iced Americano. "Then you *did* get together with this…Julie is her name?"

"We did indeed," Mike says, shit-eating grin firmly in place, "We had a little picnic down by the lake, did some antiquing—"

"Wait a minute, *you* went antiquing?"

"Joe, if there's nookie involved, I'll do a lot of things. Things I'm not proud of."

"Like the time you told Allison Messerschmidt you had been wounded in the war and didn't think you'd ever get an erection again."

"No, I was actually proud of that one," Mike says, "Best handjob I ever had. At any rate, don't tell Carol and Lars about the antiquing. They'll never let me live it down."

"Your secret's safe with me." It isn't, but…

Mike waves his hands (and his coffee) while he talks. "Anyway, after we're done antiquing, we go for a little walk in the woods. We wind up at this little place called Revelation Bluff. You familiar with it?"

"I am."

Oh boy, am I ever. Back in my day (and probably still), it's where teenagers would go to spend, uh, quality time, unseen by their parents or any other adults. In a weird way, knowing Mike has been there sort of defiles it. Speaking of which…

"All right, we head up there," Mike says, "And seconds later, Julie's sundress is hanging from a tree branch and we're going at it on this little picnic blanket. I'm glad we were in the middle of nowhere because things got *loud*. I think there are squirrels up there who are scarred for life."

They aren't the only ones. "I'm glad you had a good time," I say.

"It was fucking amazing fucking. I'm seeing her again tonight, after your dad's thing."

"You going to her place?"

"No, she wasn't too into that," he says, "And I'm bunking with Lars at the hotel, so that's a no-go. She's going to pick me up and we'll find someplace."

I prop an arm on the bench. "Isn't it a little weird she doesn't want to go to her place?"

"I don't know," Mike says, "Maybe she's got a roommate. Maybe her cats get jealous."

"Has she got a roommate or cats?" I ask.

"I didn't bother to ask," Mike says, "Look, it's not like we've got a deep, committed thing going here. It's Wednesday now. The stuff for your dad goes until Sunday, then I'm going to the Cities. I've got a Get Out of Jail Free card."

I'm not sure it's as simple as that. But Mike doesn't see complexities at the best of times. It's impossible to see them when he's getting laid. At least he's using his time constructively. (If *constructively* is the word I want.)

"I'm very happy for the two of you," I say.

Mike checks the time on his phone. "Didn't your mom say dinner was going to be at six? It's almost six now."

"I know."

He waits for me to expound on that, but no answer is forthcoming. "Is there a reason we're still sitting here? Or that we came here in the first place?"

"My brother Kevin should be at the house by now."

Again, Mike is waiting for more of an answer. Again, he doesn't get it. He lets out an impatient sigh (and Mike isn't the most patient of souls in the first place). "You're avoiding your brother?"

"More or less."

"I thought you and Kevin were cool with each other."

"We are. It's just…complicated."

It's hard to explain to Mike, who's an only child, the dynamics of my relationships with my brothers. In my younger days, Kevin was the guy I wanted to be. He was the guy *a lot* of people wanted to be: good looking, popular, charismatic, a star athlete and a straight-A student. Someone you'd hope would develop a drinking problem just to level the universal playing field. But no, Kevin went to college on a basketball scholarship, got himself into law school at Berkley and passed the bar on his first try. He married a fellow lawyer, has a growing practice in contract law and is thinking of going into politics. The lovely house and the 2.5 children go without saying.

But Kevin *does* have a flaw, at least from my perspective. It would be a little much to expect someone to meet such unalloyed success *and* be humble. Kevin isn't a braggart, because braggarts tend toward insecurity and Kevin has nothing to be insecure about. (Just ask him.) No, it's more in the way he carries himself. It's how I imagine heads of state, movie stars and CEOs carry themselves; the expectation they will be deferred to. In conversation, Kevin often talks past you, as if the gaze of the public is upon him and he must be scrupulously correct. If *you* fail to meet those standards, he will either ignore you or gently guide you in the direction he feels you ought to go. Dealing with Kevin puts you somewhere between intimidation and exasperation. And that's *before* we talk about my relationship with his wife. Ergo, hiding out, even temporarily, seemed the best option.

But all that is difficult to explain to Mike, so I just say, "We're fine. Let's get going."

"Sounds good," Mike says, hopping to his feet, his bouncy walk carrying a little extra bounce, "I hope your mom is making a big meal. I'm going to need my strength for tonight."

Dear Lord. We manage to stay off the topic of Mike's rutting as he drives the rented RAV4 back to my parents' place. The sun is creeping across the sky and a warm breeze is blowing. There are only a few clouds. I forget what it's like to have summers with very little humidity. It's such a fact of life in the Twin Cities, it's eclipsed the memory from my childhood. When we pull up to the house, a red Chrysler Pacifica minivan is on the curb. Its very ostentatiousness announces the arrival of my brother Kevin and his family.

Mike's eyebrows go up. "Nice van."

"And he took the best parking space."

We find a spot next door (right in front of the Seavers, who will probably write down the license plate number and call the police to run a vehicle check mere seconds after we leave). We head into my parents' now overcrowded house.

Surprisingly, the living room and dining room are empty. I assume Mom and Dad herded everyone into the backyard. Mom is in the kitchen, busily filling plates with raw burgers, hot dogs and brats. A huge bowl of potato salad rests on the counter. Mom glistens slightly with perspiration and a few stray hairs escape her ponytail. But her face is shining. Her family is under one roof, and she is in her glory. She turns to Mike and me as we walk into the kitchen.

"It's about time, Joe," she says, her excited voice betraying the admonishment, "We thought we'd have to start without you."

"Oh heavens, we wouldn't want that," I say, deadpan.

As usual, Mom either misses or chooses to ignore my sarcasm. "Would one of you boys mind bringing the potato salad outside?"

"Mike can handle it," I say, ignoring the dirty look Mike is almost certainly giving me, "You need a hand with the other stuff?"

"That would be great," Mom says, "Thank you."

That's a thing about my mom. She's not one of these long-suffering types who thinks it's her duty to decline all offers of assistance. If you're the sort of yamhead who will make a pro forma offer, expect her to accept it. I pick up a plate of delicious and oh-so-deadly meat products while Mike struggles with the vat of potato salad.

"Who's doing the grilling?" I ask.

"Your father," Mom says, "Owen offered, but your dad insisted."

Not surprising. Owen is a pretty good grill man, but Dad has ruled that particular roost for decades. He might retire from the store, but you'll have to pry his spatula out of his cold, dead hand. Mike and I start toward the door.

"I assume Kevin's out there?" I ask.

"Of course," Mom says, "Everybody is out there."

By *everybody*, Mom means Owen and his family are here as well. My uncle Mel had to beg off this week due to work, so he and his brood aren't here. And Gordie has been persona non grata for several months. Mike stops near the door.

"Is it okay I'm here?" he says, putting on his best smile, "This seems like a family thing."

Mom beats me to the punch. "You are more than welcomed here, Mike. You and Joe have known each other for years. You're practically family."

"Absolutely," I say, "More like a skid row cousin we don't talk about in polite company, but family nonetheless."

Clearly, this disappoints Mike. He was hoping to avoid toting the potato salad. We push our way out into the backyard.

The yard is square and housed on three sides by a tall wooden fence (built by my dad). The lawn is trimmed and free of weeds or crabgrass. There's a maple tree in the far corner that once hosted our treehouse (also built by my dad). A picnic table rests on the corner of the lawn nearest the house. A propane grill sits on a plot of cement between the house and the garage. Various lawn furniture, hauled out of the garage for company, is scattered about. Kevin, standing at the grill and talking with Owen and Dad, is the first to greet me.

"Hey, there he is," Kevin says. I get the feeling he greets a lot of people that way.

Kevin looks like he did the last time I saw him, a few Christmases ago: sandy blonde hair (like Mom), dazzling white teeth, clear skin, blue eyes, athletic build. He looks cool in his white polo shirt, black shorts and loafers. (Seriously, what is it with my family and loafers?) His movements are easy, and he seems completely in his element. I set the plate of meat down at the grill and offer Kevin a handshake. Then we realize we're brothers who haven't seen each other in a while and should probably do more than just shake hands. He pulls me into an awkward hug that best resembles Donald Trump trying to convince one of his sons he really loves them.

"How are things in St. Paul?" Kevin asks.

"Jiffy swell," I tell him, smiling weakly.

"Good to hear, good to hear," Kevin says, "I was just talking to Dad about sleeping arrangements. I was thinking Jordan and I can take my old room over the garage and Flynn and Tucker can sleep in Owen's old room. That okay with you?"

"Uh sure," I say, "I just assumed you guys would get a hotel room."

Two high-priced Bay Area lawyers, Kevin and Jordan could at least spring for rooms in town. Maybe even a suite. Kevin has never been known as a spendthrift. He claps Dad on the shoulder.

"No rooms available," Kevin says, "Thanks to the big guy here."

The big guy in question concentrates on the grill, probably so Kevin won't see him wince. I look toward the backyard and see Jordan in conversation with Owen's wife, Mary. In a way, they look alike. Both are slim, blonde and pretty. But Jordan wears expensive clothes and carries herself with a certain glamour. Mary is shy and dresses rather plainly. If I had to guess, Mary is on her way to life as a hausfrau while Jordan is on her way to an affair with her tennis instructor.

As I've said, I have complicated relationships with my sisters-in-law. Jordan actively hates me, owing to my brief but bitter affair with her sister. (The brevity due to my going back to her hotel room after the wedding reception. The bitterness due to my never calling her again.) Mary, though, is a different story. She's never said or done anything to convey overt dislike. But there's tension whenever I'm in her presence. I used to think it was because Mary, like her husband, lacks anything approaching a sense of humor while I make my living writing glorified dick jokes. Lately, I've started to think it's something deeper. I get a very strong sense of disapproval. Not over how I behave. Just over who I am.

You see now why family gatherings aren't big with me?

Kevin sips his fizzy water. (I seriously doubt there's any alcohol in there.) "You're still in St. Paul, huh? I remember when you had that crappy little apartment on Summit Avenue. The one with the lunatic downstairs. Where you living these days?"

"The same crappy apartment above the same lunatic."

My answer doesn't faze Kevin. Nothing does. Yep, this is a politician all the way. Speaking of lunatics, I take the opportunity to introduce him to Mike. They exchange a quick handshake, then Kevin downs the rest of his fizzy water.

"I could use a refresher," he says, "Joe, why don't you come with me?"

Ah. A not-at-all-subtle invitation to chat. Mike looks pained, realizing he's about to be left alone in a group of relative strangers. I'm sure Dad will let him help with the grill, just to make him feel at home. (Although, at home, Mike would never think of grilling.) I follow Kevin across the yard, toward the kitchen. His wife watches us as we walk.

"Hi Jordan," I say.

"Hello, Joe," she says, scratching her nose with her middle finger, "My sister says hi."

Behind her, Flynn and Tucker gape at me, as if to say *Oh,* this *is the rat bastard uncle Joe that mommy and auntie Carly keep talking about.* I'm a real hit with this branchlet of the family tree.

Once we're in the kitchen, Kevin dumps the melting ice from his glass into the sink and goes to the freezer for more. He speaks without looking at me.

"What's going on with Dad and Burt?" he says, his voice moving into a more business-like tone.

A strange bit of relief washes over me, as if we're on *my* ground now. (Although, there are many members of the law enforcement community who would dispute this ground with me.) I give Kevin the story while he fills his glass with more ice, and I fetch a couple beers from the fridge. (One for me, one for Mike.) I follow him to the liquor cabinet. He finds a bottle of Perrier that my parents may have had since *Family Ties* was all the rage and pours some into his glass. (Maybe he should cut that with some gin.)

"The watch might be a problem," Kevin says, "Beyond that, it doesn't sound like they have much."

"Beardsley seems committed," I say, "And he's got the ear of the mayor."

Kevin winces. "Gordie as mayor. I knew that would bite us in the ass. I just didn't realize how." He takes a contemplative sip of his fizzy water. "You talked to Eli?"

"Just for a minute or two. At the store. He didn't say much. There's something Burt said, when he was going after Dad at the Buffalos thing. He was going to tell everyone about *Taylor*. I've asked Dad and Eli what Burt was talking about, and they both clammed up. Does *Taylor* mean anything to you?"

Kevin starts to shake his head then stops. His eyes narrow, as if he's concentrating on something. "I can't say it *means* anything to me. But I remember it being mentioned."

I try to control my excitement. "When? What happened?"

"It was just a little thing. When I was a kid. I must have been about six. I remember Mom was pregnant with Owen. I got out of bed and started to come downstairs. I'd do that sometimes if I couldn't sleep. Mom and Dad would either send me right back to bed or they'd let me stay up for a minute and watch some TV with them. Anyway, they were talking, and it sounded serious, so I sat on the stairs and listened. They were talking about Will's wife leaving him."

My eyebrows go up. "Will's wife left him? I didn't know that." Come to think of it, I don't know anything about Will.

"She left him for Burt," Kevin says, "Nice, huh?" Whoa. I *really* didn't know the whole story there. "Dad was pretty pissed about it," Kevin says, "Called it exactly the kind of thing Burt would do. He kept going on about Burt and said something about wishing he'd never gone to Taylor. He wished none of them had."

"Meaning him and his other partners?"

"I think so."

"Wait, is Taylor a person or a place?" I ask.

"He didn't say. Mom asked him about it, and he said it was nothing. Right about then, they found me on the stairs and sent me to bed. That's all I remember."

That tells me something and nothing at the same time. The situation with Will and Burt and the wife is interesting. *Taylor* involves all the partners. If I talk with Will at the party tonight, the conversation will be plenty awkward, that much is certain. Kevin leans against the fridge.

"Has Dad got a lawyer?" he asks.

"You think he needs one?"

"It wouldn't be a bad idea."

Of course, a *lawyer* is going to say that…

***

"When you think about it, Gordie's right," Lars says, sipping his gin-and-tonic, "What good is pouring money into the past? We need to think about the future and how that money can be better used."

"Uh-huh," I say, "It doesn't have anything to do with Gordie not being invited to this little shindig?"

"Possibly," Lars says, "But I like to believe in the better angels of Gordie's nature."

"Hate to tell you this," I say, "But I don't think the angels are driving the bus there."

It's disconcerting to see Lars fall under whatever spell my uncle Gordie is casting (likely using a potion created from failed attempts to make methamphetamine). But as long as Gordie is not here, I can live with it.

The Porter's Bay Historical Society is housed in the former Great Northern Railroad depot, not far from downtown Porter's Bay. The society has restored the depot to its former glory. The woodwork, brass rails and hardwood floors have all been repaired, refurbished, or replaced. The platform outside is spic and span. Tracks still run past the place but are no longer used in the service of larger engines. Instead, a restored trolley takes passengers on a little excursion from the depot to an end point in Bennett Park and back again. The

Historical Society's offices are housed in the former Western Union offices in the back and the main floor is used for receptions such as the one honoring my dad.

As befitting the Historical Society, it's a genteel affair. The interior has been decked with red, white, and blue bunting (which will likely be reused in a few weeks for the Fourth of July celebrations). A framed picture of my dad is placed along one wall. There's a cash bar where the ticket office was once located and some finger food is available on a table along one wall. Henry Mancini, a favorite of my dad's, plays over the P.A. Everyone is dressed in business casual (lots of summer dresses, short sleeve collared shirts and cargo shorts) and making polite conversation. I'm sipping a cheap beer and learning to ignore the taste, if not embrace it. Lars and I stand in one corner and watch the proceedings. Lars, wearing a suitcoat over his finest black bowling shirt, is unable to contain his excitement.

"I spent time with your uncle this afternoon," he says.

"At the bowling alley?"

"He prefers to call it the Western Mayor's Office."

"Even though it's north of City Hall?"

"Visionaries don't worry about small matters," Lars says, "I got to be at your uncle's side and pick up his views on what he'd like to do with your fair city."

"Other than abusing his authority and putting his drinking buddies on the city payroll?"

"Those are lies made up by this town's jealous and resentful media."

"What media?" I ask, "This town has one newspaper and three radio stations."

"And according to Gordie," Lars says, adopting a superior air, "They're both a dick."

On the bright side, Gordie hasn't developed a persecution complex since he's taken office. He's had one his whole life. I take a healthy sip of my beer.

"Gordie now has a plan to cut funding for the historical society?" I ask.

"Absolutely," Lars says, "I realize it's a bit gauche to bring it up in this setting—"

"You think?"

"But this entire celebration of a town's been-and-gone days is an unnecessary drain on the taxpayers."

As frequently happens when dealing with Lars (and my uncle Gordie, come to that), I get a small but persistent headache between my eyes. "Lars, you realize the Historical Society gets practically no money from the government? Percentages of pennies. Most of its funding comes from private donors."

"Who are burdened."

"Whose donations are tax deductible."

Lars sniffs. "The less said about the IRS, the better."

Oh Lord. At least Gordie isn't here, so I don't have to witness Lars fawning over him. I look around the depot, which is rapidly filling up. Mom and Dad are in a corner, holding what passes for court. Eli is chatting with them again. Owen and Kevin and their wives are nearby. Will is on the other side of the room. I turn to Lars.

"I have to ask," I say, "Don't you consider it a bit ironic that you're interested in Porter's Bay's history while you're also in favor of defunding its historical society?"

"Not at all," Lars says, and somehow, I knew that would be his answer, "The Historical Society takes in money while generating nothing other than the funds needed for its mission."

"Which is basically the definition of a nonprofit."

Lars waves his gin-and-tonic, nearly hitting me in the face. "Then you see my point. Why throw money at a pig-in-a-poke when there's profit to be made?"

As you may have guessed, Lars is a hard one to figure. For all his hippy-dippy attitudes on life, he's also a ruthless capitalist. He's the superintendent of my building, so he lives rent-free (if you want to talk about not getting your money's worth on an investment...) His other income is generated by odd jobs and certain unnamed sources. The bulk of his time—when not goofing off—is spent on various get-rich-quick schemes that never generate anything but further debt.

Therefore, it's with a certain trepidation that I follow him down this particular road.

"This is your gangster tour?" I ask, trying not to wince.

Lars adopts the superior air that marks what he thinks is a great idea. "Indeed. I'm going to generate interest—profitable interest—in this town's gangster era."

Yep, that headache is just creeping across my sinuses. "Lars, I told you before, this town didn't have a gangster era. It had a couple of gangsters pass through on their way to bigger things. How are you going to generate a tour from that?"

"There isn't a lot of information *now*," Lars says, "But I'm working on it. Doing research. Going through records and documents and other artifacts."

"How are you doing that?"

"With the help of the Historical Society, of course."

"Of course." I knock back most of my beer. "What about the movie? If you're up here working for my uncle and running a gangster tour, what's that going to do to the movie?"

I should explain. A few months ago, Lars came to me with an idea to make an independent film. He had lined up backers (a couple of rich kids looking to find a purpose in life) and wanted to bring me on as the writer. My interest in film overrode my good judgment and I agreed, as long as I could also be a producer. Against all odds, this idea has not fallen apart. Lars and I have been crafting the script during several increasingly frustrating writing sessions. Meanwhile, Lars has been trying to put together the other production elements. Now I'm staring at the possibility that all my work has been for naught. (I'm sure that's going to be the end result, inevitably. I just didn't think we'd get here so soon.)

"The movie is in no danger," Lars says, "I live up to all my responsibilities. You must know that."

"I know *I* had to clear the clog in my kitchen sink because my asshole superintendent never got to it."

"I would have gotten to it eventually."

"I gave you three months. I would have had to wash my dishes in the bathtub if I waited any longer."

"I can't be responsible for your impatience," Lars says, "I tell you to have no fear, brother. We will be making a cinematic classic. I just have to figure out how to keep all the balls in the air."

This from a guy who can barely keep his balls in his tightie-whities. But at least the movie is still on his radar screen. I slam the rest of my beer and excuse myself to get another. (Seriously, *nobody* has thought to open a tap room in this town? Just to introduce decent beer into the ecosystem?) The room is filling up and getting slightly warm. Will sits in a straight back chair near the front door. After getting my beer, I make my way over to him.

"Hi Will," I say.

Will squints slightly then looks to the corner where my brothers are located. He does a quick bit of mental math.

"Joe, right?" he says, "The writer?"

"That would be me," I say. I nod toward the chair next to him. "Anyone sitting there?"

"Not at the moment." I grab a seat. "Another great turnout for your dad. He deserves it."

Will is sweating due to the heat in the room; parts of his black dress shirt are darker than others. He calmly sips his cheap beer and watches my dad hold court. I try to find a comfortable position in the folding chair (a fool's errand there).

"Things should be a little more peaceful tonight," I say.

Will's face falls. "That was a hell of a thing last night. *That* your dad did not deserve."

"Burt was pretty bitter."

"Ah, Burt had nothing to be bitter about," Will says, flipping a hand, "He always had more mouth than brains. When we got the store started, he liked hanging around and pretending he was a big man. But like I told you, he didn't have Henry's smarts and he didn't have his drive. He spent the next forty years thinking his friend had screwed him over. Sad."

"You never felt that way yourself?" I ask, "Even a little bit?"

He holds his thumb and forefinger about an inch apart. "A *very* little bit. Maybe for about five minutes. I knew it was coming and I knew Henry was right to do it. I tried to keep up with him, but I knew I never would. I didn't stew on it for forty years until I decided to make an ass of myself in public."

Will's face is turning red. He closes his eyes and takes a calming breath. I toy with my Solo cup, hesitating slightly, both to continue the questioning and to drink this piss-water beer.

"Maybe it was for the best," I say, "Eli said he and Burt started a sporting goods store, and it went under. Doesn't sound like being in business with Burt was a good idea."

"You're damn right there," Will says, "You could never trust Burt. Eli must not have learned his lesson the first time. Too bad."

"Still, it was a hell of a thing," I say, "Burt getting killed."

"I suppose. I don't know what surprises me more: that it happened or that it hadn't happened years ago."

"That many people hated him?"

"I don't know about the number," Will says, "But the people who hated him *really* hated him. Burt was that kind of guy."

So I gather. "I get the impression the cops think my dad did it."

Will snaps me a look. "Where the hell did they get that idea?"

"My dad's watch—the one the Buffalos gave him—was found on Burt. Dad isn't sure how Burt got it."

"Probably stole it," Will says, "No way in hell is your dad guilty. I've known him longer than any of these damn cops. You'll never get me to believe that."

I'm glad for Will's faith in my dad. At the same time, I can't help feeling downhearted. Word of Dad's rumored role in Burt Franklin's death is making its way around town. The erosion of my dad's hard-earned reputation has already begun.

"Still, it's weird," I say, "What would Burt be doing in Bennett Park that late at night?"

"Who the hell knows? Probably up to no good. That was Burt's style."

"Burt was shady?"

Will chuckles. "*Shady* is a good word. He was always that way. Lazy. A schemer. If the store wasn't making money on what was coming in the front door, he would have found a way to make money on something going out the backdoor. I understand why Henry didn't want him around. From what I hear, Burt never changed. He was still into that kind of stuff."

"What kind of stuff?" I ask.

"Ah, I don't know anything for sure," Will says, "You hear rumors. Just a *Keep an eye on that guy* kind of thing. And when you know the guy and it's completely in his character, you tend to believe it."

Interesting. I wonder if that's what caused his business with Eli to go under. This might merit further research (and at least open the field of suspects beyond my dad).

"Have you seen Burt much?" I ask, "Over the years?"

"No," Will says, "Didn't seem much reason to. Certainly not after…ah, you don't want to hear about any of that."

"Your wife?" I say.

There he is, folks: the elephant in the room, sucking down margaritas, acting odiously toward the ladies and generally making an ass of himself. Will stares at me for a second before he relaxes.

"Heard about that, did you?" he says.

"Just in passing," I say.

"It's not a big secret. Hell, you get a divorce, you gotta go to court and then it winds up in the newspapers. In the fine print, of course, but still…" He sips his beer. "Rosemary was my wife's name. Not going to go into all the details. It's never a simple thing. But she took up with Burt and decided she'd be happier with him. Left me to clean up the mess."

"I'm sorry."

"It happens. You want life to be smooth, but it doesn't work that way. Not for all of us."

I take a sip of beer, just to break the tension. (Nope, doesn't help.) Will stares into the distance, not really focusing on anything. At least, not anything in the present.

"Your ex wound up marrying Burt?" I say.

That gives Will a hearty laugh. It starts somewhere in his mid-section and mushrooms up through this body until it comes out like a sharp bark. It draws a few looks.

"No, they didn't get married," he says, "They shacked up for a few years, then Burt kicked her to the curb. He wasn't the marrying type. I'm not sure Rosemary was, either. I just didn't see it at the time. At any rate, Rosemary had the good sense not to come back to me. She moved to Memphis—she had cousins down there—and that was the last I heard of her. No idea where she is or…hell, if she's even still alive."

He looks into his beer while I feel like a complete shitheel for bringing the subject up. At least we'll be spared dealing with a widow who would demand justice for her dear departed scumbag.

"You still live in Porter's Bay?" I ask.

"I do," Will says, "Got a little house off 14th. Suits my needs."

"Did you spend any time with my dad after the thing at the Lodge?" I ask, dipping the alibi toe in slightly.

"Didn't get a chance," Will says, "I wasn't sure how your dad was feeling about things. Thought maybe he'd want to be alone. My daughter Alice gave me a ride home and I went to sleep." He chuckles. "Exciting life I lead, eh?"

I don't answer. Okay, so Will has an alibi, if you want to call it that. Truthfully, it's the same as my dad's. If I'm buying my dad's alibi, I have to buy Will's. For the time being.

"Burt said something about Taylor last night," I say, "That he was going to tell everyone about that. You have any idea what that's all about?"

Will looks away. "You ask your dad about it?"

"I did. He said it wasn't anything. Didn't tell me a whole lot, really."

"I don't know either. You never knew what the hell was up with Burt. Likely as not, he was talking out of his ass."

I seriously doubt that was the case, particularly when my dad and both his former partners seem so anxious to stay off the subject. If I'm going to find out anything about Taylor, I'm going to have to do it without their cooperation.

Before I can ask Will anything else, we're interrupted by a tall woman with curly hair and wire-rim glasses. If I had to guess, she's a few years younger than me. She's nearly my height at six feet, and her long arms and legs move a bit awkwardly, like a colt learning to stand. She wears a black vest over a white blouse and a pair of black slacks. She flicks me a nervous look, as if to tell me I'm in her seat. The funny part is, she's not a stranger to me.

She's the one I saw with Evan when he was talking to Burt at Nick's Corner Bar.

"Everything okay, dad?" she asks.

"Everything's fine, Alice," he says, "I was just chatting with one of Henry's sons. This is Joe. He's—"

"A writer," Alice says. After a moment's contemplation, she offers me her hand. "I've read your column."

I take her hand. "Really? You live in the Cities?"

"No. I live here," Alice says, unsmiling, "But we get the internet, too."

Ah. My urban bias is showing. Alice drops my hand. The crowd is closing around us as the place fills up. Alice stands close to Will, protectively. Obviously, I have questions, but this isn't the time and place to bring them up.

"It's nice of you to be here for my dad," I say.

Alice starts to say something then notices Will staring at her, steadily. Maybe there's some kind of telekinesis they share (similar to how Mike and I communicate in any situation involving trouble or a girlfriend…though, those two frequently dovetail together). Alice gives me some forced politeness.

"It's my pleasure," she says. I'm not sure I believe her.

An awkward second passes, then I ask, "Were you at the Buffalo Lodge last night?"

"No," Alice says, "I had…other stuff going on." She turns to her father. "Are you okay? Do you want to get going?"

"I'm fine," Will says, sounding annoyed, "I'm thinking about getting a refill."

"You sure—?" Alice says.

"Yes, I am," Will says, "I know you have to work in the morning. We won't stay late."

I turn to Alice, maybe looking for some way to ingratiate myself. "Where do you work?"

"I work for the David Jones Law Firm," she says, her voice not getting any warmer, "Up in Greenville."

Greenville is two towns up from Porter's Bay. A drive of maybe twenty minutes. Will lays a hand on Alice's shoulder and turns to me.

"You going to be at the softball game tomorrow?" he asks, "The one the Youth Sports League is putting on?"

"Planning on it," I say.

"Good," Will says, "I look forward to seeing you play."

"Don't get your hopes up," I say.

My dad was a good athlete in his day and my brothers went to college on athletic scholarships. They must have gotten all the athletic talent in the family because none of it extended to me. Will chuckles.

"I'll see you then," he says, ambling off to get himself another drink.

That leaves Alice and me alone. She looks toward the corner where my dad is standing, probably trying to think of a graceful way out of this conversation.

"I hope your dad is okay," she says, "I heard the police are looking at him. After what happened to Burt."

"It's a hell of a thing," I say, "But I know my dad didn't do anything."

"I'm sure he didn't," Alice says.

No nice way into this (and Alice isn't the sort to encourage niceties), so I dive right in. "You're friends with Evan Erickson."

Alice's eyes cut toward me. "Yes, I am. How do you know that?"

"I saw the two of you at Nick's," I say, "Last night."

"I was there to meet Evan. He had business with Burt."

"What sort of business?"

The look turns icy. "Private business."

"You understand why I ask. Given what happened to Burt and all."

"It was something about money," Alice says, "I was mostly concerned with keeping Evan calm. Not making a scene. Then we left."

"And you went home?" I ask.

Alice pauses before sipping her drink. "Are you implying something?"

"No, I just—"

"We're friends. That's all. Evan has a girlfriend."

"I didn't know that."

"There it is. He took off and went to meet some friends. And I went home. End of story."

Wow. I once tried hitting on a girl named Jen at a party. The conversation might have set the North American speed record for Going South in a Big, Big Hurry. (It ended with her calling me *a piece of shit* after less than two minutes if that gives you any idea how it went.) This convo with Alice might have just topped it.

"Does, uh, does your mom know?" I ask, "About Burt?"

"I don't know. I don't talk to her much." She finishes whatever beverage she's drinking. "If you'll excuse me, I'm going to check on my father." Alice starts to step past me then pauses. "Whatever comes of it, it's not like Burt didn't get what he deserved." Before I can ask her about that, she says, "It was nice meeting you. Have a good night."

Alice disappears into the crowd, moving as if she'd like to avoid contact with each and every person, both here at the party and in the world in general. I would love to ask her what she meant about Burt getting what he deserved. But I doubt she'd answer the question, even if she was still standing here.

After all, answering my questions doesn't seem to be anybody's priority these days.

***

One thing this evening had going for it was the complete lack of an unpleasant incident. As a result, my father isn't in need of a drink when we get home. (He's going to have one anyway, but more because he wants it than needs it.) Mom, never much of a drinker, makes her way into the kitchen for some decaf coffee (possibly the only thing worse than her actual coffee). Dad fixes himself a whisky and water from the liquor cabinet. I fetch a bottle of Grand Brewing Hefeweizen from the fridge. Dad and I settle in the living room. He kicks his feet up in his favorite chair.

"That was nice," he says, mildly, "They didn't have to make that much of a fuss. But I appreciate it."

"They made a fuss because they appreciate *you*," I say.

Dad gives that a flip of his hand. The man could never take a compliment to save his ass, a quality he's passed on to at least two of his children. He sits back in his chair, looking tired but content.

"It's been nice being a part of the historical society," he says, "They're good people."

"You're retiring from there, too?" I ask.

"Soon enough," Dad says, "I want to clear out my schedule. Take some time before I figure out what I want retirement to look like."

"That's a lot of stuff you're going to be clearing out," I say, "Chamber of Commerce, the Buffalos, the historical society, the church council."

"Owen is taking all of them," Dad says, "He's looking forward to it. He's been waiting for a while now."

"The heir apparent," I say.

"Apparently," Dad says, giving that a little grin. If you're wondering where my love of wordplay comes from…

"I don't think he could replace you, though," I say, "He's just going to take your place."

"You don't need to flatter me, Joe. You're already in the will."

For some reason, Dad's attempt at humor doesn't land with me. He could have safely retired a few years ago, but he put it off. Probably because he didn't want to face this reality: once you're retired, the next stop is death, no matter how many years you're given. But suddenly, *I'm* thinking that way about *him*. That's a reality I can't face.

Before we get too deep into that conversation, though, the phone rings. Dad shoots a look at it, disturbed. He's firmly of the *You don't call someone after nine* generation, so the phone ringing at this hour can't be good. He grabs it.

"Hello?" Dad says, "Yes, this is Henry Davis." Then his brow furrows. "Okay, I'll be there in a few minutes." He hangs up the phone and runs a hand over his face. Any trace of tiredness is gone. He turns toward the kitchen. "Katherine, I have to go down to the store. The security alarm went off."

Mom drops everything and walks into the living room. By the time she gets there, I'm on my feet. The store has had a security alarm since it opened. But the damn thing going off is a generational event. Mom stops at the edge of the dining room, holding an empty coffee cup.

"What happened?" she asks.

"The security company doesn't know," Dad says, "Just that the alarm went off and the police have been notified. I'm going down there."

"You should call Owen," Mom says.

"They already called him," Dad says, "I'll meet him down there."

"Maybe you should let him handle it," Mom says.

Dad stops before he gets to the front door. "I'm still the owner for a few more days. I can handle it."

Mom gives me a look and I instantly know what she's asking. "I'll go with you," I say.

Dad turns toward me, mildly annoyed. "I said I can handle it."

"I know you can," I say, "But that security alarm goes off about as often as Halley's Comet comes around. And I'm here for it. I'm not going to miss that."

Dad throws the door open a little wider, leaving room for me. "I never should have let you move to the big city." He heads out the front door.

I catch eyes with Mom. She mouths *Thank you.* I return it with a simple nod. She knows that whatever happened with the store, Dad is likely to downplay it. She'll be expecting a full report from me later, containing all the things Dad refused to tell her.

Joe Davis: Middle Child and Rat Bastard.

***

We take Dad's SUV down to the store. Owen is waiting when we arrive, along with two uniformed cops. Given this is late on a weeknight, a boring shift for cops, I'm surprised there aren't seventeen units and a fire truck here. Dad parks at the curb and ambles up to the scene. Owen is the first to greet him. He looks alert. (Then again, I think he sleeps that way.)

"It's okay, Dad," Owen says, "You didn't need to come down."

Dad ignores the greeting. "What happened?"

"Someone broke in," Owen says, "Looks like they went in through the backdoor."

"Did they do any damage?" Dad asks.

"No," Owen says, "They picked the lock pretty cleanly."

"Let's take a look," Dad says.

The cops lead the way inside. Owen and I follow. The route takes us to the back of the store. Dad keeps his hands in his pockets. He gives the shelves a cursory look, making sure everything is still in place. Owen looks a little sulky, having once again been reduced to *right hand man* status. The backroom is three-quarters stockroom and one-quarter office. The merchandise is stacked and neatly arranged. A large garage-style door and a smaller door border the alley. The smaller door, apparently, was the point of entry. Dad and the cops take a look.

"Nothing too complicated," one of the cops says, "Just jimmied the lock. The alarm probably started beeping. The cover on the security pad was opened, so they did make an effort to stop the alarm. They probably left by the same door."

Dad looks toward the front. "Did they take anything?"

"Nothing," Owen says, "I put the cash register money in the safe before leaving. The safe wasn't touched."

The cop points toward the front. "The safe is behind the counter, correct?"

"That's right," Dad says.

"They wouldn't have gotten that far before the alarm went off," the cop says. "I understand it's pretty ear-splitting."

"It is, trust me," Dad says, glancing around the backroom. "The office door is open. Owen, did you leave it like that?"

"Not that I remember," Owen says.

The cops slip in ahead of Dad and Owen, hands on their guns, as if the intruder might be hiding there. (Apparently, they're working under the theory Catwoman broke into the joint.) After a second of looking (because that's all the office requires), they step aside, allowing Dad and Owen to enter. I follow them in.

The office is tiny, just like I remember. There's a desk, accompanied by a few filing cabinets, and a computer on the desktop. (The computer was Owen's idea, which Dad begrudgingly agreed to.) Everything appears intact. Dad inspects the office while Owen steps outside to chat with the cops. Dad rattles the filing cabinets, but they're still locked. I look over the desk. And that's when I spot the note.

It's written on a single sheet of typing paper. It's in simple block lettering, probably written with a sharpie. It reads *You can't retire on blood money.*

I pick up the note, using just my index and middle fingers. I look toward the police and Owen, but nobody takes notice of me. I hold the note toward Dad. He takes it from me and looks it over. And this is the part that really frightens me.

Dad seems lost. He's panicked and doesn't know what to do. He looks at me as if I can figure it out. The man who always had the answers and always guided me toward the right thing, my mentor and moral compass, needs me to tell him what to do. We're through the looking glass.

I take the note, fold it into quarters and stick it in my back pocket. I raise my eyebrows slightly, making sure Dad will follow my lead. One of the cops steps to the door.

"Anything missing?" he asks.

"No," Dad says, "Everything is fine."

The cop takes Dad's word on it. Dad moves past me, heading out of the office. I pat him on the shoulder as he passes. He reaches up, grabs my hand, and gives it a squeeze. Just like he would do when I was a kid and facing something scary and he was trying to reassure me. Except this time, it's supposed to work the other way around.

And that's even more scary.

CHAPTER SIX

Parents have a weird sense of their children's innocence. In the effort to protect said innocence, it's more about the parents than the children.

My mom fought like hell to maintain my belief in Santa Claus, even when it became obvious that particular reindeer had left the barn. She went so far as to get my idiot uncle Gordie to portray Santa Claus on Christmas Eve. I thought it was rather strange I finally got to see Santa when he'd remained unseen for years. Also, Santa's stumbling, weaving and being so disoriented that he stuffed one of the presents into the dishwasher seemed rather out of character. It was only after constant badgering that my mother finally confessed the whole plot, swearing me to secrecy, lest my little brother Owen find out (although Owen was operating under the same suspicion I was). Mom hated to see Santa no longer being a part of our lives. As for me and Owen, we moved on just fine.

That's really the point. Parents who hate to see their kids swearing, having sex, developing challenging political or religious opinions, what have you, are not troubled by what their children are actually doing. They struggle, rather, to accept their own rite of passage. What does having a child who's old enough to do all these things say about me? *Parents have trouble reconciling the image of their little one with this new adult persona. But it's not just the loss of the small child. It's the loss of the parents' image of infallibility. Rather than being a parent who can do no wrong, they are now imperfect, perhaps even an annoyance* because *of their imperfection. It's not just about the child's loss of innocence. It's about the parents'.*

On the way home, Dad and I make the decision not to tell Mom about the note, at least not yet. It's a strange feeling (one of many I've had lately). From the time I was a kid, *Don't tell Mom* has been the battle cry for me and my brothers. Now Dad is in on the conspiracy. But it *is* better if Mom doesn't know. At least until we get things straightened out.

Dad is nowhere to be found when I come down to breakfast the next morning. The aroma of eggs and bacon hits me at the top of the stairs. Mom is getting breakfast ready for the family. (If it seems like we're putting Mom to intensive labor, please know that she loves to do it and it gives her peace of mind, something she could use right now.) Her face is glistening, but she's smiling. There's no sign of anybody else. I look presentable enough in my t-shirt and running shorts. I sit at the kitchen table, and Mom puts a cup of coffee in front of me. (Mental note: go out for some decent coffee later.)

"Where's Dad?" I ask.

"He's having breakfast with Eli and Will," she says, "Probably to talk about the softball game today."

Huh. I wonder if he's going to tell them about the note. It's not something I can share with Mom, so I keep the thought to myself. We sit in silence while Mom works on breakfast. The radio plays in the background; jazz interspersed with commercials and news reports. I'm left to my thoughts, which are not altogether pleasant.

What did the note mean? *You can't retire on blood money.* What kind of blood money? Does it tie into this Taylor business? Who left the note? I'm not going out on a limb to suggest it might be the same person who murdered Burt. But why leave a note for my dad? Is the murderer threatening my dad? If that's the case, we should turn the note over to the police. But Dad won't go for that. The police are likely to ask uncomfortable questions. They might also take it as proof Dad killed Burt.

"Something on your mind, Joe?" Mom asks, putting the bacon and eggs in front of me.

I snap out of my reverie. "No, I'm just trying to get my brain moving. First thing in the morning, it's kind of sluggish." Mom probably well remembers what it was like to get me off to school when I was younger. I pick up my fork and tell her, "Thanks."

Mom pours herself a refill of coffee. "You're welcome."

She gets a certain satisfaction from my good manners. She and Dad drilled that into us from the time we were young, and they did a pretty damn good job. Sure, there are a string of ex-girlfriends who will openly question my moral fitness, but my manners are impeccable. Mom continues making breakfast for the rest of the Katzenjammer Kids. Apparently, I'm up before Kevin and his wife. (They must still be on West Coast time.)

"Did you know Dad's partners very well?" I ask Mom, "Back in the day?"

Mom keeps right on cooking, the sound of the whisk clanking against the metal bowl. (She's quite the multi-tasker when it comes to cooking and conversation.) "I didn't know them very well. I met them all, obviously."

"What did you think of them?"

She stops whisking the eggs for a moment. Mom has probably never given this topic much thought. "They were fine. They were more your father's friends than mine. I thought Will was very nice. Eli was kind of quiet. Burt was…I don't want to speak ill of the dead, but I never cared for Burt."

"That seems to be the consensus."

"He was loud. And coarse. And arrogant. Your father thought he was funny. By the time they went into business together, I think that was starting to wear off."

I can't help wondering if Mom had a role in that. She will tell you she defers to Dad in most things, but I've noticed over time that she wields a quiet influence on him. If she didn't care for Burt, Burt's days as my dad's friend would have been numbered.

"When Dad bought out his partners," I say, "where did he get the money?"

"We refinanced the house," Mom says, "We were lucky. Your father had more money saved than his partners. He was good with the books, and he ran the store well. That's why we were able to pay off the house before Owen left for college. He's a good businessman."

Of that, I never had any doubt. Dad has passed the ability to manage finances on to his kids. (My meager income doesn't exactly qualify as *wealth management*, but still…) I tap my fork against my plate.

"How did he get the others to go along with the sale?" I ask, "Dad was only one guy out of four. I can't see him pulling a Godfather and bringing Luca Brazzi to the meeting."

"I'm sorry, I don't get that last part."

"Skip it. Just go back to the question."

Mom carefully flips the bacon. "Actually, the partners made it easy on him. They were all in debt. They needed money and your father offered it to them, as long as they gave him their shares of the store."

I know you're probably wondering how I don't know all this. I've known for a long time that my dad bought out his partners, but I never thought to ask about the details. I go back to my breakfast, hoping to make this next part sound casual.

"The other night, Burt said something about *Taylor*," I say, "Dad says he didn't know what Burt was talking about. Did it ring any bells for you?"

"No," Mom says, with no sense of panic, "If your father doesn't know anything about it, *I* certainly don't."

My mom has never been what you'd call a master liar. When she says something like that without batting an eye, you can take it as the gospel. Whatever Taylor is, it's known only to my father and his friends.

This pleasantness is interrupted by a knock at the backdoor. Mom is unperturbed. That's the thing about my hometown: no one calls ahead and a knock on the door is not seen as a threatening event. Mom peeks through the little window, just to see who it is.

"It's your friend Mike," she says.

Huh. I guess the year Mike spent living with his grandmother must have schooled him in the ways of small towns. Or he's an inconsiderate dickhead. Really, it could go either way. Mom opens the door for him.

"Good morning, Mike," she says.

"Good morning, Mrs. Davis," Mike says, poking his head in, "Is Joe…" Then he spots me. "Oh, I guess he's up."

"Come in," Mom says, "Have you had breakfast yet?"

"Yep, I did. They've got a really nice continental breakfast at the Kahler."

Mom pats Mike on the shoulder and goes back to her cooking. I try to cover my amusement at Mike doing his Eddie Haskell routine. The look on Mike's face, though, is anything but amusing. His skin is flushed, and his hair is piled high from running his hands through it. This is clearly not a social call. Whatever it is, he can't go into it in front of my mom. We're presented with a perfect excuse to leave when the backdoor opens again and Kevin and his brood file into the kitchen. They look fresh and perfectly coiffed, as if this wasn't first thing in the morning. Kevin gives Mom a kiss on the cheek.

"Morning," Kevin says. Then he notices our visitor. "Good to see you, Mike."

Kevin and the girls surround the table. Jordan pretends to interest herself in Mom's cooking, so as to have as little as possible to do with me or my friends. (As far as I know, Jordan's culinary skills extend only to calling the local Chinese place for takeout.) The kitchen has never felt large, and the influx of visitors makes it feel positively cramped. I scarf down my breakfast and make a clean getaway. Mike and I head for my room. As we're going up the stairs, Mike looks back toward the kitchen.

"I gotta tell you," he says, "Kevin's wife is a babe."

"Yeah, so is her sister."

Mike's eyebrows go up. "You think you could introduce me to the sister?"

"I don't think my endorsement is going to help."

"Ah," Mike says, "You slept with her and never called her again."

When we get to my room. I make sure to close the door behind us. Mike grabs a seat on the bed (mussing the Batman bedspread ever so slightly) while I spin the desk chair around and drop into it.

"What's up?" I ask.

Mike runs a hand through his hair. "Okay, this Julie chick I was telling you about? We got together last night. Wound up missing your dad's thing. Sorry about that."

"He was devastated, but I believe he'll get over it."

"Swell. So, we were looking for a place to go. I suggested to Julie that we get a drink and maybe go back to her place. She nixed that plan. We just bought a bottle of wine and went up to Revelation Bluff."

"When in doubt…"

"But I'm getting agitated. I'm thinking, 'Why doesn't this chick want me to see her place? Is she a hoarder? Does she have her dead mother buried in the basement? Is she homeless? What the hell is going on?'"

"Did you ask her about it?" I say.

"Almost," Mike says, "We got up to Revelation Bluff and I was going to ask her, but then she started blowing me and I thought, 'Y'know, I really think too much.'"

"A man's got to know his limitations," I say.

"When we left Revelation Bluff, I took her back to the gas station where she parked. Then I went to the hotel and started stewing over it." For those not in the know, Mike can stew with the best of them. "Today, I decided to follow her. I know she stops into that gas station every morning for coffee. I staked out the place, saw her come and go and then I followed her."

Oh, I'm sure this went beautifully. "What did you discover?"

"Okay, I followed her to the neighborhood by that big park. The one where they found the dead guy. What's it called?"

"Bennett Park."

"That's right. Not the greatest neighborhood, but I didn't care. Julie parks in an alley behind one of the houses. I figure out which house it is, then I go up and knock on the front door." He runs a hand over his face. "And a kid answers."

I sit up in the chair. "A kid? How old?"

"I don't know. Six, eight, ten. Too young to shave, I know that. Anyway, the kid and I stand there for a second. Then I ask if his mom's home. He yells for her at the top of his lungs. Little bastard has no volume control."

"They rarely do."

"I hear Julie yelling from another room, asking what's going on. The kid says there's a man at the door and, I quote, 'I think it's a friend of Dad's.'"

"Oh, shit."

"Shit. Yes, shit. Julie walks into the room and gets a look on her face like an armed Jehovah's Witness just came to the door. She tells the kid—I forget his name, Jeff, Fred, Rufus, something like that—to run along and play. Then she tells me to meet her around back. She doesn't want the neighbors to see us."

"Sounds like the ship sailed on that."

"Yeah, I get the feeling Cunning isn't exactly Julie's middle name. Anyway, I met her in the back, right by her car. Julie apologizes for not telling me she's married, she hasn't done this sort of thing before, she just got caught up in it, all that."

"Been there."

A little more than a year ago, I discovered my girlfriend at the time, Norah, had a husband she had neglected to mention. It didn't end the relationship, but it started a string of events that nearly put me in jail. So, I'm not about to get on my high horse with Mike. He starts pacing (inasmuch as my tiny room will allow). I worry about my old stuff: the model of the *U.S.S. Enterprise* on a shelf, my Star Wars figurines, the Night Hawk action figure, the *Happy Days* lunchbox. Even the Soul Driver poster and the Porter's Bay and Adams College pennants on the wall aren't safe. Mike is, if nothing else, a perfect bull in a China shop.

"She tells me she's not happy with her husband," he says, "Tells me he's an alright guy, but he's stuck in a dead end job, has no ambition, is fine with living in Porter's Bay for the rest of his life. She needs a little excitement. That's why she took up with me."

"Makes sense, I guess."

"Here's the problem," Mike says, "I just got out of there when the husband came home. He didn't see me, but I saw him. He's the biggest fucking guy I've ever seen. And built like a brick shithouse. I don't know what dead end job he's stuck in, but I'm guessing it's knocking down buildings. With his bare hands."

"Oh, golly."

"If this guy finds out I've been playing sticky finger with his wife, they're going to find me spread over a four or five state area."

Egads. "Are you going to break things off with Julie?"

Mike stops pacing. "I don't know if it's going to be that simple. I told her more than I should have. I told her I live in St. Paul. I told her the temp job I work at. I even told her I live in Lowertown. If I break it off and Julie gets upset, she might tell the husband and the husband will have all he needs to track me down and kill me."

"That would be tragic."

"Especially for me. Sure, there's always a chance the guy would kill himself instead of me, but I don't have that kind of luck. No, if stuff is going to get broken off with Julie, it has to be her idea."

Here we go again. A few months ago, Mike was involved with his now-former boss. He started cheating on her (if that's how I want to describe it) and decided to break things off. In the name of keeping his job, he wanted it to be her idea, so he went deep into the Bad Boyfriend Playbook. It, and many other things, blew up in his face (as they usually do).

"You think it's going to work this time?" I ask.

"Different story," Mike says, waving a hand, "Last time I was trying to be subtle-like. I had my job to consider. And

Brigid knew me well enough to get suspicious if I just did a one-eighty and turned into a complete asshole."

"That would be a one-eighty for you?"

Mike ignores me. "Julie doesn't know me all that well. If I can produce enough red flags, she might break things off. That way, everybody's happy. The husband and kids have Julie. I'll be free and safe. Julie will think she's dodged a bullet. Win-win-win."

I could point out that Mike doesn't have a history of winning, particularly in the area of relationships. But it would be a waste of time. While my closest friends have fairly diverse personalities, one thing they have in common is stubbornness. Once they've determined a certain course of action is right, they can't be dissuaded. Given everything that's going on with my dad, I have neither the time nor the energy to talk Mike out of his bullshit plan.

"Good luck to you, son," I tell him.

Mike silently talks himself into it. The sun shines through the window. Not a cloud in the sky, which means the softball game is almost certainly on. Jiffy swell. Mike looks ready to move on from his own contretemps.

"How are things going with your dad?" he asks. I tell him about the break-in at the store and the threatening note. He chews his goatee as he listens. When I'm done, he asks, "What are you going to do next?"

"I've already talked with Dad's old partners. The only other guy I can think of is Evan Erickson. He was the one having the argument with Burt, after the thing at the Lodge. I don't know what his story is but maybe he can tell me something. There's also that Taylor thing Burt mentioned. Nobody wants to talk about it. I should maybe look into it."

"Then your plan is to just keep bashing away at this thing and hope something falls into your lap?"

"That pretty much covers it."

Both the investigation and the story of my life.

***

It takes a little footwork, but I'm able to find Evan Erickson. The footwork involved remembering his parents' names (Mom came in handy for that), looking up their address in the phone book (yes, people in Porter's Bay still use the phone book), and giving them a call. His mother answers. Turns out Evan's address is easy to come by: it's hers. Apparently, he still lives in the basement of his parents' house. His mother gives me his cell phone number but also tells me he's at The Hub right now, having lunch. I thank her for the info and decide to surprise Evan.

When I arrive, the place is busy with the lunch crowd. I don't need to eat, but as I recall, The Hub has pretty good coffee. *That* I could use. Evan is at a booth by the window. He wears a blue t-shirt that could use a wash. His hair hangs into his face. He's finishing up a burger and fries. I go to the counter and order a coffee-to-go. Might as well be prepared in case things with Evan get unfriendly. I stroll to his booth.

"Evan?" I say, "Joe Davis."

After a few seconds, Evan casually points at me. "Elyse's friend, right? Didn't we run into each other at the Buffalos thing?"

"We did. You got a minute?"

"Sure." I slide into the booth. Evan sets his burger down. "I'm just having lunch," he says. "I get meals for free. My girlfriend is a server."

"Really? I used to date a girl who was a server here."

"Oh? Who was that?"

I flip a hand, letting him know it's not important. "A girl I dated in high school. You probably wouldn't remember her." I look around the place. "Which server?"

He indicates a tall, willowy blonde with a ponytail. "That would be her over there. Her name is Charley."

"Charley?"

"Short for Charlene. But don't call her Charlene. She hates it."

"Understood," I say.

"She can set you up with a free lunch, if you want."

"No thanks," I say, "Big breakfast."

Evan must sense this isn't exactly a social call. He stretches one arm across the back of the booth and lays the other on the table. (If this were a Tarantino movie, he'd light a cigarette.) "What's on your mind?"

"You know about Burt Franklin, obviously."

His face clouds. "Everybody's heard about that."

"And you've probably heard the cops are looking at my dad."

"Heard that, too. It's bullshit. Your dad is a good guy."

"Thank you," I say, "I'm trying to find out anything I can about Burt and what he was doing the night he died. See if maybe I can get to the bottom of what was going on."

Evan seems a little wary. "I get that."

"Me and some friends were at Nick's after the thing at the Lodge. I saw you there, talking to Burt. It didn't look friendly. I'm wondering what you were talking about."

Evan's arm slides off the back of the booth. He situates both hands around his plate. "Just a deal we had going. I bought a car from him a while ago. Damn thing turned out to be a crapbox. He had to know that before he sold it to me. I've been trying to get my money back. He wouldn't do it. Kept pulling that *Buyer beware* shit." He lets out a breath. "Anyway, that's what we were talking about."

"Seemed pretty heated," I say.

"We'd both been drinking. You know it goes." He forces a laugh. "Burt was pissed about having to walk over there."

"Someone slashed his tires," I say, "Don't suppose you know anything about that?"

Evan can't resist giving me a sheepish grin. "Hey, buyer beware, *seller* beware, right?"

I guess that solves The Hardy Boys and the Mystery of Who Slashed Burt's Tires. But it pales in comparison to the larger thing I'm working on.

"When you were arguing with Burt," I say, "I heard you say something like, 'You don't own me.' That was about the car?"

"That what I said? Man, I *had* been drinking. To be honest, I don't remember a lot of it."

"But you remember you were talking about the car."

"Yeah, that had to be it."

Evan tries to adopt a casual air, but his steadfast refusal to make eye contact has me a little suspicious. His hands are fidgety, probably jonesing for a smoke. Maybe he's had too much caffeine. Maybe he's had too much something else. Or maybe I'm making him nervous.

"How did you find out?" I ask, "That Burt had died?"

"Parents told me. Next morning. Actually, it was probably in the afternoon. I…was out kind of late." He gives me a dopey smile. "I was at Nick's for a little, then I went over to the Hard Times, on Lake Drive. You ever been there?"

"Nope."

"I was hanging out with some buddies. Charley was with us." He looks toward Charley, who's serving a booth in the opposite corner. "Then one of my buddies invited me over to his place. We finished the evening over there."

"Was Charley with you?" I ask.

"Yeah, Charley's real cool with my buds." He looks toward her, and his face darkens. "She doesn't need to be working at The Hub. Her family owns a pizza joint up in Center City. Ed's Pizza. But she doesn't like getting handed anything. That's why she moved to Porter's Bay and took a job here. She's f'n cool."

"Sounds like it."

"It's not like her family is bad or anything. I've hung out with her brother a bunch of times. He's the manager of the place. A good dude."

Evan crams the rest of his burger into his mouth. It would have been better to take it in two bites, but I get the feeling he's hastening to get out of here. I'm not going to let him go quite *that* easily.

"There was someone with you at Nick's," I say, "Alice, right? Will's daughter?"

Evan flinches, like a gnat is buzzing nearby. "Yeah, she was there. I mean, she wasn't *with* me. We just know each other from high school. We bumped into each other."

"And left together."

"*Just* left together," he says, "As soon as we got out, she went one way, I went the other."

"She said she was trying to keep you from making a scene."

That annoyed look gets turned up to eleven. "I guess that's what she was trying to do. I was more worried about Burt." He finishes his fries, takes a last sip of his Coke, and gets up. "I gotta get going. There's a softball game for your dad today, right?"

"This afternoon," I say.

"Cool. I'll see if I can make it."

Evan says a hasty goodbye and leaves without tipping. He walks across the restaurant and corrals Charley. They have a short conversation. Charley purses her lips and puts a fist on each hip. I'm not sure, but I could swear Evan nods his head toward me. He gives Charley a quick kiss on the forehead and beats a hasty retreat. Charley goes back to work.

I get up to leave and realize I should use the restroom. It's past the breakfast counter and down a short hallway. It is, just as I remember, immaculately attended. It gets the Joe Davis Stamp of Approval. I step out of the restroom. The backdoor to the place is next to the men's room. Two voices come from the other side of the door. One of them gets my attention.

"Charley, you know this guy is no good, right?" a female voice says.

That brings me to a halt. Charley is out back, likely taking a smoke break. The other voice has a smoker's buzz to it. I assume it belongs to another server, perhaps a confidant. I stand and listen, trying not to breathe too loud. (Some might call this eavesdropping. Those people can mind their own business.)

"You don't know him," Charley says. Her voice is more direct than I would have anticipated. It's not the voice of someone who suffers fools.

"I know him well enough," the confidant says, "Thirty years old. Lives with his parents. Works part-time in a comic book shop. This sound like a guy who's going places?"

"He's going to be fine," Charley says, her voice now a little unsure, "He's just got to figure a few things out."

The confidant scoffs. "Yeah, how to keep leaching off you. And whatever the hell else he's into."

"What do you mean?" Charley says.

"Oh, do the math, honey," the confidant says, "He goes out five, six nights a week. Gets bombed or stoned. He's not getting that money from that comic store job. And there's only so much he can get from you or his parents."

"Just, just keep that to yourself, okay?" Charley says. There's a little pause. "I'm worried about him. I think he's in trouble."

I expect the confidant to be dismissive but instead she asks, "What kind of trouble?"

"I think some guys might be coming after him. He owes them money. That's why he was working with this…this Burt guy."

"The one that got killed?"

"Yeah, him," Charley says, "They had something going on. Evan wouldn't tell me what it was. But he needed money, and this Burt guy was supposed to give it to him."

"Did Evan get the money?"

"I don't think so. Evan said Burt was being a real dick about it. I don't know if Evan got the money or not. He won't tell me."

"Honey, you're really getting yourself bent out of shape for a guy that ain't all that loyal to you?" the confidant says.

A pause, then: "Why do you say that?"

"I can tell the type. And I saw him at Nick's the other night, talking to some girl."

"What girl?"

"Didn't catch her name," the confidant says, "Tall girl, curly hair, glasses. Not as cute as you, but I don't think that makes a difference to Evan. It's not about cute and ugly. It's about similar and different. That boy has a wandering eye, and he probably always will."

That temporarily silences Charley. And it brings my eavesdropping to an end because a blousy woman with a small child in tow comes down the hall. She pulls up short when she sees me. I give her a finger wave. *Nothing to see here. Just your friendly neighborhood pervert skulking about.* The woman clutches the child. I slink past them and down the hall, back toward the restaurant.

Joe Davis: Public Menace.

CHAPTER SEVEN

Two things have remained consistent in my life: I've never been a great athlete and I've never had the brightest group of friends. This is underscored by the memory of the football games I played with some neighborhood buddies when I was a kid. Kelly Park was just down the street from my house, and we'd play there every Sunday from the time school started until the weather got too bitter to continue (usually around the time the snow started to fly, and the ground started to freeze). Kelly Park had a skating rink, a baseball field and a giant lawn that would have been perfect for football.

So naturally, we played football inside the skating rink.

I'm not sure who made this decision. I was not in on the planning. Nor, sadly, did I raise any objections. It made for an interesting form of the game, as being run out of bounds now became being run into the boards. Also, we weren't smart enough to play touch or flag football. We played full tackle football. Shockingly, we did this for years without anybody breaking a limb or suffering a concussion (as far as we knew).

My greatest moment—if that's what you want to call it— occurred when I was playing running back and our QB, Rudy, tried to pitch the ball back to me. The ball flew over my head and rolled several feet behind me. I ran back to get it and my first two attempts resulted in my kicking the ball even farther away. When I finally picked the damn thing up, half the civilized world seemed to be closing in on me. I slipped two tackles then ran at an angle toward the sideline. I outran Bob Sunde, who disappeared over the boards after missing the tackle. Gary Rusich caught up to me and tried to bring me down by my sweatpants. I kept my legs churning and willed myself to get away. I outran the rest of the opposing team and got to the endzone for an absolutely improbable touchdown. I spiked the ball in celebration.

Only to discover Gary Rusich holding the shredded remains of my sweatpants.

As I recall I made the extra point and thanked the gods my house was only a quick bike ride from the park.

Yet I'm not completely lost as an athlete. I'm tall (a little over six feet). I've kept pretty trim. And I stay active. I'm an avid runner and bike rider. I play in a touch football league in the fall and a broomball league in the winter. But whatever gift is given to athletes—a natural ability that can be cultivated—was denied to me. The scouting report on me will always read *Tries hard*, which is a euphemism for *Sucks*. So, you'll forgive me if I'm not looking forward to participating in a sporting event in front of my hometown.

And my brothers aren't helping.

"Keep your elbow up," Kevin says, casually leaning against the chain link fence, "You want a nice even swing, right through the ball."

"Make sure you stay in the batter's box," Owen says, "Don't worry about the pitch hitting you."

I turn toward him. "It's a damn slow pitch game. Even if a pitch hits me, it would be less damaging than a noogie."

"One of your noogies maybe," Owen says.

Kevin laughs. Just what I need. The two of them aligned against me. They both look ready for the game. Kevin wears a white polo shirt, black coach's pants, and a spotless pair of tennis shoes. Owen is less stylish, wearing a blue t-shirt, gray sweats, and beat up sneakers. I go back to taking warm up swings. Even with my nerves about the game, I can't help admiring the scenery. Bennett Park was like Valhalla when I was growing up. Every trip was magical. The kick ass rocket ship slide was home to the best games of tag imaginable. To one side of the softball field is the baseball stadium and an amphitheater. Up the hill are the picnic grounds and a gazebo that holds special memories from when I was a teenager. The rolling lawns gave everything a lush feel. There's nary a cloud in the sky. Even if my ultimate humiliation is nigh, this is still a great place.

Kevin turns to Owen. "Maybe he's better in the field."

"I don't think so," Owen says, "You remember? We used to call him Dr. Strangeglove."

Cruel fate—or more likely my dad's meddling—has put me on the same team with my brothers. The game won't start for another half hour but already people are filtering in. It's supposed to be an informal affair; no uniforms have been issued. Pastor Tony, the retired pastor from Our Savior's Lutheran, acts as the umpire, and spectators have been encouraged to bring picnic lunches. It looks like half the town has turned out.

I leave the batting cage and offer them the bat. "Why don't you show me how it's done?"

Kevin takes it and slips into the batting cage. He gives us a workshop on executing a smooth, level swing. All without breaking a sweat. (Seriously, could the guy at least have a bum knee? A weak shoulder? Jock itch?) I look away, knowing I'll see enough of this during the game. Owen looks over at me.

"Dad stopped by the store this afternoon," Owen says, "He had breakfast with Will and Eli. They got threatening notes, too."

I snap him a look. "How did the notes show up?"

"Will's was on the windshield of his car," Owen says, "Eli's was slipped under the door of his apartment."

"Did they look like the one Dad got?"

"More or less," Owen says, "They were phrased a little differently, but they both used the words *blood money*."

"They have any idea who could have left those notes?"

"Dad said they don't. The notes were waiting for them when they got back from the historical society thing."

This puts things in a different light. If the person who murdered Burt left those notes, that calls into question the whole issue of motive in Burt's murder. Was the murderer targeting Burt specifically or my dad and his friends as a whole? I've been assuming the former, but if it's the latter, that means Dad or one of his friends could be next. The thought makes me shiver.

"Are they going to take the notes to the police?" I ask.

"I don't think so," Owen says, "The police kind of freak Dad out at the moment." He scratches his neck. "Um, I probably don't need to tell you this, but—"

"Don't tell Mom," I say.

"Glad we're on the same page," Owen says.

Kevin finishes taking his swings and steps out of the batting cage. He flips the bat around as he walks up to us. "You figured anything out since last night?"

"Depends," I say, turning to Owen, "You remember Evan Erickson?"

"Oh, I remember Evan," Owen says, "He worked at the store for a minute-and-a-half. I had to fire him."

I give them an overview of Evan's argument with Burt, what he claims it was about, and the conversation I overheard with Charley and the confidant regarding money Evan apparently owes. Owen takes the bat from Kevin and shakes his head as he steps into the batting cage.

"That's Evan," Owen says, "He's always been a little shady."

"I hear he's friends with Will's daughter Alice," I say.

Owen pauses in the batting cage. "Yeah, I think they used to date. Back in high school. They were a couple years behind me, but I remember something about them dating."

"He's got a girlfriend now," I say.

"Charley," Owen says, taking some swings, "I've seen her at The Hub. She seems bright. No idea what she's doing with Evan."

"You think Evan and Alice are still seeing each other?" I ask, "Even as friends?"

"No idea."

"Well, they're seeing each other *today* at least," Kevin says.

He nods toward the field. Sure enough, Evan is in conversation with Alice. I do a doubletake, partially surprised, partially chagrined at getting scooped by Kevin. They're on the other side of the softball field, standing against the chain link fence that surrounds the field. They're close, their body language stiff. If I had to guess, the conversation isn't casual.

"Isn't that interesting?" I say.

"I'll take your word on it," Kevin says.

Since I've got other business to attend to and don't need to be further reminded I'm the least athletic member of my family, I decide to get a closer look at Evan and Alice. I walk along the fence paralleling the first base line. I do some light calisthenics, lest I look like I'm skulking about. (As an avid runner, I can at least do these and look competent.) A voice to my right interrupts me.

"You really need to do that for a beer ball game?"

Carol approaches, wearing a sleeveless pink blouse, faded jeans and tennis shoes. She, at least, is dressed for a beer ball game. I keep up with the stretching while she props an arm on the fence.

"Just keeping an eye on someone," I say, "Maybe two someones."

Carol spots Evan and Alice. "This is about the thing with your dad?"

"It is."

"I don't suppose your uncle Gordie is here?"

"I haven't seen him. Honestly, I'd be shocked if he showed up. He doesn't want anything to do with celebrating my dad. When the city council passed a resolution to give my dad the key to the city, Gordie tried vetoing it. They had to override it.”

Carol gives that a cluck of disgust. “Your uncle is a real piece of work.”

“He is. He’s a piece of other things as well.”

She pulls her hair back into a ponytail. “Have you heard of a guy named Vic Easton?”

I’m about to say I don’t, but then the name strikes me. “He’s a real estate developer. He lives up near Center City. I’ve seen some of his billboards.”

“That’s right,” Carol says, “And he gave a bunch of money to your uncle’s campaign.”

I nearly drop my glove. “Where did you hear that?”

“I connected the dots. I talked to the guy who owns The Hub Diner this morning. He said Gordie’s campaign was floundering last fall, then all of a sudden, he had a bunch of campaign posters and signs. He had ads on the radio. He had a billboard outside of town. He never told anyone where the money came from.”

“He certainly didn’t get it from his pizza delivery job.”

“Exactly,” Carol says, “Then later, I talked to Freja, she’s the lady who owns the coffee shop on Lake Drive—”

“Cream and Amber?”

"That's the one," Carol says, "She saw Gordie up on Revelation Bluff, meeting with Vic Eaton. You know what that means, right?"

"They're dating?"

"No, you idiot! Well, I guess we can't rule anything out, but that's not where I was going with that. They were meeting out of the public eye. Then this Big Box Bill comes up."

I groan. The Big Box Bill has been hovering around like a storm cloud. It requires a bit of explanation. As I've mentioned, Porter's Bay draws most of its income from the tourist trade. As a result, it deals heavily in *quaint*. To the untrained eye, someone feels like they've driven into the 1950's whenever they pull into town. Toward that end, mom-and-pop stores and family eateries and antique stores are welcomed. Walmarts, on the other hand, are persona non grata. The townspeople felt so strongly about it that back in the 80's, the city council passed a ban on big box stores into law. It's why my father has been able to keep a family-owned hardware store going in an age of Home Depot, Menards, and Lowes. Since Gordie was elected, though, there have been rumors he's pushing to repeal the ban.

"I've heard about it," I say, "How does that fit in?"

"Like I said, connect the dots," Carol says, "Vic Easton is a real estate developer. He owns land here in Porter's Bay.

He gives money to Gordie's campaign. Gordie gets elected. Then Gordie puts the Big Box Bill on the table."

"Gordie's in Vic Easton's pocket."

"Exactly. And I'll bet you anything Gordie will get kickbacks and other favors from Easton once this is done. Gordie needs to be impeached."

Whoa. Our own little Watergate, right here on the North Shore. "Can that even be done?"

"Yes, it can," Carol says, "I looked at a copy of the City Charter. It takes a three-quarters vote of the city council, but the mayor *can* be removed. That means if I can get at least five of the city council to vote for impeachment, Gordie is gone."

I should be concerned about Gordie being removed from office as a black mark against our family. Then again, Gordie being *in* office is a black mark on our family, so it evens out. Still, I have to tamp down Carol's zeal.

"I don't think the city council is going to make any move against Gordie unless you show them proof he's corrupt. No offense, but all you've got is hearsay."

"All I've got *now* is hearsay," Carol says, "but I'm going to keep digging. I'll find something I can use against Gordie. And I'm going to get his ass kicked out of office."

The determination Carol has, her desire to get to the truth, no matter what it takes; all of that brings a goofy grin to my face, one I haven't had in a long time.

"What's so funny?" Carol asks.

"You just…you remind me of someone," I say, glancing toward the gazebo.

Before Carol can ask a follow up question, Lars bounds into the conversation. A St. Louis Browns baseball cap squashes his quasi-pompadour and a Washington Senators jersey covers his bony torso. A pair of tan cargo shorts and some eye black under eye completes the ensemble. Carol looks him up and down.

"And which one of the Bad News Bears are you supposed to be?" she asks.

"I'm sorry, I'm not familiar with that Walter Matthau classic." Lars sets an aluminum bat on his shoulder. "What are we talking about?"

"My idiot uncle Gordie," I say.

"That man is no idiot," Lars says, "I chatted with him earlier this afternoon."

My eyebrows go up. "Oh? How did that come about?"

"Gordie was having a staff meeting at the usual spot."

"Drinking with his buddies at the Village Bowl?" I say.

"Precisely," Lars says, "I happened to be there and wanted to chat with him. I wasn't sure he'd have time to talk to one of the hoi polloi, but I appealed to his sense of citizenship."

"You bought him a beer," I say.

"I did indeed," Lars says, "I told him I was fascinated by his views and his administration. Turns out he was quite forthcoming. By the way, Joe, he's disappointed in you."

"Because I wouldn't join his staff?"

"You're right again," Lars says, "See, you know your uncle so well and yet you refuse to work for him. Why is that?"

"First, I have no desire to move back to Porter's Bay," I say, "Second, I have a moral issue with Gordie."

"And what would that be?"

"That I have some and he doesn't."

Carol covers her mouth and giggles. Lars's head snaps back. He adopts a wounded air.

"Well, if that's how you feel, I'm glad *somebody* is in Gordie's corner," Lars says, "I'm working for him now."

So much for giggling. "What do you mean you're working for him?" Carol asks.

"That's what came out of my conversation with the mayor," Lars says, "He said the people were with him, but the media continues to sully his good name."

"Your words, not his?" I ask.

"I summarize," Lars says, "But the local media—"

"Both of them," I say.

"Remain adamantly opposed," Lars continues, "I think they take it personally that your uncle was elected. Rather than seeing him as representing the will of the people, they see Gordie and his friends as a bunch of drunk shitkickers."

"His words, not yours?" I ask.

"I have merely quoted," Lars says, "But Gordie and I decided what he really needs is a new spokesperson and media consultant. And—" He throws his arms wide, cracking the aluminum bat against the top of the fence. "*I* am that person."

Carol's jaw drops. Given that Gordie's election and subsequent administration have seemed like a fever dream, I'm beyond the capacity to be shocked (though I *am* getting an enormous headache).

"What the hell, Lars?" Carol says, "You're going to move up here?"

"That's to be determined," Lars says, "I am well on my way to being a local entrepreneur. A move to this charming little burg might be in the offing."

We'll see how charming this burg remains with Lars in it. Carol gently grabs the front of Lars's jersey.

"I wouldn't get too close to Gordie if I were you," Carol says, "I think he's corrupt."

Lars waves this off. "People will always try to take down great visionaries. I know this from personal experience."

"You know a great visionary?" I say.

As usual, Lars ignores me. "Gordie will do great things in this town and—Joe, *I* was the visionary I was speaking of—I'm going to make sure he's given credit for what he's done."

"How are you going to do that?" I ask.

"I don't know," Lars says, "I've only had the job a few hours. But I'm itching to get started. Itching, I say."

Carol scoffs. "You sure that's not a tick?"

"No, I don't believe so," Lars says, "I'm looking forward to making Gordie—oh, lookie there, it was a tick—one of the most powerful men in this state."

"If that's the case," I say, "I look forward to moving."

The game is about to start, meaning I can get away from James Carville and Mary Matalin over there. Dad and Will captain the two teams. Kevin, Owen, Lars, and I are all on Dad's team. Evan, Eli, Carol, and Alice are all on Will's team. Our team is first to take the field. I'm at first base (which is where you put someone with a crappy throwing arm). I try to tamp down my nerves. Dad steps into the pitcher's circle to get things started.

The game is slow pitch, so there's a lot of hitting and a lot of poor fielding. Will's team gets two runs in the first, aided by Lars ducking a line drive at third base. Kevin and Owen even things up in the bottom of the first by hitting back-to-back homers. In the second inning, Alice surprises us all with a hard line drive into the rightfield corner. Her swing is surprisingly aggressive. If she were a better runner, she might have gone all the way around, but she only gets to second (after first missing the base and going back to get it).

We're not exactly erasing memories of the 1991 World Series here.

The game goes back and forth and, honestly, I start to lose track of what inning it is and what the score might be. Everyone seems to be having a decent time. Some highlights include Robert Humphrey's pants falling down as he was running to first, thus tripping him and allowing us to get the out, Kevin and Owen continually hitting home runs, Evan running out a triple and practically knocking Lars into the dugout, Kevin nearly throwing out Terry Schlander at first base after a hit to centerfield (if only the idiot first baseman had held on to the ball), and Carol racing in on a flyball, positioning herself perfectly, and missing the actual ball, which bounces off her forehead. At the top of the last inning. Will makes his way to home plate and jokingly waves the bat toward centerfield *calling his shot* ala Babe Ruth. My dad laughs.

"Not in this lifetime, Will," Dad says.

"Just bring it in," Will says, "And try to put some arc on it this time, would you?"

The opposing dugout is to my left. Evan approaches Alice. She gets up and goes to the other side of the bench. Evan slips a Sharpie out of his pocket and scribbles something down on Alice's glove. He moves back to the other side of the bench.

"Joe!"

That's my dad's voice. I return to the action, just in time to watch Will's ground ball strike a pebble and bounce directly into my nutsack. All systems shut down. It feels like someone is trying to pull my stomach out through my urethra. I collapse to the ground. Will runs past me, heading for second. A few moments later, my dad is standing over me. Not out of any concern for my health, mind you. He's picking up the ball and throwing it to third to keep Will from advancing. That done, he turns to me.

"Joe, what was the first thing I taught you about playing ball?"

"Keep your head in the game," I say.

"At least you remembered, even if you didn't apply it."

Dad offers me a hand and pulls me to my feet. Kevin and Owen are stretched out on the field, busting a collective gut. Will stands on second base. The waves of pain are subsiding. I let out a few breaths. Dad puts a hand on my shoulder.

"Are you going to be all right?" he asks.

"Sure," I say, "Just be glad Frick and Frack out there already gave you grandchildren."

Dad pats my shoulder and heads back to the pitcher's circle. I try to ignore the abject amusement on the faces of my teammates. Will, though, is not smiling. He's wobbling a tad. A second later, he collapses altogether.

Will is saved from completely faceplanting when Buck Johnson, the second baseman, grabs him and breaks his fall. Everyone runs toward him. Dad is immediately at his side.

"Just stand back, okay?" Dad says, "Give him some room." The crowd backs off and Dad kneels next to Will. "Can you hear me, Will?"

Will's face is white and sweaty. "I hear you, Henry. But I'm under no obligation to listen to you."

Dad lets out a sigh of relief. "Can you sit up?"

"I think so."

Will slowly sits up, dusting off his shirt as he does. The color is returning to his cheeks. Alice pushes her way through the crowd and kneels next to her father.

"Dad, are you okay?" she says, trying to keep her voice level.

Will pats her arm. "I'm fine. I'm fine."

"I told you not to play today," Alice says.

"I'm *fine*," Will says, an edge creeping into his voice, "I just got a little lightheaded. Ran down the baseline too fast."

Dad joins Kevin and Owen in helping Will up. Will takes a quick breath, making sure he's steady. He nods at my dad. Dad turns to the crowd.

"Maybe we ought to call it a day," Dad says.

"No, no, no," Will says, "Not on my account. Let's keep going."

"Forget it," Alice says, "Henry is right. Let's stop the game here."

Will is ready to argue, but players from both sides want to move on. Will takes the temperature of the room.

"Alright then, let's call it a day," Will says.

The crowd starts to disperse. Some move toward Will to make sure he's okay. I walk back toward first base, still moving gingerly. The opposing dugout is empty. I look toward the crowd. Will and Alice are preoccupied. Evan is in the crowd. I shouldn't do what I'm thinking. But I'm going to do it anyway. I powerwalk to the dugout (as best I'm able) and find the end of the bench where Alice's glove is lying. I take a quick peek at what Evan wrote.

9:30. Usual place. Re: Berringer. Please come.

I don't know what that means, but I may have to find out. I step out of the dugout and see Alice approaching. I try to play it casual. Alice cocks her head as she walks toward me.

"Something you're looking for?" she asks.

"No, I just walked into the wrong dugout," I say, "Guess that shot to the groin must be affecting me."

"Huh. Must be true about where guys keep their brains."

She pushes past me and into the dugout. I don't seem to be making many friends these days. Puts me on the same footing as Burt. I just hope we don't wind up the same way.

***

While I'm not an athlete, I *do* know what a well-earned exhaustion feels like. Running, lawn work, broomball, softball, they all give me a feel for it. Especially on a day when I've also taken a groundball to the noogs.

My brothers and I are sprawled out in the living room, all of us drinking beer. (Kevin has joined me in drinking decent beer. Owen remains committed to domestic piss water.) Lars and Carol are in the kitchen, helping my mom with dinner. (Though I suspect Lars's contributions extend only to consulting and irritating.) My dad is upstairs, napping. Kevin, who doesn't appear to have sweated during the game, reclines on the couch.

"You heard anything about Will?" he asks.

"Nothing more than you have," I say, "Why?"

"You were talking to his daughter after the game," Kevin says, "You interested in her?"

"Dear God, no," I say, and to be fair, Alice would probably say the same thing if asked about *me*, "I was just…covering something."

Owen sits forward in the armchair. "And what would that be?"

I suppose I can't leave it at that, can I? I tell them about what Evan wrote on Alice's glove. They both give me their undivided attention, which I have to confess is a new experience. When I'm done, they remain on the edges of their seats.

"Who the hell is Berringer?" Owen asks.

"You spend more time around here than I do," I say, "If you don't know who Berringer is, I certainly don't. You got any idea what *the usual spot* is supposed to be?"

"Nope," Owen says, "You got me on that one."

Kevin turns to me. "What are you going to do?"

Oof. I was hoping we wouldn't get into this. But Kevin and Owen are interested, so I'm going to have to spill. I slide closer to the edge of the sofa, unconsciously drawing my brothers into a huddle.

"I'm thinking about following one of them to the meeting," I say, "Maybe seeing if I can overhear something."

I expect this to be met with the same amusement that accompanied the bounding ball striking my bounding balls. Instead, they both get quiet.

"Which one are you going to follow?" Kevin asks.

"I'm not sure," I say, "I know where Evan's parents' house is. I'm sure I can find out where Alice lives. Whoever I choose, I have to be able to stick with them."

Kevin sits back. "Following somebody. You do this sort of thing a lot?"

"More than I should," I say.

Owen jumps in. "He does. I've heard some stories. And he helped me out a little last winter." Responding to the look from Kevin, Owen adds, "It's a long story."

Kevin lets it go. I'm getting uncomfortable with their scrutiny, so I find an excuse to step out of the living room and check things out in the kitchen. Lars meets in the dining room.

"Been meaning to tell you, brother," he says, as if we've been having a conversation for the last ten minutes, "Things are continuing to look up for my gangster business."

"Oh?" I say, "Found the contents of Al Capone's vault, did you?"

"No, but give me time," Lars says, "For now, I was able to find an old gangster hideout."

I can't conceal my look of surprise. Eighteen years growing up here, another seventeen hearing the various bits of scuttlebutt and yet I didn't realize there was a gangster hideout in Porter's Bay.

"Where is this?" I ask.

"You've heard of Dolly's Bed-and-Breakfast?"

"Sure. It's off Lake Drive, on the north end of town."

"Correct-a-mundo," Lars says, "According to my research, there is a distinct possibility John Dillinger spent the night there once."

"You're sure about that?"

Lars nods, emphatically. "Based on my research, I have absolute confidence in my speculation. That charming little house once hosted public enemy number one. It was reason enough to go talk to the owner."

As I recall, Jill, the owner of Dolly's (she's a big Dolly Parton fan and thought that name was more charming than her own), is a kind, gregarious woman. Perfect for owning a B-and-B. I can't imagine having Lars's company inflicted upon her.

"How did that go?" I ask, with a due sense of trepidation.

"Very well at first," Lars says, "I told her about my research and what I had discovered. Then I suggested she change the theme of the B-and-B. Everything is frilly and cute, but it doesn't really represent the history of the place. I suggested she change everything to a gangster theme. Make it look like an old speakeasy or a gangster hideout. Maybe a combination of both. It could be a real centerpiece for my upcoming gangster tour."

"And what did she think of that?"

"Oh, she told me to get the hell out. Ran after me with a broom. It's not easy being a visionary. You're so frequently misunderstood."

"Or worse, correctly understood."

Lars flies right by that one. "Still, the B-and-B is on a public street. The owner can't stop me from bringing the tour past her house. As long as I remain adjacent to—but not actually on—her property, I'll be fine."

"You think Jill is going to see it that way?" I ask.

"She can appeal to the city if she doesn't like it," Lars says, adding a smug expression, "But I have some connections that way."

Oh brother. "You're really going to use my idiot uncle—"

"Your idiot uncle the mayor," Lars says.

"To browbeat a local business owner into doing what you want?"

"Joe, it's the nature of business. You do what you've got to do. It's that simple."

I should talk him out of this ridiculous venture, but I don't have the time (either in this visit or the remainder of my natural life). The only thing I can do—now, as always—is stay mum and allow Lars to screw this up on his own. (I at least have faith in *that*.)

"Good luck to you," I tell him.

Lars spins on his heel and heads back to the kitchen. I stay in the dining room, wondering what to do next. I hear a *Psst* and see Kevin and Owen waving me back into the living room. I join them, fighting against the soreness from the game. Kevin keeps his voice down.

"We're going with you," Kevin says.

"Going with me where?" I ask.

Owen jumps in. "To follow Alice and Evan. See what they're up to."

Danger, Will Robinson. "You sure that's a good idea?" I say, "I don't want to get you guys in trouble." Boy, there's a complete reversal from childhood.

Kevin folds his arms. "If they have something to do with this stuff, we want to help out."

I look toward the kitchen. Unlike my brothers, I'm not worried about Mom overhearing. In fact, I'm actively thinking of ratting them out. But they might be right. I could use some help.

"All right," I tell them, "let's figure this out."

It will be nice to again work with my brothers on something. And it will be great to once again get in deep shitting trouble with them.

CHAPTER EIGHT

I've talked before about how returning to your hometown or going to a high school reunion causes you to automatically revert to the person you were back in the day, no matter how hard you've tried to get away from that person. The same principle applies to getting back together with your family.

When I go to a family event, I invariably have older relatives approach me and say, "Joe? Wow. Look how big you've gotten." This despite the fact I haven't grown an inch since I graduated from high school. They're surprised because they carry around an unchanging image in which I am perpetually four years old (and possibly a girl). The surprise comes from being confronted with the reality I am a fully grown man (or a reasonable facsimile).

If you have multiple siblings, the effect can be similar. You can be the master of your own destiny, king of all you survey (so long as your vision is limited), but the second you get around your siblings, the old dynamic takes hold. If you're the oldest, you expect to be in charge. If you're one of the middle kids, you revert to middle management. If you're the youngest, you're the follower. All other contexts can be checked at the door.

My phone buzzes, telling me I've got a call from Kevin. Oh, for garden seed. Does anyone other than me prefer texting to calling? I answer it.

"Anything yet?" is how Kevin greets me.

"No," I say, drawing the word out, "If I see something, you'll be the first to know."

"Same here. Just keep an eye on things."

"Thanks. I hadn't figured that out for myself."

Kevin ignores my snark and hangs up. I return my cell phone to the drink holder. I'm in the Ford Ranger I borrowed from Owen. (My brothers are in Kevin's rental car, my friends have commandeered our rental vehicle, and I couldn't borrow Mom's car without raising suspicion.) I'm down the street from the Ericksons' house. The sun is disappearing behind the horizon, giving everything a yellow glow. The *golden hour* is what I believe filmmakers call it. It will be dark in about ten minutes. This would be pretty if I didn't have other things on my mind. I feel good about my position. The Ericksons don't have an alley. Their garage faces the street. Unless Evan goes over a tall fence to cut through the neighbors' backyard, he can't leave without me seeing him. My phone rings, startling me. It's Owen.

"Alice just left her building," he says, his voice tight (like everything else about him), "We're following her. Anything on your end?"

"Nothing," I say.

Owen hangs up. I sit there for several moments, wondering what—if anything—I should do. Finally, the Ericksons' front door opens and Evan steps out. I slump down in my seat. Evan makes a beeline to a piece of crap Chevy and takes off down the street. I wait a few seconds, flip on my lights, and follow him.

My goal is to stay with Evan, so I'm inclined to err on the side of getting too close. Maybe I could get away with that in the Cities, but there's a lot less traffic in Porter's Bay. I hope Evan is either preoccupied or not that observant. (A little from Column A, a little from Column B…) His path takes us down a few side streets then crosses First Avenue. He's on Miller Street, going past Greenhaven Elementary (boo) and heading toward Lake Drive. I get another call from Owen.

"Alice is stopping at The Hub," he says, "Where's Evan?"

"On Miller. Closing in on Lake Drive."

"You think they're meeting at The Hub?" Owen asks.

"If they are, they aren't exactly keeping it on the downlow," I say, "Everyone in town goes to The Hub."

"Okay, keep us updated."

"Shouldn't be a problem. You call me every two minutes."

Owen hangs up. Evan approaches the stoplight for Lake Drive. The lake looms, dark and vast, in the distance. If Evan goes right at the stoplight, he's definitely going to The Hub. If he goes left, I don't know where the hell he's going.

He goes left.

Lake Drive is a two-lane road snaking next to the Lake. From here, it passes the Kahler and Howard Street. After that, you're on your way out of town and headed for Greenville. The potential options for the meeting are then fairly limited. My phone rings again. (I'm going to have to block Owen.)

"Alice left The Hub," he says, "She just grabbed a to-go coffee and took off."

"Where is she headed?"

"Up Lake Drive," Owen says, "Like she's headed out of town."

That's encouraging. At least Evan and Alice are going the same direction. This thing no longer shows signs of being a wild goose chase. Evan passes Howard Street. I'm worried *the usual place* is some remote location between here and Greenville, maybe even Revelation Bluff. How am I going to follow him up there without being spotted? That speculation ends when Evan takes a right into the fairgrounds.

The Shore County Fairgrounds sit between Lake Drive and the actual lake, on the north end of town. Every year from the time I could remember, my parents would take us to the fair, traditionally held in late July, early August. We also went to the stock car races every Saturday night in the summer. From what I understand, everything is still in place. The races won't be held until Saturday night, so the track and the grounds will be empty. The various exhibit buildings screen a good chunk of the grounds from Lake Drive. If this is *the usual place*, it's going to provide a goodly amount of privacy. I continue up the road, keeping an eye on the rearview mirror. Once everything is clear, I pull over and call Owen.

"I think they're meeting at the fairgrounds," I say.

"That's where Alice is headed," Owen says, "We can't follow her in there."

"That's what I was thinking," I say, "Will the side entrance work?"

Kevin's voice comes on (apparently, Owen has me on speaker). "We'll give it a shot. What about you?"

"If they go far enough into the grounds, I can park next to the road without them seeing me. If you have eyes on them, text me and let me know where they're at."

"Sounds good," Kevin says, "Just make sure your phone is on silent."

Yes, because I'm developmentally disabled and incapable of figuring that out for myself. But I let Kevin have the last word. (This isn't the time to assert dominance over the oldest child.)

I do a U-turn and carefully make my way back to the fairgrounds. As I approach, a car turns in and disappears into the grounds. That must be Alice. I slow as I pass the entrance. No sign of Alice's or Evan's cars. Looks like I can slip in unnoticed. I take a left across Lake Drive, kill the lights and park on the edge of the fairgrounds. I step out of the car and carefully close the door. The fairgrounds cover a decent amount of ground and the sound of the lake crashing against the shore covers some of the noise. I take my phone with me and start up the small hill toward the exhibit buildings.

At this time of the year, the exhibit buildings best resemble a collection of garages and tool sheds. They all consist of aluminum siding and A-frame roofs. The solid cement structure of the racetrack grandstand looms beyond them. The place is completely deserted. It feels like a house shuttered for the winter. Every crunch of my footsteps on the gravel seems to boom across the grounds. I use the small openings between each of the buildings to make my way through. Sweat trickles down my neck. I have to hope I don't accidently walk right in on Alice's and Evan's meeting.

My phone lights up. In the darkness, it looks like I just sent up a flare. I curl around it, trying to minimize the glare. It's a text message from Kevin, reading *Where r u?* I text him back, giving him my location. Kevin replies, *Alice nxt to midway. Not moving. No sgn Evan.*

The midway is a collection of smaller buildings on the south side of the fairgrounds. It's where the rides are placed when the fair is on. I'm not sure why the midway is a special spot for Evan and Alice, but I don't have time to speculate. I stop between two buildings and try to control my breathing. Then my phone lights up again. I cup my hands around it. The message reads *Dn't jump. Dn't yell.* I've barely had time to contemplate the meaning of that when someone's hand clamps down on my shoulder.

To my credit, I avoid crying out. There's just enough light from my phone to see Kevin and Owen standing over me. Kevin holds his finger to his lips. He points toward the other side of the Midway. Alice is waiting, her arms folded over her chest. No sign of Evan. We crouch in the shadows and keep watch.

"Boo."

In the silence, the voice sounds like a bomb going off. Everyone jumps, including Alice and my brothers. She turns and slugs Evan on the shoulder.

"Where the hell have you been?" Alice asks, her voice sharp.

Evan holds his shoulder and giggles. "I had to call Charley. She's getting off work and I told her I was going to be late."

Alice lets out a sigh. "What did you want to talk about?"

"The money."

"I don't have any," Alice says, "You dragged me out here so I could tell you that?"

Evan sways to one side. Clearly, he needed some herbal courage before this conversation. "I know you don't have it. I get that. I just thought maybe your—"

"My dad? Is that what you were about to say?"

"Well—"

"Forget it," Alice says, "He doesn't have any more money than I do. He's…he doesn't have it. And even if he did, I wouldn't ask him. My dad has enough on his mind."

That brings things to a halt, at least temporarily. Evan wipes his nose and runs a hand through his hair. (Gross.) "I just need to get some," he says, "Any way I can."

"Any way you can," Alice says, her tone dripping acid, "I heard that."

Evan hangs his head. "I'm sorry. I was desperate."

"I sure as hell hope so. It's the only excuse you've got. It's the only reason I even agreed to meet you."

"How many times can I say I'm sorry?"

"Until I stop feeling betrayed."

"I didn't know what else to do. You're the last person I wanted to hurt. I'm a fucking screwup. You know that."

A long moment goes by. Neither Alice nor Evan says anything. Neither looks at the other. My brothers and I are doing our best not to move or breathe.

Alice's tone softens. "Can I do anything to help?"

Evan opens his mouth then closes it. After a few seconds, he comes up with what I'm guessing is a different statement than his original. "I need to get the money. And soon."

"What about Eli?" Alice says, "He and Burt have been working together. If Burt had money, Eli must have some."

Evan considers this. "He might. He didn't like Burt, but they *were* working together. I have to hope, right?"

Alice puts a hand on Evan's shoulder. "How long do you have?"

"Maybe a week. Unless Berringer gets impatient, then I'm screwed. It's not your problem. It's mine."

"It doesn't mean I don't care."

Evan sways again. "This might sound way off the beam, but the lawyer you work for…"

"Don't even think about it," Alice says, "I'm not asking David for money."

"If you think about it—"

"The answer is no. End of discussion."

Evan says nothing. Alice stares a hole in him, neither blinking nor showing anything resembling empathy. I wonder what this is all about?

Then Owen's fucking phone rings.

I'm not sure what disappoints me more: that Owen left his ringer on or that his ringtone is *Wannabe* by The Spice Girls. (What the hell, man?) Everyone jumps. Owen yanks the phone out of his pocket. But he does it with such force that the phone comes out of his hand, and he's forced to juggle it. Kevin takes off running, not looking back. Owen corrals the phone and follows, but he trips and falls. I grab his arm and yank him to his feet, helping him run. (For a second, I'm reminded of when we won the three-legged race at the 4th of July celebrations.)

"Hey!" Evan shouts behind us, "Hey, what are you doing?"

Well, running is the obvious answer. Owen gets free of me, and we haul ass across the grounds and through a side gate leading to a huge gravel parking lot. We close in on Kevin, whose rental car is visible in the distance. I look back. No sign of anyone.

"They aren't coming after us," I say.

"Doesn't mean we need to stop," Owen says.

Or even slow down. Kevin gets the keys out of his pocket and into the lock cleanly. (Of course he does.) Owen jumps into the front seat, and I pile into the back. Kevin fishtails slightly as he charges out of the parking lot. I throw another look back.

"A clean getaway," I say.

"That was the only part that was clean," Kevin says.

I sit back in the seat and start breathing again. They should have left this to a professional. Or at least a spirited amateur.

***

We circle back so I can collect Owen's car, unnoticed. When I get back to the house, my brothers are still in Kevin's rented Pacifica, parked at the curb. I ditch Owen's car in front of the Seavers'. The street is dark and quiet, just like when I was a kid. I approach the Pacifica carefully. (I don't want one of my brothers to panic and attack me before realizing who I am.) Owen rolls down the window as I arrive. I lay a hand on the roof.

"What are you guys doing out here?" I ask.

"We don't want to go inside yet," Owen says, "Dad will probably ask us where we were."

"We'll tell him we went to Nick's and had a couple beers," I say.

Kevin's arm rests lazily on the steering wheel. "He'll know we haven't been drinking."

"In that case," I say, "maybe we should go to Nick's and have a couple beers."

Owen takes a nervous glance toward the house. "You want to get in the car? Mom or Dad might see you from the front window and they'll know we're home."

Great googly-moogly. They probably heard both cars pull up. But Kevin appears to be in Owen's corner. I slip into the backseat. Kevin looks like he's waiting for food at a drive thru. Owen remains still, a ball of tension. (He's always been tense but never a twitcher.) I stick my head into the front.

"This is ridiculous," I say, "We're three grown men in our thirties and we're afraid our dad is going to yell at us?" Kevin and Owen stare at me. "Yeah, I didn't believe it as I was saying it."

None of us quite knows what our next move should be. Kevin speaks to me over his shoulder.

"You get anything out of this?" he asks, "The stuff we overheard with Evan and Alice?"

This is a strange feeling. Kevin asking my opinion on something. Owen turns toward me as well. I guess I'm the resident expert on these things (though you'd be hard-pressed to know it by the performance tonight).

"Evan owes somebody money," I say, "He lied to me about the argument being over a car. This Berringer guy must be the one he owes. It sounds like Burt had money, and Evan was trying to get it."

Owen sits up, excited. "That gives Evan a motive for killing Burt."

"Not necessarily," I say, "If Burt had money that Evan needed, it gives him *less* motive. He needed Burt alive."

Kevin rests his arm on the seat. "Unless Burt wouldn't give him the money. Maybe he flies off the handle and does something stupid."

"I guess that's a possibility," I say, "It just doesn't make sense for Evan. You'd wind up with the same problem: owing a guy and having nothing to pay him with. And you'd have to cover up a murder on top of that."

Owen sneers. "Evan seem like the kind of guy who thinks things out?"

He's got me there. It's entirely possible Evan blew a gasket and only afterwards realized he created more of a mess for himself. But that's speculation, a point Kevin concedes.

"You'd need proof," he says.

"And I'm not sure how to get it." I say, "I *do* have one thing, though. Alice is tighter with Evan than she lets on. They don't talk like two people who've barely seen each other since high school. She knows about Evan's money problems, and they have a usual spot. There's more there than what she's been telling me."

"Seems you should ask her about that," Kevin says.

"Seems I should," I say, "And apparently, Eli is lying to me as well. He said he hadn't had anything to do with Burt in years. According to Alice, they're in business together."

"What business?" Owen asks.

"I don't know," I say, "But I can ask him."

There is nothing we can do for now. We sit there for a few more moments before finally deciding to head inside and face the music.

Dad is in the living room when we walk in. Normally, I'd expect to see him in his favorite chair, watching CNN or an infomercial for music he likes or a late movie (they still have those in Porter's Bay). Instead, he's wandering the living room, a slip of paper hovering just below his mouth. We stop.

"Everything okay?" I ask.

He stuffs the paper in his pocket. "It's fine."

Kevin steps toward Dad. "It doesn't look fine."

"It's nothing," Dad says, mildly irritated, "Why don't you boys go to bed?"

Owen comes around my other side. "What's going on, Dad?"

Dad tilts his head and squares us all with a look. It's the same look we'd get when we were kids and bothering him about something we wanted. It would let us know the conversation was over. This time, though, it doesn't work. Several long moments pass before Dad takes the note out of his pocket and hands it over to me.

It's another threatening note.

CHAPTER NINE

I was not a great student in high school. I've never been sure why, but I just wasn't. Concentrating in class, particularly if I wasn't interested in the class, seemed like a Herculean task. I was never on the verge of failing, but my grades were hardly reflective of my abilities and my intelligence; something my parents were quick to point out.

During my last semester in high school, I decided to show my parents up. Even though I was deep in the throes of senioritis, I lined up enough classes I liked to have a decent shot at getting straight A's. It wasn't easy, but I pulled it off. When my final report card arrived in the mail, I proudly walked up to my parents and laid my achievement before them. They scrutinized it, then my dad handed it back to me.

"Well done," he said, "Why couldn't you have done that all through high school?"

You have no idea how happy I was to get to college and keep all my report cards to myself. Then again, maybe you do.

I wonder if showing his kids various threatening letters gives my dad that same sinking feeling of handing over a substandard report card. While I'm not above engaging in schadenfreude, this thought doesn't give me any satisfaction. (Okay, maybe a little…) My brothers' faces go blank. I'm the one who has to handle this.

"How did you get it?" I ask.

"It was in the mailbox," Dad says, "Somebody must have put it in there tonight."

"How did you know to look?" I ask.

"The mail flag was up," Dad says, "I asked your mother if she was mailing something out and she said no. I took a look. That's when I found it."

I read the note. It says *The past is haunting you. Come clean. Before I do it for you.* I hand the note back to Dad.

"What does it mean?" I ask.

Dad looks over the note. "I don't know. I don't know what any of this is about."

Kevin jumps in. "Did Will and Eli get notes as well?"

"They did," Dad says, "I called them both right after I found this. Same situation."

Dad looks toward the stairs, probably hoping Mom hasn't come down without us noticing. Although, the four of us standing in a huddle won't allay any suspicions.

"Is there something about the past that we need to know?" I ask, "Burt's dead. The three of you are being threatened. Did something happen we don't know about?"

For a second, just a second, Dad looks like he's going to tell me something. But it fades. "I don't know if it has anything to do with Burt. Maybe he had something going. Maybe he used us to cover his tracks. I don't know."

I guess that's plausible. But Dad and his friends get so damn furtive when Taylor is brought up, I have to think it isn't some BS story Burt was spinning.

"I assume we're not letting Mom in on this?" I say.

"No," Dad says, "She'd just worry."

"What about the police?" Kevin asks, "If someone is threatening all of you—"

Dad's jaw tightens. "I'm not handing over the note. That's final." He starts toward the stairs then stops. "I would appreciate it if you all stayed out of this."

It's disturbing. I'm not going to lie. My dad is nervous, furtive and, dare I say, scared. Judging by the looks on Kevin's and Owen's faces, they feel the same way. Dad stalks up the stairs, leaving the three of us alone. Owen plunks down on the couch.

"What do you think?" he asks.

I sit on the arm of Dad's chair. "I'm going to talk with Eli and Will again. Maybe they can tell me something."

Owen debates this. "Maybe."

"I don't think they could tell you less," Kevin says.

We're all feeling the same thing. The most honest, straightforward, decent person we've ever known is acting like he's guilty of something. Maybe it's not what the police think it is, but it's something. We're just not sure what.

And not sure we want to find out.

***

"You said you worked on the yearbook?" Carol says, paging through it, "I thought you'd be in it more."

We're hanging out in my room before the day gets started. I'm at my desk, staring at my laptop while Carol sits on the bed, paging through my senior yearbook, completely ignorant of her status as only the second woman ever to hang out in my room.

"I was shockingly modest as a lad," I say, "I also knew my friends and family would give me grief if I had the nerve to plaster myself all over the yearbook. It was a self-preservation thing."

"That makes sense."

I'm listlessly trying to plot out my day. Alice and Evan were talking about money that Evan owed. That's worth a conversation with either or both of them. Eli claimed he hadn't seen Burt but was working with him in some capacity. That's worth another conversation. I need to put together a timeline for what Burt was doing the night he was killed. And, much as

190

I hate to think about it, I need to do some looking into Taylor, whether Dad likes it or not.

"Some of these senior pictures are hilarious," Carol says.

"If I had one piece of advice to give young dudes," I say, "it would be this: just because you can grow facial hair doesn't mean you should, especially for your senior picture. You don't want to be captured for posterity wearing Baby's First Mustache."

"You managed to avoid that."

"Because I couldn't grow a mustache at the time. Thank heaven for small favors."

Carol looks up from the book. "Baby's First Mustache. Didn't you write that in one of your columns?"

"I might have. They all run together, even for me." She flips a couple pages. "Here you are. The staff photo of *The Bay Breeze*."

A tingle goes up my neck. I try to ignore it. "I had a column. And I wrote some sports articles and other stuff."

"Why am I not surprised?"

The Taylor issue is still confounding. Where do I even start with that? Somebody other than my dad and his friends must know because threatening notes are being left. Who is that person and how do I track them down? All I can do is what I've been doing: bash around and hope I find something. It hasn't worked so far, but it's the only strategy I've got.

"Oh my God!" Carol says.

My sixth sense knows what she's found. And it fills me with dread. "What?"

Carol holds up the yearbook. "Cutest Couple: Joe Davis and Lisa Cleary."

"That was the case," I say, not looking at her, "I assure you I did not stuff the ballot box."

That's not going to put Carol off. "Who was Lisa Cleary?"

"My high school girlfriend."

"I could figure out that much. I've known you for five years and you've never mentioned her. Why is that?"

"You never asked."

I'm ducking the question and Carol knows it. She gives me a sidelong glance, waiting for me to comment. I don't.

"She's pretty," Carol says, "You guys really did make a cute couple."

I greet that in silence. I don't need to see the picture to bring it to my mind's eye. Lisa with her wall of dark hair barely contained by a ponytail, her wire-rim glasses, her intelligent blue eyes, and her prim smile. She wears a white long sleeve tee under a tan flannel shirt and sports a ratty pair of jeans. The photo was taken hastily. We were up against a deadline.

Besides, Lisa felt we should be photographed looking the way we looked in real life. She had a desire for truth and accuracy even then.

"Thank you." I spin around in the chair. "What brings you over this morning? More stuff with my idiot uncle?"

Carol closes the yearbook and sets it on the bed. "That's the deal. I followed him around yesterday."

"You're getting close to stalking, aren't you?"

"He's a public figure."

"Aren't those the people who usually get stalked?"

Carol gets up from the bed and walks over to the desk. She wants to keep the rest of the family from overhearing, even though they're well aware Gordie's an idiot.

"Your uncle met with somebody yesterday," Carol says, "It was on a dock in Greenville."

"You followed him up to Greenville?"

"It was where he was going. And Mike and Lars didn't need the rental car for a few hours. Anyway, I saw the guy Gordie met with. And I snapped a picture."

She shows me her phone. Gordie stands on a long dock, talking to a trim, well-styled guy in a polo shirt and slacks. If I didn't know better, I'd think Gordie was asking the guy for spare change. Come to think of it, I *don't* know better.

"Speaking of cute couples…"

Carol puts the phone in the pocket of her black slacks. "I did a little research. The guy is Vic Easton, the real estate developer who gave money to Gordie's campaign."

I grab the toy Batmobile from the shelf and roll it in my hands (helps me think). "Surprise, surprise."

"Exactly. They talked a while, then Gordie took off. I kept following him."

Geez. Gordie hasn't gotten this much attention from a woman in…well, ever. "And where did this journey take you?"

Carol's face wrinkles. "To a trailer park on the west end of town."

"Ah, la Maison de Gordie."

"Yeah. I couldn't follow him in there, so I parked and went in on foot. Gordie left a few minutes later. I was going to follow him again, but I thought it might be better to see his trailer. See what I could find there."

My eyebrows go up. "You broke into Gordie's trailer?"

"It wasn't like breaking into Fort Knox. Besides, after dating Mike for a year, I picked up a few things."

Jeez, I've been friends with Mike for seventeen years and never learned the art of picking a lock. Carol knocks boots with him for a year and suddenly, she's Black Widow. Maybe I need to re-examine my life choices. Then again, maybe I don't.

"You invaded Gordie's *sanctum sanctorum*," I say, "Even I haven't been there."

Carol shivers slightly. "It was everything it was cracked down to be. When I was a kid, I used to watch *Sesame Street* and imagine what Oscar the Grouch's garbage can looked like on the inside. Now, I don't have to imagine."

"Lucky you."

"It was the filthiest place I've ever seen and, again, I dated *Mike*. But it wasn't a waste of time. Take a look."

Carol holds the phone out and shows me a picture. It's a check from an organization called The Ice Dam. It's made out to Gordie for a little over a thousand dollars (a windfall in my uncle's world).

"What is the Ice Dam?" I ask.

"No idea," Carol says, "I'm going to check into it. But it was in the envelope Vic Easton gave Gordie. That's a start."

I set the Batmobile back on the shelf. "I'd love to help you, but I have enough on my plate right now."

"I get it," Carol says, "But I need to do something. Your uncle is still harassing Rajveer."

"The antique store guy?"

"That's right. Rajveer just a got a bill for back taxes the city claims he hasn't paid."

"Uh-oh."

"Yeah. It's hard to pay back taxes you weren't aware of in the first place. I don't know how Gordie thinks he can get away with this. But I'm not going to let him."

"Maybe I can talk to Gordie," I say, "Make him see reason."

"You think he's going to listen to you?"

"Does anybody? But it's worth a shot."

Our conversation is interrupted by my mom calling up the stairs, letting us know breakfast is ready. Flynn and Tucker, Kevin's daughters, peek in as they pass. As soon as they realize I've noticed them, they scurry toward the stairs. Carol returns the yearbook to the bookshelf.

"What else have you got going today?" she asks.

"I'll talk to a few people. See if I can figure out what Burt was up to the night he was killed. I might hook up with Andy and Sam. They were my best friends in high school."

"Do they live around here?"

"Andy does," I say, "I haven't run into him yet. Sam lives in Duluth. He couldn't get up here before today."

"I see," Carol says, "Going to spend the day with bros being dudes?"

"If you knew the bros and dudes involved, you'd realize how absurd that sounds."

"Have fun."

"You, too."

Carol puts a hand on my shoulder. I avoid eye contact with her. We're both sticking our noses into something others would rather we keep away from. The difference is: Carol wants to find the answers. I'm not sure I do.

***

I stop by Eli's apartment building before meeting Sam and Andy for lunch. The building itself is just off Lake Drive. It's squat and square, largely brick and about three stories high. Your typical place for the discerning citizen who prizes affordability. There's no security door to speak of. I flip open the glass door and find myself in a lobby with a tile floor, a few cheap watercolors on the wall and dirt at the edges. Before I can go anywhere, my cell phone rings. It's Mike. Against my better judgment, I answer. Mike, as usual, in the middle of a panic attack.

"I got problems," he says, as if his voice going up a few octaves didn't already indicate that, "Things with Julie are getting out of hand."

"What's going on?"

"I've been trying to break things off," he says, "Get her to see the light. Realize what a scumbag I am."

"You need someone to back you up on that?"

"No. And fuck you." He blows out a sigh. "But maybe I need to think about it. Nothing I'm trying is working."

"What are you trying?" I ask, with a due sense of trepidation.

Air rushes around as Mike paces on the other end. "I told her I have a criminal record. Been in and out of the joint most of my adult life."

"It's a shock you haven't."

"Piss off. It didn't work anyway. I also told her I've got five or six ex-wives out there. I don't even bother keeping track of them. I married them, cleaned out their bank accounts and moved on. I told her I've got more kids than I can count, and I've never met one of them. I told her I drink and do drugs. She didn't care about any of it. In fact, the drinking and drugs kind of excited her. I am completely fucked."

I sit on a bench near the front door. Mike and I have been best friends for years, but that doesn't mean I'm blind to his faults. Normally, he doesn't have to exaggerate to drive off a potential paramour. (Look no further than Carol as proof of that.) Thus, Julie's acceptance of the (barely) fake version of him is rather confusing.

"She's tenacious, I'll give her that," I say.

"I went completely the wrong direction," Mike says, "We talked about our lives. Her *real* life, in Julie's case. She's on the church council. She's on the PTA. She runs a daycare during the school year."

"Quite the goody-two-shoes."

"That's the problem. She's played it safe her entire life and now she wants a walk on the wild side. I accidently gave her everything she was looking for. I am completely screwed."

My head drops into my hand. This isn't the first time something like this has happened to Mike. This isn't the five hundredth time it's happened. I have an obligation to help him out, but right now I've got bigger fish to fry. (Huh. Come to think of it, it's Friday in small town Minnesota. There must be a fish fry someplace.)

"What are you going to do?" I ask, glancing at the clock on the wall.

"I don't know. But I have to figure out something. If Julie gets an attack of the guilts and confesses to her husband, my life expectancy drops to zero."

"And it's only at four to six months to begin with."

"Joe!"

I know. I shouldn't poke the Cocaine Bear, but it's just too damn much fun. "Look, can we put it on hold for now? Maybe we can come up with something later."

"I like that. We can do some brainstorming."

Except one rarely brain*storms* with Mike. Brain*farting* is more likely to occur. But he lets it go and I'm able to ring off. I get Eli's name off the register at the front. He lives on the second floor. I climb the bland staircase and look around. The hallway is covered in threadbare carpeting, and there are water stains on the ceiling. Eli's place is second on the right. I knock on the cheap pine door (bypassing the little brass knocker) and wait for a response. Nothing. Not even a hint of movement or stirring inside. I try again but get nada.

The door next to Eli's place opens. A woman steps out and scrutinizes me. She's anywhere between fifty and three hundred years old. She wears a floral print dress, and her gray hair is done up in one of those old lady perms that says, *No sex, no point in trying*. There's a vague smell of nicotine about her (I guess the *No Smoking* sign in the lobby is just a suggestion) and she carries a tumbler of iced tea (which may contain at least one product from Kentucky). The slash of a mouth above her jowls is set in an unfriendly manner.

"You looking for Eli?" she asks, a smoker's wheeze in her voice, "He ain't home."

"I kind of figured that."

She tilts her chin up slightly. "Who're you?"

"I'm Joe Davis."

I realize I have a very undistinguished name, not as catchy as Jonathan Creek or Richard Castle or Elvis Cole but certainly more believable. It's a mark of my father's notoriety that the woman says, "One of Henry Davis's boys?"

"Yeah, I'm the writer," I say.

The woman thinks about it. "Oh yeah, the smartass." Swell. "My name's Roberta. You a friend of Eli's?"

"No, he's more a friend of my dad's. I wanted to talk to him about something."

"Got anything to do with Burt Franklin getting killed?"

Telephone, telegraph, tell-a-townie…nice to see one of those communication forms is still in popular use. I can't help feeling Roberta's question is an invasion of privacy. (Says the guy standing outside the door of someone else's apartment.)

"I wanted to talk to him about it," I say.

Roberta leans against the doorway, sipping her "tea." "Y'know, Burt Franklin was around here that night."

Ah. Perhaps I was a little hasty in judging the nice alcoholic lady. I try to keep my excitement under wraps. "Really?" I say, "I assume you saw him?"

"He came to Eli's apartment," Roberta says, "They chatted here in the hall for a minute then they took off."

"Together?"

"Yep."

"What time was this?" I ask.

Roberta looks up as she thinks. "I'd say around eleven-thirty or so."

Interesting. Burt wasn't at Nick's after eleven-thirty or so. He was killed no later than one-fifteen. That gives me the parameters for a timeline. "Did you see Eli come back?" I ask.

"I did," Roberta says, "I can see and hear just about everyone coming and going. Apartments ain't that big and the walls ain't that thick."

"Was Burt with him when he came back?"

"No, he was alone."

"What time was this?" I ask.

Roberta's bleary eyes fall on me. "I thought you were a writer. You really a detective or something?"

"Closer to *or something*," I say, "I'm trying to help out my dad."

"Your dad's a good man," Roberta says, sipping her beverage. "It was a couple hours later. Probably one, one-thirty. Closer to one-thirty, I'd say."

Interesting. Eli is out with Burt for a couple hours. He doesn't come back until 1:30 am. That would mean he was out right around the time of the murder. He and Burt left together. Eli returned alone. (Sort of like a reverse Darmok and Jalad. Look it up if you don't get it.)

"Did you see how Eli was acting?" I ask, "Was he okay?"

"Didn't really get a look," Roberta says, "Heard him come up the stairs. I peeked out. He didn't see me before he went into his apartment." She takes another sip. "Now that I think about it, he seemed a little nervous."

"Nervous how?"

"Took him a few seconds to get the door open. Like he was fumbling with the lock. He usually doesn't do that. He's a pretty cool customer."

"That's what I've heard."

"That's the secret to life," Roberta says, "You gotta find a way to keep your equilibrium." She punctuates this with a slug of her beverage.

"Did you notice anything else unusual?"

"Can't say I did. Just Eli going out and coming back. I can't tell you much beyond that."

That's okay. I can ask Eli about it the next time I see him. "Thank you. I appreciate it."

She uses her beverage glass to wave off the compliment. "Your dad didn't kill Burt Franklin. I hope you figure out who did."

That makes two of us. Three if you count the writer *and* the detective. Four, if you include the smartass.

***

There are any number of eateries in Porter's Bay, but really, only one worth gathering at. One that brings back fond (and other) memories. I meet my friends Andy and Sam at The Hub Diner.

I met Andy Clark in kindergarten, and we were friends from then on. Back in the day, he was thin and dark-haired, with a big set of teeth and a goofy grin. He hasn't changed that much. He's added maybe a pound or two to his frame, his hair is flecked with gray, he wears glasses, and he flashes the goofy grin a little less often. But there's always been a maturity about him. He was one of those guys you knew would transition smoothly to adulthood. Sam Nelson was a later addition to the gang; his family having moved to town when we were in junior high. What he lacked in height, he made up for in personality. He had near-total recall of every decent comedy bit and standup routine from the dawn of *Saturday Night Live* to the present day. Sam's future was a little harder to predict. He could have been anything from a standup comedian to the cleverest drug mule in prison. He wound up being a dentist (so, somewhere in the middle). He's changed a bit, too. The live wire energy has been replaced by a calmer demeanor. His blonde hair has been clipped respectably short and he dresses more professionally (today, a white shirt with green stripes and tan slacks).

I grab a corner booth and wait for them. Sam strolls in like he's arrived in his living room. Andy, even though he still lives in Porter's Bay, looks like he's trying to get through life anonymously. I get up from the booth and we exchange the obligatory hugs.

"Welcome home," Andy says.

"Good to be welcomed," I say.

Sam claps me on the shoulder. "I guess the warrant has expired?"

"Yes," I say, "But the restraining order remains in place."

We slip into the booth and order a round of sodas. This is followed by spending some time catching up on what we've been doing. Andy works in sales for a local radio station. Sam's dental practice is growing. Andy is married and has a couple kids. Sam is, like me, still single, though not exactly living the life of a monk (unlike me for the last several months). This feels both familiar and strange. We spent a ton of time together in high school, and I've stayed in touch with both of them since high school. But this is the first time *all* of us have been together in seven years (since our tenth high school reunion). The conversation is pleasant, though we're only going to avoid the big news in town for so long.

"How are things with your dad?" Andy asks, fidgeting with a paper napkin.

"Still a free man," I say, "For now."

I update them on the investigation, such as it is, pausing only when the server arrives to deliver our sodas and take our lunch order. When I've finished, Andy and Sam are frowning.

"Beardsley was always kind of a Nazi," Sam says, leaning against the back of the booth.

"Ben Davenport's a decent guy, though," Andy says.

"But he answers to my idiot uncle in the mayor's office," I say, "And Gordie is completely okay with the investigation going forward. As long as it embarrasses my dad, Gordie's going to revel in it."

There is a sense of defeat among us. Sure, I can talk to Gordie, but when someone has that rare combination of ignorance and arrogance, what chance do you have of getting anywhere? Sam rubs the stubble on his chin.

"Evan's got money trouble?" he says, "I'm guessing it's gambling?"

Sam gives me his mischievous look of old. He knows something about Evan and gambling. And how the hell does Sam know about it?

"Maybe you need to fill me in," I say.

Sam looks around, making sure no one is listening in. "There's a floating card game. Guy named Berringer runs it. I've been there a few times. I'm a decent card player, but I realized pretty quick I was out of my element. And Berringer and his guys aren't the kind you want to owe money to."

Berringer. That was the guy Evan mentioned to Alice. "Evan owes him," I say.

"I know. I saw Evan there once," Sam says, "The man is lightspeed terrible. Plays loose and can't bluff to save his ass. Every time he goes in with a big bet, people know he's full of shit. When he has the short stack, he plays *more* aggressive and loses all his money. He's like the anti-Phil Ivey. If I had to guess, he's into Berringer for some serious money."

"Did Burt have anything to do with the game?" I ask.

"I don't think so," Sam says, "Burt was into practically everything else, but not cards."

I cock my head to one side. "What kind of stuff was Burt into?"

"What have you got?" Sam asks, "Loan sharking, drug dealing, fencing stolen shit, money laundering. Dude was like a low rent John Gotti."

Son of a bitch. That shouldn't surprise me. I didn't have a lot of acquaintance with Burt, but the general impression is that he was shady. (Of course, the fact that Sam knows that kind of stuff speaks to his own variety of shadiness. But he's a friend, so I'll give him a pass.)

"You think Evan owed money to Burt as well?" I ask.

"I'm sure he did," Sam says, "And I'm sure Burt would loan Evan the money. But the interest he'd charge would probably make a car salesman gag. Probably."

This makes sense. Evan has debts. He goes to Burt. What if Evan eventually gets so far into debt that Burt cuts him off? That at least gives them motive for meeting out in Bennett Park, away from prying eyes. But there's a problem.

"I can't prove it," I say, "Evan won't tell me, and I certainly can't ask Burt."

"Sorry, man," Sam says, "All I've got is scuttlebutt."

"I *do* appreciate the scuttling your butt has done so far," I tell him.

Andy straightens his glasses. "Burt wasn't completely into shady stuff. He had a real estate office."

Sam scoffs. "First, you're telling me real estate isn't a shady business. Second, I'll bet you anything Burt used it as a cover. You ever heard of him actually selling anything?"

We're interrupted by the arrival of our food. Chef's Salad for me, a burger for Sam, and a BLT for Andy. I do some thinking as I spread the blue cheese dressing on the salad. An idea is forming. Not a good one, but an idea.

"Where was Burt's office?" I ask.

"On First Avenue," Andy says, "Over a salon."

I use my fork to lightly toss my salad. "I wonder if there's anything in there."

Sam looks up from his burger. "Let's imagine it's his collection of rare tea cozies and leave it at that."

"I don't know," I say, "Maybe I should see for myself."

I can't believe I want to do this. Normally, it's Lars who recommends idiot behavior. It must be a sign of my desperation. Andy and Sam silently debate who is going to talk me out of this. Andy takes on the task.

"It's a terrible idea," Andy says, pushing aside his BLT, "You can't go around breaking and entering. What if you get caught?"

"I have some experience at entering," I say, "The breaking part is a little out of my lane."

"Not as hard as you think," Sam says.

Andy turns to Sam. "Don't encourage him."

"The man is desperate," Sam says, "Maybe we need to help him out."

"We?" Andy says, "Don't get me involved in this."

We go back to our food, letting the tension settle for a moment. I pick at the salad, giving my friends no indication I'm giving up on this idea. Sam keeps looking from one of us to the other, as if he can will some life into this idea. Andy sips his soda and gives us both a disapproving look.

"This is exactly the kind of stuff Lisa would get us into," he says, "You remember that?"

"I do," I say, a little tightness coming into my throat.

After a few seconds, Sam says, "It was fun, though. Can you remember the last time you had that kind of fun?"

Andy's face freezes. Then a grin spreads across it. "No, I can't."

"We gotta have Joe's back, right?" Sam says, putting a fist out. "Let's do it."

Andy looks around, maybe worried someone is eavesdropping. Finally, still smiling, he says, "This is insane. But I'm in."

Sam slaps the table and says, "Yes!" Andy puts his fist in, probably still not believing he's in on this. I smile as I add my fist to the group. Lisa would be proud of us.

Almost nobody else would, but Lisa would.

CHAPTER TEN

Part of the frustration of being at odds with a parent—or anyone from an older generation—is the awareness that you lack credibility. You may be knowledgeable, perhaps even an expert in your field. But you are still little more than a child in their eyes.

It's a power dynamic at least one of you has gotten used to. When even the most benign parent has been in a position of leadership for so many years, it's difficult to give that up. They get hard-wired into thinking they are the last word on everything; that they must *know more. And while children are always anxious to break away from their parents on some level and establish their own identity, there's always a bit of insecurity there. The loud voice shouting, "Mom and/or Dad is an idiot!" constantly grapples with the small voice whispering, "But what if they're right?"*

On top of that, it's a little difficult to establish credibility with someone who has pictures of you on the potty. And is willing to show them to anyone who asks. Even Batman would have a hard time coming back from that. (Probably best that things turned out the way they did for him.)

Against my better judgment, I've decided it's time to talk to my uncle Gordie. Hopefully, he'll not only stop harassing Carol's friend, he'll also let Chief Davenport put a muzzle on Officer Beardsley. It's almost certainly a fool's errand, but I feel obligated to try.

The mayor's office is on the top floor of City Hall. An elevator, which looks like it was installed when the building was first constructed back in the Twenties and has been barely maintained since, takes me up there. Many hours later (or so it feels), I step off and fight the temptation to kiss the floor.

An oak door with a brass handle and a stained-glass window reading *Office of the Mayor* takes me into the spacious outer office. Like the rest of the building, there is a marble floor, wood paneling and a high ceiling. The receptionist is an older woman, heavyset, with salt and pepper hair pulled into a bun. She wears a gray suitcoat over a white blouse. She gives me a sardonic look over the top of her glasses. The expression on her jowly face says *What fresh hell is this?*

"Can I help you?" she says, in a surprisingly deep voice.

"I would like to see the mayor," I say, "I'm sorry I don't have an appointment—"

The receptionist clearly thinks that's a hoot. "Nobody ever has an appointment. Finding Hizzoner in the office is like hitting a moving target. I should congratulate you."

Ah-ha. It seems morale is not high in the mayor's office. I appreciate the receptionist's sentiment, but I heard from Carol (who's been tracking Gordie) that he was in the office, or at least in the building. I knew my chances of catching him were good (and that might be the only good thing about this conversation).

"Is it alright if I go in?" I ask.

"Feel free," the receptionist says, turning back to the computer, "He's got somebody in there, but I don't think they're talking about anything important. As if he *ever* talks about anything important."

I like the receptionist, for her anti-Gordie sentiment if nothing else. I open the door to the mayor's office, knocking as I do. A voice says, "Come in." But the voice isn't Gordie's.

The office is large, and the mayor's desk seems impossibly far away. I find myself staring at the ceiling. A series of windows provide a peek at Howard Street, about a block away. An American flag sits in one corner and a photo portrait of Theo Humphrey, the town's first mayor, is on the wall next to it. Gordie is behind the oak desk, wearing his finest white Harley Davidson t-shirt (stained yellow at the armpits). He looks at me with the same slack-jaw and dull eyes I've seen since I was a kid. Two things make this scene hard to reconcile. One is seeing my goofy uncle in the relative splendor of the mayor's office (like watching a mule wander the Louvre). And the other is the sight of Lars at the mayor's elbow.

Naturally, it's Lars who is the first to register my presence. He straightens the suitcoat he wears over his blue bowling shirt and glides around the desk. "Joseph B. Davis, my very good friend. Come to see the mayor, have you?"

"I have," I say, "Hope I'm not interrupting anything important." Although I'm certain I'm not.

Lars steps back and folds his hands in front of him, allowing Gordie to take center stage. Gordie squints slightly and his mouth twists into a grimace. It's what happens when you have to concentrate a sluggish mind.

"Hi Joe," Gordie says, his voice coming from somewhere deep in his chest, always leaving me with the feeling it's coming from the next room, "What do you need?"

"A couple of things," I say, "Okay if I sit down?" Gordie gestures vaguely toward the club chairs in front of the desk. Turns out the chair puts me on a level slightly below Gordie. I'm sure it's a trick that predates my uncle. Gordie wouldn't be clever enough to come up with it. "First, I wanted to talk to you about Rajveer," I say, "He owns an antique store on First Avenue."

"I know who he is," Gordie says, annoyed.

"Seems like the city has suddenly cracked down on him," I say, "I couldn't help noticing it happened after he chatted with my friend Carol."

Gordie tosses aside some paperwork. "Sounds like a coincidence."

"Anything you can do to get this coincidence to stop?"

"Hey, your friend doesn't have anything to do with it," Gordie says, "This Rajveer has been skating along for a while. Ignoring the city codes and regulations. I shouldn't be surprised. He isn't even from here."

I cock my head to one side. "What do you mean?"

"The guy's from someplace in Wisconsin," Gordie tells me, "Or so he says. The only reason he came here was to open a business."

"Okay," I say, drawing the word out slightly, "I've gotten the impression you're fairly pro-business. What's wrong with that?"

"I'm pro-Porter's Bay," Gordie says, using a line I'm sure he used during his campaign, "We don't need people from out of town coming in and driving out our local businesses."

"Wait a minute," I say, "You're the same guy who wants to let big box stores come in here. What do you think *that* is going to do to local businesses?"

"It's going to make this town prosperous," Gordie says, obviously repeating talking points he's been given, "It will be the best thing to ever happen to Porter's Bay."

"Yes, but if you're so concerned about local businesses—"

"Best thing ever," Gordie says, waving any further attempts at conversation.

I slump back in the chair. "You're not going to leave Rajveer alone, are you?"

"Hey, if he walks the straight and narrow, he's got nothing to worry about from me," Gordie says, "But if he thinks he's above the law, I can't help him."

"Uh-huh," I say, "I'm guessing you're the only one who's above the law?"

Gordie gives me a faux modest look. "Well, I *am* the mayor." Swell. Just what I was hoping for. Dealing with an off-brand Richard Nixon. Before I can think up a counter argument, Gordie says, "Your friend Carol is really concerned about this guy?"

"She is," I say.

"Maybe I can talk to her about it," Gordie says, stroking his mustache, "Maybe at Nick's one of these nights?"

Ick. I don't know what I find more distasteful: Gordie thinking he can successfully woo Carol by offering to stop abusing his authority or that I would act as a pimp for the whole sordid enterprise. I'm not getting anywhere pleading Rajeev's case. I'll let Carol worry about that.

"You'll have to ask her," I say, washing my hands of the whole thing, "Meantime, there's something else I wanted to talk to you about."

Gordie lets out a sigh and turns to Lars. "Do I have anything going right now?"

Lars opens a leather-bound folder and takes out a slip of paper. The side facing me is completely blank. Lars flips over the paper. The other side is blank as well. Lars slips the paper back into the folder.

"I think we can fit him in," Lars says.

Gordie turns to me again. "Okay, what have you got?"

"Any chance you can get Cliff Beardsley to lay off the investigation into my dad?" I ask, "He doesn't have anything, and Chief Davenport would like to hand it off to someone else."

"No can do," Gordie says, "This is a local murder, and it should be handled by local cops. I trust our police department."

"If you trust them so much, why don't let Chief Davenport decide who handles the investigation?"

"Because I'm the mayor," Gordie says.

I foolishly wait a few seconds for him to expound on that. Then I realize he's not going to. His being the mayor is the end of every single discussion. It's a Get-Out-of-Jail-Free card deflecting all logic and consistency. I'm not going to get anywhere with him, and I was an idiot to even try. I stand up from the chair.

"I'll let you get on with your day," I tell him.

Gordie offers a handshake, but I turn away and pretend I didn't notice. As I start toward the door, Lars glides up next to me.

"I'll walk you out," he says.

He leads the way into the outer office. The secretary sees Lars and looks away. Lars pauses at her desk.

"Claudia, hold all my calls," Lars says.

"Hold 'em up your ass," Claudia says, not looking up from the computer, "And close the damn door on your way out!"

Once we're in the hallway, Lars jerks a thumb toward the office. "She's a good woman. Very spirited."

"I'm sure." If she's working for Gordie, she probably needs spirits to get through the day.

As we walk down the hall, Lars greets City Hall staffers, none of whom return the greeting. We stop at the elevators.

"I was wondering if you could help me out with something," Lars says.

"You need to smear some of Gordie's political opponents?"

"No! Well, not yet. Let's keep everything on the table. No, I was wondering about the gangster tour."

"You're still going to do that?" I ask.

"Absolutely. I just got permission from the city."

"Uh-huh. Did Gordie know what he was signing when you slipped it under his nose?"

"I'm not entirely sure," Lars says, "He's a little preoccupied with putting the screws to Carol's friend. And with Carol's caboose. His words, not mine."

No doubt. "How am I supposed to help you with this gangster tour?"

"I'm struggling with the script. As you may know, I'm more a big picture sort. Scripts require a certain attention to detail."

"So I've heard."

"I was hoping you could help me with a few of the entries. I can provide you with the facts. I just need someone to put it into a narrative."

I scratch the back of my head. "I don't know. I've got a lot on my plate right now."

"It doesn't have to be all that time consuming. Just a paragraph or two for each entry. I bet you could knock them out in an hour."

He's got me there. I've been known to knock out a whole column in an hour, if sufficiently inspired. What I lack in talent, I make up for in speed. My concern, though, relates to the kind of "facts" Lars wishes me to craft into a narrative. I press the button for the elevator.

"What entries are you talking about?" I ask.

"The B-and-B, obviously," Lars says, "That's going to be the centerpiece. And did you know about the loot in the basement of the Androy Hotel?"

"No, I didn't."

"I understand there is a cache of merchandise: jewels, money, gold bars, what have you. It's in a secret vault in the basement. Nobody has accessed it since the Prohibition days."

I cock my head to one side. "If it's a secret vault, how does anybody know about it?"

"I have my sources."

"Meaning you made the whole damn thing up?"

"I cannot reveal my sources," Lars says, putting a finger to his lips.

Oy vey. When is that elevator going to get here? "Lars, I don't know if I can do this—"

Lars plows forth. "And did you know the conservatory at Bennett Park is haunted?"

"I…what? No, I've never heard that. What does that have to do with gangsters?"

"Maybe nothing. Maybe everything. But I'd like to put the story on the tour."

"How do you know it's haunted?" I ask, "What proof do you have?"

"I hear things."

My shoulders sag. "This is more of that *sources* crap, isn't it?"

"See it how you will," Lars says, "But I want to make sure my customers are getting the full Porter's Bay experience."

"If you'll pardon me, it sounds like you're making up a lot of sensationalist crap to make a quick buck."

"It's the American Way."

The elevator arrives and I waste no time climbing in. "I'll think about it," I say.

"Don't take too long," Lars says, "I've got a test tour soon and I'll need the material."

The elevator doors close. Thank the gods. In spite of everything, Lars is still a friend. It would give me no joy to tell him I want absolutely no part of this horseshit. Well, it wouldn't give me *a lot* of joy.

The elevator has gone down only two floors when it stops to pick somebody up. Officer Beardsley gets on. I stiffen up. He hooks a thumb into his strained belt and hits the button for the lobby. He looks at me out of the corner of his eye.

"You got business here?" he asks, trying (and largely failing) to drop his voice an octave.

"Just talking with my uncle," I say.

"About what?"

"The usual stuff: macrame, rodeo, the novels of Balzac."

He turns toward me. "You're trying to interfere with my investigation?"

I guess there is no point in trying to keep this conversation friendly (not that I was doing a hell of a lot of work that direction). I face off with Beardsley. (I'm still taller than he is, no matter how straight he stands. That's got to piss him off.)

"I'm trying to keep my dad from getting railroaded by a cop with more ambition than brains," I say.

His mouth tightens. "I should kick your ass right here."

"That would be great. They teach you about assault in cop shop?"

"Who's going to care? The mayor's got my back."

"And I've got a column. And I will broadcast to every media outlet I can find that a Porter's Bay cop has a grudge against my family. The pictures of my assault are proof."

Beardsley's jaw works, as if he wished he had a piece of gum. When he was younger, his face had an open, good-natured quality that was undercut by a meanness in his eyes. With age, only the meanness remains. He turns toward the door and puts his hands in his pockets.

"Your dad is guilty," he says, "I'm going to prove it."

"How's that working out so far?"

A superior look comes over Beardsley's face. "You know who Cully Brown is?"

There's something disarming in his attitude. I've never liked people knowing things I don't. (Although, big picture, that covers *a lot* of people.) I particularly don't like dangerous people knowing things I don't.

"No," I say, "Who or what is Cully Brown?"

Beardsley greets that with a smirk. "You may want to ask your dad about it." The elevator doors open. He takes a step then looks back at me. "Your old man isn't who you think he is. You better accept that. And stay the hell away from my investigation."

Beardsley walks across the lobby of City Hall. I stumble out of the elevator. The sunlight creates a glare on the marble floor. Cully Brown. I had never heard that name until ten seconds ago. And yet, Beardsley thinks it's the key to taking down my father. I *will* ask Dad about that.

The question is: will he tell me anything?

***

After the pleasantness at City Hall, I decide to go for a walk. I stroll over to Howard Street. After a few blocks, I cut over and follow the trolley tracks. I'm approaching the depot that marks the Historical Society's home when I see someone sitting on the bench out front. It's Dad's friend Will. Huh. This might be worth a stop.

223

I'm careful as I approach, not wanting to startle Will. He doesn't notice me until I'm on the platform. It takes him only a second to recognize me.

"Joe!" he says, "Joe, right?"

"That's me," I tell him, "Mind if I join you?"

Will scoots over. "Have a seat."

I plunk down next to him on the bench. The view is nice. Everything about the old depot has been refurbished and well-maintained. A neighborhood peeps through bushes on the other side of the tracks. We're quiet for several moments, enjoying the weather.

"I suppose you heard about the notes," Will says.

"I did. Dad said you and Eli got them as well."

"That's the case."

"Any idea who's doing this? Or why?"

"No and no," Will says, "Somebody wants to dredge up the past, I can tell you that much. Otherwise, I don't know."

"What do they want to dredge up?" I ask.

Will turns to the trolley tracks. "I can't tell you that."

"Can't or won't?" I ask.

I'm pushing it. But I'm tired of Dad and his friends doing a Deaf, Dumb, and Blind routine in the face of the increasingly obvious fact they're covering something up. If someone is threatening them, I can't help—no one can—until I know what's going on. Will's face gets cold.

"Maybe you need to let that go," he says.

Now I'm more than a little irritated. I'm a thirty-five-year-old man. What exactly do people think they have to protect me from? Once the irritation passes, I realize Will has actually given me a decent scoop. Trying to warn me away from this is a different story than pretending he doesn't know anything. He's tacitly confessed there *is* something to know, and he doesn't want me to find out what it is.

"Does it have something to do with Cully Brown?" I ask.

Will's face flushes. "Where did you hear that?"

"From Officer Beardsley. Apparently, he knows something. Has he talked to you?"

"No," Will says, his mouth tight.

Sadly, it doesn't appear Will is going to expound on that. I keep my focus on him, as if I'm giving him the third degree (or the closest a weenie like me can come).

"Who is Cully Brown?" I ask.

"Nobody you'd know," Will says.

"Of course not. That's why I'm asking."

Will laces his fingers together and tightens them as if he's going to crack his knuckles. "Cully Brown is a name out of the past. It doesn't mean anything, and it doesn't matter."

"I think it does matter," I say, "Burt Franklin is dead, and the police are looking at my dad. For the sake of saving him, I'd like to know who Cully Brown is."

Will gets up from the bench and walks down the platform, as if trying to walk out of this conversation. I follow him. Will is burly and elderly, so it doesn't require much effort. He starts mumbling. Maybe to himself, maybe to me.

"Goddamn Burt," he says, "Couldn't leave well enough alone. Couldn't let it fucking go. Had to spill it like something broke in the shopping bag. Had to screw it up for all of us. Same damn thing he's always done."

"What did he screw up?" I ask.

"That man thought of himself and himself only." Will stops, his face flushed. "Fuck Burt Franklin! You hear me? Fuck him! I'm glad he's dead!"

Will suddenly lurches to one side. He throws an arm out to steady himself, but he's too far from the wall. I grab him around the chest and manage to slow his descent. We wind up sprawled on the platform. I get out from under Will and cradle his head. His eyes are glassy, and it doesn't look like anyone is home. His hair is damp from sweat. He's still breathing, so that's a good thing.

"Will? Will, are you okay?"

His head lolls to one side, but he doesn't lose consciousness. I fish my phone out of my pocket and dial 9-1-1. I hope they get here quickly.

So much for a peaceful afternoon walk.

CHAPTER ELEVEN

I'm thoroughly convinced that if not for my mom's nagging, my father's only two visits to a doctor would have been birth and being pronounced dead on arrival. He associates medical visits with reminders of his own mortality.

I've known others in the same boat. They hate any situation in which their own mortality becomes more vivid. They watch a gathering of friends at a funeral and wonder what it's going to look like when their own day comes. They look around a hospital room and wonder, "Is something like this going to be the last thing I ever see?" Some refuse to do any planning for their funerals because it makes them realize the manner in which they will be attending such an event.

My father is not the only one who hates seeing doctors, hospitals or funerals. I don't care much for them, either. But sometimes, you have to bite the bullet (hopefully figuratively rather than literally).

Will doesn't lose consciousness at any point. By the time the EMTs arrive, he's regained his faculties and even tries to beg off going to the hospital. But his protests are feeble and the EMTs insist he get checked out. I ride with Will in the ambulance. He asks me to call Alice and gives me her number. I do so as soon as we arrive in the emergency room. She sounds more pissed than upset and hangs up without saying goodbye.

The Porter's Bay Hospital is a five-story building just off Lake Drive. It was built when I was a teenager, taking over for the venerable building that hosted me when I was in second grade and suffered a bout of pneumonia. The emergency room is on the first floor. Everything is, as one would expect, antiseptic: beige walls and floors, the vague smell of linen. None of the staff seems to notice the patients or visitors. The EMTs wheel Will back while I give the attending nurse what information I can. I take a seat in the lobby and call my dad. He says he and Mom will be right down.

I'm trying (and failing) to fight off a serious attack of guilt. There was Will, sitting alone and enjoying a beautiful afternoon, and I come along and badger him into a collapse. I'd like to think I couldn't possibly feel worse than I do right now, but I'm sure Alice will give it the old college try. I'm relieved when my parents beat her to the hospital.

"What happened?" Dad says, by way of greeting.

I give him the whole story. I know he's not going to be happy, what with the stuff about Cully Brown and the way I tried to pry answers out of Will. Dad's face is placid as I tell the story. It's the same look he'd get when I would explain why Owen and I spraypainted cartoon characters on the side of the garage or why me and my friends felt the need to huck a slush ball at Mrs. Walker's car or why Drew Grahek's pants were at our house, but Drew was not. It's him processing the crime before lowering the boom. The literal calm before the storm. I try to remind myself that Dad no longer has any jurisdiction over sending me to my room or grounding me. It doesn't do much good. Mom remains at Dad's elbow in case he *does* lower the boom. When I finish, Dad takes a breath through his nose.

"Did he talk to you about Cully Brown?" he asks.

"No," I say, "He just told me I should stay away from this." Dad starts to step around me. I put a hand on his arm, gently stopping him. "Who is Cully Brown?" I ask.

Dad frees his arm. "Will was right. You should stay away from this. I'm going to see how he's doing."

He heads over to the nurse's station before Mom or I can say anything. I turn to my mom.

"Do you know anything about Cully Brown?" I ask.

Mom digs through her purse, looking for God knows what (lipstick, gum, the wreck of the Santa Maria). "No, I don't," she says, "I've never heard that name."

She gives me her normal open face, dashed with a touch of confusion and panic. My inclination is, as always, to believe her. But then, everything seems turned completely upside down at the moment. I don't know what to believe.

Fortunately (if that's the word I'm looking for), our family drama is replaced by another family drama. Alice comes through the door of the emergency room and blows past me and Mom like we aren't there. Her face is tight. She approaches the nurse's station and takes over the conversation with the nurse, essentially elbowing my dad out of the way. The nurse speaks to both of them, and they step away from the station. Alice accompanies Dad to the waiting area.

"Will's resting," Dad says, "He's going to be fine, but we should let him take it easy."

Mom puts a hand on Dad's shoulder and guides him to a chair. Alice looks around, obviously not wanting to join us. I step toward her.

"You got a minute to talk?" I ask.

Alice shoots me a look. "About what?"

"Life, the universe and everything. But since we don't have time for that, maybe about what's going on with your dad. And mine."

"I don't know what—"

I hold up a hand, stopping her. "Alice, with all due respect, cut the shit. I'm beyond tired of people telling me they don't know anything about something when they clearly do."

Alice glares at me (which does nothing to calm me down). Finally, she starts toward an adjacent hallway. I follow her. Dad watches us go. A few steps down the hall, Alice stops and folds her arms.

"What do you want to know?" she asks.

"Your dad got a threatening note," I say, "Two of them, in fact."

"That's right," Alice says.

"Any idea who did it?" I ask.

"No. We talked to my dad's neighbors, but nobody saw anything."

"Everyone is deaf, dumb and blind."

Alice rolls her eyes. "Whatever."

Weird. I'm maybe four years older than Alice and yet I feel like an old man talking to a sullen teenager. I decide to change topics with the young whippersnapper.

"What's going on with you and Evan Erickson?" I ask.

Alice stiffens up but doesn't look panicked. "Nothing is going on."

"What about the money he owes Berringer?"

Several things cross Alice's face. First panic then confusion then anger. Then we go back to sullen. She drops her arms and pushes off from the wall, getting up in my grill.

"That was you, wasn't it?" she says, "At the fairgrounds. You and some other guys."

"My brothers."

Why not come clean? We didn't commit a crime. It wasn't exactly moral, but when have I ever let that stop me? Besides, it's fun to throw my brothers under the bus every now and again.

"I can't believe you did that," Alice says.

"I'm trying to protect my dad," I say, "I think you can understand that."

That deflates some of Alice's self-righteous anger. "Hope you enjoyed it."

I ignore the little jab. "Evan has gambling debts. Burt wasn't going to help him out."

"Not for free. Burt wanted a favor in exchange. Evan wouldn't do it."

"What was the favor?" I ask.

"Evan wouldn't tell me."

Alice says it simply and without any furtive quality, leading me to believe she's telling the truth.

"Why would Evan ask you?" I ask, "He's got a girlfriend. He's got parents. Hell, his girlfriend's parents must have a little money. Why would he come to you?"

Alice chews her lip. "I like Evan, okay? It just…never worked out. He's bad news. I found that out in high school and nothing since has changed my mind."

"But you still care about him."

"I do." Then she shrugs. "But so what?"

Something about that hits me. I've been in that boat, though for totally different reasons. You love somebody but circumstances render that moot. Maybe it wouldn't hit me that way in other places but being in Porter's Bay makes it vivid.

"You met with Evan at the bar on the night of the murder," I say, "And you talked to Burt while you were there. What else did you do that night?"

Alice debates answering. Resignation comes over her face. She realizes I'm just going to keep badgering her—now or at some unspecified time in the future—until I get answers. Best to give me what I want. (It's not unlike me badgering my parents for a candy bar at the checkout counter when I was a kid. Nice to know I've come so far.)

"I picked my dad up at the Buffalo Lodge," Alice says, "If you haven't figured it out, he shouldn't be driving with the attacks of lightheadedness. I brought him back to his house. I went to Nick's, talked to Evan and Burt, and then I went home. That was it."

That's a sort of alibi. The part about bringing Will home is really Will's alibi. I already knew Alice was at Nick's. I'm not sure anyone saw her coming home. Maybe I can check that later. Meantime, I've bothered Alice enough.

"I hope your dad's going to be okay," I say.

Alice speaks into her shirt. "He'll be fine. Today, anyway." She pushes off from the wall. "I have to go."

She stalks past me and over to the emergency room desk. After a brief conversation with the attending nurse, Alice is directed through the doors. I stroll back into the waiting area. Mom has found herself a cup of coffee. (Great. She can try out possibly the only coffee in the world worse than hers.) I drop into a seat next to my dad.

"You and Alice have a nice chat?" he asks.

"We had a chat," I say.

Mom reaches past Dad and puts a hand on my knee. "You have to go easy on her, Joe. Her dad is sick."

"It's not good, this getting lightheaded," I say, "You think it's a heart thing?"

Mom and Dad exchange a look. It's what they do when trying to decide whether to tell me something. Mom removes the hand from my knee and Dad turns to me.

"Will has cancer," he says.

A thrill of horror goes through me. I haven't known him long, but Will is one of these people so jovial, so filled with life, you can't think of that life being in danger.

"Cancer?" is all I can think to say.

"Pancreatic cancer," Dad says, "There is…there's never a good outlook there."

Holy shit. I don't want to make this about me, but now I'm thinking of all the blundering things I said to Alice. Questioning her about Evan, her whereabouts the night Burt was killed, what her dad was doing, what have you. All the while, she's worried about her father having cancer. Nice work there, Joe.

"Wow," I say.

"They're doing everything they can," Dad says, "but Will has accepted it's terminal. Do me a favor and keep it to yourself. Will doesn't want it getting out."

"I get it," I say, "I'm sorry."

Dad lays a hand on my forearm and gives it a squeeze. "Will is a good man. He deserves better than what he's gotten. Maybe Burt was right about me. Maybe I'm not the man everyone makes me out to be." His voice gets small. "Maybe I'm not the man *I* make me out to be." I open my mouth to say something, but Dad gets up and says to my mom, "I'm going to check with the nurse. Maybe they'll let me back there."

Dad walks over to the nurse's station to plead his case. Mom and I watch him go.

"Is Dad all right?" I ask.

"He'll be fine."

"You really believe that?"

She takes a deep breath through her nose. "I'd like to."

Mom has never been able to lie to me. Frankly, sometimes I wish she would.

***

I remember binging the old *Mission: Impossible* series one summer and being entranced by it. That ability to coolly plan out an infiltration was always my favorite thing. I wondered if I would ever be able to do a thing like that. I wish someone had told me that any infiltration I ever plan would look more like *The Great Muppet Caper*. ("Peanut butter?" "Check.")

"Do you know any cops?" Sam asks Andy, "Just in case this thing goes tits up?"

Andy frowns (and he didn't exactly look exuberant before). "No one who would get us out of a B-and-E."

"Huh," Sam says, "That's sub-optimal."

Sub-optimal would be a good way to describe this whole trip. We're in Sam's hotel room at the Kahler. The room is clean but cramped, offering a lovely view of the parking lot. (You'd think a thriving dental practice would afford him a better room.) Still, this is the one place we can gather without drawing any awkward questions. And if we're going to do a break-in, I thought it best to bring along an expert in the field.

"Okay, so what does this place look like?" Mike asks, sitting on the dresser.

It's a surreal moment. Best friends from childhood, meet best friend from adulthood. Worlds are colliding. Still, even though this is the first time they've met, Mike fits right in with Andy and Sam. *I'm* the only one who is weirded out.

Andy paces toward Mike. "It's just a little office on top of a storefront."

"Accessible by the backstairs?" Mike asks.

"They're right off the alley," Andy says.

"Any residential around there?" Mike asks, "Houses or apartment buildings?"

"Houses," Sam says, "But there's a big fence running along the alley. Nobody really gets a clear look at the building."

"That's good," Mike says, chewing a corner of his goatee, "Did you see the door? What are we dealing with?"

"Just a standard wooden door," Sam says, "And your basic keyed knob. But there's a deadbolt as well."

"How are you going to pick 'em?" Mike asks.

Sam holds up his tools. "Two bobby pins. It's a simple barrel and pins lock. Shouldn't take more than a minute."

"You do this sort of thing a lot?" Mike asks.

"I've done it," Sam says.

"Excellent," Mike says.

Mike and Sam exchange a fist bump and the weirdness overcomes me again. But as I said, Mike is an expert in the field. When we were in college, he had a sideline business as a cat burglar. He wasn't exactly Public Enemy Number One. He only did it occasionally, only took small ticket items and only did it if he was broke and couldn't hit up his parents for money. He claims he hasn't done it in years, and I want to believe him. But I've had need of his skills on recent occasions, and he hasn't exactly looked…rusty. But he's given Sam his stamp of approval and that's good enough for now.

"I hope a cop doesn't come down the alley while we're in there," Andy says.

"What's the window situation?" Mike asks.

"A couple picture windows in the front," Sam says, "Just a small one in the back."

Mike flips a hand. "Keep the blinds drawn and use the flashlight on your phone. Nobody will see a thing. Who's your wheel man?"

"Joe is," Andy says.

Mike winces. He turns to Sam and Andy. "Either of you two good behind the wheel?"

"I'm not," Sam says.

"I usually do the speed limit," Andy says, "I'm told that's bad in this case."

"It's not great," Mike says. He flicks a look toward me. "You sure you want Joe handling this? No offense, but when it comes to driving, he's best left to driving Miss Daisy."

"Yeah, why would I be offended by that?" I say.

Sam waves off Mike's concerns. "If we do this thing right, we'll get in and out of there without needing a wheel man."

"I'd love to believe that," Mike says, "But Joe and I have done a few of these break-ins. How many have gone completely right, Joe?"

"Offhand?" I say, "None."

"See what I mean?" Mike says, "It never hurts to have a backup plan. Especially when you've got the albatross here with you." He holds up a hand. "No offense."

"Again…" I say.

Sam gets up from the edge of the bed. "Are you a good driver, Mike? You want to come along on this?"

"I don't think so," Mike says, "I appreciate the offer, but I've got stuff going on tonight. Besides, when it comes to one of these jobs, it definitely isn't the more, the merrier."

"Understood," Sam says, offering a handshake, "Appreciate your help."

Mike accepts it. "Good luck to you." He shakes Andy's hand then turns to me. "You got a minute?"

"Just about that," I say.

We step into the hallway. Mike's room is two floors up, so we can chat on the walk to the elevator. He looks back at the room as we go.

"They seem like nice guys," he says, "You sure they're cut out for this?"

"They'll be fine," I say, "We had a few adventures together. Back in the day."

"You never told me that."

"I have a life outside of you, Mike." We enter the empty elevator lobby. "What did you want to talk about?"

"Julie," he says, (and I should have known that), "I'm getting deeper into this thing."

"What now?"

Mike looks around, as if someone might possibly be interested in eavesdropping on this nonsense. "I've decided to come clean with her. Tell her everything. I'm not a criminal. I'm not a walk on the wild side. I'm just a dink who's between temp jobs and has no prospects. I live in fear of my mother and father. I have a *No Farting* poster in my apartment. My friends think I'm a laughingstock." He pauses. "Okay, I was hoping you'd correct me on that last one. All right, my friends *do* think I'm a laughingstock. And I've never stolen anything more expensive than a used smartphone. I've been lying to her this whole time."

Wow. Mike telling the truth. I guess they're right. Only Nixon can go to China. "Have you told her any of this yet?"

He shakes his head, "I'm meeting her in a little while, in my room."

"Good luck to you, son."

"You, too. I get the feeling we're going to need it."

Ain't that the damn truth?

***

A thing I forget about living in a small town: they get *really* quiet after dark. It's not as if they die out completely. Anyone who has been around a small town bar at closing time will know that. But the noise you find in the city is absent in a small town. No traffic, no hum of industrial machinery, no people shouting from house to house, no public transit. It's not an ideal situation for skulking and breaking in.

We're on a side street, near the alley that runs behind Burt Franklin's office. Andy's Chevy Cruze was volunteered for this mission because it's a local vehicle and won't arouse suspicion. (That line of thinking is probably bollocks, but we're going with it.) The atmosphere in the car is tense. Sam and Andy haven't done this kind of thing in years, and they were following Lisa's lead then. This time, we're on our own.

Andy chews his fingernails. "When do we do this?"

I look around. "No one has gone in the alley or passed by in a while. All the lights are off in the other businesses. I think we can do this any time we want."

Nobody in the car makes a move. You can literally hear crickets chirping. Andy asks, "Is it that time now?"

I let out a sigh. "I guess it is."

The three of us climb out of the car, carefully closing our doors behind us. (Master criminals, all of us.) There's a wind off the lake, and it's getting cool. We move into the alley, our footsteps crunching slightly on some scattered gravel. There's a tightness in my chest and I'm getting short of breath. (Joe, try not to stroke out right here.) We disappear into the shadows as we get close to the building. Andy's head is on a swivel. A set of wooden stairs, all chipped paint and splinters, leads up to Burt's office. It creaks slightly as we climb it, causing us to take the stairs at a pace one normally associates with summiting K2. I'm the first to arrive.

"Go to it," I say to Sam.

Sam removes the bobby pins from his pocket and goes about his fiendish work. It does not go quickly. I realize how spoiled I am. Mike can pick a lock in the time it takes you to say *Mike, pick this lock*. Finally, Sam pulls the bobby pins out and tries the door. It pops open.

Andy pats Sam on the back and says, "Good work."

I'm tempted to say *Took you long enough*, but that's my Mike Privilege talking. The three of us make our way into the office.

As befitting a low-rent, potential criminal hideout, there isn't a lot to the place. The backdoor opens onto a small kitchenette. The coffeemaker still has half a pot, and a few Styrofoam to-go containers sit on top of the wastebasket. The slight funk of rotting garbage permeates the place. Looks like nobody has taken out the trash since Burt's death (and I'm inclined to think it was overdue then). A thin hallway leads to the office proper. Sam and Andy stand in the kitchenette, waiting for me to take the lead. I move toward the hallway.

"Lay on, Macduff," I say.

The only door in the thin hallway leads to the bathroom, which is barely more than a WC. The office itself is cramped (all the more so for having three grown men invade it in the middle of the night). A picture window looks, I assume, over First Avenue. The blinds are drawn, so no one can see us skulking about. The front door leads to the stairs and the front entrance. A desk sits against one wall and a filing cabinet along the other. Beyond that, it's all threadbare carpeting and no decoration. Sam, flanking me on one side, looks the place over.

"This shouldn't take long," he says.

Sam is perfectly at home here (as opposed to Andy, who's hanging back as if wishing to melt into the walls). I should talk to somebody about my predilection for befriending affable low-grade sociopaths. For the moment, though, I agree with Sam.

"I'll give the desk a looksee," I say, "Why don't you guys take the filing cabinet?"

Sam and Andy step over to the filing cabinet and go right to work. I move carefully to the desk. There is no sign of a computer. Maybe it's been confiscated by the police, maybe Burt didn't have one to begin with. Surprisingly, the desk drawers aren't locked. Burt must have assumed no one was ever going to break into his office. The side drawer is empty, save for a ledger book. I toss it on the desktop to look it over. There are entries, but I can't make hide nor hair of what they mean. The entries contain dollar amounts, but the people (or businesses) are all listed by initials. If I had a guess, it's deliberately vague. Maybe Burt was lending them money, maybe he was getting money from them. Only Burt would know for sure.

"You guys finding anything?" I ask.

"Nope," Sam says, "A lot of real estate listings."

"I found a ledger book," I say, "Not sure if it's legitimate or not." I snap it shut and tuck it under my arm. "I'll take it with me. Maybe I'll find someone who knows something about it."

Andy is not down with that idea. "I don't know, Joe. That feels like tampering with a crime scene."

"Burt wasn't killed here," I say, "So, it's not a crime scene. No harm, no foul."

Andy doesn't look convinced, but he doesn't say anything. We continue to scope out the office. I go through the rest of the desk while Sam finishes up with the filing cabinet. We don't discover anything of interest. I lean against the desk, wondering if there might be something I haven't noticed yet. Nothing jumps out at me.

"You got any ideas?" I say, "Any other places we can look?"

Andy shakes his head. He's anxious to wrap this up and get the hell out of here. Sam scrutinizes the room.

"We didn't give the kitchenette or the bathroom a close look," he says.

"Because they're tiny and there's nothing to find," Andy says, "We should go."

I'm torn. There's sense in what Andy says. But Sam is right. We only get one shot at this. We should leave no stone unturned. I push off from the desk.

"Sam, why don't you take the bathroom?" I say, "Andy and I can take the kitchenette."

Sam starts down the hallway. Andy throws up his hands and follows me to the kitchenette. He's right, though. There isn't much to find. Nothing under the small sink. A rather forlorn bottle of cleaner sits on the countertop. Andy inspects the minifridge while I check out the cabinets. Sam's voice comes from the restroom.

"Hey Joe, you ever pulled an upper decker?" he asks.

"I have not," I say, "I knew a couple guys in college who did."

Andy looks up at me. "What's an upper decker?"

I hate telling him, because it's one of those things you can't unknow but wish you could. "It's when you take a shit in the tank of a toilet," I say, "Usually best done to a particularly heinous ex-roommate, ex-girlfriend or ex-landlord. They can smell something's wrong, but it takes some detective work to figure out where it's coming from. And once they *do* discover it, there's the matter of removing it. Because you can't really flush the tank."

"Are you…" Andy was probably going to finish with *shitting me* but reconsidered. "That's disgusting."

"It's one of those revenge nuclear options," I say.

"Why the hell are we talking about it *now*?" Andy asks.

"I think Sam's just trying to cut the tension."

"As long as that's all he cuts," Andy says.

I'm ready to drop this whole topic when Sam interjects once again. "I think I found something," he says.

Given all this talk about an upper decker, I'm not sure I want to find out what he's discovered. I slip out of the kitchen, Andy right behind me. We meet Sam in the thin hallway. He hefts something in his hand. I have a little trepidation about looking at it (even this far removed from high school, I don't think Sam's above some variety of disgusting joke). But I needn't have worried. Sam is holding a small black cellphone.

"Where did you find this?" I ask.

"It was taped under the lid of the toilet tank," Sam says, "Y'know, like you do."

I swipe the screen, taking it out of sleep mode. It's your standard operational smartphone, but barren of any apps. No sign of Burt's name anywhere. The realization hits me.

"This is a burner phone?" I ask.

"That would be my guess," Sam says, "Unless Burt's got a thing about keeping his cellphone in the shitter."

I look through it. The first call was placed the day before Burt's murder. A few contacts have been placed in the phone. One of them is Evan. Another is Eli. Neither of those surprises me.

"There's a call to Eli around eleven. Then a call to Evan at around eleven-fifteen. A call to somebody who's not in the contacts at eleven-forty-five. Then another call to Eli around one."

Sam peers over my shoulder. "Who was the somebody not in the contacts?"

"Don't know," I say.

It's a little late, but what the hell? I'm in this deep, right? I hit the number. The other party answers on the third ring.

"Who is this?" is how she greets me. I've only had a couple conversations with her, but the tone of her voice gives her away.

Alice.

I hang up immediately. Let her figure it out. But I have my own questions. Why did Burt call Alice the night of the murder? Was she the one Burt met in Bennett Park? If that's the case, she might be the murderer, right?

Good questions all. But they all go out the window when someone comes through the backdoor of the office.

CHAPTER TWELVE

I was fifteen the first time I snuck out of my house without my parents knowing. It didn't involve something as pedestrian as slipping out of my room and exiting via the front or backdoors. No, I discovered an escape route right out my bedroom window.

A small ledge runs below the window, barely wide enough to hold someone. A trellis runs up the side of the house, stopping at the ledge. When I was a kid, of course, my parents strictly forbade me and my brother Owen (who shared my room until I was in junior high) from climbing out onto the ledge. Owen and I obeyed the command. Therefore, the door to my room remained the only route in and out until I was in high school. How did I discover the alternative route? One night, my friend Sam climbed up the trellis, crossed the ledge and knocked on my window (scaring the living hell out of me) to let me know Beans Madden was having a giant party. I realized a route that could be traversed one way could certainly be traversed the other. An escape route was born. It was just a matter of waiting until I was old enough and independent enough to make my escape.

And I can't think of a better metaphor for my childhood.

The problem, of course, is that I keep coming back to Porter's Bay. Which in this case, is going to require an entirely different means of escape.

I don't get a clear look at the guy coming through the door. He's a little shorter than me, a little burly, and wears a t-shirt and jeans. There's also the matter of the gun he's holding. The three of us freeze.

Sam is the first to recover himself. He grabs the bottle of cleaner from the countertop next to the sink and squirts it into the face of our visitor. The guy's free hand flies up to his eyes and he shouts, "Fuck!" I recognize the voice. Officer Cliff Beardsley.

The second Sam hits Beardsley with the cleaner, the three of us start down the hall, heading for the front door. I'm not sure if Beardsley had the time (or the vision) to recognize us. But we're not going to hang around to hash things out. Beardsley lumbers blindly down the hall.

"Hold up!" he shouts, "Police! Freeze!"

But things are too far gone for that. Sam, Andy and I go out the front door (pausing only to unlock the damn thing), and bolt down the single flight of stairs. It's a small miracle we don't go ass over teakettle. The whole world is doing the "shaky camera effect" you find in most crappy Michael Bay films. (Assuming there are any non-crappy Michael Bay films.)

There's a short hallway leading to the backdoor and the fastest way back to the car.

We get through the backdoor with a minimum of fuss. A big black Dodge Ram sits in the alley; the kind of truck usually purchased by males suffering from Penial Inferiority Syndrome. It probably belongs to Officer Beardsley. I come to a temporary halt.

"We shouldn't go back to the car," I say, "If he follows us, he'll ID the license plate."

"We split up," Sam says, "He can't catch all of us."

Frankly, I'd prefer he didn't catch *any* of us. But Sam at least grasps the plan. A few gunshots ring out. One of them takes out a headlight on the Dodge Ram and the other disappears into the night. Either Officer Beardsley's vision has not cleared or he's an incredibly poor shot (it's even money). I run toward the end of the alley, moving away from Andy's car. Maybe I can lure Beardsley away from Andy and Sam.

Or I could if they weren't following me.

"What the hell are you guys doing?" I say, "The whole idea of splitting up is to, y'know, split up."

"I just started running this way," Andy says, "I didn't know Sam was going to run the same direction."

"There are only two choices," Sam says, "Why did you guys pick mine?"

"Never mind," I say, "We'll split up at the end of the alley."

We reach the street and I duck to my left. I wonder what Beardsley is going to do. Pursue us on foot? In his car? Call for back up? Shoot us all and let God sort us out? At any rate, he can't catch us all.

At least, he couldn't if Andy and Sam weren't still following me.

"What the fuck are you guys doing?" I say, "You had *three* choices this time!"

"I just started going this way," Andy says.

Sam shrugs. "I made my choice. I'll live with it."

Son of a biscuit. We haven't hung out regularly in seventeen years and we're *still* joined at the hip. It would be touching if I didn't want to murder them both. Beardsley's truck comes roaring out of the alley.

"Shit!" is all I get out before taking off again.

I turn left at the next corner, cut diagonally across the street and duck between two houses. There's a clear path to another alley and another backyard beyond that. Once I'm across the alley, I stop briefly, wondering which direction Beardsley will go next. Andy is next to me. And just Andy.

"Where's Sam?" I ask, between breaths.

"No idea," Andy says, "I took off after you and lost sight of him."

Fifty percent of the people around me listened to my orders. That's fifty percent more than I usually get. That will be a comfort when I'm hanging out in a holding cell.

I'm preparing to run to the next street when Beardsley's truck slowly cruises by. A big Maglite shines out the window. Andy and I run back across the alley, onto the first street. Just as we get there, a Toyota Corolla that has clearly seen better days slows to a halt in front of us. The passenger window comes down. Sam leans over from the driver's side.

"You guys going to get in or are you just going to stand there and get caught?" he says.

I hop in the passenger seat while Andy slides into the back. Sam mashes the accelerator to the floor before we've even got the doors closed. The Corolla roars down the street.

"Whose car is this?" I ask.

"How should I know?" Sam says.

Great. As long as we're piling up felonies… "You stole it?" I say.

Sam seems taken aback. "Hey, if somebody leaves the window cracked open and the spare keys in an obvious place like the visor, can we even call it theft?"

So, you can see where Sam was the warmup for my friendship with Mike.

The Corolla heads to the end of the street and swings a right. If we were smart, we'd slow down and drive normally. The streets are nearly deserted. There would be nothing to arouse Beardsley's suspicion. But Sam is still on an adrenaline high and going at least ten miles per hour above the speed limit. Shortly after we've passed the next street, the Ram bolts out and comes after us. Sam pushes the accelerator to the floor. Andy alternates between looking through the back window and looking at us.

"You're not really getting into a car chase with a stolen car, are you?" Andy asks.

Sam waves Andy off (and Jesus, I wish he'd keep both hands on the wheel). "It'll be fine. We're running from an off-duty cop. We just have to lose him, get you home, and pretend we had nothing to do with the break-in."

"You really think that will work?" Andy asks.

"I don't know," Sam says, "I'm terrified beyond the capacity for rational thought."

Sam zigzags through the neighborhood. The cop proves surprisingly hard to lose. He's no more than a half block back and able to match each of Sam's moves. I'm not sure if the Corolla can outrun his truck, but it can damn sure outmaneuver it. We have to hope Sam can keep this up without either crashing the car or getting shot.

Andy keeps us updated on Beardsley's progress. "We're going to have to look out for the police," he says, "Five will get you ten he's going to call this in, get some cop cars on our trail."

"One disaster at a time," Sam says, taking a corner so the Corolla damn near goes up on two wheels.

The issue now, of course, is where the hell are we going to go? How are we going to lose Beardsley? We're driving without plan or purpose. Driving just to drive. We're basically the movie *Vanishing Point*.

Sam works his way back to Howard Street. Beardsley is still only a half-block back. I don't see any other cops coming after us. I guess Officer Beardsley is determined to handle this himself. Sam ducks down some side streets. We fly past Frank Porter Park—none of us stopping to say hi to Frank—and come up on a T stop. Sam chooses to go left.

And discovers he's chosen a cul-de-sac.

We make this realization just after the truck has rounded the corner as well. There's no escape. The cul-de-sac is ringed with fine little two-story homes. A small wooded area rests beyond it. Sam takes his foot off the gas.

"Well, that sucks," he says, mostly out of shock.

Andy moves from shock to panic. "What the fuck are we going to do?"

Sam captures the moment, "Scatter!"

We've still got time enough to ditch the Corolla and head for the hills without Beardsley clearly seeing us. We vacate the car. I run toward a house at the end of the cul-de-sac. Andy and Sam go in separate directions. (*Finally*, we manage to get that right.) I'm running up the driveway of a split-level at the end of the cul-de-sac when I hear a huge crash behind me. I look over my shoulder and see the Ram merged with the back of our getaway car.

RIP stolen Corolla.

I run around the side of the split-level and into the backyard. There's a small chain link fence at the end of the yard and a wooded area beyond that. I hop the fence with little difficulty and disappear into the trees. A look back reveals Beardsley has, against all odds, cleared the fence. His gun is out, but he's not aiming at me. I keep moving through the trees.

It's not an easy run. There's no natural path, so I carve out one of my own. Branches slap my arms. I'm nearly tripped up by a tangle of weeds. Beardsley isn't slowed by any of this. He just keeps coming. Jason Voorhees, anyone? The trees open onto a parking lot. I'm looking at the back of the Kahler Hotel. Howard Street and Lake Drive loom beyond, with the lake just a little past them. I haul ass across the parking lot.

I need a place to hide. I've got friends at the Kahler. But how to get in? The loading dock is locked. The lobby has a camera. I sure as hell don't want to be recorded fleeing from a cop. I'll have to take a chance on the side doors.

I put on another burst of speed. Beardsley is slowing. Apparently, I've taxed his limit. I run around the building and spot a middle-aged couple going in a side door. The glass door slowly starts to shut behind them. I reach out and get the door just before it closes. Halle-fucking-lujah! I slip around the door and yank the damn thing shut behind me.

The middle-aged couple watches as I hustle up the stairs. The guy is a tweedy-looking sort with a bowling shirt and cargo shorts. "Excuse me," he says, "Are you a guest at the hotel?"

I stop and try to think up an excuse. All I come up with is, "Mind your own fucking business." Then I continue up the stairs.

Yes, it lacked diplomacy. But it got to the point in a big, big hurry.

The room Mike and Lars share is on the third floor. It's the best choice. Carol would only give me a lecture. I head to room three-twenty-three, doing my best to appear casual. (Between the sweating and the heavy breathing, I don't think I'm too successful.) I rap on the door. Light is visible through the peephole. Someone must be in there. A few seconds later, Mike answers. His hair is piled high, and his brow is furrowed.

"What's up?" he asks, glancing down the hall.

"I need to come in," I say, "Now!"

I push past him and into the room. He smells vaguely of smoke. I wonder if he's taking his smoke breaks outside or here in the room. Mike closes the door while I pace around.

"You didn't exactly pick the best time," Mike says.

"I don't have a fucking choice!" I say, "I've got a cop after me."

"Break-in went that well, did it?"

I give him the Netflix guide recap of the break-in. When I'm done, I go to the window and peek through the curtains. "I need a place to hide out for a little bit. Just until Beardsley is gone."

"You think he recognized you?" Mike asks.

"I don't know. I mean, it wouldn't take Hercule fucking Poirot to figure out it was me. But I don't know if he got a clear enough look."

"Meaning you can play dumb."

"And dumber, if necessary."

Mike takes an uncomfortable glance toward the door. "Look, I really want to help you. But Julie's coming over." There's a knock on the door. "In fact, she's here."

"You are not kicking me out! Beardsley is probably doing a sweep of the hotel. I'm not taking a chance on running into him."

Another knock. Mike calls over his shoulder, "Be right there." He turns back to me. "I'm trying to break shit off with Julie. I don't want to blow this."

"Mike, this is where I need to remind you that A, I know all of your worst secrets, and B, I have a public forum in which to share them."

Mike sticks a finger in my face. "One of these days, you're going to either lose that column or I'm going to kill you. Either way, your blackmail time is limited."

"Noted."

Another knock. "You can hide in the closet," Mike says, frantic, "Just get moving."

The closet is near the door and home to about seventy-three hangers, none of which are in use. It's cramped, but I can stand up straight. The place smells of mothballs. Mike slides the door shut. I hope my claustrophobia doesn't make a sudden reappearance. Mike answers the door.

"Sorry, I was just on the phone with my idiot friend, Joe," he says, "Couldn't get rid of him. You know how it goes."

Julie understands. She and Mike step into the room. She brings with her a smell of cheap perfume that overrides even the mothballs in the closet. I don't have any trouble hearing the conversation. I hope Mike finishes this break-up quickly and with a minimum of fuss. (Ah, my optimism is cute. It's like I've never met him.)

They chitchat for a few minutes. Julie's voice has a dreamy, distant quality. It either bubbles with excitement or drops to a husky whisper. Mike does a lot of stammering. He doesn't offer Julie any kind of refreshment, which is understandable since he's trying to break things off. The small talk flags, and Mike is forced to get down to brass tacks.

"I've got to be honest with you, Julie," he says, "Really completely honest. I'm not who you think I am. I didn't do any of that stuff I told you. The fact is, I'm an unemployed doofus who's been fired from his last two jobs. I should have told you the truth right from the beginning. I'm sorry."

I've got to tell you: hearing Mike be sincere tells me how well he fakes it most of the time. The only difference, as far as I can detect, is a very slight pained quality to his voice, as if someone has gently grabbed his testicles and started squeezing (which, viewed from a certain angle…) Mike and I wait for Julie's response.

"All of that is true?" she asks, "This is the real you I'm talking to right now?"

"This is me. Warts and all. Mostly warts."

"You've been lying to me the whole time?"

"Not the whole time. Just a chunk of it."

Another few moments of silence. Not seeing the action makes it worse. I don't know if Julie's tearing up or if her face is turning red and she's on the verge of a meltdown. Mike is silent, having said all he has to say.

"You did all that for me?" she asks.

"For you?" Mike says, knowing full well he did *not* do any of that for Julie, "Su…sure."

"Oh Mike, you're wonderful." Oh Mike, you're a fucking idiot. But Julie doesn't see it that way. "Just the fact you were willing to lie to me shows what a bad boy you are."

"I…that's…"

Things go silent. I can't blame Mike. The truth, sadly, has not set him free. The silence is interrupted by a smacking sound. It takes me a few seconds to identify it. Son of a bitch. They're making out. I recoil.

Julie comes up for air. "I want to be bad, Mike. Let's be bad."

The sound is faint, but I hear zippers and buckles and the soft sound of clothing hitting the floor. I take out my cell phone and send Mike a text message. **Please knock it off.** If I know Mike, he's going to ignore it. I'm trapped and there's nothing Mike can do to help.

"Take me, Mike," Julie whispers, "Take me right in this bed."

Not that he's thinking too much about me right now.

***

"That was the most goddamn disgusting thing I've ever been a part of," I say, stalking my parents' backyard, "You have any idea how traumatizing that was?"

Carol, perched in a lawn chair, peers at me over the top of her shades. "It doesn't sound like Mike had much choice. Not that he would have done anything if he *had* a choice."

"I've got to tell you, Julie's *loud*," I say, "I'm amazed someone didn't call the cops. And she's insatiable. They were up half the night."

Carol looks toward the house. "What did you tell your parents?"

"I didn't tell them anything," I say, "They were asleep by the time I got home. Nobody asked me about it this morning."

"Or about the police chase?"

I stop. "No. I'm surprised by that. I expected Officer Beardsley to crash in with a riot squad first thing. So far, all quiet on the western front."

I plunk down in the lawn chair next to Carol. She sips her coffee and looks unconcerned, even a little annoyed, with my contretemps from the night before. I try to relax and enjoy the smell of cut grass coming from somewhere in the neighborhood. It isn't working.

"What are you going to do next?" Carol asks.

"Talk to Eli," I say, "He was more connected to Burt than he's let on. And I'm going to talk to Alice. She got a call from Burt the night of the murder. Maybe I'll talk to Evan again. All that assumes, of course, I'm not going to be in jail by the end of the day."

Carol crosses her legs and bounces one foot. "This is a small town. And your dad is one of its most prominent citizens. It's not like you're hard to find."

"I know," I say, "I'd hate to have it happen before he gets the key to the city tonight. Trundling off into retirement with one of his kids in jail."

"Better you than him."

"This is what I've been saying." I run a hand over my face. "How about you? I assume my uncle is still in power."

"For the moment," Carol says. She slips off her shades. "I've been doing a little research, but I've hit a brick wall."

"How so?"

"I did some looking into the Ice Dam, the company that issued Gordie the check. According to their website, it's a charitable organization, helping further environmental causes."

"Leading one to wonder why they have anything to do with my uncle."

"Exactly," Carol says, "I decided to visit them. They have an office in an industrial complex in Greenville. At least, they have an office in theory."

The plot thickens. "What do you mean?"

"The place is abandoned," Carol says, leaning forward in her lawn chair, "I couldn't get inside, but I could see through the windows. No furniture. No computers. No phones. Hell, there was wiring hanging from the ceiling and dust about an inch thick on the windows. Nobody has been in that place in forever."

"Curiouser and curiouser."

"On top of that, I can't talk to anyone from the Ice Dam and ask about this stuff. There's no contact information for anyone. I can't even just send a general email."

"You're thinking what I'm thinking?"

"That the Ice Dam is a front company?" Carol says, "You're damn right. Then I did some looking into that check to Gordie. It was drawn from a bank here in Porter's Bay. First Federal. I went down there and asked around. Didn't get anything. 'Privileged information…privacy of our customers…ma'am, you're making a scene.' The usual crap."

"Getting hassled by The Man."

"I even went to the *Porter's Bay Times*, tried to see if the editor was interested in any of this. No such luck. They won't touch it. The editor said I have no proof and besides, he gets ad money from Vic Easton. So, that's out."

Ugh. I remember when Lisa wasn't hired for a summer internship at the *Porter's Bay Times*. All she went on to do was become a star investigative reporter for a big media company. Good to know the local press is as incompetent as ever. I turn toward the kitchen window.

"Maybe my mom can help," I say, "My parents bank at First Federal. She might know somebody down there."

"It wouldn't hurt," Carol says, with a notable lack of enthusiasm, "It's not like I'm getting anywhere at the moment."

We head into the kitchen. Mom is preparing lunch for everyone. (Turkey sandwiches. Everything lined up like she's running a sandwich shop.) The radio is on in the background. God is in His heaven, and all is right with the world. Mom looks up from her work.

"Welcome back," she says. It's her standard greeting, though we've only been gone ten minutes. "Would you like some more coffee?"

Both Carol and I say, "No." We're a little too hasty about it, but Mom doesn't notice. She resumes her sandwich making. I take up position in front of the nook that houses the pantry while Carol sits at the kitchen table.

"Hey Mom, do you know anyone down at First Federal Bank?" I ask.

"Of course," Mom says, "Your father and I have been banking there for forty years."

"Do you have any friends that work there?" I ask, "Anyone you trust?"

"I trust all of them," Mom says. She pauses with the sandwiches. "Why do you ask?"

I let Carol tell the tale, since she's been doing most of the work. My mom appears interested in everything Carol says. When the story is finished, Mom sits at the kitchen table.

"You think this Vic Easton is giving Gordie money?" Mom asks. "It would make sense, wouldn't it?"

"Do you know anyone down at First Federal who might help Carol?" I ask.

Mom thinks about it. "Marion. We used to bowl together. I bet she knows everything that's going on down there. It's just a matter of asking."

Carol, who has already made several attempts to run the information blockade, seems a little wary. "Do you think she'd actually tell us?"

"Of course," Mom says, "She might need a little guidance, though. Marion is a dear, but not too bright. Do you know what I mean?"

"Sure," I say, "You just described all of my friends except Carol."

Mom swats me on the arm. "I'm sure that's not the case."

"You're right," I say, "None of them are *dears*."

Carol butts in. "This is great, but I don't know if I'm going to get anywhere with it. The editor at *The Porter's Bay Times* still doesn't want anything to do with it."

Mom gets up from the table and goes back to the sandwiches. "Oh, that won't be a problem. Fred Meers might think he's some kind of lord and master. But he's been skimming from petty cash to pay for that new car of his. Once we talk to Jessica in accounting, Fred will play ball."

Wow. My mom has this kind of dirt? She has always exuded the kind of quiet decency that would make Betty Crocker seem like a filthy whore. (Even including the word *whore* in a sentence involving my mother feels indecent.)

"How did you find out all this?" I ask.

Mom wipes her hands on her apron. "Joseph Benjamin Davis, I have lived in this town my whole life. Do you think all I do is make meals and clean the house?"

"You have a life outside of me."

"Exactly."

Carol hops up from the table. "You said this Marion would talk to us?"

"She might," Mom says. She points to the cheese and Carol begins assisting with the sandwiches. "I've got her number. I'll put in a good word for you."

"What about the woman in accounting at *The Times?*" Carol asks.

"Oh, Jessica is very nice," Mom says, "I'll make sure she talks to you."

"That would be great, Mrs. Davis."

Mom slips off her apron. "Call me Katherine. Please."

Son of a bitch. Who'd have thunk it? All of Gordie's shenanigans and the two people he never should have crossed are Carol and my mother. He's not going to see this coming. And I'm going to enjoy it.

***

I'd love to tell you the Porter's Bay Public Library is an architectural marvel, a throwback to a different era when more money and taste floated around my humble hometown. But unlike the high school or the hockey arena or City Hall, the public library is more functional than artistic. I assume it was built in a later era. I'm not sure where the original library might have been. (Yes, yes, I know it's my hometown and I should know more about its history. But there are only so many hours in the day and that beer isn't going to drink itself.)

The library is a one-story structure with a lot of glass and very high ceilings. There are wooden tables, cubicles and bookcases. Most of the reading material is contained in the huge area to the right as you walk in. The computers are housed in a smaller area (likely where they used to keep the card catalogues) to the left. Nothing much to it. But it's one of the few places I can do some research without any scrutiny. I snag a study room and hunker down with my laptop and my notebook.

I've finally accepted that my dad and his friends aren't going to tell me anything about Taylor or Cully Brown. Time to consult my friend the internet. Taylor is too vague to look up right away, so I go with Cully Brown. It's a distinct name. A general search gives me too many possibilities. I do a more specific search: *Cully Brown, MN.*

Disco.

There's a newspaper article about a Cully Brown who died roughly forty years ago. Found dead in his car, parked next to a lake. The story says police were treating it as a possible suicide. No further information and no follow-up article. The location is interesting.

Taylor, Minnesota.

There's nothing else on Cully Brown, so I do some research on Taylor, Minnesota. It's a small town in the center of the state. It has a few lakes around it and draws on the tourist trade in the summer. Like Porter's Bay, it deals heavily in quaint and rustic. Nothing much beyond that. Cully Brown's was the only violent death the town saw in…maybe forever.

I sit back in my chair in the study room. A guy named Cully Brown dies in Taylor, Minnesota. Officer Beardsley is convinced it has something to do with Burt Franklin's murder and that my father is mixed up in both. How is he drawing that connection? *Is* there a connection or is Beardsley on a fishing trip? I do a little more research, but it doesn't tell me anything. I drop my laptop back into its bag.

I wander out the front of the library. The lawn is small, and the walk is wide. An uneasy feeling creeps over me. Now I know something about Taylor and Cully Brown. But how is it connected to my dad and his friends? It must be. Otherwise, why would Burt bring it up?

A voice intrudes rudely into my thoughts. "Joe Davis!"

Officer Beardsley crosses the street from City Hall. This will be an irony. Writer Arrested in Front of Public Library. I fight off the instinct to run. Beardsley powerwalks up to me. He wears shades. Whatever is visible on his face shows no sense of humor or trace of human feeling.

"You and your friends have fun last night?" he asks.

"It was swell," I say, "I don't get together with them nearly enough."

"You broke into Burt Franklin's office."

I give him a quizzical glance. "Burt Franklin has an office?"

"Cut the shit." He's trying to be tough but from the time we were kids, he never had that in him. Being a cop hasn't changed it. He's all gut and imagined authority.

"I'd love to," I say, wishing I had remembered to bring *my* shades, "But I don't know what the hell you're talking about."

"I got a call from Marilyn Holman last night. She lives right across the alley from Burt's office. Told me she saw three guys breaking into the place. I checked it out. They sprayed me with something then took off running. I chased them in my truck. Thought I had one of them cornered at the Kahler. But he got away." He tries to look down his nose at me, but he's still shorter than I am. "The three guys looked a lot like you and your friends, Andy Clark and Sam Nelson."

"Really? You were able to identify us even after getting sprayed in the eyes? Did you get a good look, so you know for sure it was us?"

Beardsley's face flushes. "I saw three guys who fit the descriptions of you and your friends."

"Wow. Three thin white males in their thirties. You don't see many guys who fit *that* description in this town. And you said they were running away from you? In the dark? But you know for sure that it was me and Andy and Sam?"

If I didn't know any better (and I don't), I'd think Beardsley was going to stroke out right here. "You going to tell me it wasn't you?"

"That's exactly what I'm going to tell you."

"Horseshit. You've been going around town, asking people questions, trying to prove your dad didn't kill Burt Franklin."

"Seemed the prudent thing when there's a cop going after him," I say, "And all the cop has for evidence is a gold watch."

"Then there's a break-in at Burt's office last night. And you're going to tell me you had *nothing* to do with it?"

I stand up a little straighter, subtly emphasizing our height difference. "I'm going to tell you that, yes. And as long as we're speculating, I have a few questions for you, officer. Were you on duty when you got this call?"

His jaw tightens. "No, I was at home. Why—"

"Did you call for backup? Or ask another officer to handle it?"

"I didn't know if—"

"You chased these guys in your truck. Did you call for backup then? Let them know you had suspects escaping? Or did you just decide to recklessly endanger the public?"

"I wasn't going to drive a car and make a phone call at the same time."

"You mean the phone call you should have made *before* going to Burt Franklin's office?"

If this were a cartoon (and we're not far from that), steam would be shooting out of Beardsley's ears. "Don't tell me how to do my job."

"Fine," I say, "Why don't we go across the street and talk to Chief Davenport? I believe he's the one who's supposed to tell you how to do your job."

Beardsley is, I'm sure, weighing the merits of beating the living hell out of me. But we're on a public street, right next to City Hall no less, and he can't add assault to his already lengthy list of fuckups. He makes a half-turn to leave, then spins back and puts a finger in my face.

"You stay the hell out of this," Beardsley says, "I only need one excuse to put your ass in jail. Go ahead and give it to me. Stay away from this."

He starts to walk away but stops when he hears my voice. "What happened to Cully Brown?" I ask.

"I'm going to find out. When I do, it's not going to look good for your old man."

Beardsley walks away. It takes a second for my annoyance to fade. When it does, I'm left with a hole in the pit of my stomach. I need to know what happened to Cully Brown in Taylor, Minnesota.

Maybe I *should* mind my own business.

***

My theory about not having difficulty finding someone in a small town proves true when I come across my dad's friend Eli. Yes, it happened while I was strolling past The Hub, the eating establishment for every old dude in town, so there might have been less serendipity involved than one would imagine. But I still feel validated (which I could really use right now).

Eli is at the lunch counter. He has a cup of coffee in front of him and seems in no hurry to finish his sandwich. The lunch crowd is clearing out. There is only one other person at the counter, another retiree from the look of it, sitting on the far end. I hop on to the stool next to Eli. He gives me a casual look then does a double-take.

"Joe," he says, "It's Joe, right?"

Nice to know I make such an impact on people. "It is Joe. I was hoping we could talk."

"Sure," Eli says, clearly hoping this will be a casual conversation. (Though he's perceptive enough to realize I rarely have casual conversations. Meaningless, yes, but not casual.)

"I want to talk about Burt Franklin. You were in business with him. Recently. What kind of business was it?"

That draws a bug-eyed look from Eli, who must be releasing his Inner Don Knotts. "Why would you say that?"

"I have some resources. From what I hear, Burt was into some shady business. And your name was in a burner phone I found in Burt's office."

"How, how did you find that?"

"Probably best not to go into it."

Eli sips his coffee, his hand shaking. "Yes, I've been in business with Burt. I didn't want to be. I never liked the man. But I was…I was desperate." He sets the cup carefully back on the saucer. "I lost my job a few years ago. The company I was working for laid me off. Twenty years I worked for them. I was two years from retirement, and they laid me off. Now, you tell me where a sixty-three-year-old man is going to find a job that pays him a living wage. No place."

"I guess not."

"I knew Burt had money. I hear rumors, too. I called him and explained the situation. He seemed amused. But he had a job for me."

"Doing what?"

"Being a bagman," Eli says, "I'd move money from his clients to him. That's how it started. Then I began helping him with the books."

My eyebrows go up. "I'm guessing not the legitimate books?"

Eli shakes his head. "Burt was terrible with numbers. He always had been. I took over. Showed him how to move money and track things without giving anything away."

"The ledger book," I say, "That was your creation."

"You know about that? How did…?" Then he sighs. "I know. You won't go into it. Yes, the ledger book was mine. I worked out the whole code. Burt could have never done that on his own." Eli clears his throat. "Do you, uh, have the ledger book?"

"I do. I'm going to hold on to it until stuff gets sorted out with my dad."

"And then?"

"I'll figure that out when we get there."

Eli probably got the answer he expected. The server comes by, and I order a coffee. Only after she walks away do I realize it's Charley, Evan's girlfriend.

"What kind of stuff was Burt into?" I ask.

"You name it. Drug dealing, money laundering, loan sharking. He wasn't making millions of dollars, but he wasn't worried about money. Prosecution, maybe, but never money."

"He must have made enemies in that line of work."

Eli looks annoyed. "No, everything was fine. It's not like what you see on TV. Sure, it's dangerous business, and Burt could rub people the wrong way. But he was a businessman. He made sure he worked with people who treated it like a business. Mostly."

"Mostly?"

"You get a reprobate every now and again."

"Was Evan Erickson one of them?" I ask.

"He was," Eli says, "What do you know?"

"I heard Evan needed money," I say, "I heard he went to Burt and Burt turned him down. Is there more to the story?"

"You got the basics," Eli says, "Evan's trouble. Burt should have had nothing to do with him right from the start. But Burt had a soft spot for the kid."

"Burt had a soft spot? I didn't know he was capable."

"Maybe the closest thing Burt could get to one. He used to be…involved with the kid's mother. A long time ago."

Dear Lord, no wonder the guy had a shortage of friends. I'd like to share Eli's sentiment about Burt helping Evan from some milk of human kindness. But I'm more inclined to think Burt saw a sucker he could bleed white.

"How much was Evan in for?" I ask.

"A lot," Eli says, "When you're in so deep that Burt won't bail you out, you've got a real problem."

"Burt wanted Evan to do a favor for him," I ask, "They talked about it the night of the murder, over at Nick's. You have any idea what that favor was?"

Eli takes a quick look around. "It involved that girlfriend of his."

"Charley? The server here?"

"Yes."

I recoil. "You mean he wanted to…"

"No! No, no, no. It's not as if Burt was above that sort of thing, you understand. But that was in his younger days, mostly. The man had a catheter, for crying out loud."

"Then what did he want from Charley?"

Eli looks the way Danny Glover would in the *Lethal Weapon* movies, just before proclaiming he was too old for whatever shit that was going down. "Charley's family runs a pizza place up in Center City. Ed's Pizza. Some of Burt's customers are employees there. Burt wanted to buy the place and use it as a front."

"Money laundering?"

"Yes," Eli says, "The parents own the place, but Charley's brother, Ken, manages it. And he wanted nothing to do with Burt. Burt thought Evan could get information on Charley's brother. Force him to let the sale go through."

"And Evan wouldn't do it?"

"He was going to think about it, but that's as far as we got before Burt was killed."

I watch Charley bring out a tray of sandwiches for a corner booth. She moves with an easy grace, despite the burden on her very thin arms and legs. It's easy to understand why Evan is attracted to her. I turn back to Eli.

"The night Burt was killed," I say, "You were seen leaving your apartment building with him. Later, you came back by yourself. What happened there?"

Eli shoots me a look. "How did you know that?"

"One of your neighbors told me," I say.

He frowns. ("People, what a bunch of bastards.") "We went to his office," Eli says, "He wanted me to look over the ledger book. He was certain somebody was skimming from him. He wanted me to see if I noticed anything."

"And did you?"

"Of course I did. I was the one skimming." He looks around. "I guess there's no harm in admitting it now. I was taking a little off the top. I needed more money and God knows Burt wasn't going to give it to me of his own free will. I told him something looked off, but I'd have to do more research."

"Did he suspect you were taking the money?"

"Maybe," Eli says, "Burt was fond of saying 'There's a difference between suspicion and proof.' He didn't like it as much when he was the one with suspicions."

Interesting. If Burt *did* suspect Eli and fired him, Eli would be without his main source of income. *That* would be plenty of motive to kill someone. And Eli was with Burt on the night of the murder. My coffee arrives and we wait for the server to walk away.

"What are you going to do now?" I ask, "With Burt gone?"

"I've got some money squirreled away," Eli says, "I'll be okay for a while. After that, I don't know."

I feel for him. My own income pays for all my stuff, but I don't have a lot put away for the future. And writing a humor column isn't exactly stable work.

"That's where you left it that night?" I ask, "You looked over the books, said you'd check it out, and went home?"

Eli toys with the sugar container. "Not entirely. Burt said he had a meeting in Bennett Park. He asked me to give him a ride there and then give him a ride home."

Jinkies. "You were with Burt in Bennett Park?"

"No," Eli says, "I dropped him off at the entrance. He told me to go for a drive, that he didn't want me around. He said he'd call me when it was time to pick him up."

"What time was the meeting?" I ask.

"About 12:30."

Okay, that checks out. "Did you see who he was meeting with?" I ask, "Did he tell you?"

"No, he didn't. And I didn't see any other cars in the lot. I dropped him off, drove around for about a half an hour.

Then I got a call from Burt, asking me to pick him up. When I got back to Bennett Park, Burt wasn't there. I waited for a minute, then I decided to check things out. I walked over by the playground and…there he was."

A rush goes though me. "You saw Burt dead? Have you told the police this?"

"In a manner of speaking," Eli says, "I was the one who called in Burt's murder. I couldn't just leave him lying there. But I couldn't let the police know it was me. I'd have to explain why I was in the park, what my association with Burt was all about. There were just too many questions. I put in an anonymous call and that was that."

"Save for the inconvenient fact my dad is twisting in the wind."

Eli says nothing. It's possible he's lying to me. He could have driven Burt to Bennett Park then hit Burt over the head and shot him. Or the confrontation could have happened elsewhere, and Eli dumped the body in Bennett Park. (Then again, I have a hard time picturing Eli dragging dead bodies around.)

"What time did you call the police?" I ask, "Roughly?"

"About a quarter after one," Eli says.

"And after *that*, you went home? Got there around 1:30?"

"I did. I've tried to forget what I saw, but…it hasn't been easy."

Okay, everything in Eli's timeline matches up with what I know. That's a point in his favor. I cock my head to one side.

"How did Burt get to your apartment?" I ask, "The tires on his car had been slashed."

"He got a ride from Will."

That causes *me* to do a doubletake. "Will? I thought Will can't drive."

"No, he can," Eli says, "He's not supposed to, but he does."

Clearly, Will doesn't tell Alice about that. And he didn't mention it to me, either. You see why I don't want to take anyone at face value?

"What can you tell me about Cully Brown?" I ask.

Eli nearly drops his coffee cup. That's the reaction I was expecting. I take no particular joy in it. Eli swallows hard.

"How do you know about that?" he asks.

"Officer Beardsley knows," I say, "And I did some research. I just can't figure out how all the pieces fit together."

Eli tries to drink his coffee, but his hand is trembling. "I can't help you with that."

"Why not?"

"It's not my place to say. Me, your dad, Will, Burt. We made a pact. Burt had to say something. The insufferable son of a bitch couldn't keep it to himself. He always resented your dad. Not just because of Henry's success but because your dad wouldn't let him…use the store."

It dawns on me. "As a front company."

"Yes. Even then Burt was as crooked as the day is long. We all knew better than to get into business with him. But we needed him."

"Needed him for what?" I ask.

Eli opens his mouth then closes it. He remains silent. It was a reach. Maybe I was hoping he'd accidentally spill something. Whatever it is, my dad and his friends have been keeping this secret for a long time. I won't get it from them that easily.

"You want my dad to go to jail?" I ask.

"Of course not."

"That's what is going to happen if you and your friends don't start talking. Beardsley will probably figure things out. And if he doesn't, he'll just make something up and dare you guys to prove him wrong."

It's my best sales pitch. A little bit of guilt. A little bit of threat. A damn fine piece of manipulation if I do say so myself. Eli, though, hails the server.

"Check, please," he says.

Balls. I've done all I can do here, save getting out the rubber hoses and the waterboarding equipment. The restaurant is clearing out. I finish my coffee and toss a few bucks on the counter.

"Whatever it is you guys are hiding," I say, "I hope it's worth going to jail over."

Eli just stares at the counter. I wait for him to say something, but he doesn't. I head for the front entrance, half-hoping Eli will call me back and spill his guts. Instead, I reach the door without interruption. Just as I expected.

Whatever it is they've got buried, it's buried deep. Problem is, I'm not the only one trying to dig it up.

CHAPTER THIRTEEN

Our society has created a stigma around living with our parents past a certain age. (Our age, not theirs.) There is a belief that successful people live on their own and only losers live with their parents. I would like to counter (or at least create reasonable doubt about) this idea by presenting the following two case studies (conducted in an academically-approved anecdotal fashion).

My uncle Kenny lived with my maternal grandparents until they passed away. He started a full-time job immediately after he got out of the army, paid his share of the bills, kept his room clean and did his share of the yardwork. Eventually, the house was put in his name to allow a smooth transition after my grandparents were both gone. A few years ago, he retired and sold the house and lives a comfortable existence on a lake near the Canadian border (a house he can afford because his credit rating is impeccable).

My friend Mike moved away from home when he went to college. He lived with his parents for a few months after college then moved to the Twin Cities. Since then, he's held no fewer than fifteen jobs. He's been derelict enough with his rent that three apartment buildings refused to offer him another lease. He's on a first name basis with at least four bill collectors. His current apartment could be featured in Better Hovels and Trashpiles *magazine. His retirement plans (inasmuch as he has any) likely include squatting in an abandoned warehouse.*

And yet, our society would call my uncle Kenny—a man who took care of my grandparents in their elderly years—a loser while venerating Mike—a man who is unknowingly supporting generations of cockroaches in his current apartment.

Unfortunately, when it comes to losers and winners and who lives with their parents, Evan Erickson is likely the rule rather than the exception.

The Ericksons have a lovely two-story home, not unlike my parents' place. It's all white paint and green trim. The lawn is well-manicured. There's a lovely little flower bed near the front door. The Audi in the driveway has been washed and polished. They even have one of those miniature lighthouse decorations out front for added charm. Everyone would want to grow up in a place like this. Maybe that's why Evan has no desire to leave.

I ring the front doorbell. A woman in her late fifties answers the door. She's wearing gardening clothes and her long silver hair is pulled back into a ponytail. I'm trying not to picture a younger version of her knocking boots with a younger Burt Franklin. I'm not having a lot of success.

"Hi," I say, "My name's Joe Davis. I—"

Mrs. Erickson smiles. "You were Elyse's friend. Right?"

"Yes, I was," I say, feeling slightly relieved.

"I remember you. You were always so nice."

"Thank you." I clear my throat. "Is Evan around?"

That brings Mrs. Erickson up short. "Evan? He's down in his room. Is everything okay?"

"It is," I say, "I'm just working on something, and I needed to talk to him about it."

"Of course," Mrs. Erickson says, "Just follow me."

Wow. That was…easier than it should have been. That explains why Evan gets away with the stuff he does. His parents either have an abundance of trust or a lack of curiosity. I follow Mrs. Erickson to a small door in the middle of the house. If you didn't know any better (and I don't until Mrs. Erickson opens it), you'd think it was a hall closet. She leads me down a small staircase to the basement. She pauses halfway and calls down.

"Evan, honey? You have a visitor."

A voice comes from somewhere far away. "Who is it?"

"Joe Davis. You remember him? He was Elyse's friend?"

A pause, then: "I remember him. He can come down."

Mrs. Erickson leads me the rest of the way. The basement isn't much. Gray cement block walls and a cement floor. Exposed beams and pipes overhead. A few pieces of garage sale furniture. A big screen TV and a large gaming system sit incongruously against the wall. There are a few posters by way of decoration. Old clothes, discarded food containers and dirty dishes cover the floor. It's like the guys from *Animal House* decorated a bomb shelter. The bed is on the far end of the room. It's a queen-size, like the one I have at home. The odor of pot wafts vaguely through the air. I wonder if Mrs. Erickson recognizes it. Evan is lying on the bed, an ankle propped on one bended knee, staring at his phone. He makes no move other than to brush a dirty t-shirt off the bed, allowing it to expertly cover the plate containing his roach clip.

"Hey Joe," he says, "Grab a chair. Thanks, Mom."

Mrs. Erickson takes this as her dismissal and heads back up the stairs. I find a straight-back chair and drag it through the dirty clothes to get it closer to the bed. Unlike a lot of people who are classified as neat freaks, I'm comfortable in dirty rooms (likely due to my longtime friendship with Mike). I need *my* place to be clean in order to write (orderly home, orderly mind). If others want to live in filth, it makes no difference to me. Evan fits right in with the room, clad in a dirty gray t-shirt and plaid shorts. Judging by the smell coming from the south, it appears he hasn't showered in the past few days. He sets the phone aside, burying it somewhere in the folds of the bed. He rolls to one side and props himself up on an elbow.

"What's going on?" he asks.

I suspect Evan knows I'm not here for a social call. His face is lined, and I'm wondering if he's slept much the past few days. I drop into the chair, trying (and I'm sure failing) to look authoritative.

"I wanted to talk to you about Burt," I say.

"What about him?"

"You needed money from him. Due to the gambling. The card game specifically. And you made a call to him on the night of the murder."

From the way Evan's entire body freezes up, he was laboring under the delusion I came here on some fishing expedition. He swings his feet around and sits up on the bed.

"How do you know all that?" he asks.

"I did a little research," I say, "You don't have to confirm anything since I know it already. I would appreciate it if you honestly answered some questions, though."

"Fine. Whatever you need."

I slide to the edge of the chair. "What was the conversation with Burt about?"

"He wanted a favor from me. I wouldn't do it."

"He wanted your help in taking over Ed's Pizza, the place Charley's family owns."

"Does Charley know?"

I shrug. "If she does, she hasn't heard it from me."

Evan's face tightens. "I'd appreciate it if you stayed away from her."

"We have a nice conversation here and I don't see any reason I need to bother her."

"Good." Evan runs a hand through his greasy hair. "Yeah, that's what Burt and me were arguing about at Nick's. That favor was the only way he was going to give me the money. I kept asking him if there was another way, another favor I could do for him. He said this was it. Otherwise, I was useless."

"But you called him later."

"Yeah. I wanted to meet with him."

A little rush goes through me. I think I know the answer to this question, but I ask it anyway. "Where did you meet him?"

Evan lets out a long breath. "Bennett Park. But he was alive when I left. I swear."

I hope he understands if I don't take his word on that. "What did you talk about?" I ask.

"About the pizza place thing. Again. I was trying to negotiate."

"And how did that go?"

"No dice," Evan says, "Just a repeat of the argument at Nick's. I had to screw over Charley's family. It was that or nothing."

"And what did you tell him?"

"I told him I had to think about it." He runs a hand through his hair. "Charley is the greatest. Better than I deserve. I literally didn't know what I was going to do."

It would be nice to believe that. But my small acquaintance with Evan leads me to believe he'd screw over anybody if it meant saving his own hide. As far as I know, Evan and Burt were the only ones at the meeting, so I'll have to take Evan's word on what happened.

"What time did you meet?" I ask.

"About 12:30. Meeting went for about ten minutes, and I left. Short and sweet. Well, one of those, anyway."

Interesting. Part of that tracks with what Eli told me. He brought Burt over to Bennett Park around that time. But Eli says he drove around for half an hour before Burt called him. Evan said they only met about ten minutes. What happened the rest of the time?

"You're sure it was only ten minutes?"

"Yeah," Evan says, irritated, "It wasn't like we had a hell of a lot to talk about."

"Where did you go after the meeting?" I ask.

"Over to Charley's," he says, "Spent the night there."

I'll need Charley to confirm that, but I'll keep those plans to myself. It would only agitate Evan, just when we were getting along so well. I use my foot to brush aside some clothes, revealing a hidden ashtray. I ignore it.

"You've been asking Alice for help," I say.

"That's the case. At first, I was asking for her help with money. She doesn't have any. That lawyer boyfriend of hers probably has plenty, though."

That catches my attention. "Alice is dating the lawyer she works for?"

"Probably shouldn't have told you that," Evan says, "Keep it between us, okay?"

"I can do that." I prop my elbows on my knees. "Alice mentioned something about you betraying her."

Evan's head pops up. He thinks for a second. "That was at the fairgrounds. How did you…?" Then it navigates the Ganja Straits. "That was you? At the fairgrounds?"

"Me and my brothers. What did Alice mean when she said you'd betrayed her?"

He flips a hand at that. "Just Alice being Alice. She still hasn't gotten over high school. You know what I mean?"

Sadly, I do. But I'm certainly not going to share that with Evan. "It didn't mean *anything*?"

"Nothing to me, anyway."

Again, I don't believe him, but again, I've got no ammo I can use to get answers out of him. Maybe I'll get something if I check Evan's alibi, but I can't do that here. I get up from the chair.

"That's all I've got," I say, "I'll talk to you later."

"Sure," Evan says, sounding less than thrilled.

Can't blame him for the attitude. Seeing me hasn't exactly been a boon for him. Evan walks me to the stairway. He stops when we get to the bottom.

"Just do me a favor," he says, "Far as my parents are concerned, you're stopping over here to say hi. Maybe ask what Elyse is up to. They don't really need to know any of this stuff with Burt or the card game. Okay?"

If Evan comes home with his face beaten in and both his legs broken, they might have some questions. But those questions won't be directed at *me*.

"No problem," I say. Then I feel the need to add: "I hope things work out. With the money."

"Thanks. Don't suppose you have any, do you?"

"Sorry, no. I'm pretty close to having my own leg breakers looking for me."

Evan gives me a sympathetic look. "I get it, man."

I go upstairs. I genuinely would like to help him, but I've got somebody else I need to help first. And that might mean further hurting Evan, if he's the one who killed Burt.

Pretty sure Mrs. Erickson wouldn't welcome me back if that were the case.

***

The next stop is Porter's Bay Hospital and a visit with Will. He was apparently out and about the night Burt was killed, giving Burt a ride over to Eli's apartment. The front desk tells me Will has been moved to a room on the fifth floor, overlooking the lake. He will likely be discharged by tonight. His room is halfway down the corridor, just off the elevator. The door is open, and Will is alone when I get there. The room, as could be expected, is antiseptic and clean. Instruments beeping away. I knock on the doorframe. Will turns from the TV to me.

"Joe Davis!" he says, his voice carrying down the hall, "Pull up a chair."

Said chair is about as comfortable as a fender. (Clearly, this hospital creates more back problems than it cures.) Will clicks off the TV.

"Good to see you," he says, "Hope this will be more pleasant than last time."

Will certainly looks a little better than last time, though he doesn't look entirely recovered. His voice is a little strained, his movements are slow, and he looks pale (although that could be the sun coming in the window). My face flushes at the thought of our last meeting.

"I'm sorry about that," I say.

"Don't be," Will says, lightly waving a hand, "You didn't do anything wrong. It was my own fault. Alice is always telling me to play it cool, keep my temper, all that. I never listen to her. Maybe it's time I started."

I adjust my position in the chair. "I heard about the…"

"Cancer?"

"Yeah. I'm sorry."

"Don't be. You didn't give it to me." He arches an eyebrow. "Did you?"

I smile. "Pretty sure I'm in the clear on that one."

I'm grateful for the stabs at humor. I don't want Will to get the idea I'm pitying him. That's probably the last thing he wants. Besides, I already feel like a shitheel for having an ulterior motive.

"We were talking about Burt last time," I say, "You got pretty upset."

"I'm sorry about that," Will says, "There's a lot of history there. Almost all of it bad."

"I take it Cully Brown and Taylor, Minnesota are part of it."

As expected, Will snaps me a look. "How did you find out about that?"

"Officer Beardsley knows. And I did some research. Cully Brown was found dead in Taylor, Minnesota. Gunshot wound to the head." I lean forward. "What I don't know is how it connects to the rest of you."

Will closes his eyes, perhaps an effort to calm down. "It's not my place to tell you, Joe. I'm sorry."

"Did one of you guys kill Cully Brown?"

The question pops out of my mouth, unpremeditated. It's been a nagging thought. Could my dad have been part of a murder? Is *that* the reason none of them will talk about it? Will looks toward the ceiling.

"It's complicated," he says.

"What's complicated? Did one of you guys kill Cully Brown? It's a yes or no question."

"It's not. Trust me on that. That's all I can tell you."

We let the air in the room settle. I look around. "I'm surprised Alice isn't here," I say.

"She had to run some errands. She'll be back later. She'll have to be if they're going to let me out of here."

"Sounds like you'll be out by tonight," I say, "Are you going to my dad's thing?"

"I want to," Will says, "It all depends on whether I can get out in time. And if Alice agrees to it. She's pretty much my ride these days."

"I've heard that. Doesn't apply all the time, though, does it?"

Will tilts his head slightly. "What do you mean?"

"The night Burt was killed, you gave him a ride to Eli's building."

"Heard about that, did you? I got a call from Burt. His tires got slashed while he was at the Lodge. He needed a ride to Eli's. Couldn't get ahold of Eli. Didn't know who else to try. I thought about calling Alice, but I knew she wouldn't want to give Burt a ride anywhere. I figured what the hell? Gotta take a walk on the wild side every now and again. Besides, it would give me a chance to talk to Burt. Maybe get him to lay off the stuff with your dad."

"How did that work out?"

"Didn't," Will says, "I knew it was a waste of time. Burt was nothing if not stubborn."

"I don't suppose you saw Burt holding my dad's watch, did you?" I ask.

"Afraid I didn't."

"That was all you talked about? My dad?"

"I put in a word for Evan," Will says, "Figured since he was Alice's friend, I could try to help out. Same thing as talking to him about your dad. Didn't get me anywhere."

"And you dropped him off at Eli's?"

"That was the case. Then I drove home. Got away with that one." He chuckles. "I *do* manage to swipe the car from time to time. Run a few short errands. Don't tell Alice."

"I won't." I cock my head to one side. "You know about Evan owing money."

"Alice told me. She tells me everything. She's a good girl. She's dating a lawyer. Did you know that?"

"I do."

"I wish they'd get married. I know that's old-fashioned. But hell, I'm old. Why not be old-fashioned?" He lays back against the pillow. "She loves him. Helped him out of some trouble."

"What kind of trouble?"

He flips a hand at that. "Nothing worth talking about."

I lean back in my chair. Will gave Burt a ride to Eli's apartment. That covers that gap of time. He claims he went straight home, but I only have his word on that. And I certainly can't ask Alice to back up her dad's alibi. Guess I'm going to have to take his word.

"Does Alice ever see her mom?" I ask.

"As little as possible. She was pretty angry when her mom left me for Burt. Refused to see her for a long time. Never wanted to be in the same room as Burt."

Apparently, she made exceptions, given that Alice's number was in Burt's burner phone, and they apparently talked at Nick's the night of the murder. But that might upset Will, and I can ask Alice directly about it (whether she'll answer directly is more of a mystery).

I stand, smoothing out my jeans as I do. "I'll leave you alone. Hope to see you at my dad's thing tonight."

"You will," he says, "How's your dad holding up?"

"He's doing okay. I guess. I think the threatening notes have him worried."

"I understand," Will says, "I just threw mine away. They're not worth looking at. I'd love to get my hands on the little son of a bitch leaving them." He tosses his hands up. "For all the good it would do."

I leave Will sitting in bed. He goes back to the television and waits for his freedom from hospital confinement. And waiting for other things he probably doesn't want to think about. I guess I didn't expect him to answer my questions about Cully Brown and Taylor. Maybe I'm a little relieved, too.

We all have things we don't like to think about.

***

It's not a long walk from the hospital to The Hub. If I time my arrival right, I should be able to corral Charley, Evan's girlfriend, and have a little conversation with her (despite my utterly worthless promise to Evan).

I'm walking up Lake Drive, approaching The Hub. I glance into the alley between the restaurant and the sandwich shop next door. A couple of guys are skulking around. They wear black windbreakers, despite the relatively warm weather, and smoke cigarettes. They're making a studied attempt to look casual and aren't succeeding. I hustle into The Hub.

The place is dead, understandably. It's the middle of the afternoon. Past lunch, but not quite the dinner hour. A few guys—regulars, I assume—have coffee at the counter. There is no sign of Charley. Another server, filling a napkin dispenser at a booth, addresses me.

"You can just sit anywhere," she says.

"I appreciate that," I say, "But I was looking for Charley."

"She just finished her shift. She's probably headed out the back. You might be able to catch her in the alley."

I thank the server and head around to the alley. I arrive in time to see Charley talking to the two skulkers. They stand on either side of her and have dispensed with the cigarettes. Charley looks toward me. Her eyes widen, as if pleading for help. The skulkers grab Charley and move her the other way down the alley. Somebody has to do something.

Shit. Why does it have to me?

CHAPTER FOURTEEN

One of the silliest things I've ever seen (and there's no shortage of competition in that area) occurred during my brief time as a pizza delivery guy, shortly after I moved to the Twin Cities. Some dude sent his girlfriend in to pick up a to-go order. She used his credit card to pay, and the clerk had to manually enter the numbers into our computer, since the credit card machine—unreliable at the best of times—was on the fritz. When the guy—who was apparently way too fond of conspiracy theories—found out about this, he was convinced we were stealing his credit card numbers for the purpose of identity theft. (As if we're all master criminals and this pizza delivery thing is just a hobby.) His response was to come into our store and confront us with our crimes, thus setting the stage for the idiocy to follow.

Adam was the name of the clerk who confronted this guy. Adam was one of those souls blessed with more mouth than brains. Rather than de-escalate the situation, Adam needled the guy, climaxing with this quote, "You're acting like a bitch!" What followed was an exchange of threats in which Adam and the guy stood on either side of the counter, negotiating a fight. The guy kept inviting Adam to step outside and Adam kept inviting the guy to come across the counter. I kept waiting for Don King to get involved in the negotiations. Finally, our manager, an emaciated dude in his late twenties, grew tired of the whole thing and escorted the guy out. He was met with no resistance. By now it was clear to everyone in the store we had witnessed two men trying their damnedest to look tough and not get into a fight.

That need to fight seems coded into the male DNA. Yes, there are plenty of mean motor scooters in the world, plenty of guys you wouldn't want to meet in a dark alley. But the majority of us just fantasize about that stuff, generally while watching James Bond or Jason Statham. We can maybe present a reasonable front, but when the fight moves from the theoretical to the actual, we're in deep shitting trouble.

Right now, the situation calls for a tough-guy-man-of-action and all it has is me. Speaking of deep shitting trouble...

Charley looks back at me as the skulkers drag her toward a maroon Buick. "Hey!" I shout. Because that seems like a good place to start the conversation.

The skulkers look toward me. One—a balding guy with a black mustache—points with his middle finger. "Get the fuck out of here!"

I'd be completely cool with that. But Charley wouldn't be and she's the person I'm trying to help. (Cripe, I've never done well with obligation. Only trouble arises from it.) I stand my ground, though I've started sweating.

"Leave her alone," I say.

In my head, I sounded like Clint Eastwood. In reality, I probably sounded like Eugene Levy in *A Mighty Wind*. Mustache leaves Charley in the care of his partner and starts down the alley. Mustache is burly and sports a bit of a gut. He reaches into his coat, and I know what he's about to pull out. (A bouquet of flowers would be lovely but not likely.) The partner hangs back. He has a bald head, a round face and dark glasses. Dark Glasses looks like the more threatening of the two. My feet stay planted, but the rest of me leans back. I'm either going to fall over backward or run the other way.

"What the hell is going on?"

The voice comes from the backdoor of the restaurant. The server who directed me to Charley has come across the scene. Mustache and Dark Glasses turn toward her. Two things happen in short order. Charley kicks Dark Glasses in the shin, causing him to scream and let go of her. I take five quick steps and ram a shoulder right into the small of Mustache's back. He expels some air and crashes into the door. The server is thrown back into the restaurant. Mustache's gun clatters on the ground and he follows, landing flat on his ass. Blood trickles from a cut just above his eyebrow.

I turn to Charley. "Run!"

We charge down the alley, going the opposite way from Lake Drive. Fortunately, Charley wears sensible shoes and is equipped for the chase. She's not much of a runner, moving largely like a bag of disconnected body parts, and the skirt of The Hub uniform does nothing to help. But I've got her hand and she's letting herself get dragged along in my wake. We pop out of the alley and run down the street behind The Hub. The skulkers are in pursuit.

"Where are you parked?" I ask.

"Back the other way," Charley says, "Where are you parked?"

"I don't have a car."

"What the hell? Aren't we running to your car?"

"I thought we were running to *your* car."

"Oh, for God's sake."

We start back the other direction. But Mustache and Dark Glasses run out of the alley. Their guns are at their sides. Charley and I turn back again. Behind us, the thugs are shouting threats. Charley picks up speed. (If Charley's views are similar to Lisa's on the subject, she'll be damned if she's going to die in this ridiculous uniform.) We duck into an unfenced backyard, run along the side of the house and then out through the front yard.

"Who are those guys?" Charley says.

"Friends of your boyfriend," I say.

"Friends of Evan's? Seriously?"

"Not *close* friends, clearly."

We cut through a couple more yards and find ourselves on Eleventh Street. All the neighborhoods in this part of town are laid out in a grid pattern, allowing us to cut through beaucoup properties and do a goodly amount of jay-running.

Eleventh Street is deserted. No one disturbs our little Saturday run. Mustache and Dark Glasses are still coming. They try to disguise their guns, lest they draw undue attention to themselves. We cut through another yard and come out in an alley (confusing the hell out of the kids playing there). Charley's breathing becomes heavy. Being a smoker doesn't suit this kind of exercise. Or any kind of exercise. She takes a look back.

"Those guys are going to shoot us," she says.

"No, they're not," I say, "They might shoot me but not you. That's not their job."

"What do you mean?"

"They were sent here to grab you," I say, "They're trying to threaten Evan. Killing you isn't going to get them anywhere. They need you alive."

We cut through another yard and on to Tenth Street. Still no one around. Mustache and Dark Glasses still in pursuit. We reach another side street. Charley hits a crack in the sidewalk and goes down. I stop to help her up. Mustache and Dark Glasses are closing in fast.

So, I'm grateful when a car backs out of a driveway and clips Dark Glasses.

Dark Glasses' legs are taken out from under him. He's in the air for a second before going down on his hip. Mustache stops to check on Dark Glasses, who struggles to get to his feet. A woman gets out of the car and offers profuse *pardon*s. Mustache and Dark Glasses ignore her and take off after us.

I have to hand it to these guys. They're determined.

We cut over another street and everyone is slowing. At this rate, we'll be walking then crawling. The last one to pass out is the winner. Charley grips my arm.

"I can't keep doing this," she says, her words coming out in gasps.

"I don't think we can stop," I tell her.

"What are we going to do?"

I don't have an answer. Stopping to fight is not an option. Letting these guys take Charley is not an option. Letting them kill me is *really* not an option. No idea what to do.

A car crosses the street ahead of us. It slows to a stop. The thing looks vaguely familiar, but I can't place it. (I'm a little distracted at the moment.) It's directly in our path. What fresh hell is being visited on us now?

So, you can imagine my relief when my brother Kevin gets out of the car.

He glides around the back of the minivan, shucking off his gray suitcoat and tossing it on the roof. My heart beats in my ears. Kevin puts his hands on his hips.

"Joe, what's going on?" he asks.

I stop and try to summon the breath for an explanation. "Those guys…after Charley here…guns."

It lacks a certain touch of the poet, but it communicates the basics. Kevin steps past me, waiting for Mustache and Dark Glasses to catch up. The passenger door opens and Jordan steps out. Ah, *here* is the fresh hell I was waiting for.

"Kevin, is this necessary?" she asks, not even looking at me and Charley.

My brother doesn't answer. Mustache and Dark Glasses slow to a halt, not looking any better than us. The guns remain at their sides. Kevin blocks us from them, his body language loose and open.

"Nice to meet you guys," Kevin says, his voice gregarious, as if he's being introduced to these dudes at a party, "I'm Joe's brother. You care to tell me what's going on?"

Mustache, his face red from running, does the talking. "Get the fuck out of here."

Kevin makes no move. "Joe, why don't you and your friend get in the car?"

"They're not going anywhere," Mustache says, raising the gun slightly, "Except the girl is coming with us."

Jordan, annoyed, steps past us. Kevin keeps his hands at his side. His body tenses almost imperceptibly. "I have to say, you kind of suck at negotiation," he says, "See, I'm just trying to get some information. You guys—"

Mustache brings the gun up to Kevin's face, holding it two inches from my brother's nose. "This is the last fucking time I'm going to tell you. Get the—"

Kevin's left hand comes up and knocks Mustache's gun arm away from his face. He follows that up with a straight right to Mustache's nose. Mustache's head snaps back. His knees give way. Kevin casually takes the gun from his hand.

Dark Glasses brings his gun up. Jordan boots him in what had been his good shin. Dark Glasses drops to the ground, his trademark sunglasses falling off. He lets out an exasperated, "Fuck!"

As Dark Glasses drops, Jordan takes his gun and hands it to Kevin. My brother tucks both guns into the waistband of his pants. That done, he grabs his suitcoat from the roof of the car and slips it back on, covering the weaponry.

Charley leans toward me. "You didn't tell me your brother was James Bond."

I shrug. "He didn't tell *me.*"

Kevin stands over the skulkers. "Word of advice, guys: if you're going to use guns to threaten someone, make sure the safeties are off. Otherwise, you look like a couple of jerk offs." He glances at Jordan. "Hon, would you mind calling the cops?"

Jordan seems put out, but starts dialing her phone, nonetheless. Charley waves her hands.

"Do we really have to do that?" she says.

"Are you serious?" I ask, "These guys tried to abduct you and then chased us all over hell. That's the kind of thing you call the cops about."

Charley lowers her voice. "If the cops get brought in, these guys might tell them about Evan and everything that's going on. I don't want them to do that."

Oh, for garden seed. I'm not inclined to let the skulkers off on their recognizance. Given my brother had to bail our asses out, it might be even harder for him. I look over the skulkers.

"You guys work for Berringer?" I ask.

Mustache hesitates. He's bleeding profusely from a possibly broken nose. "Yeah, we do, Evan Erickson owes him money." Mustache looks toward Charley. "We weren't going to hurt you, ma'am. Unless Evan didn't pay up."

"I'm sure that will comfort her to no end." I turn to Kevin and whisper, "I don't suppose we can let these guys go?"

"You don't suppose correctly," Kevin says, "I'm not in the habit of letting criminals go."

"Kevin, you're not a crusading district attorney," I say, "You're in contract law. You're in the habit of making corrupt bargains with white collar criminals. You can't give two blue collar bozos a pass?"

Kevin frowns then gestures toward the bozos in question. "Give me your wallets."

Mustache's face crinkles. "What do you need with them?"

"I was hoping to use the local library," Kevin says, "I figure you geniuses must have library cards I could swipe." He kicks Mustache's foot. "Just give me your fucking wallets."

The skulkers scramble to extract their wallets and drop them at Kevin's feet. He sorts through them, tossing aside cash, credit cards, condoms, what have you. He finally chucks the wallets themselves, keeping only the driver's licenses.

"Got your names—or at least your aliases—right here," Kevin says, holding the licenses between two fingers, "Anything happens to my brother or his friend, I give these to the cops. You go back to your boss and tell him to find another way to negotiate with Evan. We clear?"

Mustache looks at Dark Glasses, who just shrugs. Mustache says, "Sounds, sounds good."

"I'm so glad to hear that," Kevin says, "Now, get the hell out of here."

The skulkers stand, cautiously. Mustache's nose is still bleeding, and Dark Glasses' shins won't quite support the rest of him. They look around, then Mustache speaks up.

"Don't suppose you know the way back to Lake Drive?" he says.

"Yes," Kevin says, "But you can figure it out for yourselves. Get moving."

The skulkers hop along, going the other way down the street. Kevin turns to the rest of us, the situation under control. Jordan puts her phone away.

"You're just going to let them go?" she asks.

"It'll be fine," he says, which doesn't reassure Jordan. "Joe, can we give you and your friend a ride somewhere?"

I turn to Charley. "There a place we can talk?"

"You know where Bennett Park is?" Charley asks.

"You kidding me?" Kevin says, "I spent half my life there when I was growing up. A shame about the rocket ship slide."

Charley and I agree. Jordan has likely never heard of the rocket slide and probably wouldn't care even if she had. We pile into the minivan. Charley and I sit in the backseat. Kevin drops the guns into the center console. Jordan speaks out of the corner of her mouth.

"Hope you realize the favor we're doing you and your girlfriend," Jordan says.

"Um, she's not my girlfriend," I say.

Jordan gives me a sidelong glance. "No one ever is with you, are they?"

Charley gives me a quizzical look. I shake my head, letting her know it's a long story. And judging by the events of the last hour—and the last few days—not the worst one I could tell.

***

Kevin drops us off at Bennett Park and wishes us luck. Jordan says nothing. My gratitude for Kevin saving us wrestles with my resentment at being in his debt. But I can deal with that another time. Charley and I walk aimlessly into the park.

"Where should we go?" Charley asks.

"No real preference."

"How about the gazebo?"

"No." I say it a little too hastily. Being in the park with a pretty girl wearing a Hub uniform brings back memories. Pleasant but still painful. I gesture toward the picnic tables. "Why don't we sit over there?"

We make our way to one of the tables. Over in the playground, kids climb on the equipment. The sound of a little league game filters in. We have a view of the amphitheater. A wooden roof covers the picnic area. It's empty now, but people will be here soon for beer and grilling. Charley and I sit on either side of the table. She wipes her eyes. The adrenaline is wearing off and the reality of what almost happened is hitting her. She grabs my hand.

"Thank you," Charley says, her voice breaking slightly, "I don't know what would have happened if you hadn't come along."

I pat her hand. Charley fishes a pack of cigarettes out of her uniform and shakily lights one. She visibly relaxes with her first puff. I've never been a smoker, but I've always admired the way it puts people at ease. (The lung cancer and COPD, of course, are less admirable.)

"Okay, if I ask a few questions?" I say.

"Absolutely," Charley says, "It's the least I can do. For real."

"Evan met with Burt Franklin—here—the night Burt was murdered. Did Evan tell you anything about that?

Charley's eyebrows go up. "No, he didn't tell me that. He said they talked at Nick's and that was that. Isn't this where Burt was found?"

"It was," I say, "You'll understand why I'm curious."

Charley blows a line of smoke out the side of her mouth. "Evan didn't say anything. He looked a little upset when he came to my place, but I figured that was about the talk with Burt."

"What time did Evan get to your place?"

"About one-thirty."

One-thirty. That's about fifty minutes after his meeting with Burt. Plenty of time to kill him and move on. It couldn't have taken him nearly an hour to get to Charley's.

"What did he tell you about the conversation with Burt?" I ask.

"Just that it was about the money." Charley tilts her head. "He said there was something else he and Burt talked about. But he didn't want to tell me about it. He was worried something might happen to me if I got involved." She laughs without humor. "He might have been right. But he said he'd take care of it. Maybe he should have listened to me."

"If it means anything, I don't think Evan's in the habit of listening to *anyone*. I wouldn't take it personally."

"After today?" Charley says, arching an eyebrow, "I might take it a little personally."

Can't say I blame her. Charley is getting her strength back. There's something steely in her eyes that tells me she'd make a formidable enemy.

"Did any of Evan's plans involve Alice Grant?" I ask.

Thankfully, Charley doesn't react by standing up, slapping her hands on the table and screaming, *By Lucifer's beard, sir, how dare thee?* (I picture weird stuff. Sue me.) In fact, Charley isn't dismissive at all. She takes a drag on her cigarette.

"Maybe," she says, "Evan dated Alice in high school. Right up until her father caught them making out in the rose garden over there."

I arch an eyebrow. "Just making out?"

"They might have been a little further along than just making out. Anyway, they've always had this weird relationship. Alice looks after Evan, and you can tell she's nuts about him. Evan acts like he's embarrassed they ever dated. But he still goes to her when he needs something. I've asked him about it, and all he ever says is, 'I can't get rid of her.' If you ask me, he doesn't try too terribly hard."

I use my finger to trace something carved in the table. (I don't know if *JD* + *WR* is truly *4ever*, but I wish them the best.) "Evan didn't tell you anything about his chat with Burt?"

"No," Charley says, "Just that Burt wanted a favor and Evan didn't want to do it. That was it." She takes a long drag on her cigarette then flicks the butt on to the cement. (I find that sort of thing gross, but I let it pass without comment.) She tucks her legs up to her chest and wraps her arms around them. "I want to think Evan is a good guy. He's cute and charming. But I'm not stupid. I know a guy who's in his thirties and still lives with his parents is trouble. He talks like he's going to get his life together, and he has all these dreams. And if I could help him do that…that would be great, right?"

"It would be," I say, with less conviction than I might.

Sadly, I understand her attraction to Evan. I've been friends with Mike for seventeen years. He and Evan are of a type: good looking, gift of gab, seem to have the world at their feet. It's only when you get to know them that you realize they are each an unmade bed of a human being. Reality may be dawning on Charley. It has nothing to do with intelligence so much as an unwillingness to face facts. It's why my smartest friend, Carol, could date Mike for nearly a year before giving up the ghost.

"I just hope that's going to happen," Charley says, with less conviction than *she* might.

If Evan killed Burt Franklin, there is no chance he's ever going to realize those dreams, unless they involve sitting in the state prison in Stillwater creating toilet liquor and enjoying the company of other men. But if it's a choice between saving Evan or saving my dad, there's no choice at all.

"We should get going," I say, "Do you live far from here?"

"No," Charley says, "Just a couple blocks over. How about you?"

"I live…a ways from here. But I've got a thing to be at and it's not too far away. How about I walk you home?"

Charley gives me a shy grin. "Aren't you the gentleman?"

We get up from the table and walk across the park. I'm sure we'll just chitchat for these few blocks, talk about the weather, how the neighborhood has changed, these crazy kids and their rock 'n' roll, what have you. We'll ignore the fault line that now runs through our nascent relationship: the idea that she loves Evan and I love my dad and that I'm possibly trying to save the one *I* love at the expense of putting the one *she* loves behind bars.

But she works in a diner. She must know that bit about making an omelet and breaking a few eggs…

CHAPTER FIFTEEN

I think how we view the place we grew up is a microcosm of how we view changing times. I like to joke that my hometown of Porter's Bay hasn't changed over time, but that's not actually true. Arthur's Diner, my favorite hangout in high school, was torn down a few years after I left. The rocket ship slide in Bennett Park has gone the way of the dinosaur. It's not as if the town has undergone a complete makeover, but nothing is exactly the same. When I was a kid, I loved hearing my parents tell stories of "old" Porter's Bay; what the town looked like when they were kids. The changes from their time to mine were about as incremental as the changes from my time to now. But I looked on the past with a more benign eye. As do we all.

The past, after all, is safe. We know there was a future back then because we're standing in it. As we look at our own future from the present day, we don't know if anything is guaranteed or what it might hold. Once we get there, we'll look back on these times with the same fondness with which we look back on older times. It's the stability we didn't know we had at the time that we miss. It wasn't necessarily better. It was just familiar.

Unless you're like my friend Lars and you're just making up the past as you go along.

"I hope you've enjoyed our little excursion through Porter's Bay's underground history," Lars says, holding the PA mic just below his mouth, "Please tell all your friends. Leave us a review on Yelp. And please visit our website. When we've created one. For now, I am allowed to accept gratuities. Have a great day."

The trolley bus comes to a halt in the parking lot of the Memorial Arena. The little band of tourists clears out like they're fleeing the *Andria Doria*. Lars stands outside, wearing the same ensemble he wore in Gordie's office. (It's the only suit he brought. If he moves to Porter's Bay, he's going to have to do some shopping.) He says farewell to people who don't acknowledge him. He holds out a fedora in which he collects fifteen cents and a casino token by way of gratuity. Lars spins toward us as we exit.

"What did you think?" he asks, brandishing the hat (and losing the casino token).

Mike, unaccustomed to being diplomatic, looks down. "It was…uh…"

"It was a goddamn abomination," I say, *really* pleased I declined helping Lars with this project.

Lars's head snaps back. (I don't know if he's shocked by my frankness or confused by Mike and I switching our usual roles.) "What was the issue, brother?"

"The issue?" I say, "The issue is there wasn't a word of truth in any of that shit. John Dillinger did not have a shootout with the FBI outside of Sweet Mary's Sweet Shop and Sweet Mary herself was not wounded in the exchange."

"John Dillinger had a shootout with the FBI here in Minnesota," Lars says, assuming a haughty pose, "That's a matter of historical record."

"It's also a matter of historical record that the shootout was in St. Paul," I say, "And Sweet Mary's Sweet Shop wasn't even open in the Thirties. And there is no Sweet Mary. Bob DeBartelaven thought it would be a cute name for the place when he opened it ten years ago."

Lars flips a hand. "One takes a certain creative license."

"I didn't realize *creative license* was a euphemism for *complete fabrication.*"

"You're too hung up on details, mein Freund."

"Details?" I say, "Such as the Barker Gang hiding out in what is now Mrs. Krebbs' house and the FBI intercepting letters from Ma Barker talking about a walleye named Paul, thus leading the FBI right to them?"

"That is also a matter of historical record," Lars says.

"Except it was a gator named Joe," I say, "And the FBI found the Barker gang in Florida. You were only off by about fifteen-hundred miles."

"Dust in a windy street," Lars says, "The overriding importance is telling a good tale and showing the audience a good time."

I hold my hands out, palms down, trying to present a reasonable argument. (A fool's errand, I know, but...) "Lars, you can't make shit up for a tour that promotes itself as historical. People are going to think these things are true when they couldn't be more false."

"Oh, they could be more false. Just give me some time." Lars looks away from me. "Once the reviews come in, you'll feel differently."

Mike finally wakes from his self-induced coma. "I don't think the reviews are going to help, man. This tour is just a bad idea. It's pretty clear you didn't get permission from that one old lady to use her house on the tour. The one Bonnie and Clyde used as a hideout."

"Not a hideout," Lars says, "A love nest."

"Whatever," Mike says, "But she seemed pretty upset. She threw dog shit at the bus. At least, I hope it was dog shit."

"And a finer metaphor for this tour, you will not find," I say.

Lars vigorously waves a hand, as if wiping our concerns out of the air. "You're too attached to this town, Joe. You see only the idyllic place of your boyhood and refuse to see the dark, squirmy underbelly that pervades it."

Gross. "Lars, it wasn't just me. Nobody enjoyed this tour." I turn to a third party. "Mike?"

"It sucked rocks."

Lars steps toward the bus. "I have the backing of City Hall. We'll see whether people enjoyed my grand vision."

"Speaking of the mayor," I say, "You sure you want to put all your eggs in that basket? Carol has been doing some research…"

He invites me to continue this conversation with the hand. "Carol can make up whatever stories she wishes. Gordie is a visionary, and he will not be taken down by these small fractions of people. If Carol knows what's best for her, she'll stand down and let history take its course."

Lars grandly slaps the side of the bus. However, the bus driver, a dyspeptic looking guy in a plaid shirt, takes this as the sign to leave and starts driving across the parking lot. Lars runs after the bus. When last seen, he's chasing the bus out of the parking lot and on to 23rd Street. Mike and I make our way back to the RAV4.

"Julie wants to come to the picnic for your dad tomorrow," he says, "As my date."

"You okay with that?" I ask.

"Of course not! But I don't see how I can say no. If I do, Julie might freak out and tell her husband about the affair. I have to break things off with Julie before tomorrow."

"Why don't you two have sex while her husband sits in the closet and listens?" I say, "You seem to be pretty good at that."

"You can shut it any time," Mike says. He runs a hand through his hair as we arrive at the car. "What about you? How's the investigation going?"

"It's going," I say, "Just not sure where. Eli gave Burt a ride to Bennett Park the night of the murder. Evan met with Burt. Alice may have talked to him on the phone. Will gave Burt a ride from the bar to Eli's and then claims he went home." We climb into the car. "On top of that, I don't know what exactly Taylor or Cully Brown might have to do with it. And I don't know who's been sending the threatening notes. Other than that, it's going great."

One thing I've always liked about Mike is that he doesn't try to be comforting. I mean that as a compliment. Sometimes, there are no words to make you feel better and the attempt feels trite and useless. Mike is more adept at letting you sit with a situation than acting like a self-help guru.

"That sucks," he says.

"It contains definite suckage," I say.

I drive toward First Avenue. In a few blocks, we'll reach the spot where I turn left to go to my parents' house. Mike taps his knuckles against the window.

"What do you have going on after this?" he asks.

"Going to give Carol a tour of my old high school," I say, "Want to come along?"

"No thanks. I've got to figure out this Julie situation. I can't do that with Carol there."

"You sure?" I say, "She *is* an expert on breaking up with you."

"Go eat a bag of shit."

That's the reaction I should have expected (and, if I'm going to be honest, deserved). Mike chews his goatee, which is either a sign of consternation or contemplation (or perhaps constipation), depending on the situation.

"They haven't found the murder weapon yet, have they?" he asks.

"If they have, they haven't told me," I say, "Or the newspaper. You'd think at least one of us would know."

"I wonder what the murderer did with it?" Mike says.

I stretch a hand in the general direction of Lake Drive. "You may have noticed there's a rather substantial lake in which to toss the thing."

"I don't think so. The murderer wouldn't take that kind of chance."

"What do you mean?"

"Okay, picture yourself as the murderer," Mike says, "You've just killed Burt. You've got his gun. You need to get rid of the thing. But you're *blocks* from the lake. Sure, you could drive there, but it's the middle of the night. Only takes one bored cop to decide you look like a bunch of rowdy teenagers and pull you over. The cop comes to the window. You're on the adrenaline high to end all adrenaline highs. You're probably sweating. Your eyes are darting around. Your hands might be shaking. The cop will figure you're either up to something or geeked out of your mind. The cop searches the car and finds the gun and you are fucked. No, you can't take a chance on leaving Bennett Park with that gun on you."

I slip him a look. "Should I be at all concerned that your mind just automatically thinks this stuff up?"

"Kind of makes you want to stay on my good side." He turns toward me. "What I'm saying is, that gun is probably still in Bennett Park. The cops just haven't found it."

"You want me to go look for the murder weapon in Bennett Park?"

"Roger that."

Actually, I'm more likely to *get* rogered but still… "If it was in Bennett Park, don't you think the police would have found it by now?"

"Not necessarily. Cops aren't infallible. Besides, this department isn't that big. It's not like they've got hundreds of people linking arms and beating the bushes."

"Bennett Park is big," I say, "Not Central Park big, but Porter's Bay big. What are the odds we're going to find it?"

"You keep using this *we* word."

"If you think I'm doing this genuinely stupid thing by myself, you are sadly mistaken." Mike starts to object. I cut him off by raising a hand. "This car is now going to Bennett Park. If you're in it, you're going to have to come along."

Mike frowns, genuinely sorry he brought the whole subject up. "Once more around the park, Jeeves."

That's what you get for volunteering ideas. Follow-through can be a real bitch.

***

There was a time in my life when I would have been thrilled to make two trips to Bennett Park in one day. But the events of *this* day have rather harshed that buzz. I ditch the RAV4 in the parking lot, not far from where Burt Franklin's body was found. The park is still rather empty. Mike and I get out of the car.

"Okay, now what?" Mike says.

We step out of the parking lot and walk several feet into the grass. I stop and look around.

"From what I gather, Burt was found right around here," I say, "He was waiting for Eli when he was attacked."

"Interesting spot," Mike says, "You got those trees over there. If someone wanted to, they could hide and wait. If they were careful enough, they could sneak up on Burt and take him out before he knew what hit him. Literally."

"You think that's how it happened?"

"That's how I'd do it."

"Again, do I need to be concerned that you're so comfortable planning this stuff out?"

"I'm just trying to put myself in the killer's shoes," he says, "Try to feel what they felt. What's the word for that?"

"Empathy?"

"That's it. I'm an empathetic person. Anybody will tell you that."

"Uh-huh," I say, "If you left off the *em*, you might be a little closer to home." Before Mike can work that out in his head, I try to get us back on track. "So, somebody jumps Burt from behind, hits him over the head and shoots him with his own gun. What do they do after that?"

Mike eyeballs the nearby trees. "I'd want to get out of sight. Even if it's dark, I want to get out of sight as fast as possible. The trees are over there. Shortest distance between two points."

We walk that direction. The trees aren't much. It's not as if we've stepped into the Ardennes. They cover the top of a sloping hill. Past the trees, the lawn angles downward toward the parking lot nearest the conservatory. Mike and I beat the bushes, literally, but don't find anything. When we come out on the other side of the trees, Mike studies the lay of the land.

"What am I looking at?" he says, mostly to himself, "A parking lot, a playground, a conservation—"

"Conservatory."

"Whatever. A walking path, a rose garden, a—"

"Wait, wait, wait. A rose garden." Something about that hits me. I think back to the conversation with Charley. There might be something to it. I start down the hill, toward the garden. "Let's check it out."

Mike follows me. The rose garden sits next the conservatory, a stone's throw from the nearest parking lot. My parents would visit it in the summertime, more my mom's idea than my dad's. Lisa and I came here once, but we were more preoccupied with finding a place to make out and didn't really take things in. The garden has several sections of roses, all hemmed in by tall bushes. The spaces between the bushes allow a certain amount of privacy. Mike and I halt as we reach the garden.

"Let's split up," I say, "See what we can find."

The actual work portion of this escapade doesn't appeal to Mike, but he goes along with it, nonetheless. There are six sections to the rose garden, so we take three each. I start along the far side, nearest the conservatory. There's nobody in the rose garden at the moment, which is a relief. It might be difficult to explain crawling around, looking for either a gun or freshly turned earth.

I drop down on all fours and peek under each of the bushes. My mind keeps drifting to Alice and Evan. They both talked to Burt the night of the murder. Evan actually met Burt here in Bennett Park. Both have memories, at least, of the rose garden. If either were desperate to get rid of the murder weapon, this might be the first place one of them would go. After two rows of bushes, I haven't found anything. Then Mike's voice cuts through the air.

"Joe? You're going to want to see this."

He's a couple hedges away. I make my way over. Mike is crouched down, staring at the ground. He's created a small hole in the dirt, not unlike those I created for my toy soldiers when I was a kid. Except this one has a thirty-eight caliber pistol sitting in it.

"Jinkies," I say.

Mike sits back on his haunches. "Are you thinking…?"

"Pretty much what you're thinking," I say, "This is the weapon that killed Burt Franklin."

CHAPTER SIXTEEN

No matter what your relationship is with your parents, there is a certain vicarious thrill to hiding something from them. This hiding can take many forms.

Sometimes it's keeping information from them. You hide report cards. You intercept the phone call from the school inquiring about your absence that day. You don't tell them you got fired from the burger joint for smoking le ganja on your meal break. Sometimes, it's hiding your activities, such as sneaking out for a party or a date, hanging out with kids you aren't supposed to, visiting that bar in the next town with the lax attitude on carding because the owner has the local sheriff in his pocket. Then there's the literal hiding, which takes the form of contraband: porno mags, joints, porno mags, whiskey, porno mags and joints. Maybe some whiskey. Those things can be the most dangerous because they exist in physical form (until consumed or passed on to a friend). Kids do the hiding. Parents do the snooping. And the chess game continues.

Of course, we never stop to consider there are things our parents are hiding from us. Because, seriously, what is the fun in that?

But that's not really a topic of conversation I want to get into. At least not here. And my companion is distracted by our surroundings.

"You went to high school here?" Carol asks, staring up at the ceiling, "The place looks like a museum."

Porter's Bay High School is closed this time of year, but if you know a teacher who knows the principal, you can find your way in. Carol and I have been told we can wander the place, though some things will be closed to us. We can go into the theater, but we can't go backstage. The library is closed. The gym is fine, but the locker rooms are off-limits. (No big loss.)

"There was iron ore money back in the day," I say, "Built you a lot of nice things."

The high school is a four-story brick and cement building covering a whole city block. The floors are marble, the handles on the door are brass and the ceilings are high. There's something spooky about wandering around here during off times. Like all schools, it's more natural to see it teeming with life: shouting, pushing and shoving, hormones flying in all directions. But it's nice to see the place again. Carol and I pass the principal's office and find ourselves at the top of an ornate marble staircase leading to the front door.

"Seriously," she says, her voice echoing in the empty hallway, "It looks like they should hold a coronation here."

"The backstairs by the gym hosted a few…coronations of sorts."

"Gross," Carol says, "I suppose you're going to tell me yours was among them?"

"No. I had a little more class than that. Even back in the day."

We walk down the hallway opposite the big marble staircase. At the end of the hall is the theater and to the left of the theater is the library. Trophy cases line the hallway. The trophies gleam even in the thin light. I stop about halfway down the hall.

"Here's the crowning glory," I say, "You might even be familiar with this one."

We stare at a tall gold trophy, backed with a wooden base, representing the state high school hockey championship. To the right of it is a plaque, made by the Chamber of Commerce, listing the names of the players in gold lettering. To the left is a still image: a player in the red-and-white uniform of Porter's Bay flying through the air, his body perpendicular to the ice. The puck has somehow just left his stick and is about to get past the opposing goalie. Carol leans close to the glass.

"That's Rick?" she asks.

"The man himself. His big moment."

Rick Michaels was a friend, of sorts, in high school. He was a jock who preferred hanging out with nerds like me.

Everyone in town—jock, nerd, or other—knows who Rick Michaels is. He scored an overtime goal that seemed like a feat of levitation to give Porter's Bay the state hockey championship. I ran into Rick a few months ago because he was dating Carol. They made a nice couple, but sadly, the relationship didn't last. Carol twists her mouth to one side.

"Funny how he never wanted to talk about it," she says, "I mean, something like that…"

"Maybe he doesn't want to look back. Some people prefer the past just stays there." Carol studies the photo. She has a funny look. Vaguely pained. "Everything okay?" I ask.

"It's fine," she says.

I let it pass without comment. We keep going down the hall, past the library, where the offices of the school newspaper, *The Bay Breeze*, were housed. I spent a lot of time there, chatting with one person in particular. We step into the theater. Again, Carol's jaw drops. The place is cavernous, with ornate chandeliers hanging from the ceiling, a stage the size of an aircraft hangar, and plenty of gold and brass ornamentation. She stops just inside the door, gazing at the balcony and the box seats.

"You have got to be kidding," she says, "There was *this* much money in iron ore?"

"You ad writers have no idea how the economy works, do you?"

Carol gives me the stink eye but refrains from comment. We make our way to the back of the house and drop into two plush seats. It feels strange. Lisa and I would come here on lunch sometimes. I shouldn't be sitting here with anyone else. Thankfully, Carol distracts me with some conversation, even if it isn't the most pleasant topic.

"Where is the murder weapon?" she asks.

"In the back of the rental car."

Carol slumps in her seat. "Oh, that's great. That's exactly where you want a murder weapon to be. Have you thought of—and I'm just spitballing here—handing the thing over to the police? Seeing as how it's evidence and all."

"I'm thinking about it," I say, "I can't trust the cops. I have to work this thing out before I hand it over."

"Joe, that is a terrible idea." A thought occurs to Carol. "How did you get it out of the park? You can't get your fingerprints on it, right?"

I fidget in my seat. "Mike and I don't carry hankies. There wasn't a plastic bag or anything we could use in the rental car. Neither of us were comfortable using our shirts. We had to use a…less obvious article of clothing."

"Less obvi…oh jeez, one of you used your tightie-whities?"

"Okay, let me make one thing perfectly clear," I say, "I do not wear tightie-whities. I wear black or gray boxer briefs and have for a goodly number of years."

"Thank you for the info," Carol says, "Who had to do the dirty work, so to speak?"

"Mike. Seventeen years and he still doesn't know I can read him like a book when it comes to rock, paper, scissors."

Carol waves her hands. "Seriously, though, you've made me and Lars—but more importantly, me—accessories to a crime. The evidence of which is currently wrapped in Mike's smelly undies."

"I'm sorry about that. Look, just let me figure something out."

"Your funeral," Carol says, "Let's just make sure it's not mine as well, okay?"

"Understood."

We let that go, temporarily, and take in the splendor of the theater. Carol drums her fingers on the back of the chair in front of her. She's agitated and has no sweets. We may have to stop at Sweet Mary's before Carol starts chewing the wallpaper.

"Speaking of criminal conspiracies," I say, "how goes the good fight against my uncle?"

Carol sits back in the chair. "I got a visit from Vic Easton."

My eyebrows go up. "The guy behind my uncle's campaign?"

"The guy behind Gordie's everything. He was waiting in the lobby of the Kahler this morning. We had a chat."

"I'm guessing it wasn't pleasant?"

"Weirdly, it was very polite," Carol says, "Cold blooded and very polite."

"What did you talk about?" I ask.

"The Big Box Bill and the possibilities it would create for Porter's Bay. He let me know that standing in its way would be a big mistake. People would be upset. You never know what might happen if people get upset."

"That sounds…vaguely threatening."

"It was. Vaguely. Like I said, Easton is a polite guy. He didn't raise his voice. He didn't do anything obvious to intimidate me. But I got the impression bad stuff would happen if I didn't leave Gordie alone."

"And you're going to leave him alone?"

"Of course not," Carol says, "People's livelihoods are at stake. Besides, I'm just about to break this thing."

"Do tell."

Carol turns toward me. "Your mom and I talked to the woman at the bank. Marion. We went over a few things. You remember the Ice Dam? The people giving your uncle the checks? Take a wild guess who's a major funder—actually *the* major funder—of The Ice Dam."

"Would I be correct in guessing it was your visitor from this morning?"

"You would be. Vic Easton is also a major contributor to four other supposed businesses. All of whom have given money to members of the city council."

It slowly dawns on me. "Easton's bought off the mayor and half the city council."

"Exactly!" Carol says, unable to keep the excitement out of her voice. "And thanks to your mom's friend at the bank, I have the paperwork to prove it."

Son of a bitch. I should have let Carol handle this thing with my dad. In just a few days, she's brought my idiot uncle's administration to the brink of oblivion while I'm having trouble getting my dad *back* from the brink of oblivion. I get an alert on my phone, the sound echoing through the theater.

"We should get going," I say, "The ceremony for my dad is in a little while. I have to get ready."

"If we must," Carol says. She looks around the theater one last time. "Gorgeous place. You were lucky."

"I was."

I just didn't realize it at the time.

***

"Henry, for your lifetime of devotion to this city's well-being, your work for the business community, your work for local charities, your dedication to helping young people, for all the good that you've done: it is my honor to present you with the key to the city."

That gets a large round of applause from everyone gathered in the City Council chambers. The ceremony is being staged at the semi-circular table where the council sits when in session. Dad shakes hands with Mr. Somrock and accepts the large brass key. My family cheers loudly. I throw in a high-pitched whistle. Kevin adds a few cries of "Speech! Speech!" (The speech was planned, but Kevin makes it look like Dad was called upon to speak.) Dad grips the key and steps to the microphone, clearing his throat.

"Thank you, Bill, that was very nice," Dad says, a few beads of sweat jumping out on his forehead, "I grew up here in Porter's Bay. My mom and dad taught me to love this town. I was able to open a business and raise my own children here. It's always been important to give back to the community, Katherine and I have done our best to take care of this gift we've been given. And I'm very grateful to all of you for being a part of it. Thank you."

The crowd gives him another big round of applause. The chambers are packed. The sunlight angles through the picture window. The only glaring omission is the mayor (which makes this gathering consistent with most city council meetings). Will is out of the hospital and has joined Eli on the front row. Alice sits next to Will. Her applause seems strictly out of obligation. Dad steps aside and Mr. Somrock moves back to the microphone.

"Thank you, Henry," Mr. Somrock says, "We invite you all to join us in the old courtroom for a reception."

The crowd moves toward the double doors at the back. I join Kevin and Owen and their families in moving toward Mom and Dad. Kevin, as usual, gets there first.

"Great speech, Pop," Kevin says, "Proud of you."

The rest of us offer remarks. Dad accepts it all in a distracted way. He pushes past us, accepting pats on the back. Will and Eli greet him. They have a short conversation, out of earshot. My brothers and their families follow Dad. Mike, Carol and Lars hang back with me.

"Nice ceremony," Carol says, looking resplendent in her blue sleeveless blouse and black skirt, "But isn't it customary for the mayor to give someone the key to the city?"

Everyone turns to Lars (still wearing his ensemble from the tour, including the fedora). "The mayor had other business to attend to," he says.

"I see," I say, "Was this business at the Village Bowl?"

"Not in this case, no," Lars says, sweating, "Although the mayor is hoping to get there later. No, this is a meeting with…" He lowers his voice. "Mr. Easton."

Carol levels a look at Lars. "About what?"

"You," Lars says.

"Me?" Carol says.

Lars fingers his beard, nervously. "They're worried about the way you're poking your nose into things."

Mike tugs at the collar of his black polo shirt. "What are they going to do?"

"I'm supposed to keep Carol quiet," Lars says.

"How are you supposed to do that?" Carol asks.

"They didn't get into it," Lars says, "But Mr. Easton made it clear he wants you stifled."

"I'm sure he does," Carol says, "But it's not going to happen."

Lars thrusts his hands in his pockets. "Carol, you'd be doing me a real solid if you drop this. Mr. Easton scares me. He could do some real damage. Mostly to me."

"That's too bad," Carol says, "I told you not to get involved with Gordie. I don't have any sympathy for you."

Carol follows the crowd toward the reception. Lars seizes on me, dropping a hand on my shoulder.

"Can you talk to her?" he asks, "Make her see reason. This could be real trouble for us."

The funny part is, he might be right on that. Vic Easton seems like a load of trouble. Who knows what he's capable of? The problem is, if you're trying to get Carol to do something, intimidation is the worst strategy. And that's just when she's in a mood to be stubborn. When she believes she's right…

"I'll see what I can do," I say.

Lars, not comforted, joins the crowd. Mike and I trail behind.

"You really think this guy will hurt Carol?" he asks.

"I think he might try."

Mike winces but says nothing. For all the bantering he does with Carol, Mike hasn't forgotten they dated once and what it was he liked about her. The protective instinct remains. We follow the crowd out of the council chambers and down the hall to the former courtroom housing the reception. Mike slouches as he walks.

"T-minus fifteen hours to the picnic," he says, "I don't think I can get Julie to break things off. Everyone will see us and then her husband will come looking for me. Might as well move to Brazil."

"Why don't you make a pass at the husband?" I say, "That way he'll never believe Julie was sleeping with you."

"Up your ass."

"Wasn't where I was going with that."

We join the gathering in the old courtroom. The place doesn't really resemble a courtroom anymore. The benches and tables have been cleared. There's no witness stand. No seating. Just a big, empty room with judge's chambers in the rear. Some old pictures of my dad and the store are posted in various places around the room. There is a buffet table and a small bar. Will and Alice stand along one wall. Mike and I stop in the entrance.

"I should probably talk to Alice," I say.

Mike heads toward the buffet table while I walk over to Will and Alice. I'm not looking forward to this. Alice is prickly and Will seems fragile. Neither of them looks thrilled to see me. Will, at least, musters a smile.

"Heck of a nice ceremony for your dad," Will says, "Good speech, too."

"Thank you," I say, though I had nothing to do with either the ceremony or the speech, "Alice, could I have a minute? Just wanted to ask you about something."

Alice folds her arms. "Is it really necessary?"

"I think so," I say.

After a few seconds, Alice turns toward Will. "I'll be right back."

We step over to one corner. She stares at me over her glasses. With the plain blouse and skirt and the lack of makeup, her resemblance to a schoolmarm is nearly complete. I lower my voice.

"You talked to Burt Franklin the night he was murdered," I say.

Sometimes it's best to rip the Band-Aid right off. Alice's eyes get wide. "What are you talking about?"

"I'm talking about the burner phone I found in Burt's office. It had a bunch of phone calls on it from the night of the murder. Including one to you."

Alice straightens her glasses. "That was you that night. You called me."

"I did," I say.

"I was hoping it was a mistake."

"Sorry to disappoint," I say, "What did you talk to Burt about?"

Alice clearly wishes the floor would open under me. "He wanted to meet with me." She sighs. "In Bennett Park."

Smoley hokes. "And you met him?"

"Yes. He wanted me to help with Ed's Pizza in Center City. The place Charley's family owns. He knew I ran the office for my boss. He thought I could help him out. Said he couldn't trust the people he's been working with. Whatever that meant. If I did that, he'd consider giving Evan the money."

"What did you tell him?" I ask.

"I said I'd think about it. He told me not to take too long. We left it at that."

"You left him alive?"

Alice speaks through gritted teeth. "Of course I did."

And really, what else was she going to say? I figured I'd give it a shot. I look around. Everyone is ignoring us.

"What time did you meet Burt?" I ask.

"A little before one o'clock."

Near the time Burt called Eli. It clearly wasn't a long meeting. "Did you see Evan there?"

"No, I didn't," Alice says, "I didn't know he'd met with Burt until later."

I put it together in my head. Burt meets with Evan. He calls Alice and meets with her. He calls Eli and asks to be picked up. He's dead by the time Eli gets there. If everyone is on the level, Alice could be the last person to see Burt Franklin alive. But what are the odds everyone is on the level?

"For what it's worth," I say, "Evan is still in trouble. Two thugs tried to grab Charley."

That gives Alice a jolt. "Charley? Is she okay?"

"A little shaken up," I say, "But she's going to be fine."

"How did you find out about it?"

"I was there. Wrong place, wrong time. I've got a habit of that."

Alice looks me over. I'm none the worse for wear. "Are we done here?" she asks.

"Unless there's anything else you can tell me."

"There isn't."

Alice stalks past me and returns to her father. I walk to the bar and grab a cheap beer (the only kind they sell). My dad, of course, is surrounded by well-wishers. Kevin and Owen and their wives chat in one corner. Mom has buttonholed Fred Meers, the editor of the *Porter's Bay Times*. My family is all in the same room. This should be a happier occasion.

"Done my job for me yet?" says a voice to my right.

Chief Davenport sidles up to me. He wears his dress uniform and holds what is either a gin-and-tonic or a club soda. Something close to a smirk emerges from under his mustache, but it seems good humored. I greet him with a shrug.

"Not entirely," I say, "But I'm giving it a shot."

"So I hear. You've got Officer Beardsley pissed off."

"I'm not surprised. He tell you anything?"

"Not much. Just that he wants me to get you to stop."

"I see. Good luck with that."

Davenport swirls his drink. "You don't trust us, huh?"

"I don't trust Beardsley," I say, "And I know he's got the ear of my scumbag uncle. That pretty much makes you a eunuch in all this."

Davenport stiffens. "That what you want to go with? A eunuch?"

"I'm not trying to be insulting," I say, "Okay, with *eunuch* I kind of am. But you'll have to pardon me if I want to protect my dad."

"I get that. But I'm not as helpless as you might think."

"Beardsley found Cully Brown," I say, "Or at least some information about him. You have any idea how he found it? Or what it means?"

"No, I don't," Davenport says, "I don't know how he found out. I don't know how your father and his friends are connected to it. I asked Beardsley about it. He said he wanted the freedom to work on it himself. The mayor backed him up on it."

"So, you'll understand if I don't have a ton of confidence in you?"

"Just understand this much: I'm not going to let this thing get out of hand. Sure, life would be more peaceful if I gave Beardsley room. But I'll be damned if I'm going to let him railroad your dad. That's not how I work."

Huh. Maybe Davenport *is* one of the good guys. But I know enough about power and its use (or more accurately *abuse*) to know how cheap talk can be.

"I appreciate that," I say.

I'm not trying to do it (honestly), but my response has less enthusiasm than the good chief was hoping for. He waits for me to elaborate, but I don't say anything else. Davenport watches everyone crowding around my dad and drops a hand on my shoulder.

"I wish you the best," he says, "The rate you're going, you might need it."

Davenport walks toward my dad to offer good wishes. I trust him more than I trust Beardsley. And when Davenport offers me a warning, I believe he has my best interests in my mind and not his own. I appreciate that.

I'm just not going to listen.

***

I leave the party ahead of everyone else. Dad and Mom hang back to talk with more guests. Owen and his family remain as well, just in case Owen is needed. (He won't be, but it makes him feel important.) Kevin and Jordan take their daughters to The Hub for a late dinner. Carol, Mike, and Lars go back to my parents' place.

Mike is doing the driving. "Seemed like a nice little ceremony. What do you think the picnic will be like?"

"Like a picnic," I say, "It's sponsored by the church, so you can rule out alcohol. Besides, I think the city banned alcoholic beverages in public parks a few years ago."

Lars leans forward. "Gordie is trying to get that repealed."

"Why am I not surprised?" I say.

Carol pokes her head into the front seat. "I don't think you need to concern yourself with Gordie. I've got the editor at *The Porter's Bay Times* on my side now."

My eyebrows go up. "Fred Meers is playing ball with you? Up to now, they've buried every salacious story about Gordie."

Carol cocks her head. "Did you just use the word *salacious* in conversation?"

"I try to show off the vocabulary every now and again."

"At any rate, yes, Fred Meers at the *Times* is playing ball. He caved around the small matter of his dipping into the expense fund. Your mom is a font of useful—and salacious—information. I don't care what Vic Easton says. I'm not letting that chucklehead stop me."

Lars holds up a finger. "Now, Carol, that is not a—"

"I'm not going to let *any* chucklehead stop me."

We're about to have *Meet the Press* going on in the backseat of the RAV4. I'm just not up for it right now, so I move to forestall the debate and get back to the issue of my dad's retirement festivities.

"The picnic will be a grilling and corn on the cob and several hundred varieties of pasta salad type of affair," I say,

"A little thank you from Our Savior's Lutheran Church and then…my dad is retired."

I'll be honest: there's a finality about that which chills me to the bone. Mike eases the car to the curb. The lights are off in my parents' place and the street is largely empty. Something about the house looks forlorn. I turn to the others.

"You guys feel like coming in for a nightcap?" I ask, "My dad's got a liquor cabinet and there's some beer in the fridge."

Carol smirks. "You have your dad's permission to use the liquor cabinet?"

I flip a hand. "He hasn't marked the bottles in years. As far as I know."

We pile out of the car and walk to the front door. Mike hangs back as I put the key in the lock. (He has a fear of walking into darkened rooms…at least, darkened rooms he's *supposed* to be entering.) I lead the way inside.

That's when I notice someone has broken into my parents' house. And this someone is still here.

CHAPTER SEVENTEEN

When I was growing up, I never realized what a safe environment I lived in. My mom's parents lived on the other side of Porter's Bay. Shortly after they bought their house, some seventy years ago, the lock on the front door broke. They never replaced it. Their house remained unlocked—through evenings, weekends, family vacations, what have you—until the day the place was sold. Robberies were something that happened in other towns.

My parents were a little more cautious. Dad locked the front and back doors every night. Cars were always locked in the driveway or on the curb. Bikes were to be kept in the garage overnight. Dad had a shotgun and a handgun somewhere in the house. (For obvious reasons, none of us ever knew their exact locations.) And until we all reached the age of ten, Mom would walk us to the bus stop every morning and greet us when we got back in the afternoon. (Don't ask me why the cutoff was age ten. Maybe Mom must have figured once you reached double digits, you could handle yourself.) Even with these precautions, though, I never really felt threatened. Now, I wish I had appreciated that more.

And by *now*, I mean right this very second.

The guy who has broken into my parents' place—and it *does* appear to be a guy—is in the dining room when we enter. He's dressed in black, which is the uniform for this sort of activity, and in the dark, his face cannot be distinguished. When he sees us, he promptly does three things: swears, douses his flashlight, and runs for the backdoor.

Mike is over my shoulder. "Who the hell was that?"

"Why don't we find out?" I say.

And we're off. As the fastest runner, I take the lead. Carol follows, with Mike and Lars bringing up the rear. The intruder runs through the kitchen and the open backdoor. (Guess I know how he got in.) He's a bit hefty and not particularly quick. Once out the backdoor, he takes a quick right and runs into the driveway. He heads for the street.

And gets hit by my father's car.

A thing you need to understand: our street has always been well lit. We have a streetlight right next to the driveway. For as long as I can remember, my dad has always doused the car's headlights the second he pulled into the driveway then cruised into his parking spot. (Don't ask me why. Maybe it makes him feel cool. I just know it delighted me and my brothers when we were kids.) Ergo, the fleeing gentleman did not know there was a vehicle approaching until he was bouncing off its left fender.

The intruder is thrown a few feet and crashes into the garage door. The gun clatters on the pavement. He gets up and keeps running, though with a noticeable limp.

Dad hops out of the car in time to see me and my friends run past. "Who the hell is that?"

"I thought you'd know," I say, "He was in your house."

The intruder clears our driveway and hustles across the Seavers' lawn. It's neatly trimmed and slopes toward the street. The intruder wasn't that fast before Dad ran him over and the added limp does nothing for him. Halfway across the lawn, I hit him with a high tackle. We crash to the grass, and my momentum causes me to roll off him. The intruder tries to get up, only to be hit by a tackle from Carol. (Not bad for a woman in a skirt.) They both go down. Mike and Lars comE up fast.

"Dog pile!" Lars shouts.

He and Mike leap on top of Carol and the intruder. I leap on top of Lars and Mike. That finally subdues the unwelcomed guest. My parents stand in the driveway, watching the almost literal clusterfuck on their neighbor's lawn. I look toward them.

"Got him," I say.

"I can see that," Dad says, deadpan, "You think maybe you should let him up?"

I consider it for a second. "All right, everybody off. We got him." I turn to my parents. "You should call the cops."

Mom takes off toward the house, nominating herself for the job. Dad walks across the lawn as we untangle ourselves. Once the pile is cleared, I get a look at the intruder.

"Officer Beardsley," I say, "Maybe we should talk."

***

Twenty minutes later, Officer Beardsley is seated at my parents' dining room table. His hands are in his lap and he's staring at the floor. A couple uniformed cops are in the living room, getting statements from Mike, Carol, and Lars. Mom is in the kitchen, making everyone coffee. (She means well.) I'm in the dining room with Dad and Beardsley. Chief Davenport has just made his way in. He still wears his dress uniform, though the tie is untied, and the top button is undone. He steps over to Beardsley.

"Suppose you tell me what this is all about," Davenport asks.

Beardsley doesn't answer. Davenport looks toward Dad and me. Dad steps over to his liquor cabinet. Lying beside the cabinet is a thirty-eight. He slips his handkerchief over his hand (yes, the man carries a handkerchief, don't tell me you're surprised), picks up the gun and hands it to Davenport. The chief examines the weapon.

"This is what killed Burt Franklin?" Davenport asks.

I shake my head then catch myself and complete the motion as if I'm trying to crack my neck. Unless something has gone horribly wrong, the gun that killed Burt Franklin is still in the back of the rental car.

"No, it's not," Beardsley says, "I was…planting it here when they walked in."

"Is that a fact?" Davenport says, his voice a slow rumble. "Any particular reason you are attempting to frame Henry Davis?"

Beardsley doesn't answer. Davenport grabs a chair from the table, sets it directly in front of Beardsley, and sits. The chief's face grows cold.

"Let me make this first part abundantly clear," Davenport says, not blinking, "You are fired. Your days in law enforcement are over. I don't care if you're personally blowing the mayor, he can't save you. The next step is criminal prosecution. I know people around here love their cops. But you didn't rough up some drunk teenager at a party. You tried framing a guy everyone genuinely likes. That doesn't make you a bad cop. That makes you a dirty cop. You're not going to find any love for dirty cops around here. You understand me?"

Beardsley's voice is barely audible. "Yes."

"Good," Davenport says, "Because we got you on obstruction of justice, breaking and entering, and having a generally annoying attitude. Your only chance is to come clean. You willing to play ball?" Beardsley nods, still staring at the floor. "Can I ask *why* you thought railroading Henry Davis was a good idea?"

"I wanted the murder investigation shut down," Beardsley says, "I figured if Mr. Davis was charged, that would do the trick. And…some stuff wouldn't…be known."

Davenport sits up a little in the chair. "What stuff?"

It's silent for several seconds. The cops in the next room are listening in. So are Mike, Carol and Lars. Mom stands just behind the entrance to the dining room. Finally, Beardsley takes a long breath.

"I was working for Burt Franklin," he says, "I have been for a long time."

"Working how?" Davenport asks.

"Doing whatever he needed me to do. Carrying money, keeping guys in line, stuff like that." Beardsley looks up at Davenport. "I just fell into it and…pretty soon it was too late."

Davenport's body language is tense. "Why?"

"I needed the money," Beardsley says, "You know how much this job pays."

"I'm well aware of it," Davenport says, "Been doing it for a long time. Started out making less than you are now. Never took a bribe, never did anyone a favor that might compromise me."

"I get that, but—"

Davenport grabs the leg of Beardsley's chair and yanks it closer to him. "Don't hand me that shit about *needing the money*." Davenport's face is only an inch from Beardsley's, "You *wanted* the money. It's just an excuse for greed. I don't want to hear it."

Beardsley is close to tears. Davenport gets up and steps away, trying to calm down. He gives the liquor cabinet a long look but makes no move. I take his place standing over Beardsley.

"Did you plant my dad's watch on Burt?" I ask.

Beardsley gives me a hateful look. Davenport clears his throat, leaving no doubt that Beardsley should answer my questions. Beardsley looks away.

"No, I didn't," Beardsley says, "I don't know how Burt got ahold of it. Stole it, probably. Hell, if he didn't have the thing on him, I might not have gone after your dad."

Son of a bitch. Not only does Burt get himself killed, he steals the evidence needed to railroad my dad. The guy's the gift that keeps on giving. "What about the threatening notes?" I ask, "The ones my dad and his friends got. Did you do that?"

"Yeah, that was me," Beardsley says, his jaw clenched, "I thought it might make them nervous. Maybe one of them would make a mistake. Say or do something stupid."

"What were you doing the night of the murder?" I ask.

"You want an alibi?" Beardsley says, his tone conveying a certain repugnance.

"That's exactly what I want," I say, "If you've got one."

Beardsley shows no signs of cooperating. Davenport says, "Answer his question."

After a moment, Beardsley lets out a sigh. "I was playing cards with some guys. Over at Jim Kiel's house. You can ask Jim or any of the others. We were there until nearly two. My wife will tell you I was home by twelve-fifteen. That's my alibi."

I'd love to believe Beardsley is guilty of killing Burt, but it doesn't make sense. For him, Burt's death was the equivalent of kicking over a hornet's nest. He needed Burt alive. Besides, he can account for his whereabouts at the time of the murder. Beardsley is in the clear. That doesn't mean he's completely useless.

"Burt told you about Taylor, right?" I ask, "And Cully Brown?"

My dad, who's been standing in the corner, pushes off from the wall. "Joe…"

"He did," Beardsley says.

"What did he tell you?" I ask.

Dad marches up to me and grabs my arm. "Joe!"

A thing you need to understand: my dad has never laid a hand on me in anger. Beyond raising his voice from time to time (more to get our attention than anything), he's always been a reasonable force of authority. Even now, it's not anger I see on his face. It's fear.

Davenport gently puts his hand on my dad's shoulder. "We need to know this, Henry."

Dad lets go of my arm. "Let me tell it. I want him to hear it from me."

The sick feeling in the pit of my stomach is back. Dad gestures toward the backdoor. Davenport turns to the uniformed cops and waves a hand toward Beardsley.

"Keep an eye on him," Davenport says, "I'll be right back."

Dad leads the way out of the dining room. Mom puts a hand on his shoulder as he passes. Dad doesn't look at her. We step into the relative solitude of the backyard. The night is still. Dad walks to a spot in the middle of the yard, as if this is the most private spot on his property. Davenport and I stand by, waiting. Dad puts his hands in his pockets.

"Four of us decided to open the store," Dad says, "Burt, Will, Eli and me. We pooled our money, we borrowed from our parents…but we didn't have enough. We applied for loans, but we were young. We didn't have anything in the way of collateral. We kept getting turned down. It looked like the whole thing wasn't going to happen. Just a pipedream. Pardon the pun."

"Normally, I don't pardon puns," I say, "I'll make an exception in your case."

Dad smiles, slightly, at my attempt to lighten the atmosphere. It disappears quickly. "I didn't want to let it go. I knew if we could get the business off the ground, we could make it work. *I* could make it work. Over beers one night, I mentioned that to Burt. He asked me how desperate I was, if I was willing to do whatever it took. Maybe it was the beer talking. Maybe not. I don't know. But I listened to Burt's idea."

"What was it?" I ask.

Dad takes a breath in through his nose. "Even then, Burt had connections. I don't know all that he was into. I guess you make allowances for your friends. Anyway, he laid out an idea. Cully Brown was a bagman. He carried money from a corrupt politician to a 'businessman' in Taylor. According to Burt, the 'businessman' was small potatoes. The money was good, but Burt didn't think Cully would be dangerous." Dad looks down. "It was enough money to open the store."

"You robbed this Cully Brown guy?" I ask.

"We did," Dad says, "Probably didn't need all four of us, but we all went. We had guns. We wore masks. Cully didn't put up much of a fight. But he begged us not to do it. He said the people he worked for would think he had stolen the money. His life wouldn't be worth spit. But Burt kept the gun on Cully and took the money. Then we got out of there."

"The money went into the store?" Davenport asks.

"It did," Dad says, "Not long after that, we heard Cully Brown was dead. I don't know if he did it himself or if…someone did it for him. But we had a part in it. With that robbery. We as good as killed him. The four of us said we'd never tell anyone. After a while, we just pretended it never happened. At least, I did."

"And the others kept it quiet," I say, "Even after you bought them out."

"There was too much to lose if they spoke up," Dad says. "Maybe that's why I started doing things for the community. If I could do enough good work, I could make it right. Bury what I did. Sometimes, I even thought it worked."

For several long moments, nobody says anything. Davenport folds his arms.

"You realize this doesn't clear you of anything?" he says.

"It gives me a stronger motive, I know," Dad says, "I didn't kill Burt. I'd give you my word on that, but my word doesn't mean a lot at the moment." He focuses on Davenport. "What happens now?"

"Now?" Davenport asks, "Now, I take that corrupt son of a bitch in your dining room to jail. Then I do what I should have done days ago and call the sheriff's department.

Have them come in and clean up this mess. Assuming it's not too late."

I step over to Davenport. "What about the mayor?"

"I don't mean to offend," he says, "but from the bottom of my heart: fuck the mayor."

Well, we can all agree on that. Dad lowers his voice. (Maybe to keep the neighbors from hearing. Maybe to keep me from hearing.)

"I meant what happens with what I told you?" Dad asks, "About Cully Brown?"

Davenport lays a hand on Dad's shoulder. "You've done a lot of good around here, Henry. That's what this week's all about. People wanted to thank you." He slips a look toward the house. "Most of them, anyway. I think a lifetime of doing good is bigger than a mistake made when you were young. Forty years you've been carrying this around. I think that's punishment enough."

Dad offers his hand to Davenport. "Thank you, Ben."

I should be relieved. But I'm not. Beardsley won't be on Dad's back, but I haven't cleared him of anything. And now I know my dad was a crook. At least at one time. Davenport takes a step toward the house. I hold up a hand, stopping him.

"I think I've got something to show you," I say, "Follow me."

We leave Dad in the backyard and walk to the RAV4. I hope the neighbors won't see this. (Although, the presence of the police has likely piqued their interest.) I open the back and come out with the weapon, still wrapped in Mike's tightie-whities. Davenport makes no move to take it from me.

"Is that what I think it is?" he asks.

"A poorly maintained pair of Fruit of the Looms? Yes. But inside those are the weapon that killed Burt Franklin. At least, I'm pretty sure it is."

"And what was it doing in the back of a rental car?"

"My friend Mike and I found it. Over in Bennett Park. We're guessing it was stashed by the murderer."

Davenport carefully takes it from me and tucks it under his arm. "When were you going to hand this over?"

"As soon as I could trust the police," I say.

"Uh-huh. You realize that's not how criminal justice works, right?"

"I've heard rumors to that effect."

Davenport's eyes twinkle a bit. "I'll tell you what we find. Not promising anything."

He goes inside. I walk into the backyard. I feel like I should say something to Dad, but I have no idea what. Finally, Dad moves toward the backdoor. He stops, momentarily, and half looks toward me.

"I'm sorry," he says. Then he walks into the house, leaving me alone.

***

"Wow," I say, looking at the newspaper (yes, the newspaper), "Sunday is the slowest news day of the week. You timed this perfectly."

Carol hoists her coffee cup in triumph. "Here's to scandal and corruption."

"And the exposure of same."

We're not even attempting to keep our voices down. It wouldn't be necessary. The buzzing conversation at The Hub centers around one thing: Mayor Gordon Davis is in the pocket of a real estate developer who used a slush fund to bribe him and other officials into passing the Big Box Bill. They all plan to grow fat on kickbacks from the project. And the whole scheme is laid out in the Sunday edition of *The Porter's Bay Times*. Everyone at The Hub is either reading the paper or on their phones. Carol and I are at a window booth, enjoying the rumormongering.

"I have to give you credit," I say, my feet kicked up on the seat, "When you go after someone, you don't screw around."

"That's what Gordie gets for screwing around with *me*," Carol says, "And my friends."

Gordie was never the most popular mayor to begin with. (How he got elected remains something of a mystery.) If the scuttlebutt means anything, the prevailing opinion is Gordie should resign and possibly leave town. ("And the horse he rode in on" being a frequent addendum to those thoughts.) Even if I tried, I could not have found a better way to wipe Burt Franklin's murder off the front page.

"Speaking of friends," I say, "I wonder how Lars is doing this morning?"

Carol rolls her eyes. "I don't feel sorry for him. He hitched his wagon to Gordie. He deserves what he gets."

I swing my feet to the floor. "I should thank you. For a little while anyway, I've been able to get the stuff with my dad off my mind."

She gives me a sympathetic nod. "Have you talked to him today?"

"No. He was out when I woke up. Not sure where he went. The store's closed today. Maybe he went for a walk. He'll be at the church picnic this afternoon."

"And how are *you* doing?"

I stare out the window, at the clouds hovering over the lake. "I don't know. There's a whole side of my dad I never knew. It's like finding out not only is there no Santa Claus, but the guy you thought was Santa Claus is doing a stint for tax evasion."

"He's still your dad," Carol says, "He's still the person you grew up with. He just…made a mistake when he was younger."

"It's a mistake that perpetuated itself," I say, "Everything he's gotten was because of the store. But it was all built on…I don't know, blood money."

"That's really what you think?"

"It's what I'm thinking right now."

"Maybe why your dad is avoiding you."

"There's a comforting thought."

Carol holds up a hand. "Look, I want you to think about this: Burt Franklin was part of that robbery, and he probably never thought twice about it. He kept doing stuff like that. Your dad has spent his whole life trying to make up for it. *That* is who you grew up with."

I thank Carol. She's the only one I've told about this. I don't know how to break it to Kevin or Owen or if I even should. In the midst of this cheeriness, I'm strangely happy to see Lars. (Not my usual feeling when he enters a room.) He sports shades and wears a brown suitcoat over a wrinkled shirt and a crooked tie. His quasi-pompadour is drooping and there are bags under his eyes. He slinks into our booth, tossing a felt folder on the table.

"I'm part of an administration in crisis," Lars says by way of greeting.

"That's the word on the street," I say, sliding the newspaper his direction.

Lars, who's probably been inundated by this story all morning, ignores the paper. "Carol, I have to ask, as a favor to me, is there any way I can get you to retract this story?"

"Lars, there's a mountain of evidence," Carol says, "Your boy is going down"

He runs a hand through his hair, trying (and failing) to fluff up his quasi-pompadour. "I should have known. We've flown too close to the sun. We go too big too fast. Our vision was too beautiful to last too long." Lars turns to me. "Is there anything you can do to help?"

"Beyond coming up with six more clichés you can use?" I ask. Carol snorts. Lars's head drops. "Lars, if I can ask," I say, "Why are you still working with my uncle? You know he's corrupt. If there's ever a time to desert a sinking ship, this would be it."

Lars draws us into a huddle. "Because Mr. Easton wants me to handle this. I'm supposed to meet with the local media this afternoon."

"Both of them?" I ask.

"I have to convince them this is all a conspiracy against Gordie. That the donations are legitimate and there is absolutely nothing untoward going on."

Carol's eyebrows go up. "Despite all the evidence to the contrary?"

"I'm afraid so," Lars says, "I've been instructed to do everything shy of making up facts. And if that doesn't work, to make up facts."

"Nobody is going to believe you," Carol says.

"I know that!" Lars says, struggling to keep his voice down, "But Mr. Easton insists. He can be very persuasive. In the sense he scares the living hell out of me."

I gather the newspaper again. "Did he threaten you?"

"Not directly," Lars says, "But he went on about loyalty and being a team player. He said it in a way that made me think he was about to pull out a baseball bat and go after me like Robert DeNiro in *The Untouchables*."

"His bark might be worse than his bite," I say.

"Would you want to take a chance on that?" Lars asks.

"Probably not," I say.

Lars turns toward Carol. "Then, no retraction?"

"None whatsoever," Carol says, turning away from Lars.

He slaps the table, drawing the attention of a few neighboring patrons. They promptly go back to ignoring him. (Oh, what I wouldn't give to have that superpower.) Lars tugs at his tie.

"Then I have to do the press conference," he says.

"Where is it going to be?"

"Bennett Park," he says, "Right around the time of your dad's picnic."

My jaw drops. "Why the hell are you going to do that?"

"It was Gordie's idea," Lars says, "He thought it would look good to be associated with your dad. He might even go to the picnic afterwards."

"And almost certainly get thrown out," I say, "After everything Gordie did to encourage Beardsley, after not bothering to present Dad with the key to the city, Gordie thinks he'll be welcomed at my dad's picnic?"

Lars bites his lip. "Do you think your dad would make a scene?"

"No," I say, "He'd just punch Gordie in the mouth and go about his day."

"That's…that's no good," Lars says, "Gordie was so sure he could charm your dad into a photo op."

I can excuse Lars's ignorance (mostly). Sometimes Gordie not only acts like he and my dad aren't brothers, he acts like they haven't been properly introduced. Dad would sooner welcome a case of hemorrhoids than his youngest sibling. People gesture toward Lars and mumble. Less than a week and he's already an outcast. I change the subject.

"How's the gangster tour going?" I ask.

"Not well," Lars says, "With the kerfuffle around the mayor, I don't have a lot of authority when invoking City Hall. And that's before you consider the audience reaction to the test tour yesterday."

"Not good?" Carol asks.

"I handed out surveys," Lars says, "The response was…"

"Mixed?" I ask.

"Scathing," Lars says, "The surveys not only questioned the veracity of my knowledge about Porter's Bay history and the gangster era, they also critiqued my delivery and made several cracks about my personal appearance. I thought that last part was beyond the pale."

"People can be cruel," I say, "If accurate."

"But I have to put that on the backburner," Lars says, "Right now, I'm concerned about the press conference. I've got to do right by the mayor."

"If *right* is the word you're looking for," I say.

Lars picks up his felt folder and stands, wearily. "I'll see what he wants to do. For now, I have to figure out how to tender my resignation without letting anyone down. Particularly Mr. Easton. Who may have me murdered."

With that, Lars trudges out of the restaurant, ignoring (or simply not noticing) the stares that follow him. I'm not sure if it's because he's associated with the mayor or if he's recognized as the horse's ass who created the gangster tour. Once he's gone, Carol and I resume our coffee.

"You at least know the skinny on Taylor and Cully Brown," Carol says, "Does it get you any closer to figuring out who killed Burt Franklin?"

"Not necessarily," I say, "If the motive for killing Burt was covering up the thing with Taylor and Cully Brown, that gives Will and Eli motive. If there's another motive. then maybe Evan or Alice. Neither of them liked Burt and he was trying to screw over Charley's family."

"Feels kind of weak for motive."

"I know. It's what I've got, though."

Speaking of the devil (if that's the term I'm looking for), Charley approaches our table. She ignores Carol and speaks into my ear.

"I've got a problem," she says, "Some guys got to Evan. They beat him up pretty bad."

Huh. Guess I'm not the only one with problems…

CHAPTER EIGHTEEN

If you didn't deal with a bully when you were growing up, it's likely you were the bully. I wasn't consistently victimized and don't necessarily feel scarred by the experience. But it has made me sympathetic for those who have been. And how the matter of forgiveness can be rather complicated.

*I've read stories about victims confronting their bullies in later years and the bullies expressing regret. Maybe the bully makes an attempt to explain why they did it, and the victim contemplates forgiveness. I never buy that. Yes, I know, forgiveness is necessary to move on and all that horses**t. But all I can see is the inequity of the arrangement. The victim carried the emotional scars for years while the bully probably didn't give it much thought until confronted. Doesn't a* sorry *seem like an empty gesture? I'd be thinking, "That's fine, but until we get into the time machine and go back to make sure you don't do all this heinous s**t in the first place, your apology doesn't matter much, does it?" An apology feels like a Get Out of Jail Free card.*

If we're looking for empty gestures, just put some sugar in the guy's gas tank and be done with it.

I don't know if Evan Erickson dealt with bullies when he was growing up. But he's sure dealing with them now.

When Charley first tells me Evan has been beaten up, I imagine him lying in a hospital bed. Instead, he's at home, hiding out in his parents' basement. Evan's folks are out, and the front door is unlocked. Charley, still wearing her Hub uniform, leads me down to the basement, where Evan is stretched out on his bed. I expect to find him a mass of black and blue marks, but his face is clear. One arm is draped across his midsection, right about where the chest meets the abdomen. His face is pained. Even turning his head seems to be an effort. Charley rushes over to the bed and kneels next to him. He pats her arm.

"Hey babe," Evan says.

"I brought Joe Davis," she says.

"Great," Evan says, not giving it a great deal of enthusiasm. The old energy is gone, and Evan seems surprisingly sober (on a number of levels).

I keep my distance. "You okay? You need to go to the hospital?"

"I'll be fine," Evan says, "It's not like I'm spitting blood."

Well, he's got that going for him. Which is nice. "What happened?" I ask.

"Berringer's goons got ahold of me," Evan says, "I was coming out of Terzich's Grocery. They grabbed me, dragged me into an alley, had a little…chat with me."

"I'm guessing this chat involved several well-placed kicks to the body?" I say.

"They did good work," Evan says, wincing, "Whole thing couldn't have lasted more than thirty seconds. But they got their point across."

Charley runs a hand along Evan's arm. "Honey, you should get this thing taken care of."

"I'll be fine," he says, "Just let me lie here and heal up."

"I don't mean that," she says, "You need to get this thing with Berringer taken care of."

"I'd love to," he says, "But I don't have the money."

Charley frowns but says nothing. I get the feeling they've had this conversation before. Charley and I avoid eye contact. We share a bond now, but neither of us wants Evan to know. He tries to adjust his position but freezes up, hit by pain in his torso. I wave Charley over to me. She looks confused but leaves Evan's bedside, nonetheless.

"I'm concerned Evan might have bruised ribs," I say, "If he's not going to the hospital, he should at least put ice on them. Would you mind going upstairs and making an icepack?"

Charley looks a tad suspicious. She's not a dim bulb. She must be aware I'm trying to get rid of her. But she doesn't know why and I'm certainly not going to tell her.

"I can do that," she says. She looks over her shoulder at Evan. "I'll be right back, hon."

"Sounds good," Evan says.

Charley heads up the stairs. I walk over to the bed, pulling up a chair as I do. Evan looks a little concerned. I rest my arms on my knees and fold my hands.

"I need to explain something to you," I say, "I don't think you've been telling me the whole truth. Or possibly any part of it. So understand this: I am the only thing that might get you out of this mess. With Berringer. With the cops. With everything. I'm going to ask you some questions and if I get the idea you're lying to me or not telling me something, you're on your own. Do you understand me?"

Evan tries to take a deep breath but winces from the pain. "That sounds good. What do you want to know?"

"You met with Burt in Bennett Park the night he died," I say, "But here's something that's never made any sense to me: you already made an offer to Burt, and he turned it down. Why did you have a second meeting? You had to have something different to offer him."

Evan looks toward the stairs. "I did," he says, "Alice's boss."

I cock my head to one side. "David Jones? The lawyer? What did he have to do with it?"

"He almost got himself in some trouble. He was in the middle of a nasty divorce case. Representing the wife. He bribed a cop and set up a DWI arrest on the husband. But the cop was going to flip on Jones. Alice asked me to help."

"What did you do?" I ask.

He says it like it's obvious. "I found some blackmail info on the cop. It shut him up."

"Who knew about this?"

"Me, Alice, the lawyer, and the cop. That was the whole circle of trust."

"But you brought Burt into it?"

"I got desperate," Evan says, "I thought maybe Burt would go for it and leave Charley's family alone. Bleed this Jones guy for money. It was worth a shot. I just pulled it out of my ass. Anyway, the lawyer has a pretty good load of money. I thought Burt could use that. But he wasn't interested. He wanted the pizza place. There was nothing else I could do."

"Burt was trying to get Alice to help him out," I say, "With the pizza place thing."

"She told me. After Burt had…y'know. I told her about what I offered Burt. I felt…y'know, *bad*. I'm not used to feeling like that."

Evan and Mike should hang out more. Guilt is a completely foreign concept to them. Maybe they could work on it together. Then again, who am I kidding? They'd just spend time drinking beer and chasing broads.

"I'll have to talk to Alice," I say, "She'll probably be at the picnic this afternoon."

"My parents are going to be there," Evan says, "They want me to come, too. I'll probably go. Just to stay on their good side. I'll be fine as long as nobody hugs me."

"It's a picnic full of Minnesota Lutherans," I say, "You have nothing to worry about."

Charley returns with the ice pack. I'm not going to get any more out of Evan, so I show myself out. I tell them to call me if anything comes up and leave Charley to minister to Evan's injuries.

He's a fuck up and has a pretty girl tending to him. I'm trying to do the right thing, and everybody hates me. Yeah, life is fair, isn't it?

***

Our Savior's Lutheran Church has reserved the entire picnic area for two hours on Sunday afternoon, filling the place with an array of pasta salads and casseroles (or as we call them in Minnesota, *hotdishes*). If you're ever concerned about the mayonnaise or cheese industries going under, I present church picnics to alleviate your concerns. A couple picnic tables are pushed together to house the various goodies. Pastor Jason, an associate pastor at the church, is working the grill, providing a slew of burgers, brats and hot dogs. (Chicken? Move along, city folk.) Lemonade and fruit punch are going around and if the number of people making trips to the parking lot means anything, there's beer here somewhere.

Dad, as always, is the center of attention. There is an easel with older photos of him and the family. There will be another ceremony thanking him for his work and wishing him well in his retirement. Dad will get through it and cover his relief when it's over. I can't really read his mood. He's always been good at putting on a public face. Watching him chat and press the flesh, you would be hard-pressed to know he confessed to being part of a crime last night.

The picnic area allows for a view of the park's tiny amphitheater. I can see Gordie conferring with Lars. A few strangers—media types, I'm guessing—mill about in the seating area. Lars looks haggard and still wears his rumpled suit. He consults some notecards. There is no sign of Vic Easton, but that's probably for the best.

"This should be good," says a voice to my left.

Carol sidles up, holding a red Solo cup and drinking something that may or may not be fruit punch. She removes her sunglasses and hangs them in the bodice of her sundress.

Her wicked grin is still in place (and has likely never left her face). I look toward the amphitheater.

"It's not like Lars is uncomfortable being on stage," I say, "He was the ring announcer for that wrestling promotion. He was the emcee for James Queen's funeral. He used to work the room at that strip club he owned."

"Didn't all those end in disaster?"

"Yes, but he's comfortable with his own disasters. That's what I'm saying." I nod towards the amphitheater. "Shall we take a look?"

"Are you kidding?" Carol asks, "I wouldn't miss this."

Carol and I saunter down the sloping lawn to the amphitheater. The assembled media, consisting of two women who serve as news directors for the local radio stations and Fred Meers, who runs the *Porter's Bay Times*, are seated in the front row. The place isn't large—just a small cement stage and several rows of benches—but the acoustics are great. Carol and I can mill around the back and catch everything. Gordie, wearing his finest bowling shirt and cargo shorts, stands onstage, smoking a cigar. His hands are clasped behind his back and his chin juts out. He looks like the birthday party clown version of Benito Mussolini. At a gesture from Gordie, Lars steps up to address the assembled press.

"Ladies and gentlemen…um, gentle*man*…assuming you identify that way," Lars says, "I'm sorry, I still struggle with pronouns. But my heart and mind are open. I'm willing to learn."

Gordie growls, "Get on with it."

"Sorry, sorry." Lars clears his throat. "Thank you all for coming. I'd like to begin with a statement and then I'll take questions. I am here to address the scandalous rumors printed today in the *Porter's Bay Times* concerning the relationship between Mayor Gordon Davis and local businessman Vic Easton. The mayor wishes to state, unequivocally, that there is nothing improper in his relationship with Mr. Easton. Mr. Easton has been a campaign contributor and supporter and is only concerned with the public good. In order to refute these charges, Mayor Davis has authorized an independent investigation to thoroughly look into the whole matter and he is confident this will clear his name." Lars looks over at Gordie, who nods his approval. Lars turns back to the media. "I will open up the floor for your questions."

A woman from one of the radio stations raises her hand. She's tall and dark haired and has a husky, fluid voice. "Annie Bauhof, KRMN News. Who will be conducting the independent investigation?"

Lars rubs his forehead. "That would be…Cooter."

"And who is Cooter?" Ms. Bauhof asks.

"He is an…associate of the mayor."

"I see," Ms. Bauhof says, "The *independent* investigation is being conducted by one of the mayor's drinking buddies?"

Lars shuffles his notecards, dropping a few. "That is correct."

Ms. Bauhof remains standing. "Was Chief Davenport considered for this investigation?"

"He was considered," Lars says, "However, the mayor felt Chief Davenport could not be trusted with the security of certain…information related to the situation."

"What kind of information?" Ms. Bauhof asks.

"Information related to the case," Lars says.

"Like the facts?" Ms. Bauhof says.

Lars nods. "Like those."

Carol puts a hand over her mouth and laughs silently. Clearly, Lars wishes this interrogation would end. However, Ms. Bauhof is not letting up.

"I'm confused," she says, "If the mayor believes an investigation will completely exonerate him, why be concerned about the information Chief Davenport would uncover?"

Lars looks through his notecards but doesn't find what he's looking for. He turns to Gordie for some direction. Gordie waves a hand toward the press, letting Lars know he's on his own. Lars mops his brow with the notecards.

"We believe our investigation will uncover a different collection of facts which might contradict Chief Davenport's findings," he says.

Another newswoman stands up. She's blonde and thin. "Melanie Wehrmacher, WSPB. How can there be a different collection of facts? Facts are simply facts. One collection must be untrue. Are you saying that Chief Davenport would lie?"

"No," Lars says, "We are not saying that. We are saying Chief Davenport might be…mistaken. Vis a vis, the factual matters. We believe our findings…would be…*more* factual."

Ms. Wehrmacher and Ms. Bauhof exchange a look. Ms. Wehrmacher does the speaking. "That doesn't make an ounce of sense."

"In which case, let's move on," Lars says.

The women sit down, still confused. Fred Meers from the *Times* stands. He's bald and has what might be a permanent squint.

"Fred Meers, Porter's Bay Times," he says, "I'm curious why Mr. Easton, who lives and works in Greenville, would be involved in a mayoral campaign in Porter's Bay unless he had a vested interest?"

Lars drops a few notecards. He takes a half-look toward Gordie, who just shakes his head. Lars is still on his own. He works his mouth, but nothing comes out. Finally, he hits on an answer.

"Those questions should be directed to Mr. Easton," he says.

Fred Meers stands his ground. "But Mr. Easton is central to the allegations. He's bought franchise rights for three different big box stores, with plans to open them in Porter's Bay. Why would he be interested in Porter's Bay politics unless he wants to expand his business and use the mayor as a tool for that?"

Gordie pushes past Lars. "Who are you calling a *tool?*"

Lars puts a hand on the mayor's shoulder and guides him away, assuring him his spokesman can handle this. Gordie continues to glare at Meers. Lars steps forward again.

"Mr. Easton is simply a visionary businessman," Lars says, with less conviction than he might, "It's what good businessmen do: anticipate changes in the market and prepare for them."

"But there's a difference between anticipating changes and creating them," Meers says, "Mr. Easton appears to be using bribery to create changes. Can the mayor refute this?"

Lars mops his brow again. "The mayor objects to your use of terms like *bribery* to describe what Mr. Easton is doing."

Meers reads from his notes. "A new car for Councilman Zach Morgan. Campaign contributions for Councilwoman Samantha Papke. A large screen TV and other high-end purchases for Mayor Davis. All through various supposedly charitable organizations propped up by a slush fund created by Vic Easton. All the people I've named have spoken up in favor of the Big Box Bill. If this isn't bribery for the purpose of benefiting Vic Easton's business interests, what are we supposed to call it?"

Lars fumbles with his notecards, dropping more of them. He looks to Gordie, who is stone-faced. Lars turns to the reporters and freezes. Finally, he drops the rest of his notecards.

"You're supposed to call it bribery," Lars says, "Because that's exactly what it is. What's going on here isn't what I signed up for. I thought Mayor Davis stood for a revolution in politics. A politics for the common man *by* the common man. And I still believe in that. But I can't be a party to bribery and shenanigans. My friend Carol saw it and I did not. I'm not going to silence her or threaten her, as Mayor Davis and Mr. Easton proposed. And I'm not going to stand up here and spin lies and look like an idiot. I can go anywhere and do that. Good day to you all."

Lars slips his hands into his pockets, gives the assembled press a little bow and sashays to the edge of the stage. The cigar falls from Gordie's mouth. He grabs Lars and begins strangling his now-former press secretary. Lars tries to speak but sounds surprisingly like Donald Duck. The press leaps onstage and tries to pull the mayor off. Carol turns to me.

"Should we help him?" she asks.

"Nah, he'll be fine," I say, "Gordie will lose steam long before Lars loses consciousness. We should get back to the party."

Carol puts her shades back on. "That sounds good."

We stroll across the lawn, returning to the picnic area. Dad is chatting with Pastor Tony, the former head pastor at Our Savior's, now retired. Will and Alice have arrived. Alice leaves Will at one of the tables and goes to the buffet. I depart from Carol and make my way over.

"Had a little visit with Evan Erickson this morning," I say.

Alice continues loading a plate, perhaps wondering what she's done to deserve the curse of me. "I'm sure that was fun."

"Not particularly," I say, "Some goons got to him. Beat him up pretty badly."

Alice drops a spoonful of potato salad. "About the money?"

"That's what I gather. He's going to be okay. In fact, he might even be here today." I pick up a plate. "Evan offered up the lawyer you work for—and that you're dating—to Burt. Evan told him about the DWI your boyfriend arranged and how he got Mr. Jones out of it.

Alice steps close to me. "He told you all that?" She lets out a disgusted breath. "Great, Evan. Why not just tell the damn newspapers?"

"I'll keep it to myself if I can," I say.

"But you want to get your dad out of trouble first. So, I'll take that for what it's worth."

Sheesh. Tough room. (But she's not wrong.) "That's what you talked about with Burt when you met him in Bennett Park," I say, "He gave you the option to work for him or he'd go after your boyfriend."

Alice's shoulders sag. "Yes, that's what it was. I told Burt I had to think about it. I didn't know what to do. I didn't want to work for Burt, and I wasn't sure he'd leave David alone. He might have me work for him *and* bleed David dry at the same time."

"Convenient that Burt was killed then."

She puts the plate down. "What is that supposed to mean?"

"Just what it sounds like. There is a distinct possibility you were the last one to see Burt Franklin alive and you're up to your armpits in motive."

"I didn't kill Burt. I'm not sorry he's dead, but I didn't kill him."

"Not even to save your boyfriend?"

"I would have figured out a way. Thankfully—and yes, I will say *thankfully*—Burt was killed before I needed to do that. That's all I have to say."

Alice picks up her plate and stalks away, heading back to her father. I look down at my plate and realize I've collected a bunch of pasta and mayo-based food I have no interest in eating. I don't wish to offend, so I bring it over to my family's table and leave it there. (If I'm lucky, some daring squirrel will take it off my hands.)

Mom now handles the flow of visitors. Dad is walking over the hill, away from the picnic area. I follow and find him sitting on a bench overlooking the playground. He has a beer in his hand but isn't drinking. I make my way over. He speaks without looking at me.

"Is the party boring you?" he asks.

"I might ask you the same thing."

"Just needed a minute."

"Okay if I join you?" I ask.

He nods, and I plunk down next to him. We watch Kevin's and Owen's children thrash around the plastic equipment. Dad's face is blank, a far cry from the smiling, outgoing dude who has been working the room all week.

"There used to be a rocket ship slide there, right?" he says.

"Absolutely. Coolest thing ever. I could have cried when they tore it down, even though I was twenty and hadn't played on it in years."

"I didn't bring you kids here too often. Your mom had to do it. I was always at the store."

"No offense to you or Mom, but the playground was the important thing. Didn't really matter who brought us."

Dad sips from his can of beer. "I'm sorry you got dragged into all this."

"I chose to get involved."

"If I had gone to my grave with no one knowing about…what happened, that would have been all right with me. I guess that doesn't speak highly of me."

"It's understandable."

"It wasn't about my public image. I need you to understand that. I really *do* love this town. I wanted to do some good. But I'd be lying if I said I didn't think about Cully Brown and what we did to get the store started. Every time somebody said, 'You're a good man, Henry.' I'd think, 'You don't really know me.' As much as I love you boys…you don't really know me. I guess *you* do. Now."

Something pops into my head, something I wouldn't have dreamed of telling my father even twenty-four hours ago. But now I need to tell him.

"Last winter, I had to solve a murder for a contract killer," I say. Dad shoots me a look, but I keep going. "Her name—at least the name she goes by—is Deirdre. I'm not going to get into how I know her. But she wasn't guilty. She threatened to kill me if I couldn't prove that. And I proved it. Somewhere along the way, I thought I could…I don't know, save her. Redeem her. Something. If someone showed her decency, she might become a decent person in return."

"Did it work out that way?" Dad asks.

"After I proved she was innocent, Deirdre killed two people. She thought they were dangerous to her, even though one was going to jail and the other was scared shitless. Deirdre killed them anyway. Because that's who she is."

After a second, Dad says, "Jesus."

"One of the people she killed—a woman named Kendall—showed up in a dream of mine," I say, "Couple weeks ago. I don't remember a lot about it. I just remember there was snow falling. And Kendall and I just stood there and looked at each other."

"Did she say anything to you?"

"No," I say, "When I woke up, I realized it was because she can't say anything anymore. Because of something I did."

I've never talked to anyone about this, even my closest friends and they went through it with me. Dad stares, intently.

"Other than finding another reason to keep me up at night, thinking about you living down in the Cities," he says, "why did you tell me this?"

"Because I'm not going to stand in judgment of someone unless my conscience is clear." I look over at Dad. "You raised me better than that."

Dad gives the matter some thought, then he turns to me. "If you had a gun in your hand and the opportunity to shoot," he says, "would you have killed this Kendall person?"

"No. Of course not."

"Then you shouldn't carry the burden of her death," Dad says, "You aren't responsible. This Deirdre person is."

"And if you had a gun in your hand and the opportunity to shoot, would you have killed Cully Brown?"

Dad looks away. "Of course not."

"Maybe it's time you stopped carrying *that* with you."

He doesn't say anything. There are no magic words to take away a lifetime of guilt. Maybe, though, Dad can start down the road to forgiving himself. He pats my leg.

"Thank you," he says, "You're a good man, Joe."

"I try. I have a lot to live up to."

The men in my family are not huggers. I know that's antiquated, but it's how we do things. High school and college graduations. Weddings. Those require a hug. Beyond that, it's a pat on the back, a squeeze on the shoulder, the solidarity of a good handshake. So, it means a lot when Dad squeezes my shoulder.

"We should probably get back to the picnic," he says.

"Sounds good." We stand and walk away from the bench. "As long as we're being honest with each other," I say, "you can go ahead and admit I'm your favorite."

"I don't have a favorite, Joe."

"Sure, I know you have to say that. But it's just us here. You can be honest with me. I'm the favorite, right?"

"I'm going back to the party now," Dad says.

"I promise I won't tell Kevin and Owen. I might imply it heavily, but…"

"Goodbye, Joe."

Dad walks back toward the party. As he does, he throws a look over his shoulder. Kind of hard to tell, but I think he's smiling.

I look over the park and take a deep breath. At least Dad and I have settled things. No matter what my dad did in the past, he isn't a guy like Burt Franklin, whose various criminal activities were apparently his life's work. And he was in it right up to the end. Going after a family-owned pizza joint and possibly destroying Alice's boyfriend.

A thought suddenly occurs to me, snapping my head back. A sudden rush of thoughts. Pieces falling into place. I look toward the party. Eli and Will mingle with my dad. Alice hovers nearby. Evan approaches, moving gingerly and leaning on Charley. I run the information through my head a few times, just to make sure. It all makes sense.

I powerwalk to the picnic area. I tug at Alice's sleeve. She turns to me and groans. The hero's welcome once again. We take a few steps away from the crowd.

"Did you tell your dad about what happened with David?" I ask, "The DWI thing?"

Alice gives that a look of revulsion. "God no. Why would I tell him a thing like that? It would just make him worry. Besides, he likes David." The hostility turns to wariness. "Why do you ask?"

I don't answer. I pass her off with a "Just curious" and walk away. I can feel her watching me as I go. I slip through the crowd and find Evan sitting at a small table with his parents and Charley. As I approach, Evan can't hide his look of disgust. (There's a lot of that going around.) Mrs. Erickson lightly elbows her husband.

"This is Joe Davis," she says, "You remember? He was Elyse's friend."

Mr. Erickson, the epitome of a white man wearing brown shoes, doesn't look up from his brat. "Don't remember him." Suddenly, I'm not so disturbed about Burt Franklin bedding this guy's wife back in the day.

I push past Mrs. Erickson's embarrassment. "I just need to talk to Evan for a second."

Mrs. Erickson, glad for any way out of this situation, says, "Of course. Evan, honey, why don't you talk to Joe?" It has the same quality of *Why don't you run along and play with your little friends?*

Evan maintains Resting Stink Face but gets up from the table, nonetheless. Charley gives him some assistance, and Evan keeps a grim visage to cover the enormous pain in his torso. He's sweating by the time he gets to his feet. I guide him over to a huge maple tree. I give Charley a look, telling her this has to be just me and Evan. She doesn't look pleased, but she returns to the table.

"The thing with David Jones, the lawyer," I say, "Did Will know about it?"

Evan looks like someone just cut one. "Alice's dad? No way. Alice would've ripped my nuts off. I barely survived telling Burt."

For once, I believe Evan. There's no hesitation, no furtiveness. You can read the truth on his face (which is probably why he's such a terrible poker player). I thank him and cross the picnic area again. Chief Davenport is making his way down the buffet table. His uniform has been replaced by a maroon polo shirt and a pair of jeans. I slide up next to him.

"I know who killed Burt Franklin," I say.

Davenport stops, a ham puff pastry halfway to his plate. "Maybe you ought to share it."

We step away from the picnic area. Davenport leaves his plate behind. I try to keep my body language casual. ("Nothing to see here. Just two dudes talking about—I don't know—football and auto mechanics. Move along.")

"I think this is what happened," I say, "The night of the murder, Eli Perry drove Burt here to Bennett Park. Eli was working with Burt, and they had stopped by Burt's office to go over the books. Burt had gotten a call from Evan Erickson, asking for a meeting. Evan was in debt to some gamblers, and he needed money to bail him out. Burt wasn't going to do it unless Evan did him a favor: helping him take over Ed's Pizza up in Center City to use as a front company. Evan had another idea, though, and he wanted to talk to Burt about it. Burt and Evan met in Bennett Park."

"What was this other idea?" Davenport asks.

"I can't get into it right now. Let's just say it involved a very small circle of trust. There were only four people who knew about it. Five, after Burt met with Evan. Burt said he wasn't interested and that was the end of the meeting. But after Evan left, Burt called Alice and asked her to meet him in Bennett Park. He wanted Alice to work for him, and he used the information Evan gave him as leverage."

"I take it Alice is in this circle of trust?"

"She is. The other two can't be named just yet. Anyway, Alice said she'd think about it and then she left. Burt called Eli and asked him to come pick him up. Burt was dead by the time Eli got here. Eli was the one who called you guys."

Davenport sighs. "Going to have to get that pay phone taken out."

"The thing is: Will knew about the trouble. It involved someone close to Alice. Will mentioned it in passing when I visited him at the hospital. But nobody told him about the trouble. Near as I can figure it, there's only one way he could know."

The chief's shoulders sag. "He was in Bennett Park."

"He overheard the conversation with Alice, waited for her to leave, then attacked Burt and killed him. And he stashed the weapon here in Bennett Park."

Davenport puts his hands on his hips and takes a deep breath. He's probably known Will as long as he's known my dad. It's a small town. Everybody knows everybody, particularly if you're the chief of police. It doesn't mean you always like doing your job, though.

"We need to talk to Will," he says, flatly.

Will is on the edge of the picnic area, in conversation with my dad. Davenport and I start that direction. Will looks away from my dad and sees us coming. Instinctively, he knows why we're headed his way. Maybe he knew he screwed up the second he mentioned Alice helping out her lawyer boyfriend and hoped I would never put two and two together. He hurries down the hill, away from the picnic area.

Davenport rears his head back, as if he's about to yell. Then he realizes he'll be creating a scene. "Son of a bitch. They never make it easy, do they?"

That's been my experience. Davenport picks up speed and the two of us make our way through the picnic area, trying to create as little fuss as possible. We pass my dad, whose head swivels between looking down the hill and watching our approach.

"What's going on?" he asks.

"We need to talk to Will," I say.

This is a tricky spot. Heads are turning. People notice the pace at which Davenport and I are moving, as well as Will's hasty retreat.

So, a guy trying to kill Mike turns out to be a *good* thing.

Mike materializes from the direction of the conservatory. The guy coming after him is anywhere between six and eight feet tall and he's either spent quality time in the gym or he came out of the womb looking like Dwayne "The Rock" Johnson's bulkier cousin.

"Come here, you son of a bitch bastard!" the guy yells, "You want to fuck around with another guy's wife? Come here, you lousy piece of shit! I'll rip your fucking dick off!"

Now, Mike has never been a great runner. Smoking and a lack of interest being his primary inhibitors. But the proposed forcible removal of his schlong has inspired him. He chugs across the lawn like Adrian Peterson in the open field. He looks back to see if the guy is gaining on him. He doesn't notice all the heads turning to watch his cowardly flight. He doesn't need sympathy. He needs his johnson. He speeds toward the picnic area, shouting, "Help! Police!" Chief Davenport ignores him.

"I'm sure somebody will take care of that," he says.

Davenport and I start down the hill toward the amphitheater. Dad follows. Will can't move fast, but he's desperate and he's got a head start. There's also the matter of us trying not to draw attention to ourselves, as a full-on chase almost certainly would. Will slips around the back of the amphitheater. Davenport and I quicken the pace.

"Hey, where are you going?" a voice shouts out, "The potato salad can't be that bad!"

Andy and Sam come toward us. They must have parked in the lower lot. I hold up a hand, indicating we can't have this conversation at full volume.

"What's going on?" Andy asks.

"I think we found the murderer," I say.

Andy grabs my arm. "Who?"

"Will," I say.

Andy stumbles but keeps up with us. This isn't the end I was hoping for. Judging by the grim mood of the group, nobody was hoping for this. The amphitheater is empty when we get there. The backstage area has barely any wing space, but we check it anyway. Snake eyes. We gather on the stage.

"No offense," Sam says, "But it's not like Will is Usain Bolt. He couldn't have gone far."

I agree. It's possible that Will is hiding, but where? A lot of the crouch has gone out of his legs. There are only so many places he could be hiding. Then I spot something.

Alice rushes across the lawn. Her form isn't great (she runs like a gazelle with a lame hoof), but the speed is there. I'm guessing that's born of urgency. I step off the stage and walk up the aisle, getting a better view of where she's going. She's running toward the baseball stadium. I signal the others to follow me.

Wade Stadium is the home of the Porter's Bay High School baseball team. A large grandstand wraps around home plate and extends down the first and third baselines. Unless I'm completely mistaken, it's deserted. The front gate is unlocked. We get up the entranceway and find ourselves directly behind home plate. Several feet to our left, Will and Alice are in conversation. Will glances at us and pulls a handgun.

Okay, so the footrace portion wasn't much. Let's hope the shooting portion isn't worth writing home about.

CHAPTER NINETEEN

I've always been amazed by people who can pull a sleight of hand. Sure, it's great when magicians pull it off (I know a guy named Marks who's pretty good) but it's even more impressive when your average slob does it. That puts me in mind of my friend Stoner.

Stoner was in the group of guys I ran with in college. It was four years of regrettable experiences, some of which should have generated lawsuits but never did. The collection of us were at a party that eventually devolved into watching a movie (the thing you do when everyone is too drunk to continue carousing and the neighbors might call the cops if you don't take it down a notch). I found myself on the couch with Stoner and a young lady named Melissa. Melissa had been crushing on Stoner since three beers ago and cuddled up to him. Stoner kept a lazy arm around her and watched the movie. I sprawled on the other side of the couch, gently swaying in the breeze.

About halfway through the movie, I got up to use the restroom. As I was coming back, I passed Stoner in the hall. He stopped and reached into his pocket.

"Why don't you hold on to this for me?" he asked.

He dropped something into my hand. I knew very well what it was but still found myself asking, "What is this?"

"Melissa's bra," Stoner said.

Now, there was very little reason to hand me Melissa's bra (I don't think Stoner really expected me to return it to its rightful owner) other than to let me know he had managed to remove said item from her person. The thing is, I didn't see any movement between Stoner and Melissa beyond the seemingly innocent cuddling. And Stoner usually had more discretion than to start snogging in a room full of people. I had no idea how he procured the bra. At no time did his fingers leave his hand.

"How did you do that?" I asked.

Stoner stepped past me to get to the bathroom. "A good magician never reveals his secrets. But you may want to get rid of that bra before Melissa finds you with it."

I think Stoner has a kindred soul in Will, who managed to produce a gun seemingly out of thin air. (Although, I would have preferred he pull something as harmless as Melissa Sundeen's lacy undergarment.)

Everyone freezes in place, even Chief Davenport. Maybe the good chief is armed on his off hours, but he's smart enough not to start a firefight in Wade Stadium unless it's a last resort. (Let's hope it doesn't come to that).

"Don't get crazy, Will," Davenport says, "Give me the gun and we'll talk."

"Sorry, Ben," Will says, "We're past that." He half turns toward Alice. "Sorry about this, honey."

Before Alice can respond, Dad steps forward. "Why did you do it, Will?"

"Because Burt Franklin was a worthless son of a bitch and I'm glad he's dead." Will says it with almost no emotion, as if he's already processed what he's done and couldn't find any regret in it.

I keep my hands where Will can see them. "You were in the park that night. You overheard Alice talking to Burt."

"And Evan," Will says, "I knew Burt was up to something. I was giving him a ride to Eli's place when Evan called. I overheard them talking. Alice's name came up. Whatever Evan wanted to talk about had something to do with her. When he got off the phone, Burt said, 'That daughter of yours is pretty good with the books, right?' I didn't know what he was talking about, and he wouldn't tell me. But I didn't trust him. I started following him."

"That's how you knew he was in Bennett Park," I say.

"I grew up right near here," Will says, "I know this park like the back of my hand. Knew exactly how to listen in on Burt without him knowing I was there. I heard everything. Evan offering up Alice's boyfriend. Burt using that to try and get Alice to work for him. He hurt Alice once, when he took her mother away from us. I wasn't going to let him hurt her again."

"You waited for Alice to leave," I say, "Burt called Eli. Then you attacked Burt."

"He didn't see me coming," Will says, "I didn't have my gun with me, so I used his. Got rid of the damn thing on my way out. Or thought I did. And I left the watch."

My dad steps forward, his hands still at his side. "*You* took my watch? Why?"

Will regards my dad. "Because I hate you, Henry. I've hated you for forty years. Just never told you. Maybe I didn't want to face it myself. I went along with all this *Henry Davis is a good man* horseshit. You forced me out of the store. After that, my wife never looked at me the same way. She thought I was weak. A loser. Made it easy for Burt to move in. That's what you did for me, Henry. I hate you more than I hated Burt."

Dad's face is still. "Will, I—"

"To hell with you, Henry," Will says, "I don't want your apologies or your pity or whatever the hell you were about to give me. Maybe I should have been less of a coward. Maybe it's not too late."

Will aims the gun at my dad. Several things happen at once. Alice cries out and grabs Will's arm. I shove my dad out of the way, taking us both down. The gun fires, but Alice has redirected it. A bullet pings off one of the bleachers. Will, reacting instinctively, throws Alice aside, knocking her to the floor. He realizes what he's done and lowers the gun.

"Honey, I'm sorry, I didn't—"

That's all he gets out before Sam hits him with a flying tackle. It does nothing beyond knocking Will's gun to the floor. Andy scoops it up and hands the gun to Chief Davenport.

"Stop now, Will," Davenport says, his voice a quiet rumble.

Nobody moves. Will slowly turns and helps Alice to her feet. She can't bring herself to look at her father. Will steps over to Chief Davenport.

"Let's go," Will says, his voice hollow.

Davenport gently takes Will's arm and leads out of the stadium. Alice follows, not looking at any of us. I help my dad to his feet.

"You okay?" I ask.

Dad gives me his usual placid look. "Worried about a broken hip? It's no big deal. You're still in the will."

I'm glad Mom is not around to hear that. Dad holds up a hand, assuring me he's okay. I turn to Sam and Andy.

"Nice work, guys," I say, "You got the job done."

Sam's eyes are bright. "Kick ass, man."

Andy weaves slightly. "I didn't even think about it. I just grabbed the gun. We got lucky."

Sometimes that's how you get the job done.

EPILOGUE

With time and perspective, I now realize that going off to college isn't leaving home *in that you're not necessarily going out into the real world. But that first move away* is *significant because it's the first time you've established an identity outside of the home you grew up in.*

My mom once told me that every time she looked over one of her son's dorm rooms, she had a mix of sadness and excitement. Sadness that one of her boys was old enough to live away from home. Excited, though, to imagine us living our lives in this place, becoming grownups (or reasonable facsimiles), having independence. (If she had known what kind of crowd I fell in with at college, she might have tempered her enthusiasm.)

Returning to the place you grew up after years of living on your own, though, can be strange. You realize how comfortable you've become with your life outside of this place, so much so, you start to think of the person who grew up here as somebody totally different. You ask yourself, "Am I that person or this person?" This place is a part of you, but it doesn't feel like you belong in it anymore. It can be a relief to get away again and let the hometown drift back into the comfort of nostalgia.

After the last week in my hometown, I'm not sorry to get going. But maybe I am.

I'm in my room, carefully packing my clothes. Sam will pick me up for lunch then drop me off at the Kahler. From there, it's back to the Cities. I can't help wondering what state I'm leaving Porter's Bay in. But hey, Sergeant Pike is only going to watch my cats for so long.

Kevin pokes his head in my room. "Taking off, huh?"

"I should get back to my cats and my apartment," I say.

He leans against the doorframe. "I'm surprised you're leaving with all the excitement."

He may be right. There hasn't been this much excitement in Porter's Bay in a long time. Scandal at City Hall. Police corruption. Murder. Nobody will be sorry to see me go.

"I'm sure the rest of you can handle it," I say, zipping up my suitcase.

Kevin gives me a smile, a genuine one. "Glad things are okay with Dad."

That's as close as Kevin will come to thanking me for my role in proving Dad's innocence. Will is in custody in Duluth and the sheriff's department has taken over the investigation into Burt Franklin's murder, with the cooperation of Chief Davenport. I'll probably be called to testify, but that won't be for a while. If it happens at all.

"How much longer are you guys going to be up here?" I ask.

"We fly out on Thursday," Kevin says, "This is a nice little summer vacation for the girls. But we've got stuff to get back to."

"I get it."

Yes, there's a little implication his stuff is important, as opposed to me returning to write glorified dick jokes. But I don't think it's an intentional dig. It's just Kevin being Kevin.

"We're going to be in the Cities for a few hours before we fly out," he says, "Maybe you and I can have coffee."

"Sounds good."

Kevin steps out of the doorway but reappears a second later. "I forgot to tell you. I really liked your column on *The Hangover* movies."

"Thanks," I say, "I didn't know you read that column."

"I read all of them." Then he disappears down the hall.

A minute later, I'm ready to go. I stand in the doorway and look over my room. I'll be back here at the holidays, either Thanksgiving or Christmas, possibly both. I'll stay here again. But every time I leave, it feels like this is the last time I'll see it. No matter what happened in life, this shabby little room was safe harbor. I love my apartment. Maybe I'll live in a decent house one day. But nothing will ever quite mean what this place does. I close the door on my way out.

I head downstairs and stroll to the backyard. Mom and Dad are seated in lawn chairs, enjoying their morning coffee. The day is sunny and warm. They're looking around the yard and talking about construction plans. Mom has always wanted a gazebo and Dad is finally willing and able to build it. They get up and make their way over to me.

"Are you leaving?" Mom asks, a sadness in her voice.

"I need to," I say, "I've got to get back to the kitties."

In other circumstances, my mom might consider that a lame excuse. But since she has the sinking feeling Lenny and Squiggy are the closest things she'll get to grandchildren from my branch of the family tree, she accepts it. She gives me a long hug.

"Make sure you call us when you get home," she says.

"Will do."

Mom whispers to me. "And call your father more often. He worries about you."

"Got it."

She parts from me, her eyes a little misty. "It was nice having you all under the same roof again. Even for a few days."

"Maybe we can do it again at Christmas," I say.

"Maybe," Mom says. She does her best to keep the doubt out of her voice.

Mom steps into the driveway, as if there is something to attend to. I know very well she wants to give me and Dad a few seconds alone. Dad takes a hand from one pocket and offers it to me.

"Thank you for everything," he says.

"Anytime," I say, shaking his hand, "But hopefully never again."

"And thank your friend Carol for me. Even if she might have gotten me into deeper trouble."

I can't help but laugh. Events moved rapidly after Gordie's disastrous press conference. An emergency city council meeting was held on Monday to discuss Gordie's participation in the Vic Easton scandal and his ties to corrupt police officer Cliff Beardsley. The council formally asked Gordie to resign. He refused. The council then called a vote and the required three-quarters majority voted to remove Gordie as mayor. While Gordie holed up in his office, refusing to leave, the three city councilmembers implicated in the Vic Easton scandal resigned. After Chief Davenport approached Gordie and threatened to "haul your worthless ass out of here," Gordie finally left. A power vacuum was created by the resignation of the mayor and the loss of almost half the city council. To bring a measure of stability, the council asked my dad to step in as interim mayor.

"You're retired from the store," I say, "Now you can have a career in politics."

Dad squares me with a look. "That's not going to happen. I am the *interim* mayor. I'll keep the seat warm until the election in the fall. Then I'm out of it."

"But if people like what you do…"

"Then hopefully the next guy—or gal—will be just like me. But it won't *be* me."

I let him have the last word. I know him well enough to know a gazebo alone isn't going to satisfy Dad's craving for activity. After a few months of him getting underfoot around the house, Mom might sign off on a mayoral campaign. Who knows?

"At least you've regained your standing as a pillar of the community," I say.

Dad seems as if a weight has been lifted from him, "I may not deserve it, but…"

"You deserve it." I clear my throat. "How is Will?"

His face clouds. "Not good. The condition he's in, stress is the last thing he needs. They'll try to take him to trial, but…I don't know if he'll make it."

"I'm sorry."

"Will's not. He told Ben Davenport he has no regrets about anything he did. Including trying to frame me."

Dad stares at the clean pavement of his driveway. I feel like putting a hand on his shoulder but refrain. I finally say, "Are you all right?"

He gives it some thought. "I am. I'm sad Will feels the way he does. Instead of talking about it like adults, I ignored it and he let his hate fester until…all of this." He looks toward the sky. "But I'm not going to let it get to me. Whatever time I have left—whatever time *any* of us has left—is a gift. I'm not going to squander it worrying about something like this."

"Make sure it's a long time, okay?"

"It's not really up to me. But I'll do my best." Dad gives me a hug. "I love you."

"I love you, too."

"Do me a favor," Dad whispers, "Call your mother more often. She worries about you."

"Will do."

There's a honk at the end of the driveway. Sam and his SUV are waiting. He rolls down the window.

"Hey, Mr. D!" he shouts, "You and Joe need to get a room?"

We part and Dad looks to the end of the driveway. "I know he helped save us. But I never liked him. You know that, right?"

"I do," I say, "You hide it magnificently." I pick up my bag and start down the driveway. I stop and turn back to Dad. "You're still not going to cop to me being your favorite, are you?"

"Not at all."

"How about I'm the favorite today? You can rotate between me and Kevin and Owen."

"Drive safe, Joe."

I say one more round of goodbyes to Mom and Dad (in Minnesota, the goodbye ritual can last for *hours*) and finally get going. My parents stand in the driveway, holding hands, as Sam and I disappear down the street.

***

Sam and I join Andy at The Hub for lunch. Sam is also heading home today. He doesn't make frequent stops in Porter's Bay. This might be the last time we get the band back together for God knows how long. The Hub buzzes with conversation. The patrons smile toward me. Yes, I could be put off by their previous lack of faith in my dad, but to hell with it, this is a better situation than before.

"You gave people plenty to talk about," Andy says, popping a French fry into his mouth.

"You guys helped," I say, "Heard anything about the stolen car?"

"I haven't," Andy says.

Sam picks at his Hungarian Mushroom Soup. "That break-in was fun. We ought to do that at least once a year."

Andy looks horrified. I snicker and say, "I'll take it up with my staff."

"At least we found enough to take down Beardsley," Sam says.

"And Eli," Andy says, frowning.

The catch in finding Burt's cooked books was that it implicated the guy who cooked them. I handed the ledger book over to Eli, who then handed it over to the authorities. He is currently negotiating with the police and the sheriff's department. Andy pours ketchup on his burger.

"I heard Eli is cutting a deal with the cops," he says, "He knows the key to the books and a lot of other things Burt had going on. Eli might be able to get off lightly."

"I hope so," I say, picking up my chicken salad sandwich, "I don't want to see Eli in jail."

That seems to be the consensus at the table. I take a bite of my sandwich and watch a server walk past our table. I see The Hub uniform and get lost in my thoughts. Andy and Sam know what's on my mind. It's one of the reasons I miss these guys. Andy does the speaking.

"You ever talk to Lisa?" he asks.

I snap out of my reverie. "Just on social media every now and again. She's doing well."

Sam crushes crackers into his soup. "I saw her on CNN one night. A rare appearance."

"She doesn't like publicity," I say, "Makes the job harder. She's a reporter, not a celebrity."

"I thought that's how it would be," Andy says.

We spend the time breaking bread, trying to keep the conversation going (which is easy) and trying to avoid the topic of Lisa (which is not). Andy is finishing his sandwich when he offers up something out of the blue.

"You think you'd ever move back here?"

There's no way I can answer that question honestly. First, something in Andy's manner tells me he'd really like me to come back to Porter's Bay; that it would be fun to hang out like this all the time. Second, he still lives here. There's no way he *wouldn't* take offense to me saying *Ah jeez, are you shitting me? I'd rather drive a nail into my dick.*

"Hard to say," I tell him, even though it isn't, "I'm doing pretty well in the Cities right now. But you never know."

I credit myself with being magnificently vague. Unfortunately, I tried it on somebody who's known me since I spilled milk on him in kindergarten.

"You're never moving back here, are you?" Andy says.

"I can't see it happening, no," I say, "But hey, maybe I'll feel differently in ten years."

"You're trying not to hurt my feelings."

"Pretty much. How am I doing?"

Andy grins. "I appreciate the effort."

We finish our meals. Sam insists on paying the check. (I put up the usual fake protest, but hell, the dude is making *way* more money than I am.) We step onto Lake Drive and prepare to go our separate ways.

"I'll probably be back at Thanksgiving," I say.

"Make sure you stop in Duluth," Sam says, "We can grab a drink or several."

"I'd like that," I tell him.

We stand there, awkwardly. Even though Sam is giving me a ride, this is the last time *all* of us will be in the same place for…ever? I turn away then spin back toward them.

"You guys know I love you, right?" I say.

"Of course," Andy says, as if it should be obvious.

Sam drops into a *Dumb guy from high school* voice. "If you love us so much, why don't you marry us?"

"If we weren't all straight, I'd consider it," I say.

"To paraphrase Groucho Marx," Sam says, "We three would make a lovely gay couple."

We collapse into laughter, just like at the lunch table in the old days. We exchange awkward hugs and say our goodbyes. Then we all move on.

***

I'm legally obligated to make one more visit to Davis Hardware and say goodbye to Owen (or he'll piss and moan about it all through the holidays). Sam drops me off in front (the Kahler is walking distance from here) and I head inside. The place isn't busy. Owen is sweeping near the front counter, enjoying his second day as owner, operator, general manager, and lord and master of Davis Hardware. Judging by his demeanor (perhaps the first time since high school his ass has unclenched slightly), the new power becomes him.

"Hey Joe," he says, his voice booming (yes, actually booming) out over the store, "Stopping in to say goodbye?"

"That is the case," I say.

He sets the broom aside. "Come on, I'll give you a tour. Show you what I'm going to do with the place."

I barely avoid cringing. Yes, Dad would rearrange the store from time to time over the years, but I'm afraid Owen will try to reinvent the wheel. Thankfully, that does not appear to be the case. He's going to move a few things, maybe remodel the backroom (something it could really use, I'll give him that), and if he can take advantage of his contacts at City Hall, maybe get a new loading dock. Nothing huge, but Owen's excitement makes it seem like he's building an empire. The tour ends at the front counter.

"I made a new hire this morning," Owen says, leaning on the counter, "Evan Erickson."

My eyebrows go up. "Evan? You fired him once."

Owen flips a hand. "He could use the job. Has a few debts to pay off. He says he's trying to get his act together. I agreed to front him the money and in exchange, he'll work it off here."

"Can you trust him?"

"I think so. Evan's parents told him he'll get thrown out of the house if he loses the job, so he's got incentive."

"Good idea," I say, "It wasn't, by any chance, Dad's idea, was it?"

That takes some of the steam out of Owen's stride. "He might have mentioned something. But it was still my call."

I try not to show my amusement, as it will only set Owen off. He may own the store now, but as long as Dad is with us, he'll be the real power behind the throne. I hang around and chat with Owen. It's easy to remember all the time I spent here, either working as a teenager or playing as a kid. It's progressed from playground to place of business to…what? Some piece of nostalgia. Like the rocket ship slide at Bennett Park or Arthur's Diner, but one that has survived. Now, it's in new hands.

"I should get going," I say, "Got to meet my friends and head back to the Cities."

"Understood," Owen says, "I'll say goodbye to Mary and the kids for you."

"Assuming she's cool with that. I always get the sense Mary doesn't really like me."

"Nah, Mary likes you just fine," Owen says, "I don't think she can understand you, but she likes you. Jordan is the one you have to worry about."

"Really? I hadn't noticed."

We step to the door and shake hands. Dear God, Owen is smiling, genuinely. I find myself smiling as well.

"Take care," I say, "Of yourself and this place."

"Don't worry, I will."

"You know what? I'm not worried at all."

***

I haul my stuff a few blocks to the Kahler Hotel. My friends are waiting in the porte cochére (entirely too grand a title for the blacktop outside a two-star hotel), next to the RAV4. Carol stands by a pillar, wearing her shades. Lars looks around, furtively. Mike is perched on a stone ledge, staring at his phone.

"Bout time," Mike mumbles, sounding not unlike a surly teenager.

"You guys ready to go?" I ask.

"More than ready," Lars says, "You've got an interesting little town here, my friend, but it's a bit wackadoo. Time to go home."

I load my luggage into the car, finding various places in which to stuff it. Mike stands next to me as I work.

"Julie's not here to see you off?" I say.

Mike chews his goatee. "Oh, she saw me off all right. Told me she never wanted to see me again. Said she regretted the whole affair after seeing her husband chase me down and

417

me beg for my life. At least the husband took pity on me. Said I wasn't worth the effort. So, that's over."

"With a minimum of fuss," I say.

"And a maximum of humiliation," Carol says.

I'd like to say we all feel sorry for Mike, but none of us do. This is yet another in a series of beds Mike has not only made for himself but befouled in the process. And it won't be the last. Best to get him—and the rest of us—back to our element. We climb into the car and head out of the parking lot. Rather than take a right for Lake Drive, I turn left and head up Howard Street.

"Hope you guys don't mind," I say, "I want to take one last spin around before we leave."

Carol is up for it, though she immediately buries herself in a book. Mike does a little grumbling. Lars is strangely silent. Still, I'm behind the wheel, so they're a captive audience. I pass the State Theater on Howard Street, drive a few blocks over to pass the massive Porter's Bay High School building, then down a few more blocks to go by City Hall and the library. As we pass, Lars taps the window.

"Gordie is gone," Lars says, "Like Icarus, he flew too close to the sun."

Carol looks up from her book. "Really? Icarus? You're going with that?"

"I realize you saw things differently," Lars says, "And I will admit you were right. Gordie let the power go to his head. It was a case of Occam's razor."

I cock my head. "The simplest solution is likely the correct one?"

"No," Lars says, "What's the corruption one?"

"Lord Acton," I say, "Absolute power corrupts absolutely."

"That's it," Lars says, "Gordie had the power to make a real change. To create a political revolution. A movement that would sweep this country. Instead, he put his friend Booger on the payroll."

Carol can only shake her head. "What great movement did we lose, Lars? What was Gordie's philosophy? Get government off your back and into the bar? He didn't have one solitary idea that was practical. It was a classic case of the Peter Principle."

"Carol, don't be disgusting," Lars says.

She clucks her tongue and goes back to her book. I do my best to come between our own low rent Spencer Tracy and Katherine Hepburn (and I mean *really* low rent).

"Either of you worried about blowback from Vic Easton?" I ask.

"Let him try," Carol says.

"He said something about getting revenge for my betrayal," Lars says, "Nothing more than that."

Mike shoots a look at Lars. "You're not worried?"

Lars waves it off. "So many of my business ventures have ended with those kinds of threats, they've lost all meaning."

Despite his bravado, Lars keeps looking around, as if he's expecting an attack. Nobody seems to be paying any attention to us. Maybe Lars will calm down once we're out of town. Maybe Vic Easton considers the Twin Cities too far south to pursue petty revenge. I hope so, since Lars lives one floor down from me. Murder and mayhem can really disturb your sleep.

The route takes us past the Memorial Arena and then the parking lot that used to house Arthur's Diner, my favorite hangout in high school. I turn on to First Avenue. My old elementary school, Cobb-Cook, is visible a few blocks away. I point these things out to my friends, who are polite but not greatly interested. The Joe Davis Mundane Memorial Tour. Speaking of which…

"Sorry about the gangster tour, Lars," I say, (though I'm really not sorry).

Lars perks up. "I went about it the wrong way. I was taking a little fragment of history and trying to embellish it. Sensationalize it, if you will. And what have I been involved with for the past week? An honest to goodness murder right here in Porter's Bay."

Carol squares him with a look. "Were you involved with that? It looked like Joe did most of the actual investigating."

"I was around and have access to the principals involved. Certainly, this has more credibility than my horseshit attempts to manufacture a gangster era in Porter's Bay."

Mike pats Lars on the shoulder. "You shouldn't be so hard on yourself."

"No, I'm quoting the surveys," Lars says, "That gangster thing was a pig in a poke. The *real* blood and guts of Porter's Bay has been right in my grasp this whole time."

His disgusting imagery aside, I don't much fancy the idea of Lars having anything more to do with my hometown. Still, I don't want to offend him. A, he's my friend and neighbor; and B, it's a four-hour damn drive home. I don't want to argue with Lars the whole way. I drum my fingers on the steering wheel.

"You should be careful," I say, "I think Vic Easton will be looking for you. Might be best to steer clear of Porter's Bay for a while."

Lars muses upon this, relaxing visibly as we get closer to the edge of town. "You may be in the right. I don't know how long Mr. Easton's memory is. Better to let the heat die down."

I know how this will play out. Within two days of getting home, Lars will be wrapped up in some other scheme that's bound to fail through either impracticality or poor planning or poor execution. Or, most likely, a combination of all three. I've saved Porter's Bay from further disaster.

First Avenue empties onto Lake Drive. I go right and head south. Lake Superior shimmers in the sun. We pass the city limits. Porter's Bay begins to fall away behind us. The lake is on our left, rolling against the beach and ebbing away. My friends settle in for the drive. Lars whistles a little tune.

"Going home," he says.

I check the rearview mirror, then focus on the road ahead.

"Home," I say.

Randall J. Funk is the writer of the Joe Davis Mystery series. He is also an actor, director and playwright. His plays include *The Hound of the Baskervilles, The Mudslinger Party*, and *Bring Me the Head of Dominic Papatola*. He holds a Master's Degree in English Studies from Arizona State University. He currently lives in St. Louis Park, MN, with his daughter Bea.